DEX

KNIGHT EMPIRE
BOOK 2

LILY ZANTE

AUTHOR'S NOTE

DEX is the second book in the KNIGHT EMPIRE series, a steamy, billionaire contemporary romance saga based around a family of six brothers and their tyrannical father.

The series begins with the prequel, THE DARKEST KNIGHT. The first book is JETT, followed by DEX, and then RIO.

Each book can be read as a standalone, and is about one couple, but it is recommended to read these books in order for the best reading experience.

THE DARKEST KNIGHT

JETT

DEX

RIO

ZACH (pre-order, releasing in February 2026)

CHAPTER ONE

DANI

I TRY TO HIDE IT, THE FEAR AND WORRY WHICH STICKS LIKE A tight ball in my chest every time I see my father.

He used to be unstoppable.

A loving giant. A man who could command a boardroom and inspire his employees with a vision. Now he lies weak and frail before me, but it's his uncharacteristic quietness which disturbs me. He used to be larger than life, a jovial man whose laughter would bounce off the walls of a room and fill it completely.

He has a reputation as a visionary investor and business magnate, having expanded the company rapidly into international markets. He would regale me with stories about how he built up AO Eletronica from nothing, to becoming one of the largest mobile network operators in the world. It's not doing *too* badly, but it was once a powerhouse in Latin America, though lately it's started to slide a little.

The company isn't where it used to be. Investors are

backing off, profits are starting to dip, but we're working on fixing these things. Still, I can't shake the feeling that my father is hiding something deeper.

Something worse.

Whatever it is, it's breaking him in slow motion before our very eyes because I see a heaviness in his expression. I noticed it soon after an alliance he'd pinned his hopes on, fell away. A few months ago, out of nowhere, Paul Knight, a billionaire from the US, visited my father and suggested an idea that could help both our companies. It felt like a miracle, so timely and apt. Like my father's prayers had been answered.

Paul Knight suggested a marriage of convenience. It would be a purely transactional arrangement, with rules to keep emotions out of the equation. A proposal in which I would marry his son, Jett, for a year, thereby securing a high-profile merger between the Oliveiras and the Knights.

My father would get injections of capital, the shareholders would be appeased, and it would strengthen the public image of the company. From what I understand, Paul Knight would get access to a major emerging market.

I remember the day my father asked me if I would be willing to take part in such a scheme. He couldn't even look at me. But I took his hands and told him I'd do it. It was just for a year, and purely transactional arrangement. A marriage only on paper. I could do that. How could I not?

My parents have given me everything in life. They've supported, encouraged and loved me. Asking for a paltry year of my life to do this was nothing in the grand scheme of things, especially if it helped the business.

But the deal fizzled away and with each passing week thereafter, my father seemed to slip into himself, retreating from us.

Now my mãe sits across from me, worry etched into every

line of her face. My parents mean the world to me, and as an only child, I feel the weight of their worry and sorrow. I came back home after attending college in the US, and I still live with them in the home where I've grown up, here in São Paulo. Once upon a time this place felt grand, and untouchable. Now, it feels like a little faded, a little old, like it needs a little more care and love.

Just like my father's business.

"Papai," I whisper. "It's going to be okay." But my father's gaze is distant, like he's already given up. I hate seeing him looking so helpless and adrift.

As the VP of Brand Strategy and Corporate Communications, I can see that we've not quite managed to keep up with global tech giants, rising competition and the heavy costs of maintaining our infrastructure. Our business practices are outdated and, to our detriment, we haven't adapted to the changing market. Revenue has started to fall and investors have started to pull out. I see these as temporary setbacks and we're working on fixing these issues. We're not as bad as my father fears. The world is changing, and we can't remain at the top forever, but we're in a pretty good position, nonetheless.

My father lost all hope after the Knight deal never got off the ground. I told him we'd find another way. I told him not to lose hope, because there is another way, but he won't listen to me. He refuses to even consider my most recent idea.

"I'll marry Oscar," I say, my voice firm.

I hesitate, swallowing hard.

Oscar Ramos.

"You will do no such thing, filha." *Daughter.* They love me so much. I am so deeply aware of how much it hurts my father that the only way to help him might be through an alliance with a rich and powerful family.

My mother inhales sharply.

Oscar Ramos is a fifty-three-year-old billionaire, the head of a dynasty with questionable business practices. He's been circling around my family like a vulture, asking for my hand in marriage. He must have caught wind of the Knight deal, and mistakenly believed I was available.

But seeing my father's health go into decline, I'm now seriously considering this option, even though my heart aches. I once saw a photo of Jett Knight online. He was handsome, and young. The idea of marrying him didn't seem scary. I prayed that the deal with Paul Knight would go through.

It gave us all hope.

My father kept saying, *"Paul Knight is a good man, Daniela. A good man. He will help us. He wants business in Brazil, but he doesn't know the market, the people. We do. We will be saved."*

Jett Knight is younger than that dinosaur, Ramos. I feel like I could have married him and made it work. He also has a daughter I could have focused my attention on, but then he pulled out and now my father doesn't like the idea of me marrying Oscar.

But what other choice do we have?

My mother stiffens. "Ramos is old enough to be your father, Daniela. He's bald, and so big, and ..." She shivers in disgust.

"Looks aren't important, Mãe " I should know. I've been plagued by my looks. People don't look any deeper when they look at me. They assume I'm a princess, an airhead, that I have nothing of importance to say, that I'm just something to look at and desire.

Men especially.

I hate it.

Oscar Ramos scares me, and he makes me shiver for all the

wrong reasons. I don't want to be with him, but we're out of choices now. I grip my father's hand tighter.

"Please. I just don't want anything to happen to you. I'll do whatever it takes to help our business. It will only be for a year, Papai. And we'll go back to how things were." When my father was strong and well.

"You will not marry him," my father says weakly.

"I will," I insist. "I'll do whatever it takes."

"Listen to me, filha!" my father cries. "You will not *ever* marry Oscar Ramos."

I swallow, my throat burning. Because if I don't form an alliance, my father might spiral into depression and become so ill, I fear the worst might happen.

"What about someone else, like the Knights? Or another rich and powerful family?" I suggest.

My father shakes his head. "Paul Knight never mentioned anyone else."

I frown. "How many sons does he have?"

"Five."

I sit back, stunned. "Five? And he didn't put forth *any* of them for the alliance? You never thought to mention it, Papai?"

"He only mentioned the oldest son. He was eager for a marriage because this son was a widower with a daughter who needs a mother. I didn't want to go back and beg, Daniela. People aren't as agreeable towards arranged marriages in the US. They don't need to make alliances."

"But Paul Knight approached you, Papai! *He* needed *you*."

My father closes his eyes and lets out a murmur. "He did."

"The other sons … are they married?" My brain goes into overdrive as I try to find a lifeline away from Oscar Ramos.

"None of them are married, but as far as I understand, they are … not available."

I exhale sharply. Five sons. Surely one of them might be single and agreeable to an arranged marriage? On paper only.

An idea forms in my mind. I'm prepared to do whatever it takes to save my father's business. I was ready to marry a man like Oscar, but if there is another way …

I remember the picture of Jett Knight. He was handsome. If he was good-looking, then maybe his brothers aren't so bad either.

Also, there are potentially five of them to choose from.

If I can meet and marry a Knight, I can save my family and it won't even seem like too much of a sacrifice.

CHAPTER TWO

DEX

I LEFT MY APARTMENT HOURS AGO, LOSING MYSELF IN THE GYM until my arms and legs were cramping from exertion, and my t-shirt was soaked with sweat. I'd tried to exhaust my body and mind, tried to throw off my sullen attitude and utter boredom with life in general.

Lexi would have helped. I could have called her even now but phone sex isn't really my thing. I'm more of a physical guy. Our friends with benefits arrangement worked fine when she was here, but she took off a few months ago to work in Spain as a nanny and she's not planning on coming back for a while.

I haven't met anyone since she left. No one who would be worth hooking up with. It feels like too much effort.

But after sweating out my ennui, I step out of the gym, still feeling restless, and go upstairs to the penthouse, to see Jett. I've got something on my mind, business, mostly, but I also just want a distraction. When I knock on Jett's door, Cari opens it.

"Oh. Hey," I say, surprised.

She's always here. Feels like she spends more time at Jett's place than her own. Not that I hate her. I don't. But I do want my brother back. Before I can say anything else, my little niece runs toward me.

"Uncle Dex!" she squeals, before wrinkling up her nose. "You're smelly!"

I scoop her up and cuddle her. "That's because I've been working out at the gym, and now you're going to be smelly, too, princess," I tease, sniffing the air.

She giggles as I set her down. I glance at Cari. "How's it going? You opened your new flower shop yet?" She quit as Jett's assistant, and is now opening her own small flower shop inside a café.

"I'm still finishing off a few things. I'm opening next week."

"Good luck."

"Thank you."

Before I can ask for Jett, he steps into the living room, looking half-distracted. He's dressed casually but sharp. Obviously going somewhere.

"You're dressed up," I state.

"Hey," he drawls, buttoning his cuffs. "We're going to see Brooke's school play."

"Why don't you come along?" Cari offers, her tone teasing.

"I'd rather scrape my nails along a blackboard." I flash Brooke a smile. "What are you this time, sweetie? A chicken or some other farmyard animal?"

"I'm singing," she says, shyly.

"She's got a great voice." Jett says with pride. There's a warmth in his expression that wasn't there a year ago. He's happy. Stupidly, annoyingly, and ecstatically so. I'm happy for him, too, but right now, I just want to grab a few beers with my brother. I need to talk and find a way to distract myself from this feeling of agitation that I can't seem to shake.

I glance at the time. The night is young. There are others I could call. "You guys look busy, so I'll get out of your way."

"You sure?" Jett asks. "Stay. Have a drink."

"I was thinking of heading to a bar."

"Can't tonight." Jett studies me. "Something bugging you?"

"Nope. Work is work." I shrug. "Lexi's still away. My evenings are mostly always free. Just wanted to see if you wanted to grab a drink."

"Maybe another time."

"It's cool. Enjoy the play." But I feel worse now than when I first walked in. Jett playing happy family and exuding happiness leaves me feeling melancholy, and I can't explain why. I'm over the moon for him. If anyone needed to find happiness, it was him. Losing his wife like he did, and having to bring up Brooke, has been hard.

Overcome by the mundanity of it all, I call my youngest brother as I leave, needing to hear a familiar voice. He picks up on the third ring. I can tell from the noise in the background that he's outside somewhere.

"Hey, where are you?" I ask.

Zach laughs. "Nowhere you'd want to be."

I have no interest in finding out. "I called to see if you wanted to grab a couple of beers."

"You called Jett first, didn't you?"

I grin. "No."

"I bet you did." Zach knows I would. He feels left out, but he shouldn't. I love him just as much as I love my older brother. Feels like I can talk to Jett more, though, about life stuff.

"Alright, fine. I did. You busy?"

"Got my hands full at the moment."

"Understood." I don't want details. Zach is a bit of a ladies man. But then, we all are, even the Italian Knights, given some of the stories I hear from Rio.

Zach pauses. "You good?"

"Yeah," I say, even though I feel like I'm wasting my damn night. "Catch you later."

I hang up, exhaling. Both of my brothers have a life. They have things to do. I go back to my apartment, get dressed, and step outside. There's a sharp bite in the November air. Too cold to wander around, but I'm too restless to stay in. I still need a drink. I need to let off some steam after today's meeting with all of us, and our father. That old man has been pissing me off lately.

I pull out my phone and make a call. "You in?"

Rio answers straightaway. "Yeah. What's up?"

"Wondered if you might want to grab a few beers. At The Oasis?" A stylish rooftop terrace in Manhattan, that's been around for almost a decade. It's become our regular haunt. Where none of the others hang out.

A beat of silence. He sounds tired. "You wanna come over to mine instead?"

"Sure."

A few minutes later, I drive across town to SoHo where the Italian Knights live, my half-brothers. The secret family my father had when he cheated on my mom. The secret which drove her to her death when she found out.

But it was really me that put the nail in her coffin. It's a burden which weighs on me. A burden I try to forget by having fun with women like Lexi.

I knock on Rio's door and he answers in an instant, already holding a beer. "Hey, dude. Come in."

We're just a short drive away in Tribeca. It's done by choice, not theirs, not ours, but the old man's.

Like us, the Italian Knights also have a luxury four story

building. Rio, like Jett, gets the penthouse, because he's the oldest in his set of brothers. The guy's got a rooftop pool and garden.

I step inside the penthouse, which I've visited more times this last year than in all the time we've known each other. He's been over to my place a few times, and so far, we haven't been caught, by either sets of brothers.

It's a crazy situation, to have to hide the fact that my half-brother and I get on, but I have a sneaky feeling, as does Rio, that the old man likes this setup. He makes us attend those painful Knight family dinners every so often, but he seems to like keeping us divided, with just a thin veil of unity. A unity that's needed for the Knight empire to continue its global domination.

With six sons, the old man's legacy is assured, and by encouraging our division, he's safe in knowing we'll never unite and take him on together.

Except that Rio and I got talking about a year ago. We were going down the elevator after attending one of the Knight family dinners, and by the time we descended to the base, we were talking like we'd been friends for years.

Brothers, more like it, because that's what we are.

We discovered then that we're more alike than not. People have commented that we look alike, except that my hair is short, if a little longer on top, while Rio's hair is longer, his skin olive toned. I'd say my hair is dark brown, but his is a shade darker. He sometimes sweeps it back, and other times he just parts it down the middle, and it hangs, like he's a modern-day saint, albeit a brooding one.

Now that a few people have commented on it, I see the resemblance. We do look alike, more than we don't. We're also quite similar in personality. Neither of us likes authority. We don't like suits. We both have attitude and we can't stand the old man. That's what we call him, too.

"You hungry? We can order in," Rio suggests, sitting down. He's wearing jeans and a T-shirt, like I am.

"Yeah, sure. Jett's busy with his whole domestic life thing."

Rio snorts. "Cari's a regular now at his place, huh?"

"Dude's practically married," I say. "I'm happy for him, but it's impossible to get him out for drinks."

"You have to be happy when people find love. Don't begrudge them it."

I shoot him a look. "Since when did you turn sentimental?"

Rio just shrugs. I take a beer from his refrigerator and take a seat in one of his big comfortable couches. He sits across from me.

"How far down the list was I?" he asks, sitting back, beer bottle in hand.

"What list?"

"The list of people you called before me."

I laugh. "Relax, brother. You were top of the list."

"Yeah, yeah." He doesn't believe me, and he knows me well enough to know that he shouldn't.

"Lexi and I barely text anymore, and I'm not in the mood for dealing with a stranger at a bar tonight."

Rio assesses me carefully. "You sound lonely, dude."

I shrug. "Bored, more like."

"You need to get out there and find someone new."

I roll my eyes and take another sip of beer. But before I can respond, something catches my eye. Something sitting on Rio's fireplace.

A photo, of a woman. Framed like it belongs there. Like it's important. I freeze. The image is familiar. *Too* familiar. I get up, walk over, and pick it up by the edges. "What the fuck is this doing here?" I growl because I know exactly who it is.

Rio scrubs a hand down his face. "Shit."

I turn the photo around, studying it. "This has been sitting here for *months*?" This is the photo the old man had at the last family dinner.

"I should've put it away," Rio mutters.

I look at him, then back at the picture.

It's the heiress. She's standing outside, near a huge bouquet of flowers. Looks like the backdrop to a fancy event. Head tipped back, she's laughing, and not looking at the camera either, like she doesn't even know someone's taking a photo.

Whoever took it caught a moment, and caught the very essence of her. She's beautiful. Full mouth, pouty lips. Bright green eyes framed by thick lashes. Thick defined eyebrows, too. She's impossibly stunning, now that I find myself staring at her for longer than is normal. Her hair is medium brown, long and luscious. Loose curls, running riot down her shoulders. She has high cheekbones. Of course she would. A perfect nose, too.

And she wanted to marry Jett in a marriage of convenience. I find it suspicious why someone who looks like *her* would want to be a part of *that*. It disgusts me and makes me wonder what her real motive might be.

"Is this your shrine to her?" I look at him in disbelief. The dude looks something I've never seen him look before —*agitated*.

Rio exhales slowly, eyes flicking to the photo. "She's gorgeous, right?"

I let out a dry laugh. "No argument there, but you don't even know her."

"Do we ever really know anyone?" he counters. "You go to a bar, meet someone, it's all based on looks anyway."

I narrow my eyes. "So what, now you're obsessed with some woman you've never met?"

"It's not like that," he snaps.

"Isn't it? What conclusion do you expect me to draw from this?"

I thought Rio was way cooler than that. This is odd and confusing. I've seen this guy in action and he doesn't go crazy over a woman. As far as he's concerned, it's easy come, easy go.

He scrubs his hand over his jaw. "I borrowed it, and I meant to put it back at the next family dinner."

He stole it from my father's penthouse. *What the hell was he thinking?*

"You *borrowed* it? Also, you think the old man hasn't noticed it's missing?"

I know exactly when he took it. It was that time our father told us about the deal with the Brazilian heiress, when he expected Jett to agree to the alliance between the two families, but instead my headstrong brother turned up with his assistant, Cari, and declared his love for her in front of us all. "It was *that* dinner," I state, my mind whirring with the possibilities of what this could mean because this behavior is out of character for Rio, and now I'm starting to get worried.

"I doubt he's missed it," Rio retorts.

"Why do you have this, brother?"

"Why not?" He takes a big swig from his beer bottle, and I note that he hasn't answered my question.

"Are you seriously considering this?" I'm fearful of his answer, of the expression on Rio's face. This guy looks like he's seriously considering the marriage deal. I think it's a sick idea that only someone like the old man could come up with. "What type of woman would agree to an arranged marriage?" I ask when he doesn't answer. "What type of *guy* would agree to this?"

"Your brother was going to do it," Rio pushes back.

I've spoken to Jett about this, and he never would have. "He was never going to. The old man thought it would be a good idea, and he tried to get into Jett's head, by telling him that Brooke needed a mother, and Jett needed a wife, but you should know by now that neither me nor Jett would ever willingly adjust our lives to fit in with something the old man dictates. I can't vouch for Zach, because that guy's always had a soft spot for the old man. As for you ..." I point at Rio with the photo. "This is the last thing I expected from you, brother."

Rio looks away, and I probe deeper. "What's going on? Something you want to talk about."

All I wanted was an evening chilling and hanging out, taking it easy. Not some existential angst situation.

"You still getting over the breakup?" I prompt. He was serious about someone, and they broke up a while back. He's not like me. He doesn't do hookups or casual relationships. This guy wants something deeper. Meaningful. I guess in that respect we're different.

"That's over. Forgotten," he says, with a finality in his tone that tells me not to pursue the matter.

"Okay. And this ..." I hold up the photo. "What about this, brother?"

"She's gorgeous."

"She's not bad," I agree. This woman has movie star looks, for sure, but I wouldn't be surprised if that photo has been touched up, just like in celebrity magazines. She can't be *that* beautiful. Because, now that I find myself staring at the photo with a little more concentration, she's *really* pretty. "But looks aren't everything."

My heart sinks looking at Rio's face. I never had him down for being such a soft guy, not with that dark and dangerous persona he's always projecting. "If you're obsessed with her, why don't you just go for it?"

"What?"

"Marry her."

"I thought the old man said the deal's fallen through."

"With Jett," I point out. "But he hasn't said anything more."

"It's been a few months. Maybe she got another offer?" Rio asks, and the fact that he's asking, suggests that maybe he's been thinking about it.

"If you want her, go for it. *Do something*, instead of sitting here worshipping this picture."

"I'm not worshiping that picture," he snaps. "I just took the photo and I was hoping to put it back at the next family dinner."

"But you've been thinking about her?" I nod at the photo. Rio doesn't answer. But the look in his eyes tells me everything.

CHAPTER THREE

DANI

After sitting by my father's bedside, listening to his worries, I found Paul Knight's number in my father's diary and called him.

Others might have sent an email, but time is of the essence and it feels as if we don't have time for that.

He answered smoothly, and with great charm, in a voice rich with warmth. Perhaps it was a little *too* warm, a little *too* smooth, but I found it reassuring. It was what I needed.

"Ah, Daniela," he said, as if he'd been expecting my call. "How is your father?" His voice dripped with concern, so much so that I almost believed it.

I explained, politely but directly, that I was sorry the alliance hadn't gone through and that my father was still very eager to make a deal. I also mentioned—offhand and casually, as if it wasn't the real reason I was calling—that I'd recently discovered he had five other sons.

Because I was so worried about having to marry Oscar Ramos, I didn't dance around the topic.

"Mr. Knight, my father is most anxious for this alliance, and I was wondering if there was any possibility that one of your other sons might be more amenable to this arrangement."

He paused and I heard my heartbeat thumping inside my ribcage. Then, his voice turned warm again, almost approving.

"It's certainly worth considering. Why don't you come over, and we'll set something up? I'm sure both our families can benefit greatly from a deal of this nature."

My heart sank a little at that. I wasn't going to correct him, but I also don't fully share my father's pessimistic view that our business is failing. A man like Paul Knight would have done his due diligence and gone through everything with a fine-tooth comb. He's obviously happy with the company, and I sense he needs us as much as we need him.

Naturally, my parents were shocked when I told them I was going to New York to meet Paul Knight. My father insisted that he come along, but I told him all I needed was for him to get well again.

And to believe in me.

His reply?

Always, filha.

I'M SITTING IN THE VIP LOUNGE AT THE AIRPORT, A BOTTLE OF still water in my hand, though I haven't taken a sip.

I'll be boarding soon for my flight to New York, and I should be going over my talking points for my meeting with Paul Knight. I should be reminding myself why I'm doing this; why I'm about to step into the lion's den of one of the most ruthless business families in the world.

Instead, I'm staring at my phone, Raquel's name glowing on the screen.

I should call my best friend.

I *want* to call her.

But what would I even say? That I'm flying to New York to discuss a potential business *alliance* that could help my father's company? An alliance that involves me marrying a man I've never met? That I might walk into that meeting and have my future decided by cold negotiations between men who see me as leverage rather than a person?

That won't go over well.

Raquel would murder me.

A wry smile tugs at my lips. My best friend from childhood, the person I went to Georgetown University with and lived with while in the US—she wouldn't just murder me—she'd stage a full-scale intervention, drag me to a law office, and have me signing restraining orders against every single Knight before sundown. She isn't just protective; she's relentless. Brilliant. A force of nature wrapped in designer heels and sharp wit.

I've told her *nothing*.

I never even mentioned anything to her about Jett Knight.

I thumb at the screen, hesitating. Maybe I'll visit her before I fly back home. She lives and works in Miami. I could say I have a layover, meet for a quick drink, pretend everything is fine. But Raquel isn't the kind of woman you can lie to, a least, not easily. She *knows* me. She reads between the lines, catches the hesitations, senses the things I don't say.

She isn't an idiot. And now, if I suddenly tell her I'm flying to New York with no clear reason? She'd know something was up.

I exhale sharply and lock my phone.

The worst part is, she's going to find out eventually. I can't keep an entire *marriage* from her, if things work out for me on this visit. And when she *does* find out, she's going to *question* it. Hard.

Because men fall for me. They always have. Raquel has seen it happen too many times.

She's been my shield against them when I needed her to be, my wing woman when I needed an escape. She knows how they stare, how they follow, how they *want*. She's spent years teasing me about it, rolling her eyes at the way they trip over themselves to impress me, joking that I should be charging a *tax* for the privilege of my attention.

So when I have to tell her I'm getting married, to a man she's never heard me mention, a man she *knows* I haven't been dating, she's not just going to accept it at face value. She's going to suspect. And if she suspects, she'll *dig*.

Which means if this works out and there is a marriage, we have to be *convincing*.

My stomach twists at the thought. I don't even *know* any of the Knights yet, and somehow, I'm supposed to play the part of an adoring wife to one of them? To hold hands and smile up at a strange man like he's the center of my world, convince Raquel, and everyone else, that this marriage is *real*?

I grip the armrest of my chair, my pulse hammering.

It's not just about fooling my friends. My father and Paul Knight have been clear: *no one* outside of our families can know this is an arrangement. If the truth gets out, it could ruin everything—the business deal, the fragile alliance, the perception we need to give to the outside world, and to the investors and shareholders.

This marriage would be a merger of two powerful families, and it would be my father's chance to boost his company.

I have no choice.

I have to lie to Raquel.

If things work out, and there is a marriage, I'll have to convince her that this is love, not business.

If I fail, if somehow I can't walk away with a Knight, then I'll have no choice but to marry Oscar Ramos.

That would be a death sentence.

The boarding announcement crackles over the speakers, and I rise, smoothing down my dress. I pick up my phone one last time, staring at Raquel's name.

Then I tuck it away.

I'll deal with her *later*.

For now, I have bigger battles to fight.

***

PAUL KNIGHT PAID FOR MY FLIGHT, AND SET ME UP IN A glamorous hotel in New York, even though I insisted I could take care of it.

I arrived in New York from Brazil last night. I've been here twice, for a weekend with friends when I was studying in Washington and the second time when I ran the marathon. This city isn't completely alien to me.

Landing so late, I went straight to bed and have spent the morning getting my bearings, reading up on the Knight brothers again. I'd already done my research before leaving Brazil, but looking at photos of them online now, knowing one of them might end up as my husband, makes it feel different.

There are five of them. They all look *impressive*. Handsome, powerful, successful. But I don't care about looks. That's never been my priority. It's the person inside that I'm more interested in. I also want to know their "why?"

Why would someone marry a stranger for a year? I have my reasons, and I'd like to know theirs.

I'm due to meet Paul Knight at his apartment later this morning. He told me he doesn't want me to go to his office. He wants to talk about this informally.

I'd like to believe him, I really would, but for a man heading the multi-billion Knight Enterprises, I'm surprised he's able to make so much time for me and at such short notice.

He mentioned that he's hosting some kind of high-profile event tonight at his penthouse, and I'll have to come to that. He asked me to "Dress to impress," for that event.

For now, this morning's meeting is an informal chat about "how we can best help one another" and he's arranged for a chauffeur to pick me up.

I'm curious about meeting him.

I should be grateful that he agreed to meet me so soon. For now I'll focus on what my father told me: One year. That's all we need, filha. One year, and the cash injections from the Knights will go a long way to helping with our ambitious plans to boost AO Eletronica.

I get ready quickly, nerves frayed as my mind buzzes about what to expect. I'm nervous as I get into the chauffeured car. My heart races when I step into the elevator of the building where Paul lives. This sprawling tower symbolizes wealth in a way I didn't think was possible. As I ascend, shimmering glass and mirrors everywhere, I'm in awe of the magnificent views of the skyline.

I know this lifestyle well. The wealth, the glitz. I'm used to this life of privilege and security. I've grown up surrounded by luxury, attending exclusive events, brushing shoulders with politicians and billionaires.

I shouldn't be surprised, but this is another level.

Anxiety floods my veins, and I take a few calming breaths and try to imagine my father smiling and healthy again.

The elevator dings and the doors glide open. I step into a

world of polished marble and large expansive windows overlooking views of places I've only seen in films before.

A maid ushers me in, but I barely take in my surroundings before Paul Knight greets me.

He's tall. Gray-blue eyes. Not as warm as I expected. Truth be told, he's nothing like I expected. His voice on the phone had been smoother, more inviting. In person, he studies me with a sharp, assessing gaze. His smile is soft, but I feel as if there's something calculating behind it.

I recover quickly, returning his smile as I step forward.

"Daniela," he says, extending a hand. "Welcome."

"It's nice to finally meet you."

"Shall we?" He gestures for me to follow him.

I pass a few rooms, before Paul Knight leads me into this smaller more informal one, but I don't see photos anywhere. The entire penthouse reeks of money and mind-boggling wealth, yet there is no color. No warmth. No woman's touch. Everything is sleek and metal or glass. It's nothing like my home back in São Paulo. The home that will always have a place in my heart, no matter where I might settle in later years.

We sit. We talk. He asks about my family, my father, and my mother.

"It takes a lot to call me directly," he muses. "I'm impressed."

"I understand, Mr. Knight."

"Don't call me Mr. Knight," he corrects. "Too formal. If we're going to be family soon ..."

I force another polite smile, as the picture of Oscar Ramos in my head fades, replaced by one of the Knight brothers. I have no idea which one it will be. I look around the room and find it odd that there are no family photos anywhere. Not a single photo up on the walls.

"I was surprised to hear from you. It's been months since the previous deal fell through. What prompted this, Daniela?"

I have to be careful. I can't tell him about Oscar Ramos, or my father being so sick with worry.

"Well, Mr.—*Paul*," I correct myself quickly, "You were the one who approached my father first."

His eyes narrow. He doesn't like being reminded of that fact. He tilts his head, and I can't tell if he's surprised that I said what I did, or if he's angry.

I smile, leaning forward slightly. "My father is excited about this arrangement, as am I. It's an incredible opportunity for both of us. I truly believe we can benefit from each other."

He tilts his head, considering me. "You're not in it for the relationship?"

I blink. "It's an arranged marriage, Paul."

"In some cultures, arranged marriages lead to fruitful entanglements."

"Yes, but affairs of the heart can be unpredictable," I counter smoothly, "It might be better, for both parties, to see this more as a business proposition."

His smile sharpens, and he seems to like my answer. "I like that you're pragmatic. Business-minded, too, and you have no delusions about what this is."

"I am fully aware that this is purely business." I don't yearn to meet a man and fall in love.

Not yet.

I had two relationships while I was in college here in the US. Nothing serious. Ever since I moved back home, I've been focused on proving myself at my father's company. He gave me a prestigious role, but I work hard, long hours, to prove myself. I don't want anyone to accuse my father of nepotism.

But I see what my parents have and I want a marriage as strong and as durable as theirs. I want a man to look at me the way my father looks at my mother, when she doesn't even realize it. When she's doing the most mundane of tasks like watering a plant, or sipping her coffee. My father often looks at my mother as if she were his next breath.

I hope to have that one day.

For now, I keep mostly to myself. I've learned to bury my own needs and focus on my family and our business instead.

This marriage of convenience is a task on my to-do list. It's a goal, something that needs to be done, and once it's over, I can cross it off.

Most of the men I've met see me as a commodity. So it's going to take a special man for me to open up and trust him. To allow myself to fall in love with him.

I feel a coldness here, sitting across the room from Paul. There's a lack of spirit, but I try to remain positive. The Knight brothers are closer to my age than Oscar Ramos, and I should be grateful for that. At least I'll have more in common with them.

And a year isn't too long.

Paul tells me the rules. This will be a marriage in name only. Separate bedrooms. No emotions. No feelings. No commitment. It's a business arrangement, nothing more.

But we will have to live together.

The outside world will need to see that we are together, that the Knights and the Oliveiras make a formidable partnership. I force myself to nod as he emphasizes the business deal more than the marriage. That's a good way of looking at it.

He's watching me, waiting for an answer to a question I've already forgotten.

"I'm family-oriented," I add quickly. "I love my parents, and I'd do anything for them."

"Oh?" His eyes darken slightly, as if weighing my words. "You would do *anything* for them?"

I straighten, careful not to appear too eager. "Of course. My father built this business from nothing. It means everything to him."

Paul leans back, steepling his fingers. "Is there anything I should know?"

I swallow. Does he already suspect?

"I just want what's best for my family," I say carefully. "And who wouldn't want to come and live in America?" I throw in a light laugh. "Your sons are all accomplished men. Handsome too."

"And filthy rich," he adds.

This feels like a test. "Yes, as am I. My family, I mean."

He nods.

I sit back, feeling more emboldened now that he's talking more about business than feelings and emotions. "People use dating apps to find someone compatible. I'd rather align with someone who shares my goals."

Paul watches me for a long moment. Then, he smiles. "That is exactly the type of woman I'd hope for my sons to marry, but …" He leans forward in his expensive looking leather chair. "I've been a businessman for over forty years. There are CEOs, and captains of industry who don't have the balls to pick up the phone and call me. And yet, you did."

I flash my glitziest smile, hoping to gloss over the desperation he might have sensed in what I did, and why I did it.

"I'm not shy, Mr. Knight," I insist. "I just don't like seeing a good opportunity pass me by. If I want something, I go for it."

He surveys me for longer than I am comfortable with. This is nothing like what I was expecting. I feel like I'm being chewed to pieces by piranhas.

"It's just that people don't do what you did unless they need something desperately." It's like he can smell blood in the water.

"We both have a lot to gain from this union, Paul. You get access to the number one global telecommunications company in Latin America." We *were*, but surely he will be doing his own due diligence.

"I agree, absolutely. I was just curious to know if you were acting out of need. But I see now that you're not just beautiful, you're smart, and you've got guts."

I remain silent, because I *was* acting out of need. I no longer know how to gauge the success of this meeting. It's been nothing like I imagined.

"And that's a good thing," he continues, oblivious to the chaos churning inside me. "Because you'll need your smarts and guts, especially when it comes to my boys."

My eyes widen and I wonder if he's issuing me a subtle warning.

He chuckles. "Don't worry. They don't bite, but … I can't see them being amenable to something like this." He stands. "I wouldn't be able to sell this as an arranged marriage deal, but I've been working on this ever since we spoke. Tonight's special event is the perfect opportunity for you to meet my sons."

I raise an eyebrow. "Special?"

"A soiree. I didn't think you'd want to be presented like some prize pony at a gala." I listen intently, as he continues. "But my sons are headstrong. If I make this about business rather than a matchmaking spectacle, they'll be more likely to listen."

"Is that why your oldest son pulled out?"

Paul's lips tighten. "He had other ideas."

He doesn't elaborate.

Instead, he smiles again, smoothing over the moment.

"Tonight will be a networking opportunity for high-profile business partners. Key investors. Industry leaders. And *you*. The surprise guest."

I exhale slowly. This is bigger than I expected.

I nod. "I'm … I'm looking forward to it."

He gives me one last unreadable look. "I do hope this will lead somewhere."

CHAPTER FOUR

DEX

It's rare for all of us to be in the same place at the same time, unless it's a Knight family dinner. And tonight, while it's still at the old man's penthouse, it's *not* a family dinner.

This is a soiree, according to the email that was sent out.

As Zach, Jett, and I approach the elevator, I spot the Italian Knights, Rio, Enzo, and Matteo, already waiting. Rio cocks an eyebrow at me. I nod back. I haven't had a chance to ask him yet if he's spoken to our father about the Brazilian Beauty Queen.

Beside him, Enzo stands stiff, unreadable as always, and Matteo looks as pissed off as ever.

None of us likes coming here, at the dinners the old man hosts every month or so where he forces us to sit through an evening of veiled insults, business talk, and power plays. But tonight, it's something different. This time it's a small and intimate soiree and a chance to network with high-worth individuals, high-powered investors, CEOs and social elites.

At least there's safety in numbers and the old man will be busy mingling and working the room.

Which means I can stay for a short while, show my face and get the hell out. Jett probably has the same idea. He's brought Cari along, and I'm still trying to work out if it's a brave move on his part, or insanely stupid.

We stare at the elevator, not sure how the seven of us are going to fit in there. The Italian Knights were already here first so, when the doors fly open, they take up the back wall. The rest of us stare, with hesitation, not stepping inside.

"There's plenty of room," Enzo says.

"Let's just get in," Zach says, always the only one of us eager to come here.

We step inside, but Jett and Cari still hover outside.

"Stop being such an ass," I mutter, glaring at Jett. Now that he's all loved up, he's already acting different. Like he's not one of us. "You can squeeze in, even with that big head of yours."

Jett cuts me a look that has the power to freeze me. Cari steps in and my brother reluctantly follows. He leans against the mirrored wall, surveying us like he's already figured something out. "A soiree," he states, flatly. "I wonder what the agenda behind this is."

"The last thing we'll expect, no doubt," I say. "There's always an agenda, even if it's just dinner."

"It's never just dinner." Everyone says in unison.

"Are you sure you want to go to this?" Jett asks Cari.

She places her hand on his arm, looks up at him like he's her world. "Your father invited all of us. It would be rude not to."

I frown. "It's a bit late now, bro, you're already heading

up." He's treating Cari like she's made of glass. When did he turn into such a wuss? "It'll be easier to get lost among the guests," I offer, then turning to Cari, after remembering the last time, "Tonight won't be so bad."

"After my last visit ..." Her voice trails off. That must have been a baptism by fire. First time she came, and the first time any of us had the balls to stand up to the old man in the way Jett did.

Jett seems to be overanalyzing this evening. "But why? This is quick. Usually he tells us about these weeks in advance, and he only told us a few days ago."

"You're right. The old man usually holds these things in some plush hotel ballroom, not his penthouse," I say. "Maybe it's a party. His birthday, or something?"

"Do we even know when his birthday is?" Enzo asks.

Matteo snorts. "Does anyone care?"

The elevator ride falls silent after that.

When we step out into the penthouse, the housekeeper greets us and leads us towards the Great Room, a large, expansive open space with windows looking onto Central Park. Despite having been here many times, I find myself still awestruck at the views of the Manhattan skyline.

Before we even round the corner, I hear it already.

Music.

Not just any music.

Live jazz. There's also dim lighting and the kind of atmosphere that screams wealth and sophistication but I smell *manipulation.*

"What the hell?" Matteo says under his breath.

My mouth falls open slightly. "What is this?" I scan the room. No band, thankfully, just music filtering through high-end speakers. But the champagne towers? The waiters in crisp black-and-white suits, serving gourmet hors d'oeuvres and canapés? This signals something else.

"Are we about to stage a hostile takeover or something?" Jett asks dryly.

"Guys, calm down. Maybe Dad just wanted to have a nice evening." Zach looks hopeful. Stupidly hopeful. I can't shake the stupid out of this one. He thinks our father has a good bone in his body.

"Nice and Paul Knight don't sit well in the same sentence," says Rio, swiping a glass of champagne off one of the server's trays.

Matteo grabs a couple of canapés like he doesn't give a shit. Enzo stands with his hands in his pockets, looking effortlessly detached despite the tuxedos our father insisted we wear. "Glad I dressed up," he says.

I glance at Rio, who looks just as confused as I feel. What the hell is this about?

Then I see him.

The old man. The patriarchal figurehead of Knight Enterprises. And a bane in our lives.

He's across the room, standing in a small circle of powerful men. The type of people who make decisions that shake markets.

Seeing us walk in, he excuses himself from the group and strolls toward us, his suit impeccable, his expression unreadable. "Glad you could all make it," he says smoothly.

"This isn't a Knight family dinner," I say.

"Excellent observation," he says, in his usual patronizing tone. "Did you not get the memo?"

"I did, but this…" I gesture around. "You don't tend to do these types of evenings unless you want something."

Jett's gaze sweeps over the room. "I see a lot of heads of

industry here. Investors. CEOs. Social elites. Why here and not in some swanky hotel? What are you not telling us?"

Paul smiles. "So many questions. So much suspicion. Why not just enjoy a nice event like this for what it is?"

"And what is it?" Jett asks. "You never host an event unless there's something in it for you."

"You never do *anything* unless there's something in it for you," Rio counters, just as I was about to say the same thing.

"So?" Jett waits for the explanation. He and our father still haven't thawed from their last battle. Paul tried to push Jett into an alliance with a Brazilian heiress, and Jett shut him down, hard. But what really pisses the old man off is that Jett is in love with his assistant, and he snubbed the old man and his deal completely.

But tonight isn't about Jett.

It's about something else and I'm determined not to leave until I find out what. Our father steps to the front of the room, lifting a champagne flute. He taps the rim of his glass with a silver spoon, and a hush falls.

"My friends," he begins, his voice rich with authority. "Welcome. I'm delighted to have you all here tonight. Just a small gathering. An informal evening to bring together captains of industry, esteemed investors, and, of course, family."

Bullshit.

Then he smirks, and I know what's coming before he even says it.

"Did you know the combined wealth in this room exceeds, oh, I don't know, a few trillion dollars?"

I roll my eyes. Of course, this asshole would do the math.

Paul Knight doesn't collect people. He collects power. He likes to own the narrative, make sure every piece on the chessboard moves at his command.

And tonight?

Tonight is a goddamn power play.

I tense as he continues, his voice oozing control.

"Tonight I have a very special guest…" He lifts a hand toward the entryway, that familiar smile of his sharp enough to slice through steel. "As Knight Enterprises looks to strengthen its ties in emerging markets and expand our global footprint, it's my pleasure to introduce a woman whose intelligence, influence, and heritage align perfectly with that vision."

The moment she steps into view, I fucking know exactly who she is.

Jett curses under his breath.

I hear collective gasps around me, from my brothers.

Daniela Oliveira.

The heiress.

She's breathtaking. Tall. Voluptuous. Filling out her sparkling, shimmering, sequined dress like it was made for her.

It's also completely inappropriate. There are only two other women here, excluding Cari, and they're both wearing dark business suits. And trousers. As if they need to dress like men to fit in.

This Brazilian Beauty Queen looks like she ought to be on the red carpet at a Hollywood film premiere.

"Jesus," I mutter.

"Fuck," Jett says at the same time.

"Isn't that the woman you were meant to marry, Jett?" Zach jokes, elbowing me.

"Is that her?" Cari pipes up. She cranes her neck, her gaze fixated on the woman that Jett was once supposed to take as his wife. Just like that, Jett slips his arm around Cari's waist and pulls her closer to him. A territorial move if ever I saw one.

"Who cares?" he growls.

"She's gorgeous," Enzo adds, nodding.

"Shut up," Rio snaps. "Shut the fuck up."

I look at Rio's face and his eyes are transfixed. Paul stretches out his hand, and Daniela takes it as he leads her to the front. He introduces her as the "the family behind AO Eletronica. All the way from Brazil," Paul adds, looking jubilant. Like the cat that caught the canary.

She steps forward, her voice measured but soft. "I'm delighted to be here." She sounds a little breathless, and she's not as thin or as fragile as I thought she was. She is literally Amazonian; tall and voluptuous, with the face of a movie star. Full, luscious lips. Dramatic eyes. High cheekbones. Long, wavy dark hair.

This was the *"something"* on the old man's agenda. My attention fixes on Rio again, and I see that his eyes are still glued to this woman. The heiress is still talking but I barely hear it, because all the pieces are falling into place. Paul Knight just made this event about her.

About this deal.

About the marriage alliance.

Something in the pit of my belly tells me it's back on.

I glance at my brothers. "He can't stop himself, can he?"

"Never." Jett drains his whiskey glass.

The old man crafted this entire night around her. Then, like the goddamn showman he is, he takes Daniela's hand and leads her straight toward us.

"Surprise guest, huh?" I snap.

His expressions smacks of a win. "Daniela was in town, and it seemed like the perfect opportunity to invite her."

I don't fucking believe the gall of this man. "She just happened to be in town?" My gaze flicks to the heiress's wide eyes. She stares back at me, calm and collected, as if she's seen men worse than me. But that big, wide smile of her soon got wiped off her face.

Matteo sniggers. "Or maybe you put this event together just so you could find a way for her to meet us."

We're all thinking the same thing.

Zach offers her a polite nod. "Nice to meet you, Daniela." He extends his hand, and the heiress shakes it firmly, but she eyes us with uncertainty.

"Yeah," Jett mutters, barely looking at her as he catches another whiskey glass. Rio, on the other hand, can't seem to look away. He's transfixed by this woman.

"This is a bride auction, isn't it?" I say flatly, glancing at the Beauty Queen, and I swear I see her flinch. "Just call it what it is." I eyeball the old man.

He chuckles. "This is Dexter. You'll have to watch him, Daniela. He can be quite cutting with his remarks."

Her bright green eyes meet mine with surprising ease. What I see now is something else. Not fear. Not even interest. There's a calmness about her, like she's assessing me. Trying to figure out what kind of monster I am before deciding how to handle me.

But even though she plays it cool, I can see the tension in the way her fingers tighten ever so slightly around the stem of her glass. I can see right through her indifference.

I glare at the old man again and don't care if the heiress hears me. "You planned this."

"If my sons are too busy running from responsibility," he says smoothly, "then I have to bring opportunity directly to them."

I snort. "And by opportunity, you mean something for your own personal gain."

"That's up to you." He scans us all in one swooping one-hundred-and-eighty-degree gaze. "I'll leave you to make Daniela feel at home." He pins his gaze on Jett.

"I'm already taken," Jett growls, and tightens his arm

around Cari's waist. The heiress and Cari talk before Zach jumps in, just itching to be noticed.

My father turns to Daniela. "Please, make yourself at home, and report to me if they bite, or are rude. They shouldn't be. I've spent a fortune on educating them."

I look away, feeling abject disgust and unable to face him.

"You know what?" I mutter. "I need some fresh air."

I head towards the balcony, desperate to get away.

CHAPTER FIVE

DANI

THE PENTHOUSE IS A HIVE OF ACTIVITY, CHATTER AND PEOPLE circulating. A soirée in Paul Knight's penthouse. I still have to pinch myself.

This is such a big deal for me, for my family. I can't believe that I'm here, meeting all the Knights.

Looking around the penthouse, it was already so amazing to see during the day, but now, for the evening party, it has a different mood; opulent, rich, and discreet. The smell of money and power pervades the air.

I'm told that we're in the Great Room. It's a large open space with windows for walls on one side of the room, and with stunning views of the city and Central Park.

The sequined black, figure-hugging dress I'm wearing seems too much. With a high neck, it reveals my bare shoulders even more because I'm wearing my hair up. To make matters worse, the dress catches the light, shimmering as I walk and I suddenly feel overdressed, wrongly dressed, for a room filled mostly by with men in suits.

I wish I hadn't listened to Paul Knight. I'm already seeing that he manipulated me into wearing something I wouldn't have chosen for myself.

This dress is more for a party and not for an event like this. I wish I'd gone with my gut and worn something demure. like the smart but dressy trousers I'd picked out. But Paul insisted I wear something dazzling, something that would catch the eye of a Knight.

I feel so out of place, and I'm sure it shows. I don't know what to look at, and I know no one, apart from Paul Knight but he's busy being the host. Luckily the views from this room are stunning, and I look out often, as do most people here, but they're talking and laughing.

There are only two other women here, as guests. The others are servers, and they are so beautiful, in my country they would be on the cover of magazines, not serving food at events like this.

I arrived early, before most of the guests and Paul tried to put me at ease. He told me that his sons would be here soon and I anxiously awaited their arrival, looking around, standing here by myself. Feeling out of place and out of my comfort zone. Every now and then Paul would take me under his wing and introduce me to his friends. I tried not to shiver in disgust when most of them, not all, but *most*, raked their eyes over me slowly. I'm sure many won't even remember my name, but they looked at me like they wanted to devour me. I've seen that look in the eyes of many men.

It's a hungry look. Men can't hide their feral desires.

I approached the women guests. They're much older, both wearing pantsuits. This is so plainly a man's world and maybe they wanted to blend in, not stand out in sparkling sequins like me. I tried to make conversation but they were cold towards me, a little wary of me. But this changed when I started talking about business, and AO Eletronica. They soon took interest. It was then that they saw me as someone worthy. Someone more than the sexy dress I had on.

After that I walked around with a glass of untouched champagne in my hand, trying to be as invisible as I can be in a shimmering dress that hugs my body.

And that's when I saw them enter.

The Knights.

They stood at the entrance of the room. I recognized them from the online research I'd done. It was impossible to ignore how handsome they are. They're all so good-looking. *Too* good-looking. And they're around my age, a little older.

Not *decades* older. Not old enough to be my *father*.

I know all too well that beauty is only skin deep and I planned on getting to know them, to see if they have good hearts and good values, and to see who among them is caring and kind.

Just as I was getting ready for Paul to make an introduction, he told me to hide. I wasn't sure why, but I did as he asked, and I listened as he addressed his guests and talked about the Latin American markets.

Then, he introduced me.

That's something I wasn't expecting.

He said he didn't want to parade me like a show pony, but introducing me the way he did, seemed like he did exactly that, because I felt like a show pony. I was so nervous walking into the room and I had to keep reminding myself why I was here, why I agreed to this in the first place.

I started to see that what this man does, and says, are two different things, and I'm already unsure of whether I can trust him.

"Time to meet my sons," he said, casually opening his arm and expecting me to loop mine through it. Which I did. He then led me over to his sons, and I didn't know where to fix my gaze because when he introduced me, his sons seemed frozen for a few awkward seconds.

Then one of them said something about this being a bride auction. He seemed annoyed. So hateful. It unsettled me. Paul introduced him as Dexter and warned me to watch him. I understood why Paul had put on this event, why he'd asked me to meet him at the penthouse instead of the office.

His sons seemed to hate that I was there and I got the feeling that they're not too close to their father, either.

One of the brothers, Zach, I think, was nice and he shook my hand. But Jett, the one I was supposed to marry, seemed especially cold. He barely acknowledged me, yet his girlfriend, I presume she's his girlfriend, given how his arm was slung tightly around her waist, was friendly.

"Hi, I'm Cari. Nice to meet you," she said.

I felt relieved because her warmth felt genuine. "Nice to meet you."

"Is this your first time in the US?" she asked.

"I've been here a few times. I also went to college here."

"That's so interesting." We made idle small talk, and I sensed that she was doing her best to make me feel welcome, but I felt more out of place than ever. Worse, I felt isolated. It's obvious that I'm not wanted here. Before I started to spiral in misery, a friendly voice cut through my thoughts.

"Where did you study?"

He was young, and smiling, and I breathed a sigh of relief that someone was talking to me.

"I'm Zach, by the way." Zachary Knight. I recall reading about him online.

"Hi, nice to meet you, Zachary."

"Don't … don't call me that. I prefer Zach. I'm the youngest of this set of brothers."

This set of brothers? I blinked. Before I could ask what he meant, I caught a movement. It was one of the brothers, Dexter, the rude one. He nudged Zach's elbow. I couldn't tell if it was a warning or a joke.

Paul didn't mention anything about there being two sets of brothers. Maybe he'll tell me later. There was nothing online about that.

Zach continued. "Six brothers is a lot to remember. You're probably struggling to remember who's who."

Paul left me then, and I wish he hadn't. That's when the rude son left, too, saying he needed to get some air. I felt relieved because I wasn't prepared for anyone to be as rude to me as Dexter was.

Another brother stepped forward and smiled, looking effortlessly polished in his sophisticated tux.

"I'm Enzo." He offered me his hand to shake. His voice was deep and he seemed suave and confident. I think he's the youngest. There's something about him, something refined. Then he turned to another brother, and this one wore a chain around his neck and had tattoos peeking from his wrist, but he walked away.

"Sorry about that," Enzo said. "That was Matteo. He can be a little …," he shrugged and didn't complete his sentence.

And now, this is where I am. Standing around, trying to breathe. Trying to think about my parents, and why I'm doing this.

Enzo, Zach and Cari make small talk with me and I'm grateful that they're trying. I feel like they're nicer than the others, and they're doing their best to make me feel welcome. But I don't feel welcome at all, and I now start to wonder if I've made a big mistake.

My thoughts drift to Oscar Ramos and I start wondering if maybe I should have considered marrying him.

"This is Rio," Enzo says, breaking me out of my thoughts. He turns effortlessly to another brother, whose heated gaze I've felt on me the entire time. We acknowledge one another with a nod, and then he pulls out his hand and I shake it.

"There are too many names to remember," I admit, nervously. "I'm going to have a hard time keeping track of everyone."

"Then maybe you shouldn't agree to an arranged marriage with a stranger," someone says. It's a familiar voice. A cold voice. And it belongs to that rude man. The one who despises me even though he barely knows me. I turn and find myself staring into his cold dark eyes.

"This is Dexter," Enzo says.

"I remember. You're so hard to forget." My voice is thick with sarcasm. He looks at me, still unsmiling. As if I've ruined his evening just by breathing. He doesn't bother responding. Instead, he lifts his beer bottle, takes a slow sip, and watches me over the rim.

Tall and clean shaven, he looks like someone who spends time at the gym. Slightly flummoxed by the blatant resentment, I ignore him and turn to Rio, but I immediately regret it. Because Rio is staring at me. *Again.*

I hate when this happens. And it happens all the time.

People assume beauty is some great blessing, but sometimes, it's a curse. Because people sometimes just freeze around me. They don't know what to say. They just stare. Now I'm convinced that I should've worn something different. Something less noticeable.

Rio doesn't strike me as the silent type. He exudes confidence in bucketfuls. But right now he's looking like he's been hit over the head with something hard. He looks dazed, and I shift uncomfortably.

Thankfully, Cari jumps in. "You must find this quite overwhelming," she says, her voice gentle. "I imagine it's not easy, walking into a place like this, with all these men in suits."

I wonder what she knows about this arrangement. "It was a big decision to come here."

"When *did* you arrive?" Dexter asks.

"He talks," I remark, my voice caustic. This gets me a few laughs, but it seems to aggravate him further. He raises an eyebrow. What did he expect after his rudeness? For me to take it?

He raises a brow. "Oh, I can talk. I can talk a lot, as it happens. Just depends on if I want to."

"To answer your question, I arrived a few days ago."

"A few days ago, huh?" His voice is carefully neutral. "But I thought the deal was already over."

I laugh, but it's nervous. I don't know how to answer. He blatantly referred to the deal. He's not dancing around the issue. I stare at my glass, trying to stay cool and collected, trying not to rise to the slight edge in Dexter's voice.

"Do you want to leave now?" Cari asks Jett quietly. From the periphery of my vision, Jett glances at his watch.

"Let's go. I'd like to read Brooke a story before bedtime," Jett replies, turning his back to me. "Excuse us." He acknowledges his brothers and pointedly ignores me. I don't know why he hates me so much. He's found someone he loves. He and Cari do look good together.

I wish I could leave and go back to my hotel room, because these boys seem to hate me. Except for the two youngest ones, Enzo and Zach, and the one who won't stop staring. Rio.

Enzo excuses himself, mumbling something about needing food, and Zach follows him.

I pretend that it's okay, except I'm now left alone with Rio and the rude one, who suddenly turns to me. "You're not here to discuss global expansion and emerging markets with my father, are you?"

"Oh, Dexter," I say, offering a coquettish laugh that I try hard to make sound believable. It's evident that he thinks I'm an airhead. "I can talk about that, if you'd prefer. I work in Brand Strategy and Corporate Communications, and part of that involves managing advertising campaigns and staying competitive in all markets."

"I'm more interested in what brings you here," Dexter says. "Did my father contact you?"

He doesn't waste any time getting straight to the point. Why would he ask me this? It's obvious that these guys aren't keen on their father, which makes me worry. How can anyone not like their father? I love mine with all my heart, which is why I'm willing to sacrifice my happiness for him.

One son not liking Paul Knight, I can understand. But two sons? All of them? None of them seem to like this man. I must guard myself against their father. I must remain vigilant, because if six of his sons don't care much for him, there must be a good reason.

"No," I reply, thankful that this is the truth.

"You just got on the plane and decided to come here? To do what? To convince Jett to change his mind?" There's an edge to his voice that I don't like. I don't think I can come clean and tell him why I'm here. This was supposed to be a formal introduction, as Paul Knight said, an easier way for me to meet his sons, but it looks like they've all figured it out and are angry.

Not just with their father, but with me.

"It was nothing like that," I say calmly.

"His mind's pretty well made up," Dexter snarls. "Don't think you wearing that dress will get him to—"

"Calm down, Dex," Rio says. "Don't be an ass."

"Let her answer," says Dexter.

I wish Raquel were by my side. She'd know how to handle these boys. She'd have verbally whipped them and hung them out to dry by now. I give the rude one a pointed stare. "I have no intention of trying to convince anyone. And as for your oldest brother, I have absolutely no interest in him, because that deal never even got off the ground. We've never even spoken prior to this evening."

Dexter's face twists. "Jett was in Bermuda over the summer, having the time of his life with his assistant."

"That's information I don't need to know." My face feels hot. My insides hard and heavy. I need to get away from this man and I pity the woman who ends up with him.

"Dex." Rio shakes his head. "I'm sorry," he says to me. "Dex can get a bit … *angry* sometimes. For no reason at all, usually."

"I apologize," Dexter says gruffly. He looks at me for a beat and I can't read his expression. I don't know what to make of this man. He hasn't fallen at my feet. *Thankfully.* And he's been openly hostile. I don't understand him. And now, to confuse the situation further, he apologizes. Something I never saw coming.

He's a bit of an enigma. Turns out, I love a good challenge. "Apology accepted."

"I'm protective of my brothers." He waves his bottle at me, and I see a rare smile. The anxiety that's been tying my insides into knots, eases. I like that he's protective of his brothers, and taking that into consideration, I don't blame him for getting angry with this situation. Maybe a lot of his nastiness stems from his father? Maybe I'm not the one he's angry with.

I'm tempted to ask him about his family, to see if I can get some nugget of information, something that they aren't telling me. Information that I haven't seen online.

"How come someone like you hasn't met anyone?" he asks. I like that. He's trying to get to know me, and he's asking all the important questions. Meanwhile, Rio's staring at me like I'm the eighth wonder of the world, and I feel self-conscious again.

"Dude, get a drink," Dexter tells him. Rio gives me a disarming smile and a side eye at his brother before leaving.

"You were going to tell me why you haven't met anyone," Dexter prompts.

I like that he's curious. That he isn't taking me at face value. "I've been more focused on work."

"No boyfriends?"

"Not at the moment. I dated while in college, here in the US, but nothing serious."

"You studied here?"

"At Georgetown university."

His eyebrow starts to rise, before he schools his expression. "You last dated while in college, and not since?"

He's interrogating me, but I don't get any sleazy vibes from him. It seems like he's trying to figure out my motives. He jerks his chin, indicating the people around us. "You must be used to attention like this."

"I don't like it," I reply carefully.

"Funny that you should say that, wearing such a figure-hugging sparkly dress. You're hard to miss."

I suddenly feeling tired. Like I've had to be on my best behavior while trying to figure out all these personalities, trying to work out who would be best for an alliance.

Who out of all these brothers I could live with for one year.

Be married to. On paper.

And I'm still not sure how this would work.

"Your father suggested I dress up," I reply, noticing Matteo over Dexter's shoulder. He's laughing with one of the pretty servers. He seems flirtatious, and doesn't seem to carry himself with the same gravity as the rest of the brothers. He's the only one not in a full suit. He's wearing jeans and a shirt with a casual blazer over it.

Dexter's eyes fill with surprise. "Jesus. You've already started obeying my father, and you're not even a member of the family."

My mouth feels like I've swallowed sand. "Did *your* father force you into this?" he asks. This time, there's a softness in his eyes.

"My father would never force me to do anything."

"You're doing this of your own volition?" he cries, just as the staring brother, Rio, reappears.

I don't reply. I'm not sure how much Dexter needs to know. How much Paul Knight wants me to tell.

Dexter closes his eyes and shakes his head. "You don't need to answer. You look uncomfortable, so I'm guessing you know more than you're willing to share. I need another drink, a strong one. I'll leave you two to talk."

Rio's heated gaze on me makes me wish I could go back to my hotel room now.

CHAPTER SIX

DEX

I walk away, leaving Brazilian Beauty Queen and Rio together.

I don't trust her and I'm still trying to figure her out. Why is she here? Why would someone like her, someone looking like *that,* agree to an arranged marriage? It doesn't make sense.

I need to know what the others think. I step out onto the penthouse balcony and find Jett and Cari. Huddled together. Kissing.

Jesus. At my father's penthouse, on the balcony? They can't seem to keep their hands off each other, which is weird as hell because Cari's usually too sensible for putting on public displays of their affection. But she looks just as wrapped up in Jett as he is in her.

"Get a room, you two," I say, casually. Jett doesn't even look embarrassed. Cari turns, her expression flustered, but she doesn't move away from him.

What is it with people being in love?

"Good conversation with the Brazilian Alliance?" Jett asks. Cari swats him gently across his arm. "Don't be so nasty."

"What? It's the truth," Jett counters.

"You don't know that." She looks up at him, her eyes shining. "She's nice. I think she's really nice and brave for coming here, for meeting you all."

"You'd think Charles Manson was nice." Jett drops a kiss to her lips, but she backs off.

"I would not. I like giving people a chance, but not serial killers and their kind." Then she tiptoes up and kisses him again. "You were extremely cold and indifferent to her. You should apologize."

"The hell I will," Jett growls. They kiss again.

"Can you two stop that?" I turn away in disgust.

"What do you want?" Jett's face twists.

"I thought you were leaving to read to Brooke," I counter.

"Her nanny said she was already asleep."

"In that case, get a room."

Jett chuckles. "Lexi still away? You feeling lonely?"

"Screw you." I hadn't even thought about Lexi. But seeing Jett and Cari stare at me, arms wrapped around each other, like I'm a spare wheel on their bike, makes me want to bolt. "I'm trying to figure her out. This Daniela Oliveira," I say, putting on what I think is a Brazilian accent.

Jett chuckles. "Looked like you two were getting along."

"No. I was trying to figure out why someone who looks like her would agree to *this*."

Cari frowns. "Is it the deal still going ahead?"

"That's the only reason our father would bring her to our attention. As for the deal? I have no idea. That man doesn't tell us until he needs to," Jett replies.

I sigh heavily. "More like he doesn't tell us, but expects us to piece things together."

"This was a perfect coup we walked into." Jett rubs his hands up and down Cari's arms, warming her up.

"Why are you both so cynical?" Cari asks. "Imagine how Daniela feels, walking into this place. It's so intimidating. I think she's brave for coming here. You don't know if she's come to look for a Knight, or whether it's something else. Your father is always looking for business opportunities."

I blink at Cari. "You sound like a cheerleader for the Brazilian Beauty Queen."

"Don't call her that." Cari looks annoyed. "We women need to band together. Have you read the room? It's full of testosterone." She wrinkles her pert little nose.

"You're not wrong," Jett says. "We do need more women in business. It's a cutthroat world filled with ruthless men right now."

"You think having more women is the answer?" I ask, then think twice because of the way Cari's glaring at me. I move to deflect the conversation to something that's bugging me. "She told you she got here a few days ago, right?" I say, looking between them.

Jett frowns. "Yeah, and… ?"

"So, in a couple of days, the old man somehow managed to set this whole thing up?" I shake my head. "Think about it. He got CEOs, investors, and important people together, just like that. Normally, these people's calendars get booked months in advance."

Jett looks confused. "What are you saying?"

"I'm saying maybe he's been trying to get this deal, this *alliance* together, behind our backs, even though you told him you weren't interested. He hasn't let it go."

Cari chews on her lower lip. "That would be typical of your father."

"Yeah, yeah," I say dryly. "Welcome to the family. Oops. Sorry. Premature. Jett hasn't put a ring on your finger yet."

Cari's lips twitch like she wants to say something but thinks better of it. Jett gives me a hard stare, like he doesn't want me talking about this. "We're taking things slow."

"Cari's been working for you for three years, man. Define 'slow.'"

His face darkens slightly. But hey, the guy is happy and who am I to begrudge him his happiness?

"What do you think of the heiress?" I ask him.

Jett shrugs. "I don't."

"Come on, brother."

"I don't *think* of her," he repeats. "I never have. The arranged marriage deal was something I've never paid much attention to, even before things between me and Cari got serious. I would never marry someone for money, or to make a deal, and definitely not with someone I didn't know."

Cari rolls her eyes. "Jett, he's just asking for your opinion."

"Yeah," I add. "We all know you didn't want to marry her. You didn't want the alliance. I get that. But don't you think there's something *off* about her?"

Jett shakes his head. "I don't know. Arranged marriages happen all the time. In some cultures, they work quite well."

I take a long swig of my beer. "But someone who looks like she does, don't you think it's suspicious that she doesn't already have a line of suitors?"

Cari gives me a pointed look. "She has a name. You should say it. It seems to me that you find Daniela attractive. You should admit it."

"I do not find her attractive. She's beautiful," I say with some reluctance. "But she's not my type."

"She's more than beautiful," Cari counters, "She's Movie-star level, Hollywood-level beautiful."

Jett sighs and cups Cari's face in his hands, pressing his forehead to hers. "You are beautiful," he murmurs. "You are gorgeous, and perfect, and all *mine*."

Cari blushes, eyes softening.

Jesus Christ. "Possessive much?" I mutter.

"Shut the fuck up, Dex," Jett growls.

I roll my eyes. But my mind is still stuck on the heiress. Because I just don't buy it. "Seriously. Just think about it. You expect me to believe that she couldn't find anyone to marry her? That she—"

"Daniela," Cari says.

"Yeah, her," I continue, "she had to get on a plane and fly all the way here to make a sneaky deal with our father?"

"But it was our father who approached them," Jett reminds me. "Remember? He was in Brazil in the summer."

I nod slowly, the memory clicking into place. "I don't know if you were on the call or if it was Zach," Jett continues, "but he was talking about the company. Said he needed to wine and dine them. I'm pretty sure it's the same company."

"You're saying the old man approached them again?" I ask.

"Maybe." Jett shrugs.

I narrow my eyes. "Then why would the heiress agree? If their company was thriving, she wouldn't need to do this."

Jett shrugs. "You know what the old man is like when he wants something, he goes after it. And he doesn't stop until he gets it."

It's true, but even so, something about this doesn't make sense. I find it odd that the heiress couldn't find someone in Brazil with the wealth she's looking at us for.

Cari sighs. "Dex, you're looking for holes where there aren't any. Your father is diligent. His legal team and finance guys would have gone through everything with a fine-tooth comb. If he's going through with this deal, it means the company is legit and has serious potential."

I grunt, taking another swig of beer. She's right.

"One of you is going to form the alliance," Cari adds. "Not Jett, because he's taken, and he's *mine*." Another shiny-love-soaked glance at him. "Are *you* considering it?"

I nearly choke. "Fuck no, but I know someone who'd agree to it in a heartbeat." I look behind me, through the large windows and see Rio talking to Daniela. Jett and Cari turn their heads.

"For someone who is such a cool, hard dude, this man looks pussy-whipped without even tasting any."

"Dex!" Cari cries.

Jett looks annoyed. "Cool it with the vulgarity." He glances at Rio and the heiress again. "He does look obsessed."

"Yeah," Cari agrees, eyes wide.

I don't want to expose Rio, but the guy is making it too damn obvious.

"When did he turn into a wuss?" I mutter. "The guy is calm and sharp, with tons of attitude. He's got big dick energy that women love. But now?" I shake my head. "He looks like a wet mess over this woman."

Cari frowns. "He's not talking much."

"No. He's gawking like a spotty teenage boy at his first strip club." I sigh. "Let me go save him."

I walk back inside.

The room is dimly lit, jazz music floating through the air. The scent of expensive perfume and catered hors d'oeuvres lingers. People are talking, making deals, laughing over glasses of aged scotch.

Rio and the heiress are still standing together and it looks like they're talking. Zach and Enzo are back, too. These two are like puppy dogs. Zach more than Enzo. I'm not sure about

Enzo. He seems quiet but deadly. In any case, they don't stand a chance. The heiress is too much woman for them.

I stride over. "You okay, Rio?" I glance at the Beauty Queen. He nods stiffly. "You need another drink?"

"He sure looks like he could do with a couple of shots." Enzo grins. Rio mumbles something and disappears.

"So touchy," Zach says.

Before I can go after him, the old man steps into view.

"Daniela," he says smoothly to the woman at the center of our group, "come with me."

The heiress hesitates but follows him, seeming a little flustered. Or maybe she's just glad to be free of Rio eyeballing her so blatantly. I exhale, feeling a sense of relief that she's gone.

"What do you think she's doing here?" Zach asks.

"You interested?" I examine his face, notice that it's flushed. Notice that his pupils are dilated.

"In what?"

Jesus. This kid hasn't even pieced it all together. He's just been busy admiring the goods.

"Maybe she's here for a business deal?" Enzo suggests. It's strange that we don't often get together in a social setting like this, that it's always around the dining table or the conference room table, always doing deals. This is different, and usually when our father hosts events like these, they're in a big hotel suite, with hundreds of people around. It's easier to go all evening without running into the rest of the Italian Knights.

But being around them this evening, I see they're not so different from us. Rio and I get along, sure ... but the other brothers?

I shake the thought out of my head. It's too raw and painful because thinking about the old man's secret family brings back bad memories of things I'd rather forget. Things I'm ashamed of and hate myself for. The guilt never leaves.

I feel his gaze first, a prickling starts across the back of my neck and I realize that my father is watching me. When I turn to look, he motions me over, so I go to him, shoulders tense.

"It's been a long day for Daniela," he says. "Do you mind dropping her back to her hotel?"

I blink back shock. "What?"

Yes, I do fucking mind. I open my mouth to protest. I don't want to take her home, and I quickly scan the room looking for Rio but can't see him.

"You were probably going to leave soon anyway," the old man persists.

"I wasn't."

"You can come back," he counters.

"I *do* mind dropping her back."

"Don't be so rude," he snaps.

"No, no, it's okay." The Brazilian Beauty Queen steps around me, her deep, rich and lightly accented voice catching me by surprise. "If Dexter doesn't want to …"

Shit. I didn't realize she was standing nearby.

"Don't make me ask you twice," my father hisses.

I have no choice but to comply. I just hope Rio doesn't see me leaving with her.

"Try to be nice, Dex," my father says in a patronizing tone that grates on me. "I'm only asking you to take Daniela back to her hotel. Nothing more."

I glance at her again, and she's looking everywhere but at us. She looks uncomfortable and awkward. Like she can't wait to leave this place.

At least we share something in common.

CHAPTER SEVEN

DANI

I BARELY KNOW THIS MAN, YET I CAN ALREADY FEEL THE simmering anger lying beneath his cold, hard exterior as we walk out of his father's penthouse.

Dexter has been tasked with driving me back to my hotel, and it's clear he hates every second of it. I don't like that his father coerced him into doing this. I didn't need him to do that.

"I could have taken a taxi," I say as Dexter comes to a stop next to a black Aston Martin. It's sleek, powerful, and exudes the kind of wealth that doesn't need to prove itself.

"You heard my father." His voice is tight. "He seems to think you're some kind of precious cargo or something."

"I'm sorry for putting you to any trouble."

"It's too late for that." Anger oozes out of his every pore and I'm too shocked to speak. This man isn't even pretending to hide his dislike for me. Jaw set, silence stretching thick between us, his eyes are fixed on the road. I have the perfect opportunity to examine him closely. His hair dark brown like his eyes, is short at the sides, and slightly longer on top, with a few curls falling effortlessly over his forehead. From the side, his profile is sharp and well defined. His jaw looks like it's been carved from marble. Or maybe it's just set extra hard because he's pissed about having to drive me to my hotel.

His large hands grip the steering wheel like he's mad about something and fighting to contain himself. Broad-shouldered, but not bulky, Dexter is all lean strength, the kind that doesn't need to prove itself. He's so much more appealing than Oscar Ramos ever was.

"I don't understand why you're so angry with me."

At a red light, he finally looks at me, his gaze impassive. "What do you want me to do? Hug you? Tell you how lovely it is to see you? Ask if you'd like to go sightseeing tomorrow?" His voice reeks of sarcasm. "I don't know you, Daniela. All I know is that our father sprung you on us."

"I sense hostility between you and your father."

He lets out a sharp laugh as the light turns green. He revs the engine harder than necessary. "You think?"

"A little."

"How observant of you."

He laughs. Even though those dark, hard eyes don't turn to me often, I can feel his simmering fury in my bones. This man doesn't like me, and I misunderstood him earlier, back in the luxurious penthouse, where the music and laughter softened my interaction with him. Maybe I deluded myself into thinking he was someone he isn't, because, compared to his brothers, most of whom couldn't stop gaping at me, he seemed like the best option.

Option.

I'm talking about my future husband as an option. Not a soulmate. Not a friend and lover. But an option.

At least this option would be better than Ramos.

"What do you think of my father?" Dexter asks, glancing at me briefly before his eyes snap to the road again.

I hesitate. "He seems like a nice man."

He snorts with derision. "Nice? You don't know the first thing about him. I would caution you to be wary."

I figured out as much. Still, I don't understand why Dexter is still so openly hostile toward me after warming up towards the end. Maybe he feels tricked into meeting me, and this mood of his is to do with the way their father presented me. I understand their resentment at being blindsided, because that's not how a father should be.

"Do you have a girlfriend?" I ask, the question slips out before I can stop myself.

He frowns. "What?"

"I'm sorry. That was too personal."

"Then don't ask." His eyes stay on the road, though he glances at me every now and then, his irritation evident. "Answer me this," he says. "Is this your doing?"

I shift uncomfortably. "What do you mean?"

"You coming here, and being presented to us tonight. Don't you feel like you're in a meat market?"

"I'm a businesswoman, first and foremost," I say defensively, even though that's a little white lie. I'm a daughter, first and foremost. And I want my father to be well again. I want Papai to stop lying in bed, worrying over the company, over our future.

But I don't say any of this to Dexter. I came here to make an alliance, but the Knights don't know that. Paul Knight was careful about how to dress this up, and I'm not sure what information I'm allowed to give away to his sons.

"I don't like being tricked," he says, after a while.

"I understand," I say softly. "I would hate that too."

"Do you have a girlfriend?" I ask, again, deeply curious,

because he evaded answering the first time I asked. If he does, then he's out of the running.

"Why are you asking me such a personal question?" he asks, his eyes still on the road.

"I'm curious." I feel like a fool. I feel like I'm giving the game away. But I'm not here for long, and I need to know which of the Knights might be my best choice. If none of them are, I need to go home, and find another way.

"My father is a controlling man," Dexter says, after a while. "You should be wary of him. I don't know what he's told you."

"He hasn't told me anything."

"Then why are you here?"

"To do business."

"What sort of business?"

Before I can even think of how to answer, my cell phone rings, and it's my mãe. I glance at Dexter, see the hard line of his lips and decide that I don't want to talk to my her with this sullen angry man next to me.

The phone keeps ringing. Mãe is obviously desperate to find out how this evening went. It's past midnight back home, and I feel guilty that my parents have been up waiting for my feedback.

"Aren't you going to get that?" Dexter turns to me. Something in his eyes softens just then. "Answer your call, Daniela. It might be urgent."

So, I do. I pick up. "Oi, Mãe… já sabia que você ia me ligar."

Hi, Mom. I knew you'd call me.

"Meu anjo, estou preocupada. Você está bem?"

My angel, I'm worried. Are you okay?

My heart bursts with relief and love at the sound of my mother's voice, and to hear her words. I'm lucky that I have this type of relationship with my parents. Seeing Paul Knight with his boys, I feel incredibly blessed. I also feel homesick, and I briefly consider getting the next flight back.

"I'm okay," I tell her, speaking in my mother tongue, which is helpful, because Dexter won't understand.

"Was it good? What were the sons like?" she asks eagerly.

"Oh, you know … I'll tell you tomorrow."

"Tell me now! We've been waiting to hear from you, my love. Your Papai also wants to know."

She hands the phone over, and my stomach clenches when I hear my father's soft voice. "How was it, Daniela? Are they nice? Did you find someone you liked?"

"Papai." I would give anything to be there, with him, holding his hand, reassuring him, telling him that everything is going to be fine. Truth is, I'm not so sure anymore.

I switch the phone to my other ear, keeping it away from Dexter, just in case. "I'm good, Papai, don't worry about me. How are you?"

"I'm good, my dear. I was praying tonight would go well."

"It went fine." I keep my voice neutral. I don't want him worrying. "We'll talk tomorrow. It's late. You shouldn't have stayed up all this time for me." Guilt tugs at me. São Paulo is two hours ahead of New York and it's midnight here.

My father senses that I don't want to speak. He even asks if one of the Knights is with me. I explain that one of them is driving me back to my hotel. He sounds overjoyed and says that's good news.

If only my parents could see Dexter's face. I can't tell them how he behaved. No matter how this ends, or what further hostility I must endure, I will spare them that. I hang up.

"Your parents?" Dexter asks.

"Yes."

"You seemed worried."

My insides are in freefall. "Do you speak Portuguese?"

"Is that what you speak?"

"Yes."

He looks surprised. "Not Brazilian?"

"No."

"Is everything okay?" he asks, displaying a rare side of concern.

I falter. "Just ... old age."

"How old are you?" he cries, incredulously. His tone makes me giggle.

"I'm twenty-four."

"Seven-year age gap," he mutters.

"Huh?"

"The age gap between you and me." It surprises me that he's worked this out. "How old are *they*?" he continues.

"My parents? They're in their late sixties."

"Similar ages, then. My father's sixty-five."

I force a small smile, but my mind is racing. My father is placing all his hopes on me. I can't go back without securing an alliance. Also, Dexter was working out the age gap between us. He's older, but not Ramos-years older.

"You sounded worried about them. Are you?" Dexter prods again. I can't tell if he's genuinely concerned or if he's trying to find out more about my reason for being here.

"I'm close to my parents. They miss me and I miss them very much."

"But you've only been here a few days."

"I still miss them. It's not the number of days so much as it is the distance."

"When did you get here?"

His interrogation puts me on guard. "Why so many questions when you didn't even answer mine."

"Which one?"

"About whether you had a girlfriend."

"I'm not sure you'd like to hear the answer."

That's a warning. My mind churns through the possible answers he could give me.

"I don't currently have a girlfriend," he says, after a while. But even though he answered, I worry if he's telling the truth or convoluting it like his father would. These people are strangers to me. I was starting to think that Dexter would be a good choice of partner, but I'm not sure anymore.

I decide not to push him anymore, because I don't want him asking more personal questions of me, so we sit in silence for the rest of the journey. I'm cautious about giving too much away, and I'm also curious as to why his father hasn't been upfront with him. I suddenly have doubts about marrying into this family. Everything looks great on the outside, but a short few hours with them have exposed so much.

At least with Oscar Ramos, I know what I'm getting into.

We soon pull up in front of my hotel. Dexter turns to me. "You have arrived at your destination," he says in a robotic voice, his face expressionless.

"Thank you. I'm sorry for taking up too much of your time."

He nods, looking relieved. "Okay."

Okay? "Good night, Dexter," I say, in the breeziest voice I can muster as I start to get out of his car.

"Good night."

He doesn't look at me again and stares straight ahead as I step out. My sequined dress shimmers under the moonlight, and I pray I don't trip as I walk into the hotel. I'm sure I can feel his eyes on me.

It's only when I get into the elevator that I sigh with relief, and when I get inside my hotel room, I kick off my high heels and quickly get out of the dress. The sequins have been digging into my skin all night, and I'm itching to be rid of them.

I collapse onto the bed, exhaling heavily, glad to be back in the privacy of the hotel room, away from lecherous eyes and hostile faces. But I feel stuck. Tonight was supposed to give me a solution. A way out of marrying Oscar Ramos, but I don't think I am any better off. Most of the Knights don't even like me.

What do I do now?

A knock at the door makes me bolt upright. I grab my dress and try to quickly get into it but another impatient knock follows quickly.

"Who is it?" I tread slowly towards the door, holding the dress to me since I have no time to try and wriggle into it.

"Dexter."

I spring back in shock. "Dexter?"

"The guy who just gave you a lift here."

"I know who you are."

"You forgot your cell phone."

My cell phone. I quickly open the door, worried that Paul Knight might have called or messaged, and Dexter might have seen it.

His eyes trail down my length. It's obvious that I'm holding the dress to me, and not wearing it. I frown at him. "How did you get my room number?"

"Twenty bucks can get you a lot of information around here." His gaze starts to trail downwards again, but he quickly forces it back to my face again. "You just open the door to unexpected guests?"

"You told me it was you. You sounded like you," I protest, my fingers tightening around the fabric I'm holding to my chest like a shield.

"You have to be careful. A woman like you … here … alone. Desperate men could try all sorts of tricks."

I narrow my eyes. "Are you confessing to something, Dexter?"

"I'm not desperate, sweetheart. Just warning you to be vigilant." He shakes his head. "And opening the door *not* wearing the dress … don't do that."

"I took it off because the sequins dig in and it's difficult to put back on quickly." My pulse picks up and my voice trails off. "Thank you for this." I grab the phone from him.

Mischief dances in his eyes, while his fingers tap along the door jamb. "You're not going to ask me in for coffee?" That lazy smirk curls at the corner of his mouth.

I open my mouth, not even sure what I'm going to say to that.

"Just messing with you." He backs away, and I'm about to close the door, when I hear his voice. "Lock the door, and put the chain on."

"Why?" I frown, opening the door wider again. Surprised that he's concerned. That he might care.

"I was able to find you, and all I had to do was charm the hotel receptionist. You can't be too careful."

"Yes, sir."

I hear him chuckle, and close the door, only to be distracted by a notification ping from my phone. I startle when I see a text from Paul Knight. Just as I'm about to read it, I hear Dexter again. "I'm not leaving until I hear you deadbolt the door. And slide the chain across," he says from the other side.

I find myself smiling. There's a good man underneath all that outward hostility. Even though he's not interested in me, Dexter cares enough to keep a lone woman safe. And that tells me a lot about his character.

I bolt the door and do the chain, then hear a "Good girl."

Then silence. It's in that silence that I feel it. The pull. Not just to his body, but to the man behind the razor sharp edges, and the barbed wire comments. The one who knew I was alone and warned me, even if he wrapped his words in a thick layer of sarcasm.

I look at my phone again. Luckily I have a lock on there, so Dexter wouldn't have seen any of my messages. I read Paul's text.

> Hope you had a good evening. Did any of my sons catch your attention?

I think about it for all of two seconds. Then text back:

> Dexter

His reply is immediate:

> Good choice

> We'll talk tomorrow

I put my phone down and wonder what I've done. What death trap am I walking into?

But, considering it all carefully, Dexter is the only real option. Jett is taken. Matteo was flirting with the servers. Enzo and Zach seemed too young, too eager. Rio? He feels territorial and possessive. In awe of me. Mesmerized. A little *too* much. He's the type of man who would consume me whole.

Dexter doesn't come across like that. He's different. He's prickly and indifferent, and yet he was the only one who spoke to me and asked me questions. And he wanted answers.

I'm not thinking about marriage. I'm thinking about an alliance. An arranged marriage. A year-long contract.

Both parties get something out of this deal and at the end, we both walk away with something.

A year. That's all it must be.

But something tells me it won't be as simple as that.

CHAPTER EIGHT

DEX

My father has summoned me to his office. The soiree was only yesterday. An uneasy feeling sinks in the pit of my stomach. This can only be about one thing: last night.

All morning, I've been thinking about last night. The trickery, the surprise guest and the way we were all blindsided by our father into meeting her.

I'm meeting Jett and Zach later for drinks, and I might drop by later to see Rio. If he likes the Beauty Queen, and all signs point to my father wanting an alliance, then Rio needs to let the old man know, and fast. I sense that the heiress is eager to get the deal done.

I knock on the door and walk into the old man's office. "You wanted to see me?"

"Sit down." He gets up from his chair just as I'm easing myself into the one opposite him. He stands, hands in his pockets, staring down at me in that calculated way when he has something of importance to impart. This man likes to have the upper hand, to look down and control the room at moments like this.

"What did you make of last night's soiree?"

I knew he'd ask me this instead of admitting the truth. That he tricked all of us into meeting her.

"Did you mean to ask that, or do you really want my opinion on the heiress?" I cross my arms. I have a feeling I know why she was there, but I want to hear it from my father.

"She has a name. Daniela."

"We thought that deal was dead, that it never went anywhere with Jett. And yet, suddenly, you orchestrate an event and fly her in from Brazil?" I shake my head. "Last night wasn't about networking. We can network with those people any time of the year. Last night was all about parading her in front of us Why can't you just admit it?"

The old man glances at his watch. "She's here to form an alliance. One that will be mutually beneficial to her family and ours."

I sit up straighter. I'll be damned. He's admitted to it. "Why couldn't you tell us before?"

"Would you have turned up last night?" he asks. "I'll give it to you straight. She approached me."

I stare at him, unable to process what I'm hearing. "*She* approached *you*?" My jaw clenches. "You told us that you went to them."

"Months ago, yes, before Jett ran off to Bermuda for his little escapade."

"It wasn't an escapade," I snap. "He's in love with Cari. She's been good for him, and you should be happy for him."

"Escapade," he repeats, his tone dismissive.

"He's happy. Brooke has a mother figure she adores, and Jett—"

"I don't want to talk about Jett," the old man interrupts,

waving his hand like he's swatting away an insect. He doesn't like talking about Jett because my brother one-upped him.

Every time I'm before this man, I feel like a seven-year-old boy. How did my mother put up with him? *Why* did she put up with him?

She didn't.

She *endured* him for us. And when she found out he had a secret family, it was more than she could bear. And then I … I made things worse. I push away the dark thoughts that stalk me every time the past comes up.

My father keeps talking. "Daniela Oliveira called me because her father is most eager for an alliance."

The heiress initiated this?

"Why didn't her father call you?"

"His health is failing."

I cock my head and try to figure out what might be going on, but it would only be pure speculation. "Jett turned her down, and if she's still desperate—"

"This isn't about her. She's not desperate to make a match for love. She's doing it because she's a businesswoman and she and her father believe our families merging would be mutually beneficial for us both."

"It still smacks of desperation to me," I mutter.

"Jett," my father says, pausing to take a breath. "Jett embarrassed me."

I try not to smile at the memory of that Knight family dinner when Jett brought Cari along—something that never happens in this family. He stood up and said he wasn't going to go through with my father's arrangement. Declared he loved Cari. Made a grand statement and told everyone he loved her. "That was pretty cool," I say, proud of my older brother.

My father sneers at the memory. "And now, Daniela has chosen *you*."

The words barely register.

"What do you mean she's chosen me?" I growl. How could she? "I barely had a nice word to say to her."

I didn't lead her on. She's gorgeous and has curves in all the right places, but I like my women to be lean and athletic. There's no way she could have mistaken anything I said to her for flirting.

"You must have sent out some signals."

"Yeah, keep-the-fuck-away-from-me signals."

"They evidently worked like a charm," my father says, deadpan.

I scowl, looking up at the ceiling, wondering how the hell the heiress has interpretated so much so wrongly.

The old man gives me a wry smile. "She seemed to think you were pleasant. She likes you. I don't know what you did—"

"I didn't do anything. Trust me. I have friends with benefits—"

"And you can keep them. Have as much sex as you like on the side with whomever you want—"

I put my hand up, not needing to hear this from my father of all people. "I don't need complications like a marriage in my life, especially not an arranged marriage."

If I were ever to have the misfortune to marry, I wouldn't be fucking around on the side, like he did.

If, I were to *ever* marry, it would be because it would mean something. Because *she* would mean something to me. But this concept is something the old man wouldn't have a clue about. And, since I have zero plans to ever marry, it's a moot point.

"Don't think of it as a marriage," my father says. "Strike that word from your vocabulary, if you're struggling to come to terms with it. This is purely a business arrangement."

"Why a marriage, then? Why go to all that hassle instead of just merging or having a hostile takeover?"

"Forming an alliance benefits both of us. Arminio, her father, and I have discussed this at length. A marriage of convenience is the best solution. The company shareholders are getting skittish, an alliance with a powerful American family would do much to alleviate their concerns. For us, we get access to the telecoms market in Latin America. We get to see how it works, without starting a new business ourselves. We get access to their research, their systems, their products, their marketing. We get to see what works before we decide to go it alone."

Forming an alliance. He makes it sound like a cold and clinical process. Something that is a formality. A marriage should surely be more than that? Not that I've ever considered it.

"No," I say, determined not to let him dangle any carrot in front of me.

"She picked you, Dex."

"I don't give a shit."

Besides, Rio likes her. I can't do this to him. Even if it's just a fake relationship.

"You don't have to love her."

I let out a bitter laugh. "Of course, love is not a requisite for marriage. You, of all people, would know that."

"I loved your mother," he says in a low voice. It's rare for him to mention her. I feel like I've hit a nerve and any memory of her hits me like a punch to my solar plexus, momentarily winding me. I can't speak. I can't think.

"You don't have to do anything," he continues. "You don't have to consummate the marriage. You just need to marry her and stay married for a year. Live in separate bedrooms. Don't talk to one another if you don't want to, but you must put on a convincing show to the public. Only immediate family on both sides can know the truth."

I swipe my hand through my hair. I'm not doing this, but I am curious. "Why me?"

"You can ask her later."

I sit upright, because this man clearly has his agenda which he's following. "There will be no "later." I didn't make any moves towards her and I'm not interested."

All I can think about is Rio and how he couldn't take his eyes off the heiress. About how he's had that photo of her in his apartment all this time. I haven't seen him yet, but I'm meeting him for drinks later. We all need to discuss what happened last night.

Sometimes, I wish all of us, the Knights and the Italian Knights, could just be one big family. Sometimes it seems that we're more similar than different, and only rage separates us. Their existence drove our mother to the edge. Their existence took her from us.

But they have what we lost—a mother. Rio mentioned once that he was going to Italy to see her. That his mother lives there now that the boys are all grown up. I haven't really pushed him for much information, because talking about his mother makes me think of mine. And there are days when I can't bear to do that.

I can't agree to this. I can't do this to Rio. He's my friend and my brother. There's no way I'll marry the heiress, but I can't tell the old man about Rio's interest. We don't tell him our business unless it's a life-threatening situation.

"She picked you," my father insists, like I have no choice in the matter.

"How do you know? Have you spoken to her?"

"She came to my penthouse this morning for a debrief."

Innuendos swirl around in my head, but my father is serious. His face is set in a hard line and those cold, reptilian eyes stare back at me. I feel almost sorry that Daniela had to go to his place and have a meeting with him this morning. I remember the phone conversation she had with her parents, and how her voice was soft and filled with so much love. I didn't understand a word, but I could tell, just from the way she spoke to them, that she cares deeply about them.

"Why did she pick me?" I snap.

"We're going round and round in circles. I have no idea. Perhaps you should ask her when you get to know her better."

"That's not happening. I won't be getting to know her better."

"Surely it must count for something, having such a stunning woman choose you over your brothers? She's gorgeous. Simply stunning. Why wouldn't you be interested?"

"I barely spoke to her!"

He's such a despicable being. I'm tempted to ask him why he doesn't go ahead and marry her himself, but that would be awful for the heiress. I couldn't do that to her, put such a vulgar idea in the old man's head. I'm sure he would, if there was something in it for him, but I have a feeling that using one of us to get this deal is simpler.

"Maybe that's what she likes. The silent type. Men gush over her. They're enthralled by her beauty. She's used to it. That idiot Rio couldn't even string a sentence together from what I observed—"

"Don't call him an idiot."

My father raises an eyebrow before continuing. "Zach and Enzo would have followed her around like loyal puppies. Jett is with someone who's a decade younger than him—"

"He's in love," I interject. Jett is also someone who believes in marriage. He believes in love. I don't. I will never marry.

"Matteo flirts with anything in a skirt, and he missed this opportunity. Which leaves only you."

"I don't care. I'm still not interested. This isn't happening. The best thing you can do is tell her to get the next flight back to Brazil."

"What would you say to twelve million dollars?"

I remember the deal with Jett; the carrot the old man dangled in front of him. It was ten million. The reward has increased. "Twelve million for what?" I ask, but an idea starts to form in my head.

"To stay married for one year. You get a million dollars a month and you can walk away at the end of the year. It will be the easiest money you'll ever make."

I don't know if I can do this, not even for twelve million. Not everything revolves around money.

"I already have more than enough money," I retort. "I don't need more."

"You have access to the Knight legacy, Dex, but I'm not dead yet, so you don't own much of it. Think about it. Twelve million for a year's work. Are you really going to turn your nose up at that?"

I glare at him. "Like I said, money doesn't mean as much to me as it means to you."

There's no way I'll ever agree to marry the heiress when Rio likes her. I need to talk to him first. I shift in my chair. I already have money. We all do. But still, twelve million dollars, just to stay married for a year? Maybe I could do some good with it? I've been toying with an idea, something I've wanted to do for a long time but I kept putting off.

"Think about it," my father says, his voice smooth. "You don't even have to sleep with her, but then again, if she's willing, why not?."

I look away squirming at this so-called fatherly advice.

"She flies back in a few days' time, and she needs an

answer. You don't have long to get back to me. Think about it. Twelve million dollars for doing nothing. It's like having roommate."

Except, it's not. It's nothing like that.

I already know what I'm going to do.

I need to talk to Rio first.

CHAPTER NINE

DEX

When I turn up at Rio's place, he offers me a beer, but I wave it off, needing to have a clear head. I haven't been able to work, haven't been able to think since my meeting with the old man.

Now I need to give Rio the news that the woman he wants doesn't want him.

She wants me.

I still can't wrap my head around it. Couldn't she tell I hated her? That she's the last woman I'd pick even if we were the only two people left on earth?

"You look agitated." Rio comments, "Missing Lexi that much?"

"I wish it were that simple."

He looks concerned. "What's going on, dude?"

"Are you going to make a move on the heiress?"

He looks confused. His dark brown eyes widening, and the

corners of his lips turning up into a curious smirk. "She's gorgeous. Beautiful. Hard to resist."

"She's all of those things," I agree, "but something doesn't add up."

"Like what?"

I hesitate. "I don't know … I just can't put my finger on it."

"You don't think she's gorgeous?" he cries in disbelief. "But I get it. She's not exactly your type."

"Anyone going into a marriage of convenience for financial reasons, needs to have their head examined."

"Dude, she has her reasons, I'm sure. And she's gorgeous."

"As you keep saying." I rub a hand over my jaw.

"That woman is *hot,*" Rio cries.

I huff out a sigh. "She came to the soiree knowing exactly what it was. She was willing to be paraded in front of us like a prize at an auction."

"The old man dropped her on us like a surprise." Rio leans back, studying me.

"A bomb more like. He knew if he'd told us the truth, most of us wouldn't have turned up. He tricked us."

"It's obvious that she's here to make a match," Rio muses. "It didn't work out with Jett. Now it's one of us."

"Yeah. And you like her, so why don't you make a claim?"

Rio shrugs. "I like a bit of fire in my women. She doesn't have any."

I stare at him in stunned silence, then, "You just said she was hot!"

"I'm not denying that, but I like the chase. The thrill. And there's no chase or thrill if she's already agreed to get married. You know how I like my women, Dex. Feisty and furious. It's what makes bedtime so much fun."

"There is a chase and a thrill," I counter, frustrated. My mind races with the impression of the heiress last night, talking lovingly to her parents, and then later, when I turned up at her hotel room, of her trying to hide with the dress pressed against her. While it's true that she's not my type, I'd be lying if I said I wasn't curious to see what she was like behind that dress.

I shake my head. *I can't go there.*

Rio likes her.

"Why are you talking about her?" Rio asks, his face turning suspicious.

"Look, the old man tricked us, she's here to make a deal," I say, running a hand through my hair as I try to figure out how to drop this news. I exhale sharply.

"You look like you want to tell me something. What?"

This guy knows me too well. Better than Zach, for sure.

"She's here to marry someone, to make an alliance," I say, quoting the old man. "It's supposed to be mutually beneficial for both families. The whole point of last night was for her to pick one of us."

"Well, it figures," Rio says nonchalantly. "There's five of us. One of her. Of course, it's up to her."

I let out a humorless laugh. "Well, she uh … she picked me."

Rio's expression shifts and surprise flickers across his face. His features tighten, then he schools his face into a grin. He's not reacting like I expected. Maybe he really doesn't give a shit. He takes another swig of his beer. "She picked you, huh?"

"Apparently, but that's what I don't understand. I was horrible to her. You heard how I was with her."

Rio shrugs. "Some women like that. The offensive approach. She doesn't like me, because I was ga-ga around her. In awe. Doesn't usually happen to me, and I'm ashamed to say I must have come across as an adoring idiot. I'm sure she's had to suffer a few of those."

"But you like her. Why don't you go for it?"

Rio's brow furrows. "Because she didn't pick me, dude. She picked *you*."

"She doesn't know me."

"She doesn't know *me*," Rio counters.

"You can fix it. You're *that* guy. After a couple of dates, she'll fall for your charm. She's desperate—"

"Thanks."

"I don't mean it like that, brother. Something's not right. If the family business is doing well, and with her looking the way she does, why doesn't she already have a line of powerful men at her beck and call?"

"Maybe she's more selective. You know how so many guys with money are creeps. Nothing strange about that," Rio counters.

Maybe he has a point. Maybe I'm trying to come up with excuses to push this away. I can walk away, but the old man is persistent. He'll work through the others, through Zach, then Rio and his brothers.

"You like her. Just meet her," I plead.

Rio shakes his head, his eyes narrowing like he's made up his mind. "I don't think so. There's no challenge. I like the thrill of the chase with a woman, and with the heiress, there's no prospect of that."

"You're thinking about it wrong." I get up and start pacing. "There's no challenge because you're not married *yet*."

Rio watches me closely. "There's no challenge yet? You sound like you're trying to convince yourself of something."

I exhale loudly. "You don't even have to sleep together. You're only going to be faking it for the public, for investors, but behind the scenes, brother, sparks could fly."

"They could, with *you*," Rio throws back. I'm not doing a good job of convincing him.

I rub my forehead. "She's not my type. I just don't get it. I was horrible to her."

"Maybe she's into S&M." Rio gleefully rubs his hands together.

I roll my eyes. "Yeah. Maybe. I only spoke to her and asked questions to get intel for you."

"You don't need to do that on my behalf," Rio interjects.

"Brother, I don't care for her and I was suspicious." Now I'm starting to wonder if she assumed I asked all those questions because I was interested. I also didn't gush all over her like Enzo and Zach did.

Like Rio did.

"She picked you," Rio repeats. "What're you going to do about it?"

I hesitate, turning the thought over in my head. I stand to get million dollars a month, but the old man hasn't told me what happens if I walk away early. I decide not to tell Rio about the money. "You know what? I'm going to do it."

Rio grins. "Cool. About time one of the Knights got married."

I nod slowly. "If I marry her, the old man will think I'm doing exactly what he wants."

"He'll love that." Rio nods. "You're one of the hardest to bend, Dex."

I grin and think to myself how he'll think he's won. She'll think she's won. But I'll walk away early. Seven months later. Maybe eight months, if I can last that long.

They need a year?

They won't get it.

And in the meantime? I'll enjoy playing the game and bending the rules. More than anything, I'll enjoy pissing the old man off. "I'll just try this out and see how it goes. Have some fun. Who knows?"

Rio raises a brow. "Fun? You planning on doing the deed with her?"

I pause, my glee fading. *Not a chance in hell.* "No way." The fun will come from seeing Paul Knight's face when I renege on the deal early. But I don't tell Rio about that, either.

"It won't be easy to resist her," Rio says, wisely. "She looks even better in real life than she does in the photo."

I roll my shoulders back. "We'll see."

LAST NIGHT WAS BAD ENOUGH. GOING TO THAT EVENT, standing there like a damn pawn in my father's game. And now, less than twenty-four hours later, my whole life has the potential to be upended.

All because of something I didn't even do.

After I see Rio, I don't feel too bad. But I don't understand the quick turn of events. I can't forget how smitten Rio was by her and I think he's just putting on a brave face because she picked me. I feel bad that he's hiding his attraction for her behind a weak protestation about loving the chase or something.

It still feels wrong to go ahead with this, so I decide to run this by Jett and Zach. I head home, take a long shower, trying to clear my head. Then I tell my brothers to come over. A little while later, they both show up together.

"Has Father spoken to you?" Jett asks the second he steps inside.

"About what?" I head to the bar and get their drinks ready.

"About last night," Zach says.

I hand him a bottle of beer, and Jett a glass of whiskey. I pour myself a glass of scotch.

"Can't stay long," Jett adds, as we all sit on bar stools.

"No, of course not. Always too busy for your brothers these days," I quip.

"Don't be like that," he warns. He's extremely protective of Cari, and any jokes Zach or I make are quickly shot down. Not that we joke about her. More that we joke about *him,* and how he's so domesticated now.

"The old man spoke to me about last night." I scratch my cheek. "I might as well tell you now, before he calls us all into a meeting tomorrow."

"Tell us what?" Jett asks, guarded.

"What's going on?" Zach asks.

I exhale. "It's exactly what we thought. You know how the old man plays games with us? Last night was a setup. The heiress is here to make an alliance. She wants an arranged marriage because she didn't get one with Jett. And her family, her father, is eager for it, for purely financial reasons."

Jett and Zach exchange looks.

"And?" Zach prompts. "Get to the point. I need to be somewhere."

"Where the hell do you have to be?"

Zach ignores me. "Just spit it out."

I lean back on the stool. "She picked me."

Silence.

Then, "Who picked you?" Zach's brows pull together.

"Yesterday," I say, dragging it out. "Daniela Oliveira, the heiress, Brazilian Beauty Queen, she picked *me.*"

Zach's eyes go wide. "You're kidding."

"Why do you sound so surprised?" I ask.

"You didn't even talk to her," Zach mutters.

"Yeah, well, some of us still got it, huh, brother?" I clap him on the shoulder.

"Picked you for what ... to mate with? Marry? Talk to?" Jett asks.

I scrunch up my face in disgust. "To form an alliance. To marry her. For one year. Purely a transactional arrangement. The same deal you were meant to enter."

"You already spoke to Dad about it?" Zach asks.

"He called me in for a meeting earlier today."

Jett pats me on the back, but his expression is wary. "Are you sure about this?"

"I *wasn't*."

"He offered you money, didn't he?" Jett says flatly.

"Can we not talk about the money?" I hiss.

Zach lets out a low whistle. "You get to marry her *and* get paid for it? Why the fuck didn't she pick me?"

I down my scotch in one gulp, and Jett pours me another. Zach holds his beer bottle tight to his chest, watching me the same way Rio did yesterday when he looked at Daniela.

"You're actually going to marry her?" Zach asks, voice tight.

"Just for one year."

"I wouldn't jump into this," Jett warns.

"He's giving me a million dollars a month."

Silence.

Jett exhales sharply. "That's more than he offered me."

Zach stays quiet.

"I was expecting him to call us into a meeting today. Thought he'd come clean," Jett says.

"He had a meeting this morning," I say, my voice oddly detached. "With her. My ... wife-to-be." The words feel foreign coming out of my mouth.

"You're really going to do this?" Jett asks for the third or maybe the fourth time.

"Does this mean there's going to be a wedding?" Zach asks.

Fuck. A wedding. I hadn't really thought about the details of it all. All I know is that twenty-four hours ago, my life was fine.

I had a casual arrangement, nothing tying me down, no responsibilities.

Lexi, my friends with benefits counterpart has been out of my life for months, and that's been the biggest headache in my life so far.

But now, this.

I showed up at a networking event, thinking I'd have a few drinks, play along.

And now?

I'm getting married.

CHAPTER TEN

DANI

PAUL KNIGHT HAS SUMMONED ME TO ANOTHER MEETING, THIS time at his office. I arrived here early in the chauffeured car he sent me.

Now I'm sitting outside his office, my nerves twisting in my stomach. I told him I like Dexter, and now, in the cold light of day, I wonder how things will play out, because Dexter doesn't like me.

I assume Paul's going to tell Dexter now, in front of me. He can refuse, in which case I'll have to accept it and fly back and … fall back on the only option I have left.

Paul's assistant, a woman in her sixties with sharp eyes and a no-nonsense demeanor, glances at me from behind her desk but says nothing. And then, just as I'm trying to steady my breathing, Dexter walks in and my stomach tightens.

He stops short when he sees me. We stare at each other and I swear he almost growls, as if the sight of me makes him sick.

Before I can react, the door to Paul Knight's office swings open.

"Daniela, nice to see you." He gives me a smile that falls short of his eyes. "Dex." He nods at his son. "Come in, both of you."

I get up, half-expecting Dexter to let me go in first. Some small, stupid part of me assumes he'll be a gentleman, but he strides past me without hesitation.

Of course he would.

At least he holds the door open. I suppose that counts for something. But just as I start to step through, he shifts and blocks my entrance a little, so that I'm forced to brush past him. Our arms touch, and I catch a whisper of his intoxicating scent, feel the heat of his body. See his dark glare cutting into me as I walk past.

By the time I sit down, I'm having palpitations. I wish I had something to fan my face with. We sit across from his father, tension thick in the air. Paul's cold-gray eyes settle on me. "Daniela, I've spoken to your father. He's very happy with this arrangement."

I freeze. "You told him?"

"I told him last night."

I blink, thrown off balance. Paul Knight said he was going to discuss it with me first. He said he wasn't going to tell anyone yet.

He robbed me of something.

Everything is moving too fast and my head spins as I try to keep up.

"I didn't realize my decision was final," I say, my voice tight. "You asked me a question and I replied." I feel sick, because I've realized that not only has Paul Knight has told my father, he's most likely also told Dexter, which would explain why he's here.

Dexter snorts beside me.

"Yes," Paul answers, casually. He sits back, his eyes moving between Dexter and I, like he's enjoying my unease.

"Came as a complete shock to me," Dexter drawls. "Completely blindsided me. I had no idea you had the hots for me."

I can't face him, but I feel my cheeks burning. I try to act cool, try to think about the business side of the deal. "This isn't about attraction, Dexter. This is an arrangement. Once I removed all the other possibilities, you were the only one left."

He snorts. "You tell yourself that."

He's going to have so much fun rubbing my face in it. I address his father. "I assumed Dexter and I would get to discuss this further before we firmed up our agreement, before I told my parents, but you robbed me of that."

"And now here we are," Paul says smoothly, spreading his hands as if that explains everything. Ignoring every concern I have.

"This is moving very quickly," I say, trying to slow things down.

"You shouldn't have told him your choice. You could have delayed things. You're the reason things are moving quickly," Dexter points out, his voice unreadable.

"I thought we'd get to *talk* about it first," I fire back, then glare at Paul. "You said you were going to talk to him about it."

Paul leans back in his chair. "I did talk to him about it. I don't see the point of beating around the bush. You flew all the way here because you wanted this alliance. Your father wanted this alliance. You told me *who* you wanted. I spoke to Dex and we're all go. Why the hesitation?"

This is nothing like how he promised me it would go.

Dexter's words echo in my mind.

Be careful of my father.

Paul studies me. "Daniela, if you don't want this, you can back out. Get on a plane and go back to Brazil."

I narrow my eyes. *Why is he so eager?* "I know why I'm in a rush to get this done," I say slowly, "but why are *you*?"

Paul smiles, but there's nothing warm about it. "Once I make a decision, I move with it. I'm not one for waiting around."

Dexter speaks up, his tone edged with amusement. "Your father owns the biggest telecommunications company in South America. And whenever there's something that's 'the biggest,' 'the best,' 'the most competitive' ..." He pauses, glancing at Paul, "... *our father* always wants a piece of it."

My stomach sinks.

I barely keep my expression neutral as disappointment weighs on me. I just pray we can help our company with this alliance and get some kind of investment, some collaboration with the Knight name. The name doesn't mean anything in South America, but ever since the market shifted, investors have been backing away. Merging with a solid company, by having a high-profile wedding will help. As will the promised cash injections.

"I was planning to fly home tomorrow or the day after, and tell my parents in person, then make plans," I say.

"Your plans have already been made," Dexter announces, pointedly looking ahead.

"How do you know?" I ask, horrified.

"My father will have taken care of it, didn't you, father?" He looks at Paul.

"I'm working on it. Almost done." Paul steeples his hands.

"When are we getting married?" I ask, as my insides toss and turn with anxiety. "And where?"

"Don't ask me, ask your fiancé."

Dexter groans. "I'm not her fiancé. We're not engaged."

"You'll need to propose, and buy her a ring that's impossible to ignore."

"Fuck." Dexter sinks back into his chair, and my heart plummets in my chest. This is going to be ... difficult. Dragging this man to the altar. He hates me and I'm already convinced that he's going to make everything infuriatingly impossible.

"We have no chemistry," I lament. "I don't see how this will work."

Maybe Rio might be a better choice?

Dexter leans back in his chair, frowning. "This is a business deal. We don't have to do much convincing."

He's so cold today. Last night when he knocked on my hotel door and returned my cell phone, he was warmer. I felt like we could make this work. This morning? I see it will be impossible.

Paul gives a dismissive wave. "You will. The world needs to know that this is not a business deal, but a whirlwind romance leading to marriage." He nods at me. "Your father says it's important that Brazilian media buy the story. The investors are the ones you'll need to convince. Now," he continues, his voice measured and firm. "I need to run through the rules, and you both need to adhere to them."

I jolt to attention.

"There mustn't be a whiff of scandal. No drama. Nothing. I suggest you take the time to get to know each other." His eyes shift between me and Dexter. "You need to be clear on your backstories. You live on different continents. How did you meet? Why are you getting married so quickly? How did you propose?" To Dexter, "I suggest you buy a ring, soon."

Dexter leans back in his chair, arms crossed. "You mean you didn't buy one for me? What about the press release to announce this marriage?"

His father doesn't blink. "I thought I'd leave that to you, Dex." His gaze lands on me. "You need to be mindful," he says slowly. "If we present this as a marriage, nobody asks questions. Nobody talks." He pauses. "No one can know the truth outside of the Knight or the Oliveira family. Is that clear?"

I nod. "Yes."

"Yes," Dex mutters.

Paul shifts his weight, his expression cool. "You will be married for a year. As for living arrangements, Daniela, you will live with Dex in his apartment."

My throat closes.

Paul raises a brow. "Did you think I was going to send my son to Brazil?"

"Fuck that," Dexter snaps.

"I'll live here," I say.

It's happening too fast.

I hadn't even thought about living arrangements. About switching countries. About moving away from my mother and father and living here, with the Knights, a family I don't know.

"You both need to show that you are very much in love."

"Oh, joy." Dexter lets out a huff.

"I'll draw up the contract for your father to review," Paul says, casually.

Dexter sits up. "I need to see it."

I agree. "We should be part of this discussion."

Paul's lips press together and I sense something I don't like. "For now, you two need to get to know each other. Let your father and I handle the contract." He glances at his watch. "Now, if you don't mind. I have another meeting."

"I'd still like to see a copy of the contract," I insist.

"We insist," Dexter says. *We insist.* His reply sets my heart aflutter.

"Of course. I'll get the legal department to draft it up and send it to you both."

I hate how smoothly he dismisses us, like we're side characters in our own deal. We both leave the office. Dexter shoots off, walking so fast before disappearing. And I'm supposed to marry this man and make it look believable?

My mind is a whirr of different thoughts. My father isn't well and maybe Paul knows. Maybe that's why he's rushing this?

That's why I have no time.

I consider calling Raquel. I also need to speak to my parents. Paul broke the news to them that I had the right to tell them about. He probably told them not to contact me, but they'll be wondering why I haven't called them.

I head straight for the washroom, needing a moment to calm my twisted nerves. Try to settle the tight knot balling in my stomach.

My phone buzzes and I snatch it up, my stomach twisting when I see a text from Dexter.

Meet me in the lobby. Now.

I reply:

Now?

He texts back:

Yes now.

I let out a sigh. I desperately need to make some phone calls, but first, I need to figure out what the hell Dexter Knight wants.

CHAPTER ELEVEN

DEX

I send the heiress a text, because my father is moving way too fast. Either she knows something I don't, or the old man is withholding something from me.

I look up to find her walking towards me. She looks sad, and it makes my stomach tighten. She's away from her family, and everything familiar. Dropped into the Knight family like a grenade, and I have to suffer the consequences.

This poor woman has no idea of what she's walking into. I remember her conversation with her parents. How much she loves them. How much she cares. How she's doing this for them.

Jesus.

She's in for a shock.

Her eyes, no longer dazzling, but a muted dull green now, fix on mine, and I swear my heart flips a little. I can't remember the last time that happened and it startles me in a way I'm not prepared for. I didn't expect to feel anything for her, yet something about the way she moves, the way she looks at me, makes my stomach knot. My heart begins to race, which is crazy because I haven't even seen her woman naked, and already she's having an effect on me.

She crosses her arms. "You needed to speak to me."

"We should get our stories straight. Get to know each other," I say. "I need to get you a ring or something."

"I believe its customarily a ring." Her expression is guarded, like she doesn't quite trust me. "I can use something I have from my jewelry collection if that makes it easier for you."

"We need to play the part, so I'll buy something appropriate. I mean, we're getting married, aren't we? It's the least I can do."

"Yes, we are."

I scratch my ear, glance around the marble floored lobby. Wave at some people I know. "I don't know anything about you." My gaze meets her eyes again.

"You don't," she agrees, a little too quickly. "And I don't know much about you, except that you didn't want this."

"Well, you picked me. It's crazy, but here we are."

She exhales, eyes flicking away momentarily before coming back to mine. "I picked you because… because you didn't fall all over me."

I let her words sink in, and try to understand. "I've had it all my life," she says, something raw and honest in her expression. "I'm sorry if you think that's arrogant. It's just … you're *different*. You don't stare at me like I'm a commodity. You push back. You ask questions."

She stops like she's said too much, but I already get it. Guilt gnaws at me like a starving rat. I wince, thinking of the Brazilian Beauty Queen label I tagged on her, and in doing that, I reduced her to something plastic and pretty.

Men want to fuck her.

Women hate her.

It must be awful for her that people only see her as a beautiful face and body. They dismiss her as vapid, but the more I'm getting to know her, Daniela is anything but that.

I don't know whether to pity her or admire her for putting herself out there like this. For stepping into what's basically a cattle market.

"Why the rush for this marriage? Is there something you're not telling me?"

She puts a hand to her chest, expresses surprise. "No."

My gut tells me not to believe her. "Your father's company, AO Eletronica, is in good shape?"

"Yes." She pauses. "My father wants the credibility that comes with having an American co-partner and your father wants a share of the South American telecom market. What better way to do that than with a strategic alliance?"

I study her for a long second, try to find cracks, a sliver of information she lets slip. But she's good. "I understand your disdain for me, Dexter, but we are businesspeople. If we look at this as a business deal, we'll can get through this."

"Then we should get together and try to get our stories straight. Like the old man advised us to."

"Why do you keep calling him old man?" she asks innocently. "Do you have no respect for your father?"

"Welcome to the Knight Family." I get ready to leave. "I have a meeting I need to be at. I'll pick you up from your hotel at seven?"

"Seven is good."

I check my phone, a habit as easy as breathing, to see an email from my father. He wants us to meet in the conference room later this afternoon.

Great. I can hardly wait.

I'VE BEEN FOCUSED ON URGENT EMAILS AND TASKS FOR THE last few hours, and now make my way to the conference room where we've all been summoned.

The Italian Knights are already there. Rio nods as our eyes connect. Matteo keeps tapping the pen on the table. Enzo sits there, quietly. He also nods when I catch his eye. The only one who doesn't acknowledge me, or Jett or Zach, is Matteo. That asshole has an attitude.

"What's this about, Dad?" My eager younger brother asks, as the old man walks in, his movements sharp and precise.

"This is about something Jett should have done, but didn't," my father replies smoothly.

Screw him. I wish he'd stop poking his finger at Jett, but I have a feeling he's about to announce the marriage of convenience.

Jett leans back in his chair, unimpressed. "Let me guess," he says flatly. "You're still bitching about the arranged marriage. The one I wanted no part of."

"Doesn't matter now," my father says coolly.

I sit up and exhale, wanting to steal the old man's thunder. "Because I agreed."

No reaction from Jett or Zach. They already know.

"You're actually doing it?" Matteo asks, his brow lifting a little. "Agreeing to an arranged marriage?"

"Shut up and listen," Rio mutters.

Enzo stares at me quietly.

I feel the weight of all their gazes on me, as they digest this new information, and judge me.

"Why would you marry someone you don't even know?" Matteo asks.

I don't answer.

The old man glances at his watch, like this is some quick memo about a minor schedule change. Not a potentially massive decision for Knight Enterprises. Not a huge change in the trajectory of my life.

"You all met Daniela Oliveira at the soirée last night," he says.

"Yeah, thanks for the advance notice on that," Jett drawls.

"She was nice," Zach offers.

"Very pretty," Enzo adds.

"Well, she's not for you to look at anymore," my father says flatly. "She's agreed to marry Dex."

Matteo is texting on his phone.

Enzo shrugs. "Still pretty, though."

"That doesn't change," Zach agrees.

"She'll be your brother's wife soon," my father says sharply. "Have some respect."

"As if you know anything about respect," Matteo mutters, just loud enough, and without looking up.

The old man ignores him. "I'll keep this short. No one outside this room, apart from Daniela's parents, can know this is an arrangement. It must appear as a proper marriage." He clasps his hands together. "Call it an alliance if you want. A merging of two powerful companies."

Jett exhales sharply. "What's in it for you?"

The old man's mouth curves. "Like I told you before, access to the South American market."

"Access? Or, if I know you, you're probably planning to take it over. Slowly. Over time," Jett says.

The old man's smile doesn't falter. "Fifty-fifty deal. They stay married for a year. We gain insight. Access to their books, their operations. We send our people in. We have meetings. We don't have to move there, and they don't have to move here. Apart from, of course …" He turns to me " … your *wife*."

I feel heat course through my veins. That name. That label. It sounds surreal. "She's not my wife yet."

"She will be soon enough," he continues. "The public will see a Knight marriage. This will be interesting. The first of this generation. We have a reputation to uphold. Let's make this count."

Jett exhales loudly. "People already assume you only do things for money. I wouldn't worry too much about your reputation."

The old man levels him with a look. "It's important for AO Eletronica. This must look like a genuine union. I don't want bad press, rumors, or speculation." He flicks his gaze back to me. "Just keep her sweet. You don't have to sleep with her. You'll have separate bedrooms. She'll live in your apartment, but there must be none of your usual shenanigans. No hookups or scandal."

Fuck.

"But I thought you said I could—"

"I've changed my mind. I don't want anything to jeopardize this arrangement."

Not that I was planning on doing anything. I just wanted to see why the old man has suddenly changed his mind from telling me I could have as much sex as I wanted, to being squeaky clean.

I'm not that type of guy. I don't cheat. Even if I'm in an arrangement like this crazy one I'm about to get into. The old man's change of heart tells me he has a lot riding on this.

Still, a whole year without sex isn't going to be easy. Like my right hand isn't already overworked enough.

"Prepare to clear your schedules in the coming two weeks. I'll send out a memo about the wedding timeline."

I tense. This shit is getting real.

"You're getting married in Brazil," he announces calmly, adjusting his cufflinks. "I'll confirm the timeline shortly."

I open my mouth, then close it promptly.

What the hell?

And then, "If I'm getting married," I say slowly, "shouldn't I at least … I don't know … talk to *her* about it?"

Paul waves a dismissive hand. "No need. This is an alliance. A business deal. Just buy a ring. Get your stories straight. The rest—cake tastings, photographers and what not—I've delegated to a wedding planner. I'll speak with Daniela's parents so that they think they have some input, but we drive this show."

Jett lets out a dark chuckle. "How romantic."

Paul ignores him. "Get it done. Get it over with. Plenty of photo ops. The press will love it."

My pulse hammers in my ears. The break-neck speed of this gives me whiplash.

"We'll leave in the family jet. All of us," he announces, throwing a grenade at us.

There's a chorus of objections from the brothers. The old man's expression hardens. He levels each of us with a stare. "I know that as a family—"

Scoffs. From Rio. Matteo. Jett.

He ignores them. "We are a family," he states coldly. "Bound by blood."

More scorn.

Rio tilts his head, eyes sharp. "We only ever have meetings when it's about business. And once in a while, you throw some food on the table at your place to make it look like a family gathering."

The old man gives a tight smile. "Isn't that enough?"

"It's a long flight to Brazil," Matteo moans.

No one says anything.

But the weight of everything, the wedding in Brazil, the flight, being cooped up together, hangs heavy and smothering in the air.

DANI

I SHUT THE DOOR TO MY HOTEL ROOM, PRESSING MY BACK against it as I exhale. My heart is racing.

I'm meeting Dexter for drinks tonight and all I feel is apprehension. But that little conversation we had, just me and him, without his father, without anyone else, it was … *nice.*

Bearable.

I need to stop thinking about him like that. He doesn't want this. I get that. He has no ulterior motive for doing this. I'm helping my father, but he doesn't seem to even like his father.

At least he's doing it, because yesterday, he was against it and today, he agreed.

And me?

I need Dexter so that I don't end up marrying Oscar Ramos.

Now that it's official, now that we're getting married, it's finally time to tell my best friend. I glance at my phone.

Missed calls.

A string of messages from Raquel, ever since I texted a few days ago that I was in New York, but I never told her why.

I video call my parents first, taking a deep breath. "Papai … it's going ahead."

"Meu amor, we know!" My mother's voice bursts through the speaker, filled with excitement. "This is wonderful news! Have you got a picture of him?"

"No, Mãe, but I … I will."

"Is he good? Is he kind?" my father asks. His voice is quieter, careful. I hesitate to answer. "Which son is he?"

"The second one. Dexter Knight."

"A photo, meu amor," my mother begs.

"I'll send you one later, Mãe. We're going out this evening."

"You are?" My mother clasps her hands together, eyes shining like I've just won a Nobel Peace Prize. "This is so much better than we thought!" She sighs happily. "Arranged marriages do work, Daniela. So what if you didn't date him first? Do it the other way around. Equal minds, equal hearts. Love will soon follow."

I swallow. She doesn't fully understand why we're doing this.

"And his father?" my father asks.

"Paul Knight is drawing up a contract," I say carefully. "He said we'll both have a chance to review it." I look at my father, for some input, but he's quiet. "But Dexter and I thought we needed to be involved from the start."

"It's not necessary, not now. Don't complicate things, filha." His voice is firm. "You and Dexter, you both should just focus on the romance."

My stomach tightens.

"Papai," I start. "There's no romance here."

"There must be something if you've agreed to meet him," my mother says lightly. I close my eyes. I don't know how to explain to them that this isn't a love story.

Just as I begin to question myself again, about what I'm about to do, I hear a ping on my phone. It's Raquel. Again. I read her text.

> If I don't hear from you soon, I'm heading out
> on a search and rescue mission.

I quickly say goodbye to my parents, and tell them to get some sleep and that I'll call them tomorrow. Then I to call Raquel because I can't stall her any longer.

She picks up on the first ring.

"Daniela, where the hell are you?"

"I'm in New York."

"I know you're in New York, but where? Seriously, you've been acting weird for the past few weeks, and I … I don't know. Is there something going on that I need to know about?"

I laugh, remembering our late-night talks in college, the boyfriend drama, breakups, tequila-fueled pep talks in the early hours of the morning.

"I've met someone," I say. "And we're getting married."

The conversation falls silent.

Then, "You *what?*" Her shriek is so loud I move the phone away from my ear.

"I love him," I blurt out. How easily the lie falls from my lips.

"You're getting married?" Raquel repeats, slow, like she's making sure she heard me right. "And *this* is the first I'm hearing about it?"

"It's … complicated."

"Complicated how?"

I inhale a shaky breath. "It's been an on-and-off, international kind of thing."

"An on-and-off, international *kind of thing?*" Raquel echoes, incredulous.

"He was in Brazil a few weeks ago. Over a month ago, actually." Another lie. I hate myself.

"Aha. In the summer you said something was going on but you weren't sure what."

I swallow. That was when the whole Jett situation was happening. "Things are clearer now."

"Things are clearer *now*? What the hell does that mean?" Her voice sharpens.

"We had … uh … things to sort out."

"Let me get this straight. A few months ago, you weren't even sure what was going on, and now you're in New York, about to get *married*?"

"We haven't set a date yet," I admit. "But it'll probably be soon."

"Are you pregnant?"

"No!"

"Is he holding a gun to your head?"

I roll my eyes. "Raquel!"

"I'm just checking! You drop off the face of the earth, then out of nowhere, you're engaged?"

"I-I love him," I insist, the words making me shiver.

"You're stuttering."

"It's cold in New York."

"You stutter when something isn't right," she says. "You know what? I'm coming to see you."

"No. No! Don't do that. Please don't do that."

"Where are you staying?"

"How about I come and see you before I head home?" I suggest.

"We'll see about that. "I have to go now."

"Me too. I'm meeting Dexter this evening."

"Dexter?"

I wince. "My *fiancé*." I stare down at my ringless ring finger.

"Dex-ter," Raquel repeats, drawing out his name. Suspicion drips from her voice.

A text comes through. From Dexter again. "The Bluebell Manhattan," I murmur, reading it out loud. That's where he's taking me. Another text message pops up.

I have the ring

My breath catches in my throat. I need to be careful.

"I have to go," Raquel announces, "but we need to talk, and soon."

My heart sinks.

Lying to my best friend is possibly harder than living with Dexter will be.

Possibly.

CHAPTER TWELVE

DANI

This place reeks of decadence. It's discreet and stylish. Filled with the type of people who came to Paul Knight's soiree.

Dexter picked me up earlier, not from the hotel door, but from the car. He called me, and I went downstairs. I'm dressed more appropriately this time. A sleek, navy jumpsuit. Simple, yet flattering.

He gave me a casual glance, his eyes not even taking in what I wore. Not that I wanted him to. I don't. But this is why he's different.

We drove in complete silence for twenty minutes.

Interesting.

Now we're sitting in a place called The Midnight Lounge, in a booth of thick and luxurious blue velvet seats. This place reeks of elegance and luxury. I find myself admiring the rich textures of the furniture and furnishings, while the scent of money hangs in the air, along with the spicy floral notes.

This place has the same floor-to-ceiling windows as Paul's penthouse. With sweeping views of the skyline.

"You didn't have to impress me, Dexter."

He barely lifts a shoulder. "We need to put on a front. I'm obeying my father's orders."

"Do you always "obey?" I find his choice of words interesting, but I've learned a lot about the Knight family dynamics in my short time here. Dexter flashes me a smile that is cold and detached. It sends a strange shiver down my spine.

I study him, taking in the way his dark hair is styled. The slightly longer curls on top, styled just enough to have a natural wave. The dim lighting makes his sharp jawline more defined. And those eyes; dark and intense bedroom eyes. He's good-looking. Frustrating as hell, but good-looking, and I find myself staring at him for longer than I should. I find it harder to look away. Maybe because he isn't fawning over me, the way most men do. This man seems completely uninterested.

I just wish he liked me. It would make things easier.

A tall and smartly dressed man comes over, all in black. He and Dexter shake hands and Dexter introduces him as his friend, Luke. "This is my fiancé, Daniela," Dexter says, smiling at me with such warmth, it makes my skin prickle with goosebumps. He can be charming when he wants to. I immediately hide my left hand, the one that doesn't yet have a ring.

"You got engaged? Congratulations!" Luke exclaims. "I never thought I'd see the day when you'd want to settle down, but I guess you found the right woman."

Dexter flashes a wolfish grin. "I sure did."

"You never let them go, once you find them," his friend says, smiling at us both.

Dexter reaches across the table for my hand, making a show of our togetherness. "That's why I put a ring on her finger. I don't plan to *ever* let this one go." His words send goosebumps running down my skin. He says it like he means it, but I know better. He's so smooth. So charming. Such a good liar. I just pray his friend doesn't ask to see the ring.

"I'll leave you to enjoy your evening. Congratulations to you both. Nice meeting you, Daniela."

After he leaves, Dexter and I immediately withdraw our hands. Then a server brings over an ice bucket in which lies a bottle of champagne.

"With compliments, from Luke," he says.

"Jeez. He's really pulling out the stops." Dexter's voice drops as he pulls out the bottle. "Cristal. This is one of the most prestigious champagnes in the world."

I wince. "I hate lying to people."

He grimaces like he's in pain. "Me too. Luke's a good guy, but if we send this back now—"

"We can't."

"What would you like to drink?" he asks, scanning the menu.

"How about this expensive champagne?"

"We can open that later. I'm not really a champagne type of guy."

I can see that about him. "I'll have a cocktail. Something light and fruity. The Bluebell," I say, opting for the signature drink.

He orders scotch, and after the server has taken the order, he leans back, lacing his fingers together on the sleek and shiny table. "I guess we need to decide how we met."

I sigh, that is the task for this evening. "We should try to keep the story close to reality."

"You've done this before, haven't you?" His voice is suspicious.

"No. Have you?"

"No. But you seem pretty eager about it."

I roll my eyes. "Look, I don't want to keep repeating this. I only want to help my father. You're suspicious of me, maybe you're wondering why I haven't met anyone, but you're not a bad-looking man and I'm not bad-looking either—"

He cuts me off. "What? Did you just say you're not *bad looking*?" He shakes his head. Then, he schools his surprise, nodding. "Yeah, I guess you're not bad looking."

It's strange. In this moment, I like him a little more. "Thank you." I tilt my head and give him a wide smile. "No food stuck in my teeth? No mustache?"

He exhales a laugh. "No."

"No booger up my nose?"

"Jesus, Daniela."

"Just checking." I grin. "So, I must be presentable."

"This is definitely better than what you had on the night we first met." His eyes casually sweep over me.

I freeze. "Excuse me?"

"You weren't wearing anything," he reminds me.

I blink. "*What?*"

"When I came to your hotel room, you could've been naked behind that door, for all I know."

"I was holding up my dress!" I cry out in exasperation.

He shrugs. "Exactly. You weren't *in it.*"

I narrow my eyes. "Were you curious?"

"Nope."

"Not even just a little?"

"Absolutely not."

I sit back, studying him. "You really don't fancy me, not even a little bit?"

He leans forward and whispers, "Daniela, you're the last person I'd want to marry. What we're doing now, pretending to be madly in love, it's all lies. You know that."

I arch a brow. "What if I were the last person on earth?"

"Same. There were two other women at the soiree that night," he says smoothly. "Both in their fifties. Both wearing trousers. I'd have picked them over you any time."

I gasp. "You're dead serious?"

"Damn straight."

I burst out laughing. It's so unexpected, because I've never had any man say that to me. While his words feel refreshingly different, they also leave a sting. Because at last I've met a man who interests me, but has no interest in me.

Our drinks arrive and Dexter lifts his glass. "Let's toast to something."

I pick up my cocktail. "Like what?"

"Our impending wedding."

"Our surprise wedding."

"That too." He lifts his glass and drains it completely dry. Shock lances through me. He must be stressed. Maybe he's uncomfortable being with me, and that's why he's drinking so fast.

I groan. "We need to work on our stories."

"We do," he agrees. "People always ask how people met. What are you going to tell them?"

I take a slow sip of my drink, thinking. "I'd say we were both at a carnival," I begin. "I won a giant stuffed panda, but I couldn't carry it, so you, being the chivalrous man you are, offered to hold it for me."

He narrows his eyes. "I'm already regretting this story."

I grin, feeling the tension between us soften. Feeling slightly more at ease with him. "And then, just as we were standing under the Ferris wheel, bam! You asked me out on a date."

He shakes his head. "Absolutely not."

"Why not?"

"Because which Ferris wheel? Which carnival? Why would someone you like and me meet at a place like that? We live in different countries, also, I can't remember the last time I went to a carnival. And, did you go alone, or with friends, if so, where were they?"

I'm impressed that he's giving this such careful consideration. "Maybe we should work on our proposal story instead? How did that come about?"

He shrugs. "The usual. We went out for dinner. Had a lovely time."

"What did we eat?"

"Truffle risotto. It was out of this world."

"I love truffle risotto!"

He nods. "Good to know. At the end, I ordered you a pudding, and inside was a ring."

I wrinkle my nose. "Boring."

"Predictable," he admits.

"Have you ever actually come close to actually proposing?"

"No. Never."

"Good thing this marriage is fake, then," I mutter.

He exhales a laugh. "We probably shouldn't be saying that out loud."

I'm more curious than ever now about his former girlfriends. I swirl my cocktail, feeling a little flirty. "Maybe we should've done this 'getting to know each other' part at your apartment instead."

He cocks a brow. "Are you coming on to me, Miss Oliveira?"

I roll my eyes. "You wish."

"Soon to be Mrs. Knight."

I stiffen. "Nope. That doesn't work."

"Why not?"

"Daniela Knight?" I shake my head. "It's like chalk and cheese."

"That's because we *are* like chalk and cheese."

I sigh. "Okay, fine. We're getting to know each other." I rest my chin on my palm. "Tell me something about you."

"I like to have a lot of sex."

I blink. "Did I need to know that?"

"You're going to be my wife, aren't you?"

I straighten up, feel the heat inching along my cheeks. I can tell by the way his eyes twinkle, that he's noticed.

"I'm joking!" he cries, probably because he's realized how awkward I feel. And why do I feel awkward? He was joking.

I frown. "Why tell me, then?"

"So you understand what this isn't."

Ouch. Way to put me back in my place. Not that I was harboring any ideas. I just liked that we were starting to feel comfortable around one another.

"I understand that this isn't a real marriage," I say, carefully choosing my words. "It's a marriage on paper only, and neither of us will become romantically involved with one another or with other people, for the duration of this alliance."

He nods. "You understand completely."

A beat of silence. I want to know what a man who likes to have a lot of sex will do in the sandy desert of a one-year loveless alliance.

"You asked me about my previous relationships, but I didn't get a chance to ask you about yours."

"What do you want to know?" He picks up the second glass of scotch he's ordered. I've only taken a few sips of my cocktail. But I can tell this man is buying some time. He's hiding something.

"Tell me about your relationships."

He brushes something off his dark shirt. "Don't have one at

the moment. I tend not to go for relationships, per se. I'm more of a friends-with-benefits type of guy."

A gasp falls from my lips. I pray he didn't hear it. "Why?"

He lazily puts his arm up along the top of the booth. "I don't like getting involved. I love sex, and I already told you that, but commitment scares the shit outta me."

"Why?"

He inhales a long breath, stares down at his drink. Wraps his palm around it, as if deep in thought, then fixes me with a cold stare. "We don't need to become each other's therapists. You don't need to psychoanalyze me."

Touchy.

The cutting sting of his barbed wire words is a subtle warning to stay away.

"But you asked, so I guess you deserve an answer about my previous hookup." He clears his throat, eyes averted. "She's abroad. Working in Europe. Has been for a few months and won't be back for a while. Don't worry. I won't even look at anyone while we're married."

I clench and unclench my hands which are on my lap. What do I say to that? Thank you? I appreciate that?

"Your turn. Tell me something about you," he prompts. "What's your favorite color?"

"Green."

"What shade of green. There must be a gazillion."

"The shade of green that's earthy and solid, like the one we have at home."

He peers at me. "What color is that?"

"You'll see when you come over."

He chortles. "I get to ask another question because your answer is so vague. Tell me something else."

I sip my drink. "I'm a black belt in jiu-jitsu."

He sits up straighter. "What?"

"You heard me."

"You're a black belt? In jiu-jitsu?"

I nod.

He stares like it's the most impressive thing he's heard. "That's ... fucking *awesome.*"

I raise a brow. "You sound surprised."

"Because I am." He leans in. "What else?"

I hesitate. "I go to the gym. I run."

"Big deal. So do most people I know."

"I've also run marathons."

His eyes widen. "F—" He stops himself. "You've run marathons?"

"Yes."

He exhales. "You really are full of surprises. Where?"

I sip my drink, watching him. "The São Paulo International Marathon, the London Marathon and the New York City Marathon."

"Color me shocked." He slumps back against the velvet booth, but this time when he looks at me, there's admiration in his eyes. "You love your parents," he states.

"Doesn't everyone?"

"No." We stare at one another in silence. He doesn't want me to probe, yet he's digging deeper. "You adore your father."

"I do. He's a wonderful man."

He shakes his head. "Yeah. We really are nothing alike." He doesn't smile this time, and it feels like the air has suddenly chilled.

"Serious question. What's your biggest weakness, Dexter?"

His lips tug up at the corners. "Women who ask too many questions." Then, softer, his voice dropping lower. "And people I can't protect." A server passes by. "Another round of drinks?" Dexter asks me.

"Maybe we should open the champagne? It was nice of your friend to offer it."

"I guess it was."

I sit back and watch Dexter pour champagne into our glasses. This evening isn't as bad as I thought it would be.

<hr>

DEX

I SIT BACK IN MY CHAIR, TAKING A SIP OF CHAMPAGNE AS Daniela tells me about her college life here and then about her life in Brazil.

My gaze drops to her outfit. It's a slinky dark blue jumpsuit and it shows off her curvy hips and small waist, and with a neckline that reveals nothing, but hints at plenty. She's luscious, no way about it.

This evening could have gone worse. So far it's not been too bad. It's not like pulling out my toenails with a pair of pliers, which is what I feared.

When I told her I'd have picked the other women at the soiree over her, the way she threw her head back and roared with laughter, it hit me then. She's beautiful. I found myself staring at her, mesmerized by the soft, bare expanse of her neck, and by her sense of humor. This woman has the confidence to laugh at herself.

She's like no other woman I've met.

When the drinks arrived and we made a toast, I had to knock back my scotch to steady my nerves and quench my suddenly dry throat because Daniela is so utterly captivating when her defenses are down.

Then she had to go and tell me that she's a black belt in jiu-jitsu and my opinion of her went up a notch. And then she had to throw in that she's run marathons around the world.

Of course she has.

She just caught my eye in a way I didn't expect. And not only that—she's funny. She's sarcastic and sharp, and I like that.

I *really* like that.

But something still feels off. A woman like her has everything. She is everything. So why is she still single?

Then again, I already know the answer. She told me herself.

And this is an alliance. It's not about love. This is business.

And I can't let myself forget that.

I do not fall.

I refuse to fall.

I glance past her, toward the bar, wanting to see what Rio is up to. The dude is propped against a stool at the bar at the far end, watching me. Every now and then, he turns slightly and winks. He's perfectly positioned. Daniela's back is to him, so she has no idea my wingman is here. I told him to join us, but he refused. Said it would seem like we were ganging up on her.

"Dude," he said, "this is supposed to be an intimate date. You don't want me in the way."

I told him never to use the word intimate when talking about me and the heiress. But now … I'm starting to wonder.

I shake the thought out of my head, as quickly as it landed.

We're not going there.

She's agreed to an arranged marriage. I don't care that her family is wealthy. I don't care that she has a charming smile or that she laughs at my sarcasm.

I don't care. And yet, this isn't as bad as I expected. She's saying something. I blink, realizing I haven't been paying attention.

"You're not listening to me," she says, giving me an accusatory state.

"I'm sorry."

"Are you waiting for someone else?"

"What? No."

"Then why do you keep looking around?"

I almost tell her about Rio, about how he's perched at the bar with a smug grin, watching all of this unfold. But I don't.

Instead, I clear my throat. "Look … this is an awkward situation for both of us." I pause, tapping my fingers against the table. "I need to tell you something. After our meeting with my father this morning, he called a meeting with my brothers."

"And?" She shrugs like it's nothing.

"He told them we were getting married soon, within a few weeks."

Her lips press together. "Best to get it over and done with."

I exhale. "Right?"

"He sent me an agenda."

That makes me laugh. "Of course, he did."

She sighs. "My parents need to make arrangements. Your father is taking control. It all feels so … impersonal. Not like how a wedding should be."

"That's because it's not a wedding," I say, my voice low. "We don't love each other. Jeez, we don't even like each other."

Her gaze sharpens. "You don't like me?"

I wince, choosing my words carefully. "You picked me, Daniela, and I'm not sure why. I wasn't exactly my charming, best self."

"You have a charming, best self?"

I laugh. I actually laugh, not just at the way she says it, but because of her deadpan expression. Her delivery is perfect. "Tell me," I say, crossing my arms. "If this were a real date, what would have happened by now?"

She stares down at her drink. "I don't really go on many dates."

What the fuck? "What do you mean? Because you're too pretty for most guys?"

She looks up, and the hurt in her eyes makes me feel like a douchebag. "No. Because men only want one thing."

I blink. "You really believe that?"

"In my experience? I *know* that."

Something sharp twists in my gut. I don't like the sound of that.

She shrugs, her expression nonchalant. "Men expect something after dinner. I've never really met someone who sees me for who I am." Her voice is casual, but there's something in her tone that makes me pause.

I study her, really look at her. The way the light hits her face. The way her eyes shine with something I can't quite place. Then it hits me like a slap to my face.

This woman has a fear of being seen.

The way she looks, she turns heads. She gets noticed. I know, because I saw the reaction to her that night at the soiree. Just like I've seen the reaction to her as we walked in here. She meets my gaze. "I don't know you, Dexter."

"But we're getting to know one another," I say softly, starting to see the real Daniela.

"You know that I'm more than just my hair, or my smile, or my eyes, or my body, don't you?"

I shift in my chair. "You're so much more than that." The air between us lightens even more. "Tell me more about the jiu-jitsu."

Her brows push together, like she's trying to figure me out. Then she launches into a story about how she started training.

"What made you start running marathons?" I ask.

"A friend of mine got me into it," she says. "Raquel. She started running in college, and I joined her."

I sit up. "Raquel?"

"She's my childhood friend. My wing woman."

I chuckle. "What are we going to tell her?"

Daniela hesitates. "I told her about you."

"Already?"

"She's inquisitive."

"Her reaction?" I ask.

"She's shocked."

"Why?"

"Because I haven't mentioned any guy in a long time and—"

I arch a brow. "You haven't been dating?"

"Not for a while."

"Why?"

She shrugs. "I dated in college. Had a couple of boyfriends. But I was more focused on my studies."

Studious, too. The more I get to know this woman, the more I'm starting to see that Daniela Oliveira is the dream package.

"After college, I went back home to Brazil," she continues. "I didn't really date after that. Just focused on helping my father with the business."

She hesitates. Just slightly. Like she was about to say something else, but held back. I lean forward. "You'd tell me, right?"

She frowns. "Tell you what?"

"The real state of your father's company." Her eyes flick to mine and we just stare at each other. I don't know what it is, but something shifts in my stomach and I force myself to look away. "More champagne, or another cocktail?" I ask.

"Another cocktail would be nice. Champagne goes straight to my head."

I almost tell her we could order food. This wasn't supposed to turn into dinner, but … it really isn't such a bad way to spend an evening.

"We haven't decided on our proposal story. We should, because people always ask that question."

She's right. "We do need to figure that out."

"Do we need to take this back to your place?" This is the second time she's hinted at that. Maybe she's testing me.

I glance at her. "Are you coming on to me again, Daniela?"

"Don't flatter yourself."

I chuckle lightly. I really do love her humor. "Let's say we met through a friend."

"That won't work. Raquel has the nose of a bloodhound. She's a corporate lawyer and she'll find holes in our story."

"Will I have the pleasure of meeting this friend?"

"Of course you will. I've known her all my life, and she'll be at the wedding."

I pull a box out of my pocket. "I forgot." I lower my voice. "The ring."

Her mouth falls open. I feel like a jerk now, because I bought a cheap little thing. Nothing exclusive or special, not from an upscale jeweler. No Tiffany or Cartier here. I spent ten thousand dollars on it. It's a large square pink diamond set in a chunky rose gold band, with small diamonds all around. I slip it under the table, looking around the room. People are talking in hushed tones. Rio seems busy. He's talking to someone.

"You should just slip it on under the table," I whisper.

"Okay." She reaches under and our hands meet. The first touch of her soft, warm fingers, make me jolt. Not with fright. With an electric tingle. Like something inside me has awakened.

"I've got it." She sits back. I sit back, slip the ring box back into my pocket. "Why, thank you, darling." She waves her hand at me, showing off her ring proudly, before flashing a smile that has more megawatts than the pathetic two carat ring on her finger. Looking at it now, it's flashy, and totally impersonal. The kind of ring that screams "this is for show" rather than "I care about you."

"You like it?" It seems like the appropriate thing to say, even though I feel like I should have given her something classy.

"It's lovely, Dexter. A little too big, but it will do, also, I don't like ostentatious things, but, as you say, this isn't for real. But thank you."

She doesn't like bling. "Noted." I lean back in my seat, watching her, and I forget that this is just business. In fact, I'm starting to feel a little off kilter the more I get to know this woman.

Most of the women in my circle are materialistic, and they don't even bother to hide it. The more expensive and gaudier a trinket is, the better.

Daniela's genuine appreciation and joy surprises me again. More than that, she calms that unsettled feeling I've been wrestling with for too long. Being with her does something to me and I feel like I can breathe and be still for the first time in a long time.

There is so much more to her than I first saw, and as I start to pull back the layers slowly, a sizzle of excitement zaps through my veins. I want to discover more about who she is underneath her beautiful exterior.

Because I have a sneaking suspicion that her beauty goes all the way through to her core.

And if that's true.

She's unique.

Truly one of a kind.

Which means, what the hell am I doing?

CHAPTER THIRTEEN

RIO

I SIT AT THE BAR, FAR ENOUGH FROM DEX AND HIS NEW FIANCÉE that she can't see me. Although she's not really his fiancée. The dude hasn't even bought her a ring.

He wanted me to sit with them, to interrogate Daniela together. The guy's not even thinking straight.

I told him, *Dude, we can't do that. We can't gang up on her. It wouldn't be fair.* And, if I'm being honest? I acted like a complete sap the first time I saw her and I don't want to face her. I blame my behavior on the dry spell. That's all it was.

I take a sip of my Negroni as I glance at them. They make a good-looking pair. If only Dex would let his damn guard down. He's a tough one. Jett is too. Hell, Jett's worse. He's arrogant and always looking down on me, Matteo and Enzo. Like we're beneath him. The three of them, Jett, Dex and Zach, they've never made it easy for us.

Us having to fly to Brazil together, in the private jet, feels like it's the old man's way of forcing into pretending we're family. So that we look like a united family at the wedding.

But we're not a family.

We have never been.

The old man keeps us together to benefit him, to keep the legacy intact, to make sure the empire grows. But the bonds between us don't exist. Mama still travels back and forth between Italy and New York.

It couldn't have been easy for her to have moved here from the country she lived in and loved for all of her life. She had to, because Paul Knight demanded it. And she broke it off with him, as soon as she discovered the secret that shattered two families. She stayed here for a decade, and moved back to Italy, but we travel there a lot to see her, me, Matteo and Enzo. Mama says she'll come back here when she has grandkids.

As if that's ever going to happen.

Not from me.

Dex and I have talked about our mothers. Me mostly, because he clams up when he tries to talk about his mom. I don't push him. I figure he'll tell me when he's ready. But we talk about how our father's adultery wrecked two families. Sometimes I think about what it would be like if we all sat at a table, his brothers and mine, not because we were summoned to a Knight family dinner by the old man, but because we wanted to hang out together.

Because the truth is, we are all brothers.

We just don't act like it.

Matteo, Enzo, and I stick together. We had to. When our father moved us here, we had no one else. Mama came for a while, because we were teenagers when hell broke loose. When we realized that the nice American man who visited us occasionally, the man we called Papa, also had another secret family in the US. I remember the day we found out the truth.

That the man we called Papa had another family. That he was already married when we were born. And his wife—Jett, Dex, and Zach's mother—had died. It was suicide, we later discovered. It happened after she found out about Mama and us. She couldn't take it.

Mama was so upset. Not only that the man she loved had another family, and was married, which made her suddenly a mistress, but now she had to carry the weight of a woman who had killed herself. Mama felt it was her fault, even though she'd had no idea the old man was already married.

I push the thought aside and glance back toward Dex.

Oh, hell. Is he actually laughing?

I watch as Daniela leans back in her chair, and throws her head back, as if she's laughing, too. With her back to me, I can't tell her expression, but … these two look like they could be on a real date.

Dex has taken off his jacket, his broad frame relaxed, his sleeves rolled up. That's a flex pose if I've ever seen one. I've seen this guy in action and I can tell that he's trying, but also holding back.

Like he's stuck.

I finish my drink, then, just as I turn to order another, a woman slips onto a barstool two seats away from me.

The way she looks steals my breath away.

She's stunning.

My eyes fixate on her full mouth and those beautiful lips stained heavy in a rich red lipstick. It's the kind of lipstick that makes a statement, and this one says, "watch out". Her long curly brown hair tumbles down her back, and thick dark lashes frame her big dark eyes. The bar is mostly empty, which means she's deliberately chosen this seat.

My gaze lingers on her for half a second too long and when she catches me staring, I look away.

Damn.

"Sorry," I say smoothly. "Didn't mean to stare."

She tilts her head. "That's okay."

I expect her to leave it at that. Maybe flash a polite smile and look away.

"Can I buy you a drink?" she asks.

I blink.

Well, *hot damn.*

That doesn't happen often.

A beautiful woman sitting at a bar offering to buy me a drink?

Bold move.

I lean back, studying her. "You always go around buying drinks for strangers?"

"Let me guess," she says, resting an elbow on the bar, those rich red satin lips curving slightly. "This makes you uncomfortable."

"I wouldn't say uncomfortable."

"Confused, then?"

I try not to wince. "Intrigued."

"Ah." She leans in slightly. "And let me guess, you were about to say that if you had been the one to ask, I'd be expected to bat my lashes and say yes?"

"That's exactly what I was thinking."

"Hell no." She flags the bartender down. "If I want to buy you a drink, I'm going to buy you a drink. What's your poison?"

This woman has some balls. I tilt my glass toward her. "Negroni, or Añejo. I'd like Añejo now. It's—"

"Aged tequila," she says. "I'll have the same."

This just got even more interesting.

She looks around at the bar, examining the different jewel-colored bottles, admiring the décor. Ignoring me.

I see what she's doing.

Playing hard to get.

Waiting for a reaction from me.

Fuck if this type of chase doesn't turn me on.

Finally, I give up. Also, because I don't know how long I have here, or if she has a date, in which case, I'm out. It's something I need to find out. "So," I say, turning to face her fully. "What brings you here?"

"I'm in town on business."

"Business?" I raise a brow. "What kind of business?"

The server sets our drinks down and she picks up her glass, takes a slow sip, and meets my gaze over the rim.

"I'm a corporate lawyer."

I mask my surprise.

Because she doesn't look like a corporate lawyer. I shouldn't be so chauvinistic. Women can be brilliant and beautiful. She must have caught the flicker of disbelief in my expression because her eyes narrow.

"What?" She arches a brow, daring me to say it.

"Nothing."

"You thought I was some pretty little rich girl, sitting at a fancy bar waiting for someone to pick up my tab?"

"Wouldn't dream of it."

She eyes me carefully, like she's assessing me. "And you?"

"I'm a businessman."

"You're too slick to be an average businessman."

"Nothing average about me."

She tilts her head. "You give off shady vibes."

"Shady vibes? Please don't hold back."

"I don't." She gives me another perfect smile. Damn.

I laugh. Fully and completely. Deeply amused, and surprised. This woman has intrigued me like no other. I raise my glass in her direction. "Guilty as charged."

We stare at one another, and I feel the undeniable, dangerous pull that vibrates between us.

I take another sip, contemplating this strange situation I find myself in. I don't know her name. She doesn't know mine. But something tells me, when she does, things are going to get real.

This.

This is what I was talking about when I told Dex I like the chase. The heiress giving herself to a marriage deal is boring. Dex can have her. But this feisty woman with brains, *with balls*, this is a chase I can get behind. She already has my attention.

Until she glances over her shoulder and looks in the same direction I've been looking.

What the fuck?

"Who're you checking out?" I ask, an edge to my tone.

"The guy there. Who is he?"

"Why?" My insides harden. She's here to check out Dex. Fucking Dex. That man has women falling at his feet, whether he wants them or not, they still fall. Just like the heiress did.

"Just curious."

I'm about to open my mouth and ask her why the fuck she's curious, but I zip my mouth. I don't usually meet two gorgeous women in one week, so this is most peculiar. I try not to give a shit that she's eyeing up Dex.

"He's with someone." Realizing that she's interested in a guy who's obviously with a partner, I immediately check out of our conversation.

DEX

· · ·

Daniela and I are getting along better than I ever expected.

Maybe because there's no pressure. No romance. No pretending this is something it's not. It's purely a business agreement, nothing more. Maybe that's why I feel more relaxed, maybe that's why I can laugh, talk and joke with her. Maybe that's why she's at ease, too. It's better than many first dates I've had.

Daniela and I have even ordered appetizers.

"So much for just showing up for drinks," I said when she agreed to get food.

She waved it off. "It doesn't mean anything. We're just hungry."

And she's right. It doesn't. And we are. I'm famished. But I lean across the table, my voice dropping an octave lower. I look into her eyes. "If my wife is hungry, I'm going to make sure to feed her."

Those bright green eyes turn darker as her pupils dilate, her lips slide apart and she's momentarily speechless. I've lost my tongue, too, and have no idea why I said that. The word "wife" feels foreign on my tongue and yet so … suggestive. A visual crashes into my head of me feeding her. Slipping something between her luscious plump lips. Suddenly my pants feel tighter. Heat pulses between us. Words not spoken evoke ideas, for me at least. And Daniela, too, judging by the way she's looking at me.

"Wife to be," she says, her voice wavering.

Bingo.

She feels something. I know it as sure as I can feel my cock springing to attention. I lower my head and wonder how this has happened. We haven't even touched.

Then, when I least expect it, she asks the question that slams into me like a bullet to the chest.

"What happened to your mom?"

Just like that, the mood changes. My guard slams back up so fast it's like a physical reaction. I grip my glass, trying to decide if I want to answer.

"I'm sorry to ask," she says gently, obviously seeing the change in me. The air just chilled a few degrees. "It's just that I feel it's important."

I exhale slowly, buying myself time. Instead of answering, I turn the question around. "How long have your parents been married?"

She doesn't hesitate.

"Thirty-six years."

My brow lifts in shock and awe. "That's a long time."

"They're happy," she says with absolute certainty, like I'd asked her if she breathes air. I nod, letting her talk. She tells me how they met. How they built her father's company from the ground up. How they had problems conceiving. "They went to expensive clinics," she says. "Flew across the world looking for solutions. But it never worked. But miraculously, they managed to have me." She gives a soft laugh. "They tried over many years. It just goes to show you that money can't buy everything."

"I disagree. In my experience, I've seen that it can."

She cocks her head, watching me. "But money can't buy *everything*. It can't buy happiness, or joy, or satisfaction. Those emotions come from a deeper place."

Her words stump me, and I dwell on them as she continues talking about her father's business. I half-listen, half-think about what she said.

She's right.

Money didn't save my mother. It didn't stop her from—

"And what about you? Your parents?" Daniela turns the

question back on me and I tense. "How long were they married?"

I should shut this down and tell her it's none of her business. But before I can stop myself, the words slip out. "She died when I was eleven."

Her eyes soften. "That must have been really hard."

I'm surprised I even answered her. But for some reason, it doesn't feel dangerous to talk about this with her. Which makes me feel even worse. Jett and Zach know, of course. We've talked about it, and they think I'm being dramatic. They tell me it wasn't my fault, but they don't understand.

Nobody does.

"She and I argued before she died." My voice is quieter now. "It was stupid. A small fight. But it was the last conversation we ever had."

Daniela watches me, listening. Really listening.

It makes me do something I never do.

I keep talking.

"I don't know how much you know about my family. My father had ... a mistress."

Her eyes open wider. She didn't know. She wouldn't.

"We have—" I exhale. "We have half-brothers. Rio, Matteo, Enzo. They grew up in Italy."

She listens without judgment.

"My mom didn't know," I say, staring at my scotch. "Not at first, but when she found out ..."

I stop.

Daniela is silent, waiting.

"She drove off a bridge. On purpose."

Her hand moves instinctively toward mine. I should pull away, but I don't. Then her fingers wrap around mine, warm and gentle.

"I'm so sorry," she whispers. I stare at our hands and I want to move mine away, but it feels reassuring. Her hands are so soft and small compared to mine. Her skin is warm and soothing, infusing me with heat and chasing away the coldness of my past. Her fingernails, painted a soft pink, catch the lights, but it's my ring on her finger that holds my gaze captive. Something about it grounds me. Tethers me to her, in a way the paper contract doesn't.

I want to tell her to drop it.

I don't.

Instead, I say something that only Jett and Zach know about.

"The last thing I said to my mom was that I wished she were dead."

Daniela inhales sharply. "Dexter …"

I let out a humorless laugh, shaking my head. "It was silly. I was an evil child—"

"No child is evil, Dexter."

"You don't know what I was like back then, when my parents would argue and yell at each other. We didn't know then that it was because the secret had come to light. After that my parents used to fight all the time, not physical fights, they just threw verbal punches. I became angry and confused, and bitter, not understanding what had happened. But when I said that to my mom, she looked at me like I'd cut her in two. I wanted to rush up to her, and hug her and say I was sorry, but my stubbornness, and my anger, stopped me. Hours later we heard the awful news, that she'd driven off a bridge. That she was no longer alive. I'd give anything to turn back the time and run up to her and hug her. I'd give anything to take my words back. But I can't."

"Dexter." Daniela sniffles. I look up and see her looking so sad.

"Jett and Zach say it wasn't my fault. That she was already

so broken by our father's deceit." I pause. "But I feel like it drove her to the edge. Like she wouldn't have done what she did had it not been for me and my viciousness. She had three boys to live for. But then my father cheated on her, and I told her I wished she were dead …"

Daniela's eyes turn misty. This woman barely knows me, and yet, she's sitting across from me, looking like my pain is her pain. Feeling it.

"You can't think that what happened to your mother is because of something you said. Dexter."

"Cause and effect. I said those words and she died."

"It wasn't your words. Your father had a secret family. That would have broken her."

I exhale. "Mom died about a month later after she found out about them."

"Dexter. If I could take away your pain, I would." Her whisper curls around my heart, offering compassion.

My chest tightens. "Why would you?" I say roughly, the shutters coming down all around me, keeping me in my safe space. "You don't know me." I choose not to get close to people for this very reason. I know what love can do, and I don't want to make myself vulnerable to anyone. Ever.

Daniela meets my gaze. "I don't have to know you to see the pain in your eyes."

Hell.

We haven't even had sex. This is the kind of thing that happens post-sex. Sometimes, before I shut it down.

It's not supposed to happen here.

Not now.

Not with her.

I jerk my hand away, my entire body tensing.

She immediately retracts, looking down. "I'm sorry if I … if I overstepped."

I clear my throat, nodding.

It's fine.

It's not fine.

I glance up and spot Rio, just as the appetizers arrive. Suddenly, I've lost my appetite. This was too close. It felt good for a second, being heard. Being listened to. Having someone feel my pain and try to make it better.

But then, in the next second, I remember—

This is an arrangement. Nothing more.

This woman will be out of my life in less than a year. After seven months, she'll be nothing more than a memory.

What the hell am I doing? I pick up my drink, gripping it tighter than I should. I'm so fucking stupid. I glance at Rio again.

Daniela notices. "What is it?" She turns in her chair, then her body stiffens and she jumps right out of her seat and walks to the other end of the room. To the bar. Where Rio is sitting.

I bolt up and rush to her side. "What are you doing?" I ask, but her eyes are blazing.

"Meu Deus," she mutters under her breath.

Fuck. She saw him. But I don't understand why she's so angry. "What are you doing, Daniela?"

She doesn't answer.

She just heads toward Rio, and I frantically try to figure out what beef she has with him. At the same time, I see the woman sitting next to him. They're turned towards each other, as if they like each other.

Did he bring a date here? I catch a glimpse of bright red lips and long brown curls, a sharp profile, and an expensive business suit.

To my utter shock, Daniela doesn't reach for Rio. She taps the woman on her shoulder, and suddenly it feels like shit is about to go down.

CHAPTER FOURTEEN

DEX

I can't believe what I'm seeing. The woman jumps up from her seat, looks at Daniela, and throws her arms around her.

"Are you spying on me?" Daniela demands, her voice sharp with surprise. "When did you get here? How? Why didn't you call me?"

A firehose of questions spills from her mouth, and her friend barely has time to answer. They keep switching between Portuguese and English, and I catch about half of it, but I don't need a translation to see that these two know each other well.

Rio and I exchange looks. I raise a brow at him. *What the fuck, dude?* I silently ask. Do she and Rio already know each other?

How?

"Hey, Rio," Daniela says after a moment, once the commotion between her and her friend dies down.

"Daniela." Rio greets her smoothly, then looks at me.

Daniela's gaze moves between us, narrowing slightly. "You brought him along?"

I can't lie to this woman. "He wanted to be my wingman."

"I offered to come along," Rio corrects, coughing lightly.

"Are you both together?" I ask, my gaze bouncing between Rio and the woman.

"You're sitting like you know each other," Daniela points out. She turns to Rio, her eyes sharp with suspicion. "Are you on a date?"

"Ha-ha. Very funny." Rio rolls his eyes. He's been quiet up until now, probably just as thrown as I am.

I flick him a look. *Please, dude, please tell me you haven't made a move on her.*

Daniela's friend snorts, holding up a hand. "I wouldn't be caught dead with this man."

"You sure about that?" Rio growls. "You came and sat next to me, and bought me a drink."

"This is Raquel," Daniela tells me. "Remember? I mentioned earlier about my best friend from home, the one I ran marathons with—" As if she's just remembered something, she switches gears mid-sentence and her arm slips around my waist.

Oh.

Oh.

The acting starts now. I grin and pull her close. She's not soft and lush, like I expected, especially with those curves. Daniela is all lean muscle and firm. The way I like it.

"Hi, Raquel," I say smoothly. "Daniela has told me so much about you."

Raquel's eyes snap to Daniela. "You told him about *me*, but you didn't tell me about *him*."

"I was going to … in person," Daniela hedges. Her friend narrows her eyes and folds her arm, disbelief oozing out of her. "Why are you here, Raquel?" my curious fiancée-to-be asks.

Her friend hesitates. "I got worried."

Worried? What the hell was her friend worried about?

"Worried about what?" Daniela laughs, and we all break out into awkward chuckles.

They don't discuss this further, but I'm curious. Raquel turns to me, her gaze narrowing. "So, *this* is Dexter? Dexter Knight." She spits out my name like it's a curse. "You're doing this? You're marrying a *Knight*?"

My ears go on alert. I grin at her. "You're talking about us as if we're famous."

Raquel folds her arms, like she's getting ready to take me to trial. "Oh, they're famous, alright. In every environmental law circle from D.C. to São Paulo." She glares at Daniela. "Your fiancé's family buries lawsuits like they bury toxic waste, quietly and with no accountability."

A sniff of disgust as she looks at me.

"The Knights are everything I've spent my career fighting against. They're corrupt, ruthless and untouchable. And now one of them has you in his pocket."

"Dexter is wonderful," Daniela coos, ignoring her friend's disdain and smoothly slipping into a role that I sense makes her uncomfortable. If I can sense it, I'm sure her friend can, too. Daniela then lays her head against my shoulder, playing her part perfectly. "He's just the sort of guy I never thought I'd meet, and yes, I guess what they're doing is wrong, but, hopefully, over time, they'll learn to do better, and to be better ethically?" She gazes up at me adoringly, fluttering her eyelashes .

I stare down at her, and plaster on a loving smile. "With you by my side, I'd want to be better."

I hear Rio snort. Daniela's friend doesn't look convinced, either. "How did you two meet?" she asks.

Rio watches, his gaze knowing, as if he's waiting for me to slip up. Raquel folds her arms even more tightly.

"Did you know they were getting married?" she asks him.

He shrugs. "Didn't you?" Perfect reply.

She exhales sharply.

"Why so cold all of a sudden?" Rio asks her. "I thought we were getting on just fine."

Raquel glares at him, then me. "Tell me how you met," she says, voice tight as she easily ignores Rio. "I need to hear this."

We're all standing around now, the energy tense.

"Shouldn't we sit down and get more drinks?" I suggest.

"No," Raquel snaps. "I'm not going anywhere until you tell me what the hell is going on."

I exhale through my nose. "What do you think? That I kidnapped her? Held her hostage? That I'm forcing her into this?" I hold up Daniela's hand, to show off the engagement ring.

It feels like destiny, the way things are unfolding. The ring and us being caught and having our alibis straight.

Except … *fuck*. We didn't discuss the very thing Justice Raquel is enquiring about. She cuts Daniela a sharp look. "This isn't like you, Dani."

Daniela stiffens. "What do you mean?"

"This makes no sense," her friend says flatly. "Tell me how this happened." She waves a hand between me and Daniela. We remain standing, arms around each other. Trying to look casual, even as I'm feeling something strange, with Daniela flush against me. I try to push it back down. Hide it away. Rio doesn't sit. He stands with us. I think this dude might actually be afraid to sit back down with this chick.

"We met at a tech conference. In São Paulo." Daniela says, easily.

Rio coughs lightly. I think I hear a "Bullshit."

"Do you mind?" I hiss. He picks up his glass and drains it dry.

"You met ... in *São Paulo*?" Raquel asks stiffly. "You expect me to believe that you ..." Her head whips in my direction, "You flew to Brazil for a tech conference?"

"You'd be amazed what I'll do to avoid my father," I answer quickly. This woman is too inquisitive for my liking. "I was invited to speak. It was a panel on sustainable tech investment. Very niche. Very exclusive."

"He filled in for someone last-minute," Daniela adds. "I was there representing my father's company."

"And you ... just happened to sit next to each other?" The friend glares at us skeptically.

"Sounds like fate," Rio murmurs.

"I challenged him during the Q&A." Daniela looks up at me adoringly. I wish she really meant it.

"Atta girl," Rio says.

"In front of a packed room. She basically accused me of being all buzzwords and no substance." I press a kiss on her head.

Raquel arches a brow at Daniela. "That sounds like you."

Daniela giggles. "He was asking for it. Quoting stats from 2016 like they were groundbreaking."

I smile down at my fiancée. "She was the only one in the room who didn't fawn over me. I was intrigued."

"Aroused more like it," my wingman mutters.

I turn to him, afraid he'll blow our cover if he keeps this up. "Will you quit the commentary?" I snap, before turning back to my interrogator. "And yet, I couldn't stop thinking about her all night."

"How romantic," Raquel says in a flat voice.

"Not all love stories start with roses. Ours started with professional humiliation and warm canapés," I retort.

"Uh-huh." Raquel looks like she's still trying to make up

her mind. "And you've been secretly dating ever since? Is that the story?"

"It's not a story, Raquel. We kept in touch. It was … gradual. You know I don't do instalove." Daniela pats my arm, then, slides her hand up and down gently, as if convincing Raquel suddenly requires more effort.

"Real slow burn. Like gasoline on a match," Rio says, taking another drink from the server.

Raquel eyes him. "You're awfully vocal for someone not involved."

He grins. "These two were meant for each other. It's a beautiful love story. It really is."

"One last question." Raquel pins me with a stare. "Name one thing on the menu at that private dinner."

Jesus. And then it comes to me. "Truffle risotto. It was overcooked."

"And the wine was Chilean. Which was offensive, frankly." Daniela doesn't miss a beat.

Raquel huffs, leaning against the counter with her arms crossed, lawyer-brain in full effect. "Fine. You pass. *Barely*."

"Cross-examined and passed. Do we get a trophy?" Daniela asks.

"No, you get to keep your dignity. Barely." Her friend pouts, and with her bright red lipstick, it's hard to ignore.

Rio winks at her. "Told you. It's a beautiful, unforgettable love story."

My head snaps to him. "Remind me why I let you come here?"

"Comic relief. Obviously."

DANI

I'M COMPLETELY UNPREPARED FOR THIS. FOR RAQUEL TO TURN up like this, unexpectedly, for her to be flirting with Rio Knight, of all people, and for me and Dexter to have to show, on demand, that we're happily and madly in love.

But it seems to have worked. I think we've convinced her of how we met. I don't know why I came up with a tech conference, although I did recently attend a tech conference and maybe that bubbled to the surface. Still, there's no denying how eerie it was that Dexter and I just made that story up, on the spot.

If we're not careful, we'll end up finishing each other's sentences, too. I find myself acutely aware of the way his hand, large and soft, fits around mine. How his hard body presses against me, his arm wrapped around my back has me breaking out in a rash of goosebumps.

From excitement, not cold.

I love the way his fingers splay on my hip, his thumb hypnotically stroking back and forth. How my skin slowly prickles with an expectant thrum.

"Why don't we all sit down and you both join us? Dexter and I were just making wedding plans," I say, forcing a bright smile.

My heart almost jumped out of my ribcage when I registered Raquel sitting on the bar stool. She's so hard to miss. Those glossy, long curls, that thin, nipped-in waist, the way she moves with the kind of confidence that only someone who has never second-guessed themselves a day in their life can. And, of course, she's dressed in a designer business suit, perfectly tailored, and wearing sky-high stilettos.

And wearing her signature bright red lipstick.

But for her to be sitting with Rio of all people.

Why was she talking to *him*?

When did he get here?

Why is he here?

Does Dexter not trust me?

Or does he not trust himself?

It's too much to process all at once.

I was worried about how we'd do this, but so far, we seem to be keeping our cover. Raquel is suspicious and she was relentless in her questioning, but it seems like we've passed the test.

I'm still uneasy because she's going to pick at every word, every action, every glance between Dexter and me until she finds a crack. She knows this isn't me.

I feel Dexter shift beside me, his palm resting lightly on the small of my back. His touch is meant to be reassuring, but instead, it sends a jolt of tension through me. Not because I don't like it.

Because *I do.*

That's the problem.

Raquel's sharp gaze flits down to Dexter's hand, her lips pressing into a thin line before she looks back up at me. "Wedding plans?" she asks slowly, like she's rolling the words around in her mouth, tasting them, testing them.

I lean into Dexter's touch and lift my chin. "We were just discussing venues."

"Really?" She quirks a perfectly arched brow. "Because when I spoke to you earlier, you made it sound like this was barely a relationship, let alone something serious enough to be planning a wedding."

I let out a light laugh, the kind that should come naturally to a woman deeply in love. "I wanted to surprise you, like I said. You know how it is, Raquel. Things move fast when it's right."

Dexter makes a low, approving sound and leans in, his lips brushing against my temple. "I love this woman with all my heart." His voice is rich and smooth, laced with just the right amount of devotion.

I blink.

Dios. Okay. That was ... *convincing.* With my heart hammering in my chest, I turn to him, forcing warmth into my gaze as I play along. "You make my life complete ..."

Dexter's mouth tilts into a smile that would fool anyone. Anyone except maybe Raquel. She glances between us, suspicion still etched into every line of her face.

"Huh." She taps her manicured nails against her arm. "And when exactly were you going to tell me about this engagement?"

Dexter and I answer at the same time.

"Soon," I say.

Raquel's lips part, her head tilting.

"But you found out this way," Dexter chuckles, smooth as ever, and tightens his arm around my waist, pulling me closer. He turns to me, and before I can process what's happening, he cups my jaw and his lips brush mine so lightly. My lips feel scorched as he leaves his imprint on me.

For a man who can be so guarded, so emotionally distant, he blows hot and cold so fast, I feel like I have whiplash from his changing moods. His gaze lingers over my mouth and my lips instinctively part.

Time slows down. I think he's waiting for my permission. Sweat forms along my nape. Raquel's eyes feel like a lead weight on my chest, making it harder for me to think.

To breathe.

I tilt my face upwards and press my lips to his, but it

happens so fast. The way Dexter's mouth presses against mine, how my eyes flutter shut and I'm suddenly lost in a world of warmth and sweetness.

Then it turns slow, and lingering. I catch a hint of his cologne, dark and spicy. Dangerous, too. Like him. My arms close around his neck and I press myself against him, mewling against his mouth when his kiss turns hard, and crushing and bruising. It feels so intimate, like we're in the middle of making love, not standing in a bar, putting on a performance for my inquisitive friend. I hear a guttural moan deep in his throat, and feel the press of something poking against my stomach.

Oh my.

"Get a room, you both." Rio's voice breaks our spell and we pull apart. Dexter's eyes lock with mine. I'm left feeling breathless, giddy. For a guy who doesn't want any of this, he's a pretty good actor.

Not to mention an amazing kisser.

My insides are in upheaval. My breasts heavy. Blood thunders in my ears. I can't reconcile the cold man I met that first night with this passionate lover I now find myself staring at. This feels too real for my comfort. His thumb brushes over my cheekbone. "Right, amor?"

I smile back, feeling like a woman madly in love.

"It feels like I'm watching a porno." Raquel huffs in disgust.

"And you would know this how?" Rio asks, eyes wide.

Raquel cuts him a cold look, before turning to us. I feel that we've managed to fully convince her. But the way Dexter kissed me, he's convinced me that he loves me, and it feels bittersweet because I know how much he doesn't want any part of this.

I have a long, cruel year ahead of me, and I'd better keep my wits about me.

The spell breaks after that.

We move apart.

There's been too much shock and interruption, and our evening is ruined. Our appetizers go untouched and we all decide to head back. I feel a pang of disappointment.

This could have turned into something special, and I hate that we were denied that.

CHAPTER FIFTEEN

RIO

That was an unexpected evening. I saw Dex and Daniela, saw their downturned faces.

It looked like they were having a great time, but after the way the evening ended, it made sense for us all to go home.

Dex took Daniela back, and to my surprise, Raquel agreed for me to drop her back. Now she's sitting beside me as I'm driving, her arms crossed, staring out the window and looking pissed as hell.

I want to kiss her right now, but there's no way it's going to happen. Back at the bar, before all hell broke loose, sparks were zinging and zagging between us. I felt them, and I know she sure as hell did too.

"What's wrong, princesa?"

She turns to me, her expression sharp as a blade. "Don't call me that."

"Why not?" I chuckle, loving the fact that I can get under her skin so easily. "It suits you."

"I am not a princess or diva, I assure you."

"You sure about that?" I throw back, with a grin, which pisses her off even more. I can see there's nothing dainty or princess-like about her. This woman has balls and attitude, and I *love* that about her.

We were sparking and combusting and getting on like wildfire, until Dex and his fiancée turned up and threw cold water over our conversation.

Things haven't been the same since.

"You're a Knight." She practically spits it out, like the word physically disgusts her.

I grin. "I am."

"And he's your brother."

"Half-brother, actually."

"Still a Knight."

"Still a Knight," I agree. "A Knight in shining armor."

She groans, shaking her head.

"We were having such a nice time," I say, wanting to see her reaction.

"Were we?" She glares at me. "And then I find out you're one of *them*."

"What exactly do you have against me? You liked me before you knew my name."

"I know exactly who your family is. I know what Knight Enterprises does. I'm a corporate lawyer, and I specialize in environmental law and high-profile lawsuits against unethical corporations."

I grin. "That so?"

Her nostrils flare. "Your company always manage to wriggle out of accountability."

I chuckle. "I haven't done anything to *you*, princesa."

Her glare sharpens. "I told you, don't call me princesa." She whips out her phone and starts texting. I guess our conversation is over.

I grin wider.

I'm going to have so much fun with this one.

DANI

IT MAKES SENSE FOR DEXTER TO DRIVE ME BACK TO MY HOTEL while Rio takes Raquel back.

I can feel the awkwardness settling between both cars, like an invisible barrier neither of us knows how to break. Everything changed in the blink of an eye. Tonight was going so well.

I almost let myself believe that Dexter and I were something more. A couple. Not that I'm in love with him or anything, or even *that* attracted to him, but I like him more than I did before.

He opened up. He was vulnerable. He shared something real with me, and I have a feeling it's not something he does often.

We were connecting.

Later, when he kissed me, that kiss stole my breath away. Not just because of how it felt, but because he made the first move. I didn't expect it. There's only so much of an act we could have put on in front of Raquel, but it's clear Dexter wanted to convince her.

Why did she have to show up?

I don't know if things would've gone further between us tonight if she hadn't, but now I'll never know.

The car is silent as Dexter drives through the dark streets. He hasn't said a word, and the tension in the air is suffocating. I glance down at my phone, desperate for something to do. That's when I see the email.

I gasp, my eyes widening, because I don't believe it.

"What is it?" Dexter glances at me in concern.

I swallow hard. "Your father."

"What's he done now?"

"He copied you in on it, too."

"What has he done?" Dexter repeats, his fingers tightening around the steering wheel.

"He sent an email to both of us."

"About?"

I hesitate before reading it aloud. "Subject: Wedding Arrangements."

He makes a disapproving sound. "Go on."

I clear my throat, feel the blood rushing to my ears as I stare at the email. It looks so formal. Like a work email. An agenda. Not something for a wedding. I start to read.

Subject: Wedding Arrangements

Dexter, Daniela,

I have spoken with your parents, Daniela, and we have finalized the necessary arrangements for the wedding. The details are as follows:

- The marriage will take place 2 weeks from today. Daniela, this allows you some time in which to return home and make necessary preparations for your wedding dress, etc.
- The civil ceremony will be conducted privately, on the same day, to ensure legal formalities are completed without unnecessary delays. I have

expedited the marriage license and secured a judge to officiate.

- The public ceremony: the event the media and guests will see, will follow in the afternoon. It will be held at an appropriate venue with a carefully selected guest list. If you so choose, you may elect to get married at your family home. I believe this is something your parents would prefer."
- The wedding details, including logistics, press coordination, and venue selection, are being handled between myself and your parents. There is no need for additional involvement on your part.
- Attendance will be limited to immediate family, key business associates, and select high-society figures. The event will be elegant, controlled, and executed with precision.
- The media coverage will be strictly managed to ensure the correct narrative is presented.
- Daniela, I understand your parents may wish to incorporate certain traditions. Within reason, some accommodation can be made.
- My sons and I will arrive the day before the wedding, and we will return the day after the wedding.
- There will be no honeymoon.

This is a high-profile event, and I expect both of you to conduct yourselves accordingly. There is no room for complications or delays. We all have businesses to run, and this event must not get in the way.

Paul Knight

"Two weeks?" I gasp. I knew this was moving fast, but I hadn't expected it to be this fast.

"Screw him," Dexter mutters.

"How can he do that? We need thirty days."

Dexter lets out a humorless chuckle. "My father can do anything. He's taken care of it, if you reread the bit about him expediting the marriage license and securing a judge. He's paid someone to get this done fast."

I take a steadying breath. "He thinks my parents want me to get married at the family home. I'm sure he put that idea in their heads—"

"That's my father," Dexter says, annoyingly.

I grit my teeth. "I know what my parents would prefer. They want a church wedding."

"I'm sorry, Daniela." Dexter's voice is soft and reassuring. "This isn't a real wedding. We're playing a part. Actors in a production to fool family and friends and the business community."

Something about the way he says it, so detached, so dismissive, grates on me. I think about the kiss we shared. The words we shared. It didn't feel like an act then.

"Getting married at my family home is fine. This is just temporary. It's not real," I say flatly, forcing myself to get used to this, even though it's already starting to leave a bitter taste in my mouth. I read the email again, my stomach twisting. I blink at the screen in disbelief. "Your father just spelled out our entire wedding in a cold, detached email."

"Welcome to the Knight family."

He's said this before, many times, and now, more than ever, I wonder what kind of trap I've walked into. He looks at me. "You wanted this," he reminds me. "You flew all the way from Brazil for this."

There's a bite to his words. He sounds annoyed. I turn to

him, studying his profile. What's gotten into him? This isn't the man who kissed me. This isn't the man who let his guard down in front of me tonight.

"Why are you so angry all of a sudden?" I ask quietly.

His jaw tenses. "I'm not angry. I'm just reminding you that this is a ruse. Try not to forget that."

I try not to gasp. "Didn't feel like a ruse when you kissed me."

His lips curl into a slow, infuriating smile. "Oh, sweetheart," he murmurs, "I've charmed the pants off many a woman."

I don't like the way he calls me sweetheart. I loved the way he called me "amor" earlier, when he kissed me. It felt like he really meant it.

"You've been with women you feel nothing for?"

"It was just sex. I haven't hidden that from you."

Just sex. He sounds oddly cruel and cynical. Like he's a different Dexter. Not the charming, funny, flirtatious guy I just spent the evening with. It frightens me a little, how he can flip so quickly. How his emotions go easily from soft and caring to something cold and clinical.

He stops the car outside the hotel. I go to open the car door, but hesitate. "I guess this will be the last time I see you?" I want to return home tomorrow. I need to be back at home, to be with genuine people, people who love me.

He looks at me, his mouth open like he wants to say something. His fingers grip the steering wheel so hard, the skin across his knuckles is tight. I wait, anticipating what he wants to say, but as the last second, he turns his head, glaring out of the window.

"See you at the wedding." His voice has that detached tone again. It's like he's another person. The cold Dexter I met that first night at the soiree.

I get out of the car, heart heavy, and head into the hotel, feeling as if I've been on a rollercoaster ride ever since I arrived in New York, not even a week ago.

My life has changed, or is about to change, completely, and I feel like I have no control over my future.

I'm completely deflated.

So much has happened tonight. With Dexter, with Raquel. Everything felt like it was going well … until it wasn't.

And now, my best friend from childhood has turned up out of nowhere, throwing another layer of chaos into the evening. I don't know what the night would have looked like if Raquel hadn't arrived. Maybe things with Dexter would have played out differently. Maybe I would have had a moment to breathe, to process the kiss, to figure out what the hell we're doing.

But that moment is lost to me forever. My heart sinks when I walk into the hotel lobby only to see Raquel.

"At last! You took your time." She jumps up and rushes to me. I love her. I really do. She flew all the way here for me, and I know she means well. But I don't need this right now.

"Hey."

I throw my arms around her, hugging her tight. Another performance. Another act. I have to pretend I'm happy, even though I feel anything but.

All I want to do is go upstairs, lie down, and think about Paul Knight's email.

I have two weeks.

Two weeks to marry Dexter Knight.

But more than that, I want to think about Dexter himself. The way he can be so soft and easy to love one moment, and then cold and distant the next. How the hell am I supposed to survive a year of *this*?

"How did you get here so fast?" I ask, stepping back.

Raquel grimaces. "I couldn't wait to get out of that car with *him*."

I arch a brow. "Rio?"

"Oh, so now you talk about them like they're family."

I hear the sharpness in her tone, the disapproval just beneath the surface. I force another smile. "Well, they *will* be family soon."

Just thinking about it sends a shiver down my spine. Paul Knight as my father-in-law. Dexter my husband, and Jett, and the rest of the Knights for my brothers-in-law.

God help me.

Raquel exhales sharply and loops her arm through mine. "Come on, let's have a drink."

I groan. "I really can't. I've had way too many with *lover boy*."

Her eyes narrow. "I've been waiting for a while. Were you two making out in the car? Why is he not with you now?"

I laugh, shaking my head. "Too many questions."

She fans herself dramatically. "That *kiss*, though. Scorching. Made my toes curl and I wasn't even being kissed. How did all of this even happen?"

I sigh. "You *heard*."

"I did, but I want details. Explicit details."

"Come upstairs. We can talk, but I really need to pack. I'm taking the first flight out tomorrow, whatever time that may be."

Raquel frowns. "Already?"

"I need to go home. See my parents. Be around people I actually love and care about. I can't take it here anymore."

"What do you mean *actually* love and care about?" Her hawkish eyes and ears miss nothing.

"I need to make preparations. We're … we're getting married in two weeks' time," I say breezily, then wait for her reaction.

"Two weeks?" she shrieks so loudly, the receptionists at the desk look up. "Are you pregnant?" Her face is a picture of so many mixed emotions.

"No! We're both busy people, and I love him, Raquel." I bite down on my teeth, hating the constant lying. But I have to do it all over again and pretend. Be convincing.

I'm so tired. So, *so* tired. This evening has been a roller coaster of emotions. For a split second, I'm on the verge of telling her the truth about the arranged marriage, about my father being worried about his company, about his health, about this whole agreement. That I flew here of my own accord. Instead, I smile. "I love this man, so very much."

She tilts her head. "A Knight?"

"He's a good Knight. The way I see it, why waste time being apart when we can be together?"

Raquel studies me, something unreadable in her gaze. "I've seen you with him. I can see you have feelings for this man. Maybe you just fell for him. I never thought it would happen to you, but if you're happy, I'm happy."

Oh. Well.

This is unexpected.

"I'm happy I have your approval."

She hesitates, looks at me, as if she's not sure she's given me her approval. I let the moment slide. "I have an early morning flight back to Miami," she announces.

I shouldn't feel relieved that she's leaving, but I do. Guilt immediately follows, because I'm also deeply touched that she flew all this way for not even twenty-four hours.

Just to make sure I was okay.

I'm blessed, and so grateful for the women in my life and the power of their friendships. By the time we get to my room, we both kick off our shoes, and I slip off my earrings, my bracelet, my watch. I made an effort tonight. I feel like Dexter noticed.

Raquel eyes me critically. "You're so dressed up."

I nod toward her sharp-cut suit. "So are you."

"I came straight from work after you called me. I just hopped on a plane. I heard you mention the name of the hotel, so I went there."

"How did you know I was staying here?"

"I called your parents."

Smart woman. I really have to be careful around her. But, I love her with all my heart. She has my best interests and she really did drop everything to come here. I should be glad that she's my friend, that she cares so much, but this ruse Dexter and I are going through, just got harder.

DEX

No sooner have I stepped into my apartment, kicked off my jacket, and toed off my shoes, there's a knock at the door.

What now?

The last thing I want is to deal with Jett or Zach. I'm not in the mood to talk to my brothers about tonight, or about anything, really.

But when I pull open the door, it's Rio. Of course. The concierge must have let him up without question. He's one of the few names on the approved list. He steps inside, pacing immediately. "You want to tell me what that was about?"

I arch a brow. "You tell me."

He stops mid-step and turns, giving me a knowing look.

"We're talking about you. What was that? What's with the *kiss,* dude?"

I exhale slowly, already regretting letting him in.

"You really do like her, huh?" he presses.

"No. This is—" I stop myself. What exactly is this? I'm not sure when, or if, I'm going to tell anyone my real plan. That I'm walking away before the year is up. That I'm doing this to spite the old man.

"Have you two kissed before tonight?" Rio asks, his tone lighter now, teasing.

"No."

"You sure about that?"

I roll my eyes. "You know I only met her a few days ago."

"So … your tongues tangling forever wasn't part of the act?" He digs deeper.

I glare at him. "What do you think?"

"I think you liked it. I think you like *her*. I think you want her. In your bed."

I ignore the thought, but my chest feels suddenly tight, like it's getting harder to breathe. "It's an act, brother."

"Dude, it didn't stop you from kissing her like you meant it. Just be careful. I don't want to see you getting hurt."

"That's not going to happen. I like my relationships uncomplicated. Hookups, that's all I need. All I'm interested in." I mutter a "Jesus," as I walk past him into the kitchen. "You want a drink?"

"Yeah. Badly."

I grab a bottle and pour.

"Should you be drinking, though?" I ask.

Rio cocks his head. "I was under the limit. We paced ourselves."

I nod, handing him the glass, then start thinking about me and Daniela and how we were about to start on our appetizers.

Maybe later we would have ordered food, had dinner, even though we initially weren't going to.

I could have sat there and talked to her all night. I had so many questions I wanted to ask. So much more I wanted to know about her.

But just now, as I drove her to her hotel, I acted like a douchebag. So cold and aloof. Pushing her away. That's what I do in these situations.

Daniela spells trouble for me, and if I'm not careful, I'll do something I might regret. Because that kiss? That kiss awakened something in me. Something that's left me feeling rudderless.

If she'd invited me up what would I have said? Worse, what would I have *done*? I reverted to who I am when I need my barriers in place. I turned into an ass to maintain some distance. Now I feel bad because I can't forget the look in Daniela's eyes as she walked away.

Screw this alliance.

I'm already starting to regret it because I'm afraid. Afraid of this woman who sees deep into my soul.

She mesmerizes me. Intrigues me. Holds me captive. This date, that kiss, it leaves me feeling uneasy.

This woman wasn't even supposed to be a blip on my radar, but she's the whole damn map. Ocean, land, sky. Every coordinate I never meant to chart.

CHAPTER SIXTEEN

DANI

I LEAVE EARLY IN THE MORNING. RAQUEL TEXTS ME TO WISH ME a safe journey and to tell me she'll see me soon. My heart sinks, because lying to her is excruciating.

Hours later, my parents pick me up from the airport, accompanied by a bodyguard. I fall into their arms the second I see them. I'm so thankful to be back in the warmth and familiarity of my home, surrounded by people I love.

The Knights are so different. Cold, and uncommunicative with each other. I'm not sure I ever want to fit into their world. But I'm helping my father, and that's the only thing that truly matters. My decision to marry Dexter is further cemented when I see Papai again.

He looks better. His face is a little fuller, his posture stronger. My mother's eyes shine as she clasps her hands together, her expression tender and full of love.

"Ah, minha bela ..." Her voice is full of emotion. She dreams of a happy ever after. There were moments yesterday when Dexter and I were getting to know one another, that I had a glimpse of how things could be, if we allowed ourselves to be more.

I hug my parents and we hold onto each other for longer than usual before getting into the car to go home.

Then it starts, the conversation shifts quickly to my fiancée and the wedding.

"How is he? What's he like?" My parents want to know everything about Dexter. I tell them what they want to hear, but I embellish the truth, cover Paul Knight's coldness with a warmth he doesn't have.

I don't want my parents to worry and they will, if they know what type of family I'll be joining. My mother can't stop talking about the wedding, and at the same time lamenting that Paul Knight has restrained her from doing so many things she'd set her heart on.

My father takes her hand, caresses it in his, reassures her that this is temporary, and that one day, when the real suitor comes, they'll be able to give me a dream wedding, the way they want to. My mother catches me watching, "Only if Daniela wants it," she says quickly.

Over a home-cooked meal, I tell them more, and gloss over the truth. But the part about my date with Dexter, that part, I don't have to fake.

Because I *did* feel something.

He opened up to me, and we connected. I think I reached a part of him that he tries to keep hidden from everyone, even himself.

But as I replay that evening in my mind, I wonder if he felt a connection to me. Maybe that's why he could talk and share in a way I never expected him to. As my mother steps away to get dessert, my father shifts closer to me and takes my hand, his grip gentle and warm. He thanks me for my sacrifice, but I shake my head. "No, Papai. It's not a sacrifice."

His eyes fill with sadness. "It is, filha. I shouldn't have to ask this of you …" His voice wavers as he looks away.

"Papai, this is just an alliance." I try to soothe his fears away. "A marriage on paper. Two strong dynasties coming together. Nothing more, and it's only for a year. Raquel is close by, and I can go and visit her. I can also come home every other month, hopefully. You will see, a year will go by so fast."

"He's a good man?" My father seems desperate for me to say yes.

I hesitate. "He seems nice, Papai." After last night, it doesn't seem so impossible. "Better than Oscar Ramos," I add.

His lips press together, and relief floods his eyes.

I've decided that I won't go shopping for my wedding dress. I'll just browse online, because I have work to do, and tomorrow I'll go into the office. My father is only now starting to look better, but I think he should stay at home and fully recover. I've been away from work, leaving suddenly without an explanation and now I have to somehow break it to my colleagues that I'll be getting married and moving to New York.

"How are the wedding preparations going, Mãe?" I ask my mother. "Is there anything I can do to help?"

"It's all being taken care of, filha. Don't you worry. We've hosted parties for three hundred people here, this will be easy. Less than one hundred people." She looks a little downcast.

"The smaller the number, the better, Mãe."

"We will put the Knights up in one of our other homes here in São Paulo. The wedding of course, will take place here, at the family home. Is that agreeable to you?"

I sigh. "It is. It's fine." I would have wanted some other place, but this isn't about me. This is about Paul Knight's wishes and, I remind myself, this isn't real. My parents exchange a look.

"It's fine," I say again, not wanting them to worry.

My mother studies me. "You know, it's not impossible that you might fall in love with Dexter."

It both amuses and irritates me that she refers to him by his name. As if she knows him well. I give a small, tight smile. "It's not impossible," I echo, because she so badly wants to believe it.

"You're doing this to help the family and the business," she continues. "It's how it used to be in past times. Arranged marriages worked. Dexter is young and handsome. And the two of you …" She trails off.

"Mãe," I say cautiously.

She grins. "I haven't seen a photo of the two of you together, but … my Photoshop skills aren't bad."

She turns her phone toward me and proudly shows off a picture of me and Dexter that she has cobbled together. It looks like she found his image online and plastered it next to an image of me. It looks strange.

"Mãe!" I groan.

She just laughs.

"I'm going into work tomorrow."

She frowns, not liking the sound of that. "Why?"

"I'll come with you," my father offers.

"No, you're taking more time off," I remind him. "You're resting, Papai."

"I'm better now." He exhales. "I've been going in for a few hours a day. I can't be seen as weak. With you marrying a Knight, I need to show strength. Be the man I used to be ."

I hate that he says that. I want him to be the big strong, giant he used to be, and to believe in himself. I keep telling myself that what I'm doing will help his road to recovery. "Papai, you don't need to go in."

He doesn't like my answer. "You're getting married soon. Why should you be going to work?"

I swallow. "I've been away for so long. It will just take my mind off things until ..." I inhale slowly. "Until Dexter gets here."

They both nod, eyes bright and eager as they hang on to my every word, hoping I'll say something nice about my future husband and this situation. "He's arriving with his brothers," I continue. "The day before the wedding. They're only staying for two nights. They leave the day after the wedding."

"Why the rush?" Mãe exclaims.

"Business. They have a global enterprise to take care of," my father reminds her.

"We'll have them over for dinner as soon as they arrive," my mother insists. "We won't have much time to spend with them, or get to know them, reading the email your father-in-law sent."

"The civil ceremony will be the same day?" I ask, wondering if anything has changed between the email Paul Knight sent out, and whatever discussions he and my parents have had since then.

My mother nods. "It will. Perhaps straight after the wedding ceremony. The garden will be done up. We'll have a tent on the grounds for the wedding reception later that evening," my mother continues. "And that will be a bigger event."

"Not that much bigger," my father says. A worried frown creases his brow. He's trying to toe the line, to do what Paul Knight says. My stomach feels heavy as I contemplate what a year of being in that family will do to me.

"Must we have a reception?" I ask.

"Of course, we must have a reception, filha." My mother

looks at me like I'm a child demanding the impossible. "If the wedding is small, we need a big party. We must invite those we couldn't invite to the wedding."

I force a smile. "Okay."

But I don't feel okay.

My heart races at the thought of my impending wedding day. It was hard enough putting on a show in front of Raquel. But with my parents watching? And guests? I'm not comfortable duping so many people.

"It will be fine," my mother assures me.

I nod. "It has to be."

One day, when this is all over, when I meet the man of my dreams, I'll give my parents a real wedding. I'm not big on weddings myself, but I know they would want something more than what Paul Knight has orchestrated. I feel so controlled by this man already, and I hate it.

"I'll get the coffee," my mother says, and bustles out of the room.

"Two weeks," my father murmurs. "He gave us two weeks."

"Why is this happening so fast, Papai?" I need to know the reason behind this.

"It benefits both of us, Daniela."

It feels like a boulder is resting on my chest. "Is there something you're not telling me, Papai?"

His jaw clenches, and I brace myself. "The company, filha. Things change. We could use the cash injection sooner rather than later."

"I understand. I feel sad that I'll be living there for a year."

"I know, filha." He looks so sad that it breaks my heart, and now I wish I hadn't said that.

Why are we doing this?

Surely marrying Oscar Ramos would be easier? I wouldn't

have to move abroad, and I can handle the devil I know better than the devil I don't.

But the thought of living with Oscar Ramos makes me shiver involuntarily. This is a marriage on paper, and I feel confident that Dexter would stick to the rules. I can't say the same for Oscar.

This is better. This way. The Knight way.

"Will Paul Knight visit here often?" I ask.

"He'll run the company remotely," my father informs me. "He'll have a few of his people installed here, for the duration of the year."

I bite my lip. "That's what I expected." But my spirits sag with the confirmation that he'll mostly be in New York, and most likely a part of my life, in some way or another.

"Sleep now, filha." My father's voice softens. "You don't have to go to work tomorrow. Take a day off. Prepare for your wedding, for the things you need; your wedding dress, your clothes and whatever else a bride needs."

"I'll invite a few of my friends," I murmur. "Most of them were international students anyway."

"Raquel will be here?"

"She's my closest childhood friend, I couldn't possibly dream of getting married without her." But all the same, I hate that I'm lying to her. I will need her by my side. For support, even if she doesn't know much. My parents will have their closest friends and extended families.

And the rest?

The Knights.

This wedding is going to be so much fun.

Not.

CHAPTER SEVENTEEN

DEX

We travel in the family jet. Another first for us.

It's the first time we've traveled with the others—Rio, Matteo and Enzo. We've seen one another over the years, at meetings, the Knight family dinners, and at high-society galas and events. We run into one another in the offices, in the elevator, in the lobby. Like we would with normal work acquaintances. No one would ever think we were family. But we are. Bound together by our father's infidelity.

But in recent years, Rio and I have become friends. It's not common knowledge. Still, it's been interesting watching the others trying to avoid one another.

Traveling together, just us, in a confined space, where no one can leave, has been eye-opening to say the least.

The old man announces that we're expected to go straight to the Oliveira's family estate once we land. Daniela's father has arranged a fleet of SUVs to come and get us from the private airstrip. They've also kindly put us up in one of their private estates, not too far from her family home. But before we can go there, we're to have dinner with the family. The Italian Knights groan, but I already knew this, because Daniela told me.

"Is this really necessary?" Matteo whines.

Rio looks visibly annoyed at the bickering. "They invited you for dinner, just go, eat and be nice."

"Do we *all* need to go?" Zach asks.

"No, just you, Zach," Rio snaps.

"We *all* need to go," I bite out, finishing my second glass of Scotch. It's a long flight and we're only halfway through. Things are getting real, and I'm feeling something unfamiliar, out of my depth, uncomfortable.

I'm going to Brazil to marry a woman I barely know. A woman who intrigues me in a way that scares me. I like my walls to be up. My boundaries in place. I like to fuck without emotional ties. I've only kissed Daniela, and I can't stop thinking about it. I'm worried that this marriage of convenience is going to turn out to be a fucking big inconvenience to me. Because Daniela excites me, and living with her is going to be my worst nightmare.

Zach looks cross. "I barely know them."

"And her parents barely know us. They're giving their only child away, to someone they don't know, and they want to get to know Dexter, and his family. You can't blame them," Cari replies.

"I could never do that," Jett says, looking pensive as he watches Brooke stick flower tattoos all over his forearms.

Zach seems especially whiny today. "I just want to take a shower and go to bed."

"My daughter is handling this better than you!" Jett hisses, cutting eyes at Zach. My youngest brother is beginning to seriously piss me off.

Cari's right. I don't blame her parents for wanting to get to know us better. I'm also curious about meeting Daniela's family. I want to get to know the people who raised her, the parents she speaks so highly of. I want to see what it's like to be part of a normal, loving family. But I also feel bad for them because they seem to have accepted the old man's demands without a fight.

Knowing this, the least my brothers can do is to shut the fuck up and eat dinner. I give Zach a pointed look. "Don't be so fucking whiny and disrespectful. It's kind of them to offer."

We sit in our two groups, for most of the plane ride, though Rio and I change seats a lot, moving around the plane. He senses my unease and tries to reassure me. He's also sniffing around. Trying to gauge how I'm feeling, but we don't risk talking too much about that. The old man has great hearing, and I'd rather he not get any intel into my private thoughts.

WE DRIVE UP TO THE HOUSE. IT'S CREAMY STUCCO, FRAMED BY ivy and low-hanging trees.

Nothing like the sleek, glass and metallic structures I'm used to. This is a *home*. Warm and inviting. I feel sorry that Daniela has to leave this and come and live with me, a stranger, in New York. Worse, she'll be with the Knights, and we're such a dysfunctional family. Heck, being around the old man at his dinners, we don't even feel like family.

The front bursts with color—flowers in colors of pink, purple, red and yellow. There's a soft green trim around the windows, and something about it sticks in my head. Daniela said she liked the color green because it reminded her of home. I wonder if it's this shade of green.

The front door opens before the cars have even fully stopped, and Daniela and her parents come out.

My gaze fixes on my wife to be. We haven't spoken, or texted ever since she left. I thought she might reach out, and maybe she thought I might, but neither of us did, and now it feels strange to see her again. She's wearing a cream sundress, with tiny green florals that echo the garden outside. Flat sandals that make her look casual and graceful at the same time. My brain short-circuits because I forgot just how pretty she is when she's not trying. Not dressed for a deal, not posturing, just being her. Her hair is up in a loose twist, with some locks falling over one shoulder.

"Get out, lover boy." Rio pokes me in the side.

If I was in denial all through the flight, it now hits me low and hard as I'm about to face her. The pull to this woman. She's not safe, not from someone like me. If she were my hookup, I'd never let her go.

But she's not.

She can never be.

She's not that type of woman.

Daniela wants something real and lasting, and I'm just a temporary band aid, a tool to help her father. This woman is real and warm. Beautiful inside and out. We haven't even had sex, but already she has a hold on me.

Her eyes land on mine as soon as I get out. There's a brightness about them, not just the color of her irises, but they sparkle as she watches me. I could stare into her eyes all day long and never tire. But then the light dims, just slightly and she looks wary, as if she's not sure which version of me she's about to get.

Her mother, wearing a printed yellow dress, clutches a dish towel in one hand like she dropped everything just to come say hello. Her father smiles, his face wrinkling in a matrix of lines. He's wearing an open-collar shirt and slacks. Soft eyes, and a wide, genuine smile.

"Dexter," he beams, ignoring the old man completely for the moment. "Welcome. It is so good to finally meet you."

"It's great to meet you, sir." We shake hands, and then he draws me in for a hug. It's unexpected. Yet warm. Grounding. I've never hugged my father, and this stranger, my father-in-law to be, does it like it's the most natural thing in the world.

"Dexter." Daniela's mother looks as if she's trying so hard to hold back, but she can't. She hugs me tightly. She's short and slightly portly, which means I have to lean down to hug her back. She doesn't let go quickly. Seems like she's trying to absorb me in that warm, loving hug, murmuring something about how I'm family already and how handsome I am, and how Daniela told her I was charming. Still hugging me, it's like she's trying to extract out my essence, trying to get a feel for who I am, this stranger who'll be marrying her daughter.

When she finally pulls back, she puts her hands to her chest, still holding the dish towel, and beams at me. "I am *so* happy to meet you, Dexter."

"The honor is mine, truly, ma'am."

I've felt the heat of Daniela's gaze on me throughout this entire exchange, and I turn to her, feeling a little overwhelmed.

"Dexter," she says softly, stepping toward me with a practiced smile. "I'm so glad you made it." I notice the shift in her tone, how bright and breezy she sounds, just enough for her parents' benefit. If she's putting on a show. I can play along.

Reaching for her hand, I lean in and ghost a kiss against her cheek, lingering a few seconds longer than necessary. "Wouldn't miss it for the world," I murmur, just loud enough for everyone to hear.

We exchange a look. It's guarded, yet curious. As if we're both trying to read the other. And damn it if she doesn't make my chest feel tight again, just by her presence. This. This is what scares me. And this moment, even if we're playing along, makes me wonder how long I can keep up this pretense.

Because I'm not pretending to be excited at seeing her. Quite the opposite. I'm tamping down my excitement.

The old man watches with what I imagine must be mild distaste; families hugging, people who are genuinely happy to have met. These are things he's not used to. He plays civil, shaking hands with Daniela's parents and exchanging just enough pleasantries to keep up appearances. The rest of my brothers trail behind, shaking hands, making jokes, letting the charm drip smooth as honey.

They're used to winning people over. We all are.

We step inside the house and I look around. It's the kind of house you instinctively lower your voice in, like it's a special place, like a library or a place of worship, sacrosanct and deserving reverence. A cushion from the real world. A place where people go to rest and recharge.

We pass by a ceramic vase on the table in the hall. The floors are old wood and plants are dotted everywhere. I glance at the family photos along the hallway, and get a feeling of how lived in this place is.

Like, *actually* lived in.

Enjoyed and used well.

A home where memories and history are made, and imprinted on the walls. I see the green that Daniela talked about, a vibrant olive green that's everywhere. Catching a glimpse of one of the rooms with it's double doors wide open, I see big, soft, comfortable-looking sofas, with trim and cushions neatly arranged.

These things are clearly her mother's touches, but Daniela grew up with this warmth and coziness. Surrounded by love and laughter. Affection and understanding. The things we Knights didn't have, but desperately wanted.

I try to get my bearings, try to figure out why this house smells like cinnamon and something floral. Why my chest aches a little walking through. It hits me, as soon as we're shown into what looks like the dining room. Slow-cooked garlic and onions, fresh herbs, something rich and savory simmering on the stove.

Daniela's father asks if we'd like to freshen up and tells us where the bathrooms are. Pre-dinner drinks are offered.

I take the opportunity and rush to splash cold water on my face, then take a few deep breaths to ground myself. For some reason, I feel anxious, but I quickly push this thought aside and join everyone again.

Daniela's parents are warm, and friendly and urge us to make ourselves at home. We follow them into a large room that is light and airy, with soft terracotta walls and high ceilings. We take our place around a huge, long, rustic wooden table set with hand-painted dishes and fresh tropical flowers, radiating warmth, tradition, and quiet wealth.

A housekeeper hovers in the background, looking at Daniela's mother, waiting for her next instruction.

DINNER GOES UNEXPECTEDLY WELL. THE ROOM IS LOUD, WARM and jovial, the air filled with chatter and a reassuring hum that floats around the table.

People are talking. The Italian Knights and my brothers, they're talking, to one another, and having fun, it looks like. Maybe it's the long flight, or the soft and easy vibe we're surrounded by, or even the warm night in an unfamiliar yet beautiful setting.

It's nothing like the Knight family dinners.

Only the old man sits stiffly, jabbing his fork into the food, like it annoys him. We don't bother with him, though I catch him and Daniela's father talking now and then.

There's enough food to feed fifty. A fish stew in a broth of coconut milk, a chicken dish, infused in garlic and onions and what Daniela's mother tells us is okra. There's warm, chewy cheesy bread, fresh out of the oven, placed in baskets around the table. Cheesy rice, fresh salad, some kind of sweet corn dish that her father insists I must try.

Daniela's mother fusses over us like we're her brood and she thinks we're starving. The housekeeper is in and out of the kitchen, replenishing the food and drink, letting nothing stay empty.

I'm halfway through my second helping of food before I realize I've barely said a word. It's not because I'm being cold, it's because I can't stop eating. Everything on the table tastes like it's been made a hundred times before, with love and care, from recipes passed down from someone's grandmother. I've never had food like this. Not at some five-star restaurant, not growing up, not ever.

This is a home that feeds more than just hunger. It fills a deeper need. Something that makes me feel like I belong.

Noticing my empty plate Daniela's mother beams. "Would you like more, Dexter? I can bring you another bowl."

I open my mouth to politely decline. Knight men don't usually go back for thirds, let alone seconds, not unless it's catered and plated by a Michelin chef. But instead, I hear myself say, "Yes, please. This is incredible. Honestly, it's the best meal I've had in years."

Her hand goes to her chest, eyes shining with something that could be pride, but looks like affection.

"You serious, dude?" Rio doesn't hold back.

"I'm hungry!"

"You still need to fit into your wedding suit." My father's

voice is like water over a fire. The air chills and silence falls, but it only lasts for a few seconds, before everyone starts talking again, ignoring the old man and his comment. Daniela glances at me, startled, then looks away quickly, like she doesn't want me to see her smile.

For dessert, there's a banana upside down cake and chocolate truffles, which Daniela's mother insists we all have at least two of. So I do. It would be rude not to. After dessert, I'm so full, and feeling bloated, I excuse myself, and head to the washroom, but it's not just that. I need a damn second to breathe. It's become a little overwhelming. The house is warm. Too warm. Too many voices, too much laughter, too much contrast of how family life could be, and what ours isn't.

After the washroom, I slip outside, tugging my collar open as the night air hits my face. It's cool and quieter out here. The rise and fall clicking sound of cicadas fills the night air, and it reminds me of the summer nights in Bermuda, when we visited Aurora, our family home there.

The garden smells like earth and flowers and a hint of citrus. I think of Daniela growing up here and playing, spending her childhood. Having met her parents, having had the privilege of spending an evening here, a dull ache sticks inside my chest. If our mother had been alive, if she hadn't driven off that bridge. If I hadn't said what I did, she might still be alive.

I bury my thoughts at the sound of footsteps behind me.

"Beautiful night," says a voice. It's Daniela's father. He's holding two brandy bowls and hands me one.

"Thank you." I take the glass, even though it's not my drink of choice.

He chuckles. "You're being welcomed into the family."

I nod, then swirl the liquid around in the big glass, before taking a small sip. The brandy hits my tongue with a slow, smoky sweetness, smoother than I expected, but still too soft, too polite compared to the sharp, unapologetic burn of my usual scotch.

Daniela's father stands beside me, as if we've done this many times, and this is just me and Daniela casually visiting them for dinner. I brace myself for small talk, polite conversation or awkward small talk, but he quietly gazes out at the garden.

"She always loved this spot," he says after a while. "She would sit out here for hours, reading, daydreaming, playing with her friends."

"You have a beautiful home, Mr. Oliveira."

He pats me on the shoulder gently. "No Mr. Oliveira, please. We will be family soon, filho."

"Fil-ho?" I peer at him.

"Son," he says simply.

And, just like that, something splinters inside me. It's one word; small, soft, and trivial, yet, a word which carries so much weight.

A word I have never been called.

It lands like a thunderclap, hard hitting and loud. My own father has never called me that. Not even by accident. Not even when pretending at playing happy families. And now this man who owes me nothing, gives it to me freely.

I'm feeling too emotional to say a word, so I nod, hoping I don't turn into a mess. This is so unlike me. Falling apart, trying hard not to.

It's the flight, it's being here, being fed, and the thought of tomorrow and all that will bring.

He lets out a quiet laugh. Then his tone shifts to something gentle, but grounded. "Dexter, there is something I need you to know. This marriage is a financial solution, an alliance, a merger of two families, but my daughter is the most precious thing in the world to us. She is the best part of this family."

He looks me straight in the eye. "I don't need you to be perfect. I just need you to take care of her. Protect her. Be good to her."

Be good to her.

The words hit me like a wrecking ball. I'm not here to be good. I'm here because I made a deal with a devil. I'm here because this arrangement gives me leverage. And a million dollars a month, of money I don't really need, but hey, if I can have it, why not.

I'm here because I want to piss off the man who never cherished my mother, or protected her or was good to her. He said he loved her, but I doubt he loved her the way she should have been loved. He cheated on her, after all.

I'm not here because of Daniela. Or love.

And yet.

Being here in her garden, her father's words linger in the quiet, and something shifts inside me.

Guilt, maybe. Or regret. Or the slow, creeping realization that this family is the kind I never had, and now that I've stepped into their warmth and love, it's something my heart seems to want.

"I'll do my best," I say finally, struggling to steady my voice. It's a truth encased in the silky glove of a lie. Now that I'm here, I'm starting to see how big a deal this is to Daniela. Going to a new country where she knows hardly anyone. It can't be easy for her. Moving to New York, leaving her country, her friends, her family. Moving in with me, a stranger.

Living together, putting on a façade, for a whole year.

Except it won't be a whole year.

Daniela has a lot to give up. A lot to lose, even if she's doing this for altruistic reasons, her life will be interrupted. Her life, as she knows it, will be put on hold. Mine will be disrupted, but to a much lesser extent.

"Daniela is stubborn, fiercely loyal and she has a heart that is too big for her own good," her father adds.

"I've noticed," I say quietly.

He nods, then sips his drink. "Just take care of her, Dexter. This year won't be easy for her, and we want her to be happy. Having met you, my wife and I feel she's in good hands. You are a good man, Dexter." He touches his chest. "I can tell."

Then he pats my shoulder again, firm and approving, before heading back inside, leaving me alone beneath the stars, staring at a garden that smells like home and feels like a promise I never meant to make.

CHAPTER EIGHTEEN

DANI

DEXTER SEEMS SO MUCH MORE RELAXED NOW THAT HE'S HAD dinner. My mother fusses over everyone. She overfeeds, over hugs, over cares and she overdid it with Dexter.

Maybe "overdid" isn't the right word. She wasn't putting on an act. My mother loved Dexter the moment he got out of the car. I could see it in the way she hugged him and held him. Like she wanted this to be true. For him to be a man I chose, a man I'm deeply in love with and want to spend the rest of my life with.

But the reality is such a stark contrast.

We don't know one another. We had a great time at the hotel, finding out about one another, but we aren't in love. We aren't even "in like."

We're simply making the best of a tricky situation, and we'll be married for one year exactly.

To benefit both our families in some financial capacity.

When he stepped out of the car he looked unsure. I detected

something alien in him. Uncertainty, even. But during the meal, he looked so relaxed, and the brothers were all talking, in a way they weren't on the night I first met them.

If nothing else comes from our being together, I want Dexter to feel loved and needed, to feel like part of a family, and my mother is the best person to make someone feel that way.

But, Dios, he looked so good. *Too* good, even coming straight off a long ten-hour flight, this man stole my breath away. Crisp white shirt, sleeves pushed up just enough to show his forearms, tailored pants, that slightly messy hair that looks like it's been through his hands a few too many times. He shouldn't have this effect on me, because this isn't real, but he does, and I don't know what to do with it.

He's a man who doesn't want to get involved, and it would be so wrong to get involved. I must focus on my father's health and business, and let those be my driving force.

But Dexter makes me sit up and take notice. During these past few weeks, I've found myself thinking of our conversation, lingering over our kiss, feeling something deeply buried inside me light up like a fire.

It's something I'll work on and try to stop. Not fan the flames of desire I mostly feel when I think of him.

We have a year. And the most important thing is that AO Eletronica benefits.

Not me.

My heart sinks when I watch my parents. This is so real to them. I want to shake them and remind them that this is an alliance and nothing more, but I'm fearful now that they're buying into this story.

One look at Dexter and they're acting as if this fairytale could turn into a happily ever after.

When he gets up to use the washroom, I consider going

after him, to try to get a moment alone with him, to see how he is, but I don't want so many pairs of eyes on me, so I leave it. Then when I notice that my father is missing, I get nervous. I have a feeling he wants to talk to Dexter alone, but my father doesn't know Dexter, and I don't want my father giving him any "advice".

I find him outside, exactly where I thought he'd be, and thankfully, he's alone. I step outside, my sandals silent against the stone. "There you are," I say, light and careful, because I can't gauge his mood. "I figured you might want an escape route after dessert number two."

He turns at the sound of my voice. "You say that like you didn't go for seconds with the chocolate truffles."

"Brigadeiros."

"That what they're called? They're insanely delicious."

I grin. "I consider them to be a food group."

He holds my gaze and something inside me lights up like a star. This feels so intimate, and real. But then my insides heat up when Dexter gives me a look, half wary, half something else. Something that feels like longing, or maybe regret.

I force myself to take a breath, remind myself that this is a performance, and we are merely actors reciting our lines. But when his mouth curves, and his eyes turn soft, I feel light and giddy again.

Is this how our year together will be? Full of ups and downs? Me not knowing if he's being genuinely nice to me or mocking?

"Your parents are … something else."

I cringe a little. "They can be intense. My father especially, though my mother isn't far behind." I put my hands to my face, thinking of how she was practically force feeding him. I move my hands away. "I'm sorry. I hope you didn't find this too much."

"No." He cuts in. "Your parents are wonderful people. Truly wonderful. The best kind," he says softly, looking out into the inky darkness. For a moment it seems like he's talking to himself. I feel like I need him to just be. "You're very lucky," he tells me.

"Thank you."

"I understand now, in a way I couldn't before, why you're doing this."

A soft breeze blows, wafting the scent of jasmine and lemon leaves. I wrap my arms around myself, listening to the familiar hum of the cicadas in the trees.

"You were very good with them, Dexter. The last thing I wanted was for you to feel put upon."

"I don't feel put upon." Then, quieter, "I just feel like this matters more than I expected it to."

I look at him and see something vulnerable in his expression. Maybe uncertainty about tomorrow and the consequences of our marriage, or maybe, it's the quiet panic of someone who isn't used to being cared for.

I feel like he's still trying to make sense of it all. Not just our alliance, but my parents, and this evening. My family life.

"You have a lovely home," he says.

"Thank you. There are a lot of memories here."

"It seems lived in, homey. Cozy, but with old style elegance."

"It is all of those things, and I will miss it dearly." I feel so incredibly sad at the thought of leaving.

"It's only for a year," he tries to reassure me. "Then you'll be back here and it's like none of this will have happened ... us, the wedding ... the fakeness of it all."

"I can't believe the day is almost upon us." I feel subdued at his words. I miss the man I had drinks with at The Bluebell.

"Are you ready for this?" he asks.

"Getting married to you?" I get shivers just hearing the words out loud.

He nods.

"I feel like I'm about to take a jump off a cliff and there's nothing but darkness beneath me. I don't know if there's water, or stone, or just an abyss."

"Feels like that, doesn't it? But this will all be in your past one day. You'll forget about it. I know this is a big deal for you."

"Isn't it for you?" I ask.

He opens his mouth to say something. But stops himself.

I gulp, thinking about his friends-with-benefits arrangement. What if he's having doubts and can't go through a year without having his needs meet? The look he gives me lances my heart. "You have noble reasons for doing this. I don't. I'm not a noble man, Daniela."

I flinch inwardly.

"I'm not a monster, and I won't do anything to hurt you, but this ... this is an alliance, and not a day or a moment goes by that I don't remember that."

Asshole.

"I'm sorry. I don't mean to sound so cold," he says, looking sad, even confused.

"I understand. You didn't want any of this."

"I didn't, but now it doesn't seem so bad."

"You have me to blame for your predicament. Had I not picked you ... you wouldn't be here."

"It isn't a predicament, but you're right. I guess I have you to blame for this." He smiles, as if to soften his words. "My father could never have made me marry you, if I didn't want to."

What's he trying to tell me? Or am I reading too much into

his words? "We did get on well on our getting-to-know-you date," I say.

"Surprisingly well."

"I don't want to be your enemy, Dexter. I want us to be friends."

"We're getting married tomorrow, sweetheart. We're going to be more than friends."

I don't understand him. One minute he's stating the cold hard truth of this marriage of convenience, then next he's flirting with me.

"Don't worry," he adds quickly, "I won't lay a finger on you." Our gazes lock and I feel my cheeks blush. I don't know what to say to him. "Unless you want me to," he adds.

The scoundrel. He really does think I'm like most of the women he's met. That I'll crumple at the morsels of attention he'll throw my way.

I rush to reassure him. "I won't. Believe me."

"You sure about that?"

I arch a brow, then look away, because Dexter, when his gaze burns through me, makes me feel like I'm at his mercy.

How can there be so much chemistry and sizzling attraction between us? So much heat and desire. And how can he be kind and also annoying so much of the time?

As they get ready to leave, I remember the little gift I bought for Brooke. Jett's carrying her in his arms, and though she's not asleep, she keeps yawning.

"I got you something," I say, taking out a gift bag.

"Oh, you didn't have to," Cari says, taking the bag for Brooke.

"You … you didn't have to," Jett says. "But, thank you."

"It's only a little something."

Cari opens the bag and lifts out a little family of wooden elephants. A mommy, a daddy and a baby elephant.

The little girl immediately fully comes to life, a big grin lighting up her face as she tries to hold the elephants, but Cari insists they leave them in the bag. "Thank you," she says to me.

"You're welcome."

We all say goodnight. Then Dexter, putting on another show, maybe because we both feel like we're being watched, hugs me tight. "That was so sweet of you, to give Brooke those gifts."

He looks genuinely surprised. I smile at him.

CHAPTER NINETEEN

DANI

My family home has been transformed into a breathtaking wedding venue. I feel a little sadness as I stare at the gardens where I played as a young girl.

Not once did I ever envisage in my future, being married to a stranger, a man I barely know.

But Dexter isn't so bad. I feel something for him, but I'm not sure what. I try not to dwell on our moments together. Try hard not to think too much about that evening at The Bluebell Manhattan, or how we laughed and kissed in front of Raquel.

A few of my friends and cousins are here, fussing over me, smoothing down my dress, giggling and fawning over me. Telling me yet again how quick this is, how I've taken them all by surprise.

I hate lying. Keeping up this charade is going to sap my energy, and the day hasn't even begun. I wonder if I'll survive this one year of married life. The thought of being Dexter

Knight's wife sends shockwaves through me, even though I should be used to that idea by now.

Feeling a flurry of movement, I turn to find Raquel marching towards me. My heart blooms at the sight of her. She's been by my side ever since she flew in late last night, after the Knights left.

This morning she helped me get dressed, and now she's standing before me, her mouth wide open. "Oh my! What a vision. I'll never forget you like this, Dani." She smooths down my veil. "I don't want to mess up anything. You look so beautiful!" Tears well up in her eyes as she clasps a hand to her chest, just like Papai and Mãe did when they first saw me. They were both on the verge of tears, and it splintered my heart to see them like that, knowing this is fake, and empty and hollow.

We hug again, more like I put my arms around her and cling to her tightly.

"Hey," she whispers when we pull apart. She's still holding my arms. "What is it?"

"Nerves," I whisper, remembering that the façade must be the strongest around my friend. Raquel is such a champion of justice and truth. She's a good person, fighting all the bad things in the world. Corruption and greed. She and Paul Knight would hate each other.

I wonder how she and Rio will react when they meet today.

"Just nerves?" she asks, the bloodhound in her coming out.

"I'm happy," I insist, more to convince her than anything else. "Dexter is such a wonderful man. He will take good care of me."

Raquel looks at me like I'm a stranger. I have to admit, those words sounded alien even to me. I'm rambling in my nervousness.

"You don't need him to take good care of you, Dani, you

can do that yourself." She assesses me like she's trying to figure out what the hell is really going on.

If I'm not careful, my emotions will get the better of me. As it is, my stomach feels weird. A dizzying sensation has been floating inside me all morning. I can't back out now. Papai needs me to go through with this.

I keep reminding myself that Dexter isn't *that* bad. He's not Oscar Ramos. If I hold that thought when I start to falter, it will always tether me back to the reason I'm doing this. Marrying a man who is nothing like Ramos.

"He's a good man."

Raquel's brows push together. "Are you trying to convince me, or yourself? What is going on, Dani?"

"Nerves. Just nerves." I need to keep my mouth shut. "Has Rio seen you yet?" I ask, trying to deflect.

There's a knock at the door, and one of my cousin's pokes her head in. "Are you ready?"

I take a deep breath and walk out to find my father, looking proud and distinguished and so incredibly happy. I take his arm, and immediately feel uplifted. We're getting married outside and it's the middle of summer here. Quite the opposite to New York. The buzz of cicadas fills the air, and the scent of tropical flowers wafts all around me.

I force myself to focus on my surroundings, and not my idle thoughts. White roses and orchids surround me, their delicate scent thick in the warm São Paulo air. The music swells as we step onto a long stone pathway, lined with candles and petals, which leads to an elaborate floral arch—the place where my fate will be sealed.

My heart hammers. Every step forward is a step toward an uncertain future but I refuse to walk into it blindly. I tell myself this is just about helping my father's company.

Rows of ivory colored silk chairs adorned with strips of

golden organza are arranged with perfect symmetry. Brazilian high society, CEOs and businesspeople, and, of course, the Knights are all sitting. The Knights are in the front two rows, and on the other side, my family, immediate and extended.

The divide feels palpable. The Oliveiras are smiling, and warm and exuberant as they look at me with pride and admiration in their eyes. The Knights seem cold in comparison, rigid, and with somber expressions.

Only Cari and Brooke are smiling. Cari's wide smile warms my heart, and Brooke waves at me. I chuckle and nod at her.

The entire event is an illusion, but the few faces that are genuine and hopeful and happy, lift my spirits, and right now, I'll take any little lift I can get. I try to convince myself this is more than just an alliance. I know what people say about arranged marriages; that they're nothing more than business transactions, a cold exchange of power and wealth.

Maybe that's what this started as. But to me, I feel like it could be more. Dexter doesn't love me, nor I him, but we can be friends, and we get on. We genuinely care for one another.

We can get through this in a civil manner. I feel he likes me more than he cares to admit. I care about him. I see the wounded man, and where others might see his cockiness, I see it as a front for the deeper hurt and guilt he's carrying.

I lift my gaze to find him standing at the altar looking stunning in a perfectly tailored outfit. The fabric clings to his broad shoulders, the crisp white of his shirt stark against the dark suit. His hands are loosely clasped in front of him. His expression? Unreadable. He doesn't look happy.

But he doesn't look devastated, either. He just looks like a man playing his part. I want so badly to believe this isn't just an act, that it isn't just a deal. That at some point, Dexter and I might be more.

But then his gaze catches mine and something flickers in his eyes. Not regret. Not reluctance.

Amusement.

Arrogant, lazy amusement.

Like he knows exactly what I'm thinking, and he's enjoying the *game* he's playing.

Not the wedding.

Not the moment.

A sharp ache spreads through my chest but I lift my chin. And I refuse to break.

DEX

I FEEL NOTHING.

That's the lie I tell myself. Because something is going on, and I'm trying to push it away. I don't believe in love, and if Daniela thinks she's going to change that, she's in for a rude awakening.

She's doing this for business reasons, for money, for her father. For me, it isn't about money. It never was. I'm doing this to piss Paul Knight off. To make him think he's won, only to walk away before the year is up, leaving the deal in ruins.

I smile and remember that I'm playing the part of an adoring bridegroom. I stand at the altar, my posture relaxed, one hand casually tucked into my pocket. My brothers and father are in the first few row of seats, while Daniela's family are on the other side. They're a big family. She has no siblings, but she has so many cousins and aunts and uncles.

In comparison, we are so few. Rio winks at me, and I grin back at him, before quickly schooling myself to be somber again. Matteo is on his cell phone. Enzo looks around, calmly surveying the crowd. They know exactly what this is. A farce.

Jett is silent. Watching. Unreadable. He's been here before, trapped in our father's manipulations. He doesn't want this for me. But he also knows I won't listen to anyone. Beside him, Cari holds Brooke on her lap. Cari looks tense, like she can feel the weight of this for Daniela. Maybe because she's experienced it for herself. She's been where Daniela is, standing beside a Knight, hoping for something real.

Brooke watches with wide eyes, looking between Daniela and me, frowning, as if, even at her age, she can sense that something about this isn't right.

Zach seems to be the only one who is genuinely smiling. As if he's enjoying this. As if he thinks this is real. He leans over to whisper something to Cari, and she giggles. I'm curious to know what he said. He's probably making a bet about whether Daniela will slap me before the night is over.

My gaze returns to Rio again. I need to know he's okay with this, now that this is the moment where it's all happening. He looks too still, too pensive almost as if he might be thinking that he could have been up here, marrying Daniela instead of me. A prick of guilt stabs me, but then I see him looking around. And I see who he's looking at.

There, in the first row, is Daniela's friend. The one in the bar. The one Rio was flirting with. The corporate lawyer with the big red lips.

I let out a sigh of relief.

Rio and I are good. He's not sitting there wondering about Daniela. The man has moved on. He's on a chase. Going after Raquel, I'm sure of it. But, if I'm being truthful, it's not only that I was worried about hurting Rio, but something like jealousy prickled along my spine at the thought of him lusting after my wife. My *pretend* wife, sure. But still … I didn't like it.

Our father sits upright. His back ramrod straight. His gaze directly in front, stone-faced, emotionless. I wonder what machinations are going through his head? What he's thinking. What sort of a deal he's struck. I'm about to play along with his demands and then I'll turn the game on him.

This is his victory. I'm doing what I'm told. Marrying the girl. Securing the business deal. He doesn't realize I'm already planning to destroy it all.

And yet … when Daniela comes into my line of vision, something in my chest tightens. She looks beautiful. Too beautiful for words. The kind of beautiful that tempts a man to forget his own rules.

But I won't.

Not now.

Not ever.

Because I'm not Jett.

I'm not going to be a fool for a woman.

My lips turn up at the corners instinctively, and I break out into a genuine smile, because … because *this could be real*, a voice in my head says. Sometimes when I wake up, it feels real. Until I remember.

Daniela looks stunning, and that dress hugs her every curve. She's smiling at me, not a wide smile, but a smile that needs reciprocity, a sending-out-feelers smile, as if she's trying to gauge my thoughts.

That's when it comes flooding back in vivid color. The kiss. Something that was supposed to be flirty and fleeting, but it set my soul on fire.

Who am I kidding?

I haven't been able to get Daniela out of my head since that night. But I remind myself that this is just an arrangement. One that Daniela instigated.

CHAPTER TWENTY

DANI

THE OFFICIANT SAYS THE VOWS IN PORTUGUESE FIRST, THEN English, for Dexter's benefit.

His voice is steady, reverent, the words floating through the warm evening air but I barely hear them. My hands tremble slightly as I take Dexter's hand and instinctively give a gentle squeeze, but he doesn't squeeze back. Doesn't offer comfort.

I convince myself that it's fine as I recite my vows. But they feel real. Like I believe them. Like I mean every word. When it's Dexter's turn, he delivers his lines effortlessly.

Like a man closing a business deal.

"I do." The words mean nothing to him.

But when he slides the ring onto my finger, something feels different. I see it on his face. A glimmer of uncertainty. Or maybe a realization, confirmation, even, that he doesn't want to do this. Something about the sight of my hand wearing his ring unsettles him. It's so clear to me, but thankfully, no one will notice.

What are we doing?

I press my lips together, trying to compose myself. Trying to forget the lies and deceit of this moment that binds us together as husband and wife. A few seconds later, just as my thoughts run rampant, the officiant announces us husband and wife. Dexter takes both my hands in his, and we stare at one another.

Smile, I tell myself, because this still feels strange. I'm about to turn around to face our guests and get ready to walk back down the aisle, but Dexter doesn't hesitate. He leans forward, his hand cupping my jaw, his fingers firm but measured. Then he tilts my face up to his and kisses me.

It's controlled and precise. A kiss designed to convince the audience. More than a press of the lips, but otherwise emotionless. Nothing like the *other* kiss. The one filled with heat, and passion.

The one that seared my soul and imprinted his lips on my mouth, his hands on my face.

This is a plain and emotionless kiss to solidify the farce. I feel somehow ... *cheated.* And disappointed. As if the suppressed longing in my heart has been kicked back. He pulls away quickly and takes my hand as we turn to face our guests. Then we walk back down the aisle as husband and wife.

It's my fault, for expecting something when there is nothing. For foolishly believing we could be the couple we were at the bar.

Dexter has shown me who he is and I have to forget that other man—the one who opened up to me and kissed me like I've never been kissed before. That evening he was simply playing a part for Raquel, and I should never forget that.

As we walk down the aisle, my fingers grip his arm lightly, as if I dare not encroach his personal space. I glance at him but he's looking at his family. A heaviness settles over me as I imagine what they must be thinking.

Playing the part of Dexter Knight's wife isn't going to be easy.

OUR WEDDING RECEPTION IS ABOUT TO START IN THE LARGE tent that has been set up in the grounds.

It's draped in soft white and gold fabrics and chandeliers are strung across the ceiling, their warm twinkling lights glistening in mid-air. The night sky is a deep indigo, dusted with stars and streaked with the brushstrokes of sunset-lavender and gold.

Earlier, immediately after the wedding, as the champagne was being poured, and canapés were passed on silver trays, Dexter and I quietly slipped away to a private room for the civil signing. A registrar was waiting to handle the paperwork. We gave our signatures, but the ceremony was cold, emotionless, brief. In that moment, the transactional nature of our marriage became so clear to me.

I felt sad and alone, as we walked back to join the guests. I noticed a couple of photographers snapping photos of us, no doubt for leaking to the press.

We were hand in hand, but I quickly realized this was just for show. We mingled with our guests, drifting through the garden, sipping and laughing beneath the late-afternoon sun, the sound of clinking glasses and soft Brazilian jazz floating through the air, but I couldn't shake my melancholy.

Now the air is thick with the scent of jasmine and night-blooming flowers, and the rich aroma of Brazilian cuisine served on silver platters.

Dexter and I take our seats at the high table adorned with flowers and candles, our chairs larger and more elaborately dressed than the guests' chair, resembling thrones. To everyone watching, this is a stunning, extravagant wedding. The merging of two powerful families. A cause for celebration.

In reality this couldn't be further from the truth. This wedding, and our marriage, is like a landmine. Everything looks normal and calm, until one day I'll step on something that blows up in my face.

The live band begins to play a soft, romantic samba, the melody floating through the air as our first dance is announced. My stomach twists at the sound of our names. I glance at my husband. How strange that word feels on my tongue. Dexter downs the rest of his scotch, setting the glass down with slow, practiced ease before turning to me.

Then, he extends his hand and the moment I place my palm in his, a shiver runs through me.

Not from nerves.

From *him*.

"Shall we dance?" he asks, his eyes suddenly soft and caring. The aloofness from earlier has vanished. It seems like he's embracing this role with renewed vigor.

"Must we?" I whisper.

He leans towards me. "We need to convince our guests, Daniela."

I'm tired, and my guard is down. This has been a long day and it has sapped all my energy. But his voice, low and close, and like a whisper to my heart, makes my spine tingle. It's not a command, or a suggestion. It's something darker, protective, and for me, it's dangerous.

"Okay. Maybe we should." I give in. We stand up and his hand glides around my waist, broad, warm, ridiculously steady. He guides me onto the open space beneath the chandeliers. The music swells. It's Brazilian, and universal at the same time.

Romantic and intimate with soft sultry vibes. Perfect for small steps and bodies flushed close together.

His grip is light but firm, his movements smooth, practiced. Dexter doesn't strike me as a man who dances, so I am apprehensive at how we will be on our first dance together. Showing our duped audience that we are husband and wife so madly in love.

But when his arm tightens around me and he pulls me close against his chest, it reminds me of how real things feel between us sometimes. How dangerous that is, for my sanity.

"Relax," he murmurs, almost against my temple. "Just follow my lead."

He changes character so quickly and easily, it's frightening. "You're leading?"

"Yes, wife." Smoldering dark eyes meet mine, glittering with promise. What will the night bring? My parents have given us a private suite nearby for our wedding night. I've tried not to think about it but the night will draw to a close in not too many hours from now.

Dexter moves slowly, but deliberately. His steps aren't polished but his confidence carries him. We sway to the music, slowly, eyes locked, bodies pressed. Heat building between us.

I'm acutely aware of everything. His hand resting on the small of my back. His jaw brushing mine when he turns his head. I feel dazed and dizzy. Drunk on the idea of love. Because Dexter is a very good actor. For someone who was so against this, this man has mastered the art of playing a loving husband.

We're meant to be playing a role but this feels so real.

I'm not supposed to feel anything, and yet, I do. I let myself sink into the moment, loving the way Dexter's hand moves along the curve of my back. The way his breath ghosts against my cheek as he leans closer, causing shivers to skitter along my skin.

To our watching guests, we look perfect. It even feels real to me, despite what this is—an alliance. Not for love, but for business.

How well we deceive everyone.

I look up at him, searching for something, needing to find something real. Confirmation that he feels what I'm feeling. Electricity zapping along my skin, turning my insides light and giddy.

His hand tightens when I move my fingers to his shoulder. Not possessive, but aware. Like he's noting every breath I take. Every tremor I'm trying to suppress.

"You're trembling," he murmurs.

"So are you," I whisper back, averting my eyes. Trying to steady my heart, slow down my pulse. I can't. I feel Dexter around me. Like he's a part of me now. Potent and powerful.

The moment fills with silence, and everything we're trying not to say.

"I didn't expect this part to be hard," he mutters.

"What part?" I glance up, my eyes catching his just long enough to lose my footing emotionally.

He holds my gaze. "The pretending."

My breath catches. Just slightly. Hope rises from the base of my belly. He gently swipes his thumb across the fabric of my waist. It's a subtle movement, and no one will notice. But I feel it like it burns. Like he's branded me, just with this subtle, imperceptible movement.

"You're quite good at this," he murmurs, his voice low, just for me.

My fingers tighten slightly where they rest on his shoulder. "I could say the same for you," I whisper back. "I didn't have you down for a dancing type."

"I'm not." His mouth tilts, but his eyes stay serious. "You make this easy."

My heart flips in my chest. I'm in danger of having feelings for my husband. But I can't admit it.

Not here.

Maybe not ever.

He dips his head, his breath hot against my ear. When his lips brush my skin, shivers prickle across my neck. "When I said you were good at this I meant you're good at keeping up the pretense."

My heart sinks. He pulls away and spins me out. The cold blade of disappointment sinks into me. Then he pulls me back in, closer this time. Too close, and our chests nearly touch.

"It's easy to pretend." I remain defiant, but say it with a smile, even though inside I'm hurting. I hope I have the strength to get through this night, and all the other nights. Three hundred and sixty-five of them.

"Our first dance, amor. The first of many things." His fingers press lightly against the small of my back.

I let out a gasp. His touch makes my body react in ways that feel dangerous. Like I could give into anything he demanded, if he so wanted it. I look around, trying to focus anywhere but on my husband's handsome face.

I see Paul Knight, sitting at the table, surrounded by his sons. He watches the dance like a king surveying his empire. I'm sure he sees this as a victory, and then I remind myself that this is a victory for my father. A way for him to be well again, to have hope again, to have the business regain its previous status.

Cari smiles at me, and I sense that she feels for me. Maybe, with her woman's intuition, she sees through the way I look at Dexter, the way I'm trying not to look at him, but can't help it.

She's probably been where I am, with a man who seems unreachable, hoping for something real. I smile back. We've barely exchanged many words, but I make a note to seek her out when I move to New York. I'll need my allies there, when I'm living with Dexter.

Damn that evening when we went out for drinks. If he'd been the same person I met at the soiree, I would handle this better. I wouldn't have had a peek into who he can be when he allows himself to open up and be vulnerable.

I venture a glance at him, to find his eyes on me. My heart jumps with joy, and gratitude, at the look he gives me. I remember him telling me he wasn't interested in this alliance, that he wanted no part of it, but this look? This look says otherwise.

"Don't stare at them." He leans in again, and this time he nips my earlobe gently. My eyes widen in shock. A line of shock touches my breast, reaches between my legs. Leaves me wanting him.

"You bit me."

"Because you're so tempting, wife."

What is it with the wife?

He's obviously loving the label, but I wonder if he's playing with me again? We're supposed to convince our guests, but now he's taking it too far.

"Look at me, meu amor," he orders. "Look at me like you want to kiss me again."

My heart jolts, because of his term of endearment, and the way he says it and the way he looks at me. I can't help but stare at his lips, thick and plump, and perfect for kissing. Lips too beautiful for a man. Lips that fit over mine so perfectly. Like they were made for that sole reason.

"You want it again, don't you, Gatinha?"

Gatinha. Little kitten.

I let out a gasp, impressed, and excited. On edge. "You've been reading your tourist phrase book. I am impressed."

"For you, meu amor. Anything."

I look at him in confusion. He's talking way more intimately than he needs to be. He doesn't need to remind me of that kiss, or say these things to me, when we could just dance and be silent, and play the game.

We continue dancing and swaying, and keeping up the pretense but with every passing second it becomes harder to remember that this is merely an alliance,

I'm not sure why he's doing this, going overboard and playing with my emotions.

"Careful, Dexter." I crane my neck up at him and whisper directly into his ear. "Try not to get swept up in the occasion. You need to walk away from this untouched."

"What makes you think I won't?" He holds my gaze for longer than he should, and I'm in danger of being the one who won't be able to do what I've just told him.

When the song ends, our hands linger. Neither of us lets go first. But then he steps away first, his expression composed, like a blank canvas. The guests erupt into applause. We walk back to our table and take our seats, but when I lean back against my chair, needing to ground myself and take a breath, Dexter lifts my hand and kisses the back of it.

Cheers break out, and our guests look at us, expectantly.

They believe this.

Even though it's only a kiss on my hand.

"We need to give them more, Gatinha." Dexter twists towards me, and his eyes hold my gaze.

"Why am I your little kitten?" I ask, curious.

He leans closer, so that our faces almost touching. A charge of excitement skitters up my arms. "I like the way the word sounds on my tongue."

"Not because I'm cute and fluffy?" I'm conscious of his hand still in mine, but now he's stroking it with his thumb. Shockwaves of pleasure ripple out over my skin. I press my thighs together because I need to get control of my senses. Of the way my body reacts to him.

"Nothing cute and fluffy about you. You're all curves but toned. Just the way I like."

"Just the way you like," I murmur seductively, because my fevered body is alive and wants more. More of him holding me, and touching me, and calling me Gatinha. "I'll take that as a compliment."

"It's the truth."

I giggle, and he instinctively kisses the back of my hand again.

"I have claws, Dexter. Be careful," I warn him, trying to maintain some distance because we seem to be hurtling towards one another at breakneck speed. If this continues, I'll want more than just a sizzling kiss tonight.

"I am being careful, meu amor. I know exactly what this is." He whispers the words close to my ear, so that no one will be able to lip read them. But his breath, and his nearness make me shiver. "Are you cold, or just naturally excited by my touch?" he asks, amused.

"Cold," I lie.

"In this heat?" He glances at our guests, then turns to me again. "They want something more, Gatinha. We should give it to them."

"Give them what, exactly?" I stare around in confusion, but he's right. Our guests are looking at us.

"Lean in to me," he orders, sending a charge of excitement through me.

What is this? Some sort of slow torture?

Naturally, I do as he says, and am about to ask another question when he cups the back of my neck. My breath hitches at the touch which both electrifies and grounds me. The air in my lungs empties. I feel like I'm on a ride at the carnival, paused atop a tall rollercoaster and about to hurtle down at breakneck speed. Dexter leans in slowly, then pauses, his glittering dark eyes locked on mine, giving me a chance to pull away.

I don't.

I *can't.*

Then he kisses me.

It starts gentle at first. A mere press of his lips on mine. I prepare myself for the emotionally empty kiss earlier. But then his mouth claims mine, hot and firm, and his tongue meets me, dueling ferociously, like he can't taste me fast enough.

I can't get enough. He ravages me with a fire that surprises me. This time Dexter isn't gentle or cautious. He's like a man who's been fighting the urge for too long. A man who is finally letting go.

My traitorous hand rises to his chest, fisting his shirt. Even if I wanted to resist, slow down, hold back my emotions, it's impossible. I am irrevocably consumed by his lips, his tongue, his raw heat. His passion.

All that bottled up emotion pours out as we kiss hungrily. He angles his mouth, deepening the kiss while his other hand slides to my waist and he pulls me to him as if he can't bear to have me apart.

The world around me blends into darkness, but I hear gasps. Cheers. The clink of glasses. It feels like everyone's watching but I don't care.

Nor does Dexter.

Suddenly, this doesn't feel like a performance anymore. This is more than life imitating art.

I feel lost when Dexter moves away, breaking for air. His lips part slightly, and I feel his breath, hot and ragged, against my mouth. I only get a few seconds to recover, to breathe, before his tongue meets mine again in a slow, lazy stroke. My insides feel light and trippy. Liquid heat coils deep in my belly. My hands grip his shoulders, as I steady myself, anchoring to him, because my world is spinning out of control.

This kiss is a tell.

A confession.

It's everything we don't say but feel. The lust, the tension, the fear of wanting it all pours out of us in every moment our mouths remain melded together.

Dexter finally pulls back, a crack of light between us, his forehead pressing against mine. I feel his chest heaving, feel my lips hot and bruised.

"Where are your claws now, Gatinha?"

"Still there," I whisper, barely able to speak.

His eyes darken, the faintest smile tugging at the corner of his mouth. "They feel like heaven."

DEX

I DON'T KNOW WHY I SUGGESTED WE KISS.

I do know.

I orchestrated that kiss, because I haven't been able to stop thinking of her. I wanted her lips on mine, and that kiss at the altar wasn't the time or place for reliving our first kiss.

But that kiss just now.

Un-fucking-believable.

Daniela blinks at me a few times. Our guests clap excitedly. But we don't see them. Or look at them. We only have eyes for one another. I don't even want to see what my brothers' reactions are.

If she were a hookup, we'd have fun getting her out of that wedding dress tonight.

But she's not a hookup.

She's nothing of the sort.

And that type of relationship? That's clearly not going to happen. But, at this rate, I'm not going to be able to sleep tonight, unless I take a cold shower or two. We can't have the type of night that a kiss like this leads to.

We both lift our glasses and sip at the same time. Thankfully, dinner is served and I manage to distract myself. With the food slowly being served, the mood changes from celebratory to muted conversation. Daniela and I eat in silence as mindful servers tend to our every need.

After we've eaten, we make small talk, commenting on how good the food is. We talk about the wedding, and the guests. She points out members of her extended family, her friends, and Raquel.

Family members and business moguls move between tables, discussing alliances, financial strategies, and what this marriage means for both families. The reception buzzes around us; champagne flutes clinking, conversations dipping between business deals and false pleasantries.

I should be paying attention to the spectacle, watching how my father networks and ingratiates himself with those he deems worthy. But I find myself watching Daniela as she talks to the guests who come up and congratulate us. Most of them are people she knows, as only the Knights came from our side, not our friends or business associates. I'm sure my father will have something planned for us when we return home, some PR stunt to celebrate the first Knight wedding.

When we return home.

My insides feel heavy when I think of what that will entail.

Daniela will move into my apartment, my comfortable haven of security, my bachelor pad. I'll have to share with her.

Only for seven months.

Maybe less.

The more time I spend with her, the more uncomfortable I get about continuing with this ruse. Watching her, I can't help but admire her poise and her politeness, at her smiles and bubbly laughter as she converses easily with the guests, most of whom I don't know.

I marvel at the way she takes my hand and introduces me to them, gushes about me, telling them how we met and how much she loves me and how she knew I was the one for her.

She's an accomplished liar

And a beautiful one at that.

We're sitting on our thrones again when her expression tightens. It's so pronounced, that I sit up and take notice. A shadow falls over our table.

"Ah, Daniela." The voice is rich, and practiced. Confident, but too familiar. I glance up, my fingers tightening around my champagne glass as a portly man and many years older invades our space like an insect that doesn't belong.

He looks to be in his late fifties, maybe early sixties, silver hair slicked back, suit impeccable, posture dripping with entitlement. The kind of man who doesn't hear 'no' very often.

I don't know who the hell he is. But my wife does, and she stills beside me, her fingers curling into her lap.

Not a good sign.

"I was surprised to receive an invitation to your reception," the man muses, not looking at me once, his gaze lingering on Daniela like he's memorizing every inch of her. "I'm delighted to be here. I couldn't miss it, of course. Such an important union." He reaches for her hand and she gives it, reluctantly. I know her well enough to know this much. He lifts it toward his worm-like lips and kisses it. Too slow. Too long.

A beat passes. One second too many.

Daniela looks uncomfortable.

I don't like it. I *really* don't fucking like it. I lean towards her, possessively, taking her hand out of his, as if I own her. As if she's mine. And she is. For now.

"That's enough." My eyes cut into the man's face. My voice comes out sharper than I expect, cutting through the music and chatter.

He doesn't react immediately, but looks at me, then, and just smiles, as if he's enjoying himself, as if he knows something I don't. "Oscar Ramos," he says, giving me a sickly smile. "A pleasure, Mr. Knight. Congratulations are in order, I believe."

I believe? I don't shake his hand, or reply. Instead, I weave my fingers with Daniela's, her hand secure in mine.

A flicker of amusement crosses his face as he stares at my wife again. "I see you've done well for yourself," the man continues, his tone sweet as honey. "But then you were always full of surprises, Daniela."

Her shoulders stiffen. There's something in the way he says it. Something laced with meaning. A veiled threat, hidden beneath politeness. I lean forward slightly, keeping my voice measured, firm. "I don't like the way you're talking to my wife."

The man's lips curve, as if my words amuse him. "I didn't mean anything by it." His gaze flicks back to Daniela, slower than I like. "I only hope, my dear, that you got exactly what you wanted."

Daniela's jaw moves as she swallows. I feel her tension, and graze the fingers of my other hand lightly over her bare arms, a movement the slimy old snake observes pointedly.

"You're cold, meu amor," I say to her. She turns to me, her face flushed, but I feel her relief as her gaze melds with mine. She's scared. Or nervous. Clearly, there's more going on here than I know but I intend to find out.

The man steps back with a final nod, which I see from the periphery of my vision, even though my eyes are fixed firmly on Daniela. "A long and happy marriage to you both," he says, but neither of us acknowledge him and he leaves as quickly as he arrived.

Daniela exhales. It's quiet, barely noticeable. I watch the way her fingers press into her lap, the way she tries to wriggle her hand entwined with mine, the way her shoulders are still too tight, too tense.

"You know him." It's not a question. She nods, but doesn't elaborate. I don't like this. "Who is he?"

"No one important." She clasps her hands in her lap.

Lie.

I tilt my head. "Try again."

She hesitates, for a nano-second, before pasting on a bright, practiced smile.

"Let's not do this now, Dexter."

But she's clearly rattled. I see it. I feel it. And I don't fucking like it. I should let it go. Should remind myself that this isn't real, that she's just another pawn in this game I'm playing against my father.

But something about the way she looked just now, nervous, guarded and vulnerable, burrows into my skin like an infestation. Something gnarly and unwanted that I need to root out.

And I realize something. I don't want *anyone* making her feel like that.

Ever.

Not Oscar Ramos.

Not anyone.

"I've got you," I whisper. Her eyes moisten, and it hits me hard. Like a punch to my jaw. "Did he hurt you?" I hiss, under my breath. She gives a subtle nod, then looks down.

I reach for her face, my thumb stroking over her skin, and I feel something I haven't in a long time; I feel possessive over a woman. A woman I care about. A woman I would die for and kill for.

A woman I barely know.

CHAPTER TWENTY-ONE

DEX

WE GET THROUGH THE REST OF THE EVENING WITHOUT ANY more drama, though I look around for signs of that entitled prick, but I don't see him.

Oscar Ramos. There is more to this man and his story with Daniela, and I intend to find out exactly what the hell it is.

The rest of the night goes well. The wedding reception is flawless, a perfectly orchestrated spectacle, just as expected.

Daniela and I make our rounds, shaking hands, smiling, playing the role we've been assigned, of the happily married golden couple. She's a natural at this, slipping effortlessly between Portuguese and English, charming guests, introducing me with that well-practiced grace of hers.

When we reach the Knights' table, Cari stands to hug Daniela. "We must get together and do something," Cari says warmly. Brooke tugs at Daniela's dress, beaming up at her. "You look really pretty."

Jett offers a firm handshake, murmuring his congratulations. The rest of them all follow suit, Zach, Matteo and Enzo.

"Where's Rio?" I ask, seeing the empty chair.

"Having fun." Matteo points casually to one corner of the room. Rio is deep in conversation with Raquel. Sonofabitch didn't waste much time there.

My father clears his throat. "Wonderful, wonderful reception. Beautiful wedding," he announces, his voice cutting through the hum of conversation. Beside me, I sense Daniela's shoulders stiffen. I don't blame her. Compliments from my father always come with strings attached.

"And now, I'd like to announce a surprise gift for you both," the old man continues, brushing imaginary lint from his sleeve.

"A surprise?" I don't like the sound of this one bit.

My father keeps talking. "Such a beautiful wedding. The least I could do was arrange a beautiful honeymoon for you both."

A what, now? What the hell is he talking about? He specifically stated there was to be no honeymoon.

"A honeymoon?" Daniela whispers. She places her hand on the back of a chair, her fingers gripping tightly.

"I thought we were going back to New York," I snap.

My father shakes his head. "No, no. You newlyweds deserve and should enjoy your honeymoon."

We will? I almost ask him to repeat himself. He's changing the plan, the same plan he laid out in explicit detail through an email, the one that had clear instructions: there was to be a wedding, a brief reception, and then we all return home.

We were supposed to have breakfast tomorrow with Daniela's family, before flying back on the private jet. This was always supposed to be a lightning-fast trip, despite the distance, but things have now changed.

Now, there's a honeymoon.

I'm completely blindsided. And suspicious, too. My father doesn't do anything because it's a nice gesture. He's motivated by greed and I have to wonder, how does he stand to benefit from this?

"Why?" Daniela asks, a slight tremor in her voice. I suspect it for the same reason I feel unnerved. Neither of us had a honeymoon on our radar. My father gives her a long, unreadable look. "It's a wedding, Daniela. And honeymoons always follow."

That smile, it sends a chill down my spine. I know that smile. It means he's holding back information, making moves behind the scenes.

"We were all supposed to return home together." I force my voice to stay level. I don't like the way my father has suddenly changed the terms. In answer, he just smooths his hand over his tie.

"My assistant will have emailed you a copy of the resort. It's private, and exclusive. Take time off, enjoy yourselves. We'll speak later."

Daniela looks at me, and I want to reassure her, because, just like that, our plans have been rewritten. We're not going home. Instead, we're stuck here, trapped in a luxury honeymoon we never planned,.

I don't like surprises.

And I don't trust this one.

***

DANI

. . .

WE REACH THE SMALL PRIVATE VILLA MY PARENTS ARRANGED for our wedding night. I wish they hadn't. Between them and Paul Knight, it seems our parents aren't making it easy for us.

The driver has already dropped off our overnight bags and now as we walk inside, this is all too real. We're here, alone, just the two of us.

The villa is an open-plan space, modern yet intimate, with soft lighting and wide glass doors leading to a terrace. The centerpiece of this place is a massive four-poster bed, draped in sheer, billowing fabric that catches in the warm night breeze. Romantic and clearly designed for newlyweds.

But we aren't newlyweds. Not really.

Exhaustion and frustration cling to me like the heavy beading of my wedding gown. Dexter, however, looks annoyingly unbothered. The second the door clicks shut, he yanks off his tie and tosses it onto a chair, rolling his shoulders like a man who just closed a deal and is already thinking about the next one.

I stand in the center of the room, still in my gown, watching him unbutton the top of his shirt.

Waiting.

For what, I don't know.

He doesn't say a word.

Instead, he heads straight to the minibar and pours himself a drink, quickly draining the glass dry. He lets out a deep sigh. "I needed that."

"Our wedding day was that stressful for you?"

"On the contrary, I quite enjoyed it. You?"

"It was unforgettable." It's the truth, but now silence falls and stretches out between us like a lazy yawn.

"Are we going to talk?" I ask, wanting to know what's going through his head, this mercurial man who seems to like playing games.

"About?" He pours himself another drink then lifts his glass, taking a slow sip before finally turning to me, that lazy, insufferable smile back in place.

This isn't the man who danced with me, and held me, then kissed me in front of our guests. Not the man who held firm and possessive when Oscar Ramos came over and made my stomach turn.

He seems casual and unbothered.

My stomach twists. Is he serious?

"About the surprise honeymoon your father has unexpectedly gifted us," I snap. I have been preparing myself for life with Dexter when I move in with him in New York. I've calculated that he'll be in the office for most of the day, and I'll work from home. We only have the evenings and weekends to navigate, but I plan to visit Raquel a few times, maybe even arrange a few girlie weekends away. I also want to get to know Cari better. But the thought of this honeymoon, and nights cooped up with this man makes me suddenly nervous.

"My father is a man who makes many unexpected moves. Get ready for it Daniela. And, welcome to the family."

Something sharp pierces through me because he keeps saying that. "What is that supposed to mean?"

He moves closer, swirling his amber-colored drink around in his glass as he stands before me.

"It means …" His voice dips lower, "that this is a business transaction and we must play the part. My father is doing this for optics. Nothing more. Maybe your father also needs things to look right, which might be why we're here." His arm sweeps around the room. "This is all probably part of the act, too. Just play along with the charade. I am."

I lift my chin. "Are you?" I'm not so sure. That kiss at our reception was as unexpected as it was passionate. It also didn't need to happen, so, why did he kiss me? I need to find out.

"What was with the kiss, when we were sitting on the thrones? It wasn't necessary."

"We had to play the biggest part today, when all eyes were on us." Dexter's voice is as infuriatingly smooth as ever. "Kissing you and making it believable were all part of the act."

It stings when he says the words out aloud.

Part of the act.

He leans against the wall, watching me with a glint of amusement. "Just go along with the pretense. Unless…" He sniffs under his arm, then lifts his hand to his face, inhaling dramatically. "Do I smell or something? You seem repulsed by me."

He's baiting me, and I refuse to take it.

"I don't find you repulsive, Dexter. Just annoying."

His gaze narrows and he watches me, tracking every shift in my expression like he's reading something between the lines. Then, with infuriating ease, he reaches out, dragging a single finger down my bare arm. A slow, deliberate touch. I feel a spark, a sizzle, and try hard to hold firm.

"Just annoying," he muses. "I'll take that. After all, we barely know each other." His eyes flick toward the bed, hard-to-miss and the cause of my palpitations. "And now we have to sleep together."

"Share a bed," I correct, ignoring the way my skin still tingles from his touch.

"Sleep together," he echoes, his tone laced with suggestion.

He's toying with me. Enjoying himself. The second glass of scotch has loosened his restraint further, making him bolder.

I let out an exhausted sigh. "This is purely a transactional arrangement." I lick my lower lip, and I see the way his gaze hooks and holds my mouth. He notices everything.

"I know that."

"I'm exhausted. Sleeping with you tonight will be ..." I hesitate, struggling for the right words.

"Easy?" he offers, with an annoying grin. "Because you'll fall asleep in seconds?"

I scowl, but my stomach tightens at the lazy rasp of his voice. "I can doze off within seconds. I expect I will."

He chuckles, low and smug. "You sure about that?"

My breath catches. There it is. The charged undercurrent neither of us wants to admit to. I lift my chin. "I think you're more affected by this than you want to admit."

"I could say the same for you," he throws back. Then I see it; a flicker of raw emotion behind his cool, confident exterior. Then, just as fast, it's gone. He steps back, shaking his head like I'm amusing.

Like I'm wrong.

"Sweetheart," he says smoothly, "I don't believe in love."

It should sting. But it doesn't. Because I see him. I smile, slow and knowing.

"Maybe not," I retort.

His frown deepens. I know this game isn't over. It's just beginning. I turn my back to him. "Help me out of this, please. I can't reach all the buttons."

He does nothing and I give him some time. Because this dress is a masterpiece of silk and lace, fitted through the bodice, the back lined with a trail of impossibly tiny buttons. A design meant for a bride on her wedding night. A dress meant to be unfastened by a husband.

"Jesus," he rasps, his tone laced in irritation. "Y-you want me to undo all these?"

I glance over my shoulder, letting my gaze drop to his hands. Big, strong. Completely ill-suited for the delicate task ahead.

"This is a purely transactional arrangement," I remind him, teasing. "It should be easy for you. Like assembling a boardroom deal … or fixing a broken cabinet."

He mutters a curse, but his fingers brush my skin near my shoulders and a jolt of heat zips through me. I brace myself, to not flinch from his electric touch. To not react, but his touch is slow and careful. My breath hitches when his knuckles keep skimming my bare skin. I bite my lip, willing myself to ignore the way my stomach tightens.

"How the hell did you even get these done up?"

"I had help."

"Who?" He fumbles with the buttons, his fingertips grazing my back as he works down. I laugh, because he sounds a little, dare I say it, *unhinged*? Jealous even. I love it.

"Raquel." I feel the need to put him out of his agony.

"Who is Oscar Ramos?" he asks suddenly.

I stiffen. "A businessman."

"I didn't like the way he looked at you."

I stay quiet.

"Is there something I should know?"

"No."

"I didn't like the way he looked at you," he repeats. I wait for more questions, but he doesn't push, and I respect him for that. He just keeps going, undoing button after button, his movements growing slower. More deliberate. His knuckles graze my spine again, and I shiver.

His fingers still.

The last button is undone.

I exhale, about to step away, when the dress slips, sliding off one shoulder. I turn slightly, catching the expression on his face. Knowing full well what I'm doing.

Dexter Knight is never at a loss for words. But right now?

He looks like he's been struck dumb. His gaze tracks the silk and my naked shoulder.

His jaw tightens.

My stomach clenches.

I should tease him. Tell him to put his tongue back in his mouth. But the way he's looking at me makes my pulse pound in my throat.

"Thanks," I murmur, my voice husky as I fix the shoulder back on. Then I step away, moving toward my overnight bag in the corner of the room.

And then it happens.

I lean down to grab the bag, and the dress, delicate, weightless and with all buttons now undone, slips off entirely and pools at my waist, exposing my champagne-colored satin bra. A soft gasp catches in my throat.

Before I can react, he's there. Close. His body heat pressing against my almost-bare back. My insides sizzle with want, and when Dexter's fingers brush mine and I suck in a breath. My heart pounds so loudly I'm sure he can hear it. I make the mistake of turning around and his gaze rakes over me slowly. I see him trying hard not to look at my bra.

In that instant we're frozen, caught in the weight of something dangerous. Something electric. Something that pulls us together like magnets.

"I'll get that," he says roughly, breaking the spell. He steps back, muscles flexing as he lifts the bag. And just like that, the moment shatters.

But the tension still lingers.

"Thanks," I manage to say, scrambling to hitch my bodice up to preserve my dignity. I look around wondering where I'm supposed to get changed.

As if he's just realized my dilemma, he says, "I'll give you some privacy. I'll be outside."

This place, with everything in one room, the windowed shower unit in the corner, all beautifully done, but so … naked. He can see me having a shower. See me getting dressed. Thankfully, the toilet is behind a partition. At least he can't see me …

For most newlyweds this place would be perfect.

For me and Dexter? It's like an escape room we're stuck in.

CHAPTER TWENTY-TWO

DEX

I WAKE UP GROGGY, DISORIENTED, MY BRAIN SLUGGISH AS I adjust to the dim light filtering through the villa. It takes me a second to remember where I am.

The private villa. Our wedding night. Daniela. She's curled against me, even though this bed is huge. Big enough to fit half the Knights on it, and yet, when we got in, we made sure to stay as far apart as possible. A solid meter of space between us, maybe more.

So how the hell did we end up like this?

She's lying on her side, her body molded to mine, one arm slung over my stomach, her breath soft against my skin. My arm wraps around her protectively, keeping her close. Liking the feel of her soft skin against me.

She went to bed in silk pajamas that were delicate, expensive-looking. I'm in a T-shirt and light shorts, even though I normally sleep naked. Figured that wouldn't be the best idea tonight.

It took me forever to fall asleep. The heat. The awareness of her in the room. Remembering last night; and the sound of the shower running while I forced myself to stay outside. All I could do was imagine her stripping, stepping under the water, steam curling around her. My frustration was already stretched to the limit like an elastic band about to snap. I'd be lying if I said I didn't feel something.

Damn it, just undoing her dress buttons was the sexiest thing I've done in a while. And I've done some really sexy— some might call them depraved—things when I'm with a woman.

Undoing buttons? Sexy as fuck. Who would have thought? I had to fight not to react when the dress slid off her shoulder. Harder still when it slipped lower, leaving her standing there in that strapless satin bra.

And now she's here. Arms wrapped around my chest like she's a part of me. I should move her away, but I don't.

Because I like this.

She stirs, letting out a soft sigh, her body pressing even closer. She smells fresh and light, something feminine and warm, and this epitome of the perfect woman feels deliciously soft against me. I hate the way we fit together more perfectly than I wanted. The way lying in bed with her feels like something that makes sense. Something that could be.

I lie there, not moving, barely breathing, until she shifts again, her hand sliding lower.

My stomach tenses.

Damn.

She's not awake. She has no idea her palm is now resting just above my lower abdomen. Three more inches and …

Dammit.

Her hand moves.

Right over my cock. I'm wearing shorts, but still, her hand

is resting on my cock. And now my body? Oh, it's fully awake. I try not to think about earlier. About the way her dress slipped down to her waist. About that kiss. But my dick has other plans, thickening beneath my shorts, tenting the fabric.

I barely have time to react before she stirs again, mumbling something.

"Dexter," she whispers, her voice sleepy, breathy.

Should I answer her?

"Don't do that," she moans, her voice incredibly husky.

My eyes snap open.

What?

"Huh?" My voice comes out rough, startled. I jerk her hand away, my entire body tense.

She lets out a sharp breath, and then bolts upright. The dim light is enough for her to see what's happening. Her gaze drops to the very obvious problem in my shorts, and it makes her gasp.

"What were you doing?" She scrambles back to her side of the bed so fast she nearly falls off.

I sit up, running a hand through my hair, holding up the other one in surrender. "I didn't touch you. I didn't do anything. You did this." I gesture at the hard length pressing against my shorts.

Her mouth opens and closes.

"I swear to you, I woke up and you were wrapped around me. You had your hand on my stomach, and then you moved it down over my … I'm a decent man, Daniela. Respectable. I would never do anything. I hope you know that."

Her hand flies to her mouth, her eyes wide. Shock. Horror. Embarrassment. I can't tell which, because I'm still fighting to get my body under control.

"If that's the case, I… I'm sorry." She blushes.

I narrow my eyes, feeling mischievous. "Were you dreaming of me?"

"No!"

"I think you were," I say smugly. "You said my name."

"I did not."

"You were dreaming. How would you even know?"

"I wouldn't dream of you."

"You literally said, 'Dexter, don't do that,'" I tease, making my voice mockingly breathless.

She glares at me, jabbing a finger in the air. "I remember now. I did dream of you. We were strangling each other, and I won."

"Oh, sweetheart," I say lazily, leaning back against the pillows. "You've definitely got the hots for me."

She huffs, turns her back on me, and scoots even further away from me on the bed. If she moves another inch, I swear she'll be on the damn floor. I exhale, running a hand over my face. It takes me forever to fall asleep again. I toss and turn, but it's too damn hot, and I can't sleep in these clothes. I'm not used to it.

With Sleeping Beauty marooned on her side of the bed, I strip naked and pray I pass out before this night gets any more complicated.

Because, right now, I'm not sure I can handle waking up to her again.

***

DANI

It's really hot. That's the first thing I register when I wake up.

The second thing is far more alarming: Dexter is naked. Completely, unapologetically, *naked*. My brain short-circuits, and I scramble to process the fact that my brand-new husband is sprawled out beside me like some shameless Roman emperor, all golden skin and zero shame.

My gaze trails lower, below his belly and I shriek. From shock. From his nakedness, and his *size*. And that he has a semi-erection. The sheets barely cover him, and the heat isn't the only reason my face is on fire.

He shifts beside me, stretching like a well-fed lion, his muscles flexing with a lazy sort of ease. Then, just to make things worse, he cracks open one eye, completely unbothered.

"You been watching me?" he murmurs, his voice thick with sleep, but the corners of his mouth curling up. I quickly move the bed sheet to cover him and I clutch the other edge of the sheet and hold it to me.

"Why would you do that?" I jerk my chin at him.

He frowns, rubbing a hand over his face. "Do what?"

I gesture wildly. "This! The …" I squeeze my eyes shut, willing my sanity to return. "Sleep naked! You were fully dressed from what I remember."

He lifts his side of the sheet, peeks down at himself and shrugs, completely unfazed. "It was so hot, I couldn't sleep."

I gape at him. "So your solution was full nudity?"

"I always sleep naked. Don't you?"

I make a strangled noise and whip around, facing the wall like it holds all the answers to my terrible life choices. Spoiler: it does not. Behind me, I can feel his amusement, the sheer arrogance radiating off him in waves.

"You should try it sometime."

"Never," I hiss.

"You're overreacting," he says, sounding far too

entertained. "It's not like I planned to traumatize you. Trust me, I was far more concerned about not melting in my sleep."

I groan, throwing an arm over my face. "This marriage is already a disaster."

Dexter just laughs, deep and low. "Come on, amor. Don't act like you didn't luck out."

I can't see him, but I just know he's sniggering. I am *never* waking up before him again. And that image of his nakedness? I can't get it out of my mind. And now I'm feeling all hot and flustered.

WE LEAVE THE HONEYMOON SUITE BEHIND, STEPPING OUT INTO the bright morning sun. The villa has been ours for less than a day, and yet, it feels like a different world compared to the one we're about to step back into.

Breakfast was a lavish affair, hosted by my parents with all the warmth and grandeur they could muster. A grand send-off for the Knight family before their late afternoon departure. They only arrived two days ago. My parents asked me why they wouldn't stay a few days, that surely the jetlag would kill them?

I don't tell them that they can't really stand to be together. That they don't like to be around their father if they can help it. I tell them that they need to get back to work, and that's also true.

And now, we linger outside, waiting for the SUVs that will take them to the airfield. I feel my mother's eyes on me. She keeps sneaking glances, hopeful, like she's clinging to some fairytale in her head. She probably still believes in the idea of happily-ever-afters, that love will somehow bloom between Dexter and me. Maybe that's why my parents suggested we spend our first night at that place. I'm convinced it was my mother's doing.

But nothing could be further from the truth.

Papai, on the other hand, looks worried. The happiness he wore earlier has dimmed, his expression tight. He's been doing better lately, stronger than he was a month ago, when we decided I had to make an alliance with one of the Knights. I thought today would be easier for him, that he'd finally feel some relief now that the deal is sealed. But there's something else weighing on him. Something I don't understand yet.

"These are for you, Daniela." A small voice pulls me from my thoughts. I glance down to see Brooke standing in front of me, holding out a tiny bunch of wildflowers. A genuine smile tugs at my lips as I crouch down. "Oh! Thank you so much, these are beautiful."

Brooke beams, her small fingers tightening around Cari's hand. Just behind them, the Knight men surround Dexter, their voices low, their postures commanding. Whatever piece of advice they're giving him, I doubt it's anything warm or sentimental.

Cari winces. "Sorry, we picked them from your grounds ..."

I wave it off. "It's perfectly fine."

Cari leans in for a quick hug, but I tighten my arms around her, holding on just a little longer.

"We'll catch up when you move in," she promises.

"We will." At least, I hope we will. It's been impossible to connect with anyone through all of this, but maybe that will change when I move to New York.

Sometimes I catch Cari watching me. There's something behind her gaze, something unreadable. Pity? A warning? Or something else entirely, something she isn't saying. She wishes me a wonderful honeymoon before stepping away, leaving me to face the rest of the Knights.

They stand in a line, as if sending me off on some grand adventure. My parents hover nearby, glowing with pride. At least, my mother does. My father still looks tense.

I greet him with a warmth I don't feel, and I hate the way I'm getting used to lying and pretending so easily. Dexter shakes hands with the other brothers, the ones he calls the Italian Knights. But with Jett and Zach, it's different. He bearhugs them, the bond between them obvious. He's gentler around Cari and Brooke, careful.

Then, at the very end of the line, his father waits.

"You're not getting on?" Dexter's voice is cool, his shoulders stiff. Paul smiles, the picture of control.

"I want to spend a few days here, soaking up the wonderful hospitality of your in-laws."

Dexter's face hardens.

I glance at my father. No wonder he looked worried. Now, I'm worried too.

"Why is that?" Dexter asks.

Paul's smile doesn't falter. "Like I said, to enjoy the hospitality. And the weather."

"We should have *all* stayed, then," Dexter says flatly.

"You know how busy we are," Paul replies smoothly. "Business doesn't stop. But for the honeymooners? It can." He flashes a smile that turns my insides cold.

The SUVs pull up, and the Knights start piling in. "See you soon," Dexter calls out, voice tight.

"Rio's missing," I whisper to Dexter.

His lips curve up into a smile and I hear a chuckle. "Jeez."

"Him and Raquel?" I suggest. I also haven't seen her. She was supposed to come and join us for breakfast.

Dexter's eyes meet mine. "They're consenting adults," he says, with a shrug.

My parents hold hands and go back into the house. Dexter

and I remain standing until the line of cars is out of sight. For the first time since I've known him, he looks less cocky. More vulnerable. Like he's lost.

And I realize that's exactly how I feel too. Like I'm out of my depth. Alone. In a world I don't fully understand, surrounded by people I don't truly know.

I reach for his hand, seeing him look so alone. I don't want that for him. This might not be real, and even though we're nothing but business acquaintances, friends, at a push, I need him to know that I'm here for him.

He presses his fingers in mine, and I exhale a breath.

DEX

I DON'T LIKE THIS. NOT ONE DAMN BIT.

Paul Knight lingering here means trouble.

When I glance at Daniela, her expression is tight, her lips pressed together in worry. She's figured out what kind of man my father is. Smart girl. She knows he's dangerous, that he doesn't just hang around for no reason. If I were in her shoes, I'd be worried about my parents too.

After seeing my family off, I feel unsettled. Out of place. It's an unusual feeling, like I don't belong, like I've stepped into a world that isn't mine.

And then Daniela smiles at me. Without hesitation, she takes my hand, squeezing lightly.

"Don't worry, you'll see them again in a few days." Her voice is warm and reassuring. It's exactly what I need. I want to believe her but a heavy feeling hangs in my stomach. I offer a weary smile, feeling not so lonely now.

"We should get ready to leave," I say. We're expected to arrive in Bahia later this evening. I pray that I don't do anything stupid when we're on our honeymoon. It's going to be a torturous three nights, and I barely survived last night.

THE JET HER FATHER PROVIDES FOR OUR HONEYMOON FLIGHT IS smaller, more understated than what I'm used to. It's not a Knight Enterprises jet. No state-of-the-art tech, no marble finishes, no custom upholstery. But it's functional, and that's all that matters.

The truth is, I don't care about the jet. I care about the fact that I'm stuck on it with Daniela for the next two hours, because last night, something changed.

Falling asleep tangled together, waking up with her curled into me, her body warm and soft against mine, shifted things. And then, of course, the moment she saw me naked.

I need distance.

I decide to ignore her completely. Which is difficult when she's sitting across from me, fresh-faced, effortlessly stunning. She's not even wearing anything overtly sexy. Just a breezy white linen dress, casual and comfortable. But somehow, that makes it worse.

She's too at ease. Too cheerful. Like she's picked up on my mood and decided to fix it. It puts me to shame.

"One is better," she says, nodding toward our security detail as my bodyguard boards behind us.

"You're a Knight now. You come under our protection."

"They're hardly discreet."

Up until now we had two men, identical to every other high-end security operative, dressed in all black, wearing mirrored shades, built like linebackers with short buzzcuts.

They might as well have "bodyguard" stamped on their foreheads. One was the security detail provided by her family, and I had my own. We decided to get rid of hers and settle on having just one man.

"I need to work," I say, opening a folder, pen in hand, forcing myself to focus. Out of the corner of my eye, I see Daniela stiffen. Maybe it was the flick of my hand dismissing her. Maybe it was the coldness in my voice.

Something about it annoys her.

"You work all you want," she mutters, ordering a cocktail from the hostess before pulling out a book.

The two-hour flight is silent.

I pretend I'm unaffected, but I'm rattled. Shook. Trying to ignore the battle raging inside me. Trying to figure out how the fuck I'm going to survive a year in close proximity to this amazing woman, when one night with her has left me feeling so adrift.

When I first agreed to this, I thought I could handle it, but no amount of pissing the old man off is worth this. I'm going to have a permanent hard-on and it's going to be the death of me.

Hours later, we land in Bahia, on a private airstrip , where a sleek, black SUV waits on the tarmac and takes us to the resort the old man chose.

When we get there, the concierges unload our luggage as I take in the surroundings. This sprawling beachfront resort is elite. Ultra-private. With powder-white sand and impossibly clear water, its hidden away from the world. It has full catering, a personal staff, and, of course, security.

We're met by a welcoming committee. Smiling attendants, ready with cool towels, trays of champagne, and fresh floral garlands. A few familiar faces dot the resort. Hollywood actors. CEOs. Industry titans. Daniela notices them too, her gaze lingering as a few approach us.

"Well, well, well. Dexter Knight, finally tamed," a hedge fund billionaire shakes my hand before turning to Daniela. "And this must be your lovely bride."

He lifts her hand to his lips, holding it just a second too long. My jaw clenches, but Daniela plays the part well, offering a polite smile, engaging in easy conversation.

I don't like it.

I don't like the way his eyes rake over her, as she stands there, poised and effortlessly beautiful. She's accustomed to how men like him think and behave, but I don't like it.

"Excuse us. My wife and I need to freshen up." I take Daniela's hand away from his, clasping it in mine. The gesture is smooth, possessive. Maybe too possessive.

The Guest Relations Director personally shows us to our villa. I know his job title because he's proudly wearing it as a badge, and he has people take care of our luggage. He opens the door, and I see a champagne bottle waiting on ice.

I watch Daniela, see the way her eyes light up. "I've never been someplace like this before," she gushes.

"That's because you've never been married before, sweetheart."

"I haven't, and now I consider myself to be the luckiest woman on the planet, darling," she says loud enough for the guy to hear.

"We'll take it from here," I tell him. He nods with a smile then disappears discreetly.

"This is beautiful!" Daniela says as soon as we step inside the villa. I find her excitement endearing.

I have to agree. It's breathtaking. It has a sleek modern design with glass and stone in hues of white and sand. It's large, bright, and airy. High ceilings. Open-plan layout. Floor-to-ceiling windows revealing an uninterrupted view of the ocean. The private infinity pool stretches toward the horizon, shimmering under the golden afternoon sun. Every detail screams indulgence.

"Surely you've been to places like this?" I ask, puzzled. She's from a wealthy family. Resorts like this shouldn't be such a big surprise to her.

"I have, but this is on another level."

I guess it is. The old man really wanted to impress, though, this isn't like him. We were all supposed to return to New York today. Him sending us here takes away the suspicion of what he's still doing here, looking around AO Eletronica.

I follow Daniela as she opens the door to what seems to be the huge master bedroom, with an enormous bed on a raised dais.

As if performances will take place on that bed.

As if ...

She opens the balcony doors and there, right in the middle is a hot tub tucked into the sunken stone floor.

She blushes, before gliding past me, and opening another door.

This looks like the second bedroom. It's not as big or as opulent, but still reeks of luxury. One side of the suite looks onto the resort, onto the infinity pool and recliners and tables of people relaxing by the pool side. The other side has the most spectacular panoramic views of the ocean.

"I'm getting changed," she announces. I'm curious to see which room she takes. The concierge left our suitcases in the middle of the open plan living area. But Daniela doesn't come into the bedroom.

When I go to retrieve my luggage, I see her suitcase placed out of the way, against one of the walls. I'm curious, but decide to play it cool, and take my suitcase into the master bedroom.

I've barely finished taking my clothes out of my suitcase, while running the "I don't care about her" mantra through my head, when Daniela, my sexy and gorgeous new wife, walks in a few minutes later.

Flowing cover-up, sheer enough to reveal the outline of her bikini. Hair loose, skin glowing, the afternoon light catching on her cheekbones.

She's stunning, and I hate the way my stomach tightens at the sight of her. I recall the way she snuggled up to me, the way her hand caressed my cock. Her breathless whisper of my name. Her skin has already deepened to a soft golden tan. She looks dewy, radiant, like she belongs in a place like this.

"You have work to do, I imagine," she says, casually.

"I've got a lot to catch up on," I lie. The emails and catching up on updates will take a while. I'm glad I'll be distracted for a while.

"Best get on with it." She turns on her heel and walks away, her back straight, her chin high.

It was an act. The wedding, the romance, the costumes, the smiles.

Now, it's just us.

And reality.

Alone, in a romantic setting, For honeymooners. It's going to be nothing but slow, painful torture.

CHAPTER TWENTY-THREE

DEX

I'VE SPENT THE ENTIRE DAY WORKING. OR AT LEAST, THAT'S what I tell myself. In reality, I've been sitting in my private villa, watching my wife.

That word doesn't seem so strange anymore. I quite like it. From where I'm sitting, I have the perfect vantage point to see her at the infinity pool, stretched out in the sun, those curves impossible to ignore. She looks gorgeous. People keep coming up to her, congratulating her on our marriage, smiling, flattering her.

It's not just her looks. God knows, she's stunning. Dani has a heart of gold. She hates that people notice her looks. It's why she picked me, because I didn't fall at her feet.

Yet, there's something between us. Something that burns, sizzles. My lips still remember our first dance, our kiss.

I want more, and I wonder if I'll ever get the chance. I don't know how she feels about me. She's made it clear this is just a business arrangement, a deal to save her father's company. An arranged marriage with a clear-cut expiration date.

But we connected, and that is hard to forget, even as I work, and she sunbathes by the pool.

My brothers are almost home. I've been texting Jett, Zach, and Rio, but Rio isn't answering. I text Jett, needing his opinion as to why the old man stayed behind. His reply is dry and predictable:

> Shouldn't be surprised. He's obviously there to spy on the business.

I text back.

> Do you think something's not right with the deal?

Jett's reply:

> Our father wouldn't have agreed to this deal otherwise

I text Zach, asking for his thoughts. His response?

> Any photos from the honeymoon?

My reply:

> Sick

The hours pass and I catch up on my workload. My schedule is all over the place. After our honeymoon, we head back to Brazil for a day because Daniela insists on spending time with her parents. After that, New York.

And then … reality.

I'll have to get used to her invading my privacy, her

presence in my penthouse, the way she'll set up her life inside mine.

Hopefully, the renovations will be done by the time we return.

By the time I finally look up, the sun is high, and I'm roasting. I glance outside and narrow my eyes. Daniela is standing near the infinity pool. Talking to someone. Wearing that damn sexy strapless bikini.

My insides are molten lava when I recognize the guy. He's a Hollywood superstar. One of those action-hero types. And he's standing too damn close to her, his hand hovering near hers, his body angled toward her like he's claiming her space. She's smiling, nodding politely, but I know that look. It's the look of a woman trying to disengage without making a scene.

Jealousy creeps in before I can shove it down. I don't like the way the guy lingers, the way Daniela tries to walk away, and he won't let her. She didn't ask for that attention. She hates it.

I move before I think, striding out, across the pool area, heat pulsing through me, not from the sun, but from something darker, something possessive. By the time I reach them, I barely hear what the guy is saying. Daniela turns toward me just as I take her hand, pulling it free from his touch.

"Hey, sweetheart," I say smoothly, my grip firm around her wrist. "Everything okay?"

Daniela blinks up at me, her lips parting in surprise. And then she kisses me. It's instinctive, natural, the way our bodies fit together like they've done this a thousand times before. Her tongue swipes my lower lip and a buzz hums inside my body.

My hands encircle her waist as I claim her mouth, can't help myself as my tongue meets her. I press against her, eliciting a soft moan and causing her hands to slide around my neck. I tighten my grasp on her waist, my fingers tracing over her soft, warm and slightly damp skin. I fight the urge to explore. To slide my hands inside her tiny bikini bottoms. To reach down the front and explore her folds. To dip my head lower and suckle her breast.

Whoa. My imagination raced ahead. Thoughts I'd managed to suppress, with great difficulty, now resurface as our mouths crush together, our tongues dueling and dancing. Those tempting ideas take hold of me again.

This woman is so luscious to touch. So soft and inviting. She's almost naked, save for tiny bits of fabric strategically placed over her body. I have fisted myself to orgasm, while showering, trying to prepare myself for being around her each day.

It's slowly killing me.

"Thank you," she murmurs against my mouth as we slowly pull apart. I barely heard what the man said before we kissed and now he's gone.

"Thank *you.*"

"For saving me," she says, looking hot and flushed and sexy as hell.

"This is going to be a thing with you, isn't it?" My gaze drags down her body before I can stop myself. Her bikini hugs her curves like a lingering lover. Water droplets fall into the crevasse between her breasts, dripping down over the full and luscious globes. I try to swallow. Try to breathe, but I'm enraptured by how smooth and bronzed her skin is, how it glistens in the sun. My eyes slowly roam over her full, plush hips, and those long, lean legs that go on forever. I shake my head, trying to dislodge the idea of them wrapped around my waist.

"Kissing you?" she asks.

"Needing to be rescued on account of all the attention you seem to get."

"I don't need rescuing, Dexter. I can take care of myself."

But you're my wife.

There's no way I'm going to stand by and watch some sleazeball try to get her attention. There's no way I'm going to let my wife squirm and try to squiggle her way out of it. I'll be there, no matter what. Every part of her body is made for sinning. I should look away. I should move. I should say something sharp, something detached. Instead, my voice comes out rough. "I should get back to work."

"Are you *still* working?" There's a hint of playfulness in her eyes. Yesterday we were playing the part of being married, and today it almost feels like we really are.

"I've got a little more to do and then I'm done. Maybe we can have a late lunch together?"

"I've had my lunch, Dexter. I didn't ask you because you seemed so busy." Her fingers slowly trail up my arm, and when I don't move, she strokes my face, her thumb hovering just over my lips. I love this, and I'm tempted to ask what she's doing, but I get it, especially when I see that people around us are staring.

"You're learning fast, Gatinha."

Her face lights up, and I have a feeling that she loves me calling her that.

"People are watching, and we have to give them a show."

"Are they?"

She raises an eyebrow. "We have to keep up the pretense."

I step closer, close enough that I can feel the heat radiating off her skin. "I guess we do." My fingers instinctively wrap around her waist. She jumps, and her eyes turn darker. My cock jumps to attention as I see her thick, plumpy lips, her face upturned and just inches from my face.

"Can you take it?" she asks. "This charade."

"It means nothing to me," I whisper.

Lies.

This time, I lean in for another kiss, my hands framing her waist, her curves pressing against me.

She's barely wearing anything. Just a bikini that she fills out in all the right places. And if I'm not careful, I'm going to be carrying way too much heat.

"It also means nothing to me," she rasps, pressing her body against me, suggestively. Too close. Too flush. Too sexy. Then she does the last thing I could ever imagine her doing. She reaches down, and her fingers barely graze my hardened cock. I twitch, feeling that touch everywhere. I think I've imagined it, but her eyes hold mine and her fingertips dance over my length, like she's daring me to do something. Reciprocate. Or wait for her next move.

I'm too focused on how this feels, on what might happen next, to do anything, but savor the moment. She strokes me gently, in that tight, small space between us. Fuck, if this doesn't feel like heaven. I'm so hard, I could come over her hands if she keeps this up.

This can't happen, so I lift her fingers, and bring her knuckles to my lips, pressing a kiss there.

"We're good actors," I murmur entwining my hand in hers. We're also totally screwed. "I should get back to work." I get back to the safety of the villa and wonder how the hell I'm going to get through this honeymoon.

Things are moving so fast and my feelings for Daniela have evolved. I've done a one hundred and eighty degree turn with her.

But I didn't want this.

She did.

Now I don't know what to do. I'm a man who has built his life on control. On emotional detachment. On never letting anyone get too close.

I don't do relationships. I can't love.

I *won't* love.

And yet, ever since I stepped into this woman's orbit, something inside me has shifted. Maybe it's because the dynamics are different. Daniela is a woman who is perfectly fine without me.

I like that about her.

She's strong. Independent. Snarky and unafraid to put a man in his place. And she's got a good body; hard and firm, honed from jiu-jitsu and running. Yet she still has curves in all the right places.

She had the guts to fly out alone to meet my father and negotiate a deal. But still, the nagging question lingers. Why this alliance? It smacks of desperation. Or is it something else? She has alluded to her family business going through some struggles and has admitted they could use an injection of capital.

But something in my gut tells me it's more than that. I hate that I don't have the answers, but what I hate even more is that she's perfectly fine without me. I feel tempted to do the one thing I swore I wouldn't. To stop pretending. But if I gave in, where would that lead?

She thinks we have twelve months but seven months from now, I'll walk away. We'll part, go our separate ways, and life will go on.

That was the plan, but I'm suddenly not so sure.

DANI

. . .

If Dexter wants to play games, he can. I know men like him. Men who run when they feel trapped.

But I haven't trapped him. His own father did that.

Though I did choose him. Would it have made a difference if I'd picked Rio? I shudder. No. Not Rio. He's too much like Oscar Ramos. He hunts, and chases.

Dexter is different. Aloof. Detached. He also told me once that his father couldn't have forced him into marrying me. He's his own man and he'll do whatever he wants. Then why would he agree to this?

I spend the rest of the day on my own, making the most of my solo honeymoon. Time flies as I read by the pool, swim in the ocean, then, occasionally, slather myself with suntan lotion before lying back on the recliner with a cocktail and a book.

By six o'clock, Dexter still hasn't come out. I should check on him and make sure he hasn't passed out. Make sure he hasn't been bitten by some poisonous insect.

But I won't. He's expecting me to.

I was so relieved when he came out to rescue me from that odious celebrity, that I couldn't help but lean in and hug him out of sheer gratitude. Except, it just felt so natural when I ended up kissing him.

What I didn't expect? Him kissing me back.

My brain went into a daze as soon as he touched me, pressing me tight against him. His firm body, impossible to ignore. His hardness, a shock. I did that, to him?

My heart leaps with the thought of Dexter becoming sexually aroused. His lips, his sweet mouth, the taste and feel of him. My legs almost buckled and I tightened my hold on him, as if clinging to stay upright. My breasts pressing into his hard chest made me want to stay there. Being around him I'm in a state of constant arousal. This is something that is new to me; having a man foremost in my thoughts. Desire pulsating through every vein. I need Dexter more than I've ever thought it was possible to need anyone.

I hate that he keeps himself to himself, inside, working. As if he doesn't feel anything for me.

This is a game to him, and I mustn't forget that he's a Knight. No matter how much he thinks it doesn't affect him, his mother's tragic passing, and his father's iron fist, I know it does.

Because the truth is, Dexter is all kinds of messed up.

CHAPTER TWENTY-FOUR

DEX

We have dinner on the terrace. The infinity pool is empty and guests are dining out by the pool, while some, like us, are dining on their terraces, enjoying the sunset.

The staff are wonderful; always there, always watching and at the ready, tending to our every need. The heady infusion of salt and jasmine fills the air, and I feel more relaxed than I have all day. It was harder forcing myself to stay inside to work, knowing that Daniela was taking it easy.

In trying not to think too much about her, I didn't really get much work done. Now Daniela sits across from me. Her Kindle rests beside her plate, and she appears to be transfixed, her attention on the screen as she scrolls through a book.

I watch her, irritation simmering low in my gut. "That's rude," I say finally.

She lifts her head lazily, lips curving. "But *darling*, you worked all through the day, and I didn't want to disturb you." Her voice is sweet as honey.

"You can disturb me now. We're having dinner. I'm here, aren't I?"

Her smile widens. She leans in slightly, lowering her voice. "Because of our deal."

I ground my teeth. I was hoping that after I saved her from that over-muscled action man, when she kissed me and I kissed her back, things would be different between us.

I thought we'd reached a good place. Talking, laughing, pretending, and ... kissing. I dare not hope for more, even though I can't stop thinking about her. My cock stands to attention whenever my wife is around.

We finish the meal in silence and neither of us want dessert. I'm relieved that we can return to the villa and I'll find a way to keep myself busy, but Daniela orders a lemon tea, which makes me irritated because now, I have to be civil and wait with her.

She continues reading, while I sit there, watching and wondering what I've gotten myself into. Wondering how I'll navigate the waters back home, when we have to live together.

"I've had a long day. Swimming in the sea, enjoying the infinity pool ..." She closes her eyes momentarily and places her palm at the back of her neck, massaging it gently. "I think I'll get a massage tomorrow. I'm so tense all over."

I watch, knowing how easily I could relieve that tension for her. My eyes fall to her halter-neck black and green dress and her bare shoulders that are golden under the terrace lights.

She's fucking torturing me.

It gets worse when her fingers trail absentmindedly across her collarbone, drawing my attention to her ring and the diamonds catching the light, and to her soft golden skin.

I watch mesmerized and she catches me staring when she opens her eyes. We stare in silence for a few seconds, before she abruptly gets up. "Good night." She pushes back her chair.

Her lemon tea is barely touched. I don't intend to sit here alone, so I follow her back to the villa.

No sooner do we step inside then Daniela heads toward the main bedroom. Now we're presented with another problem. There's only one master bedroom, with a huge bed.

Although there's also a guest room.

"Where are you going?" I ask.

She pauses, glancing over her shoulder. "To sleep in my bed."

Her bed.

I arch a brow. "Ah. There's another room, and there's also the sofa."

She turns around fully and faces me. Her luscious lips curve into a smile while I try to fight the thought that this woman is so tempting.

"Dexter, *darling*, you can sleep wherever you want." She turns away but I grab her wrist and hear it, the soft gasp, the way her breath hitches in her throat. Her skin is warm beneath my fingers. Soft and velvety. The type of skin I want naked against me as I lie in bed. I keep my grip, for a beat too long, feeling the heat of her pulse beneath my fingertips.

"You're being unusually cold towards me," I murmur. "I thought we would be closer, given that I rescued you earlier."

That was my dick talking just now. I don't know why I said that. Daniela doesn't flinch, nor does she pull away. She stares at me as if she's trying to figure out what I'm thinking.

I want so badly to kiss her. Maybe just a peck on the cheek, maybe something more. Something like the melting, scorching fuck-me kiss we shared earlier. The type of kiss that moves onto something more.

"Goodnight, Dexter. Sleep wherever you want. This is your honeymoon as well." She disappears towards the master bedroom, no doubt to read on her fucking Kindle.

I let her go and head over to the bar where I pour myself a drink, and try to figure out how I'll get through this night.

DANIELA IS COOL TOWARDS ME THE NEXT MORNING, AS WE'RE having breakfast on the terrace.

A few guests mill about in the infinity pool, and beyond that, a few of them are swimming in the shimmering, turquoise blue ocean.

The day is bright, the sun bearable, with the threat of getting stronger. "Sleep well?" Daniela asks, a cold edge to her voice.

I sip my coffee before answering, because I quite like the idea that she might be pissed. That she might have wanted me beside her in bed last night. That she might have missed me.

I wanted to be there with her, but for the sake of my sanity, I slept alone. Butt naked, restless as hell, tossing and turning like a fish on a hook, knowing that she lay in the next room. "Like a baby. You?"

"Out like a light." She shrugs, then stirs her coffee. "There could've been fireworks outside, and I wouldn't have heard."

I refill our glasses of fresh-squeezed juice. The day has barely started and already I feel the oppressive weight of our alliance.

"I have more work to do," I announce, not because I *want* to work, hell, I'd rather do anything else but that, but because I *need* to. My father is still in São Paulo, undoubtedly sniffing around my father-in-law's business, and I need to stay ahead of him.

Daniela lifts her glass, and eyes me casually. "I expect nothing less from you, Dexter. Just because we're married doesn't mean our lives have to change." She says the words easily, but a stupid part of me wonders if she means them. Or if she also wonders if things could be different between us.

"Good to know," I say, my voice even.

She sets her juice down and glances at me, her gaze deceptively casual. "We'll have separate bedrooms back in New York, won't we?"

That sounds like a plea. I lean back in my chair. "For sure. There's no way we could …" I gesture between us. "This is … not that."

Her lips press together, and she looks uneasy. "You don't have to spell it out every time. I know our agreement. What this is and what it isn't. I have no illusions."

When she leans back, the sunlight catches the subtle bursts of gold in her green eyes. Today, she's not in some sheer cover-up that lets me see things I shouldn't. Instead, her outfit is soft, patterned and opaque. Still, the way it hangs loosely over her skin, makes my imagination go haywire.

I can't seem to get a break. Will our entire year be like this? If so, I'm going to be a wreck. I push my chair back and set my napkin down. "I should get to work."

She looks at me as if she's about to say something and I wait expectantly.

"Have a good day at work, darling." It's mock exaggeration. A casual turn of phrase from a doting wife. She's playing a role. That's all.

"Don't strain yourself too much on the recliner," I quip.

I step into the cool interior of the villa's study. The ceiling fans hum lazily above me, circulating the crisp air. The French doors open to a perfect view of the terrace.

And her.

Daniela tugs off the cover-up, letting it slip from her shoulders like silk, revealing a bikini that's just … fucking illegal. Then she sits beneath an oversized umbrella, leisurely slathering sunscreen over her smooth skin before picking up a book.

Just like that I imagine my hands slipping and sliding over her body. My hands smoothing that lotion over her body. Spreading it out, rubbing it in gently. Feeling her under my fingers, touching her, and making her want me. As expected, my cock jumps to life, and I drop my head in my hands.

Wrong thought. Wrong visual.

What the hell am I doing? If this were real, we'd be in bed right now, fucking like feral animals, tearing into each other the way I know we could. I exhale sharply and pull my laptop closer. I need to focus. I need to do *something*.

Like cold water over my thoughts, I look through my diary and discover, with great dismay, that I have a call scheduled with the old man. Knowing him, he's probably poking his nose where it doesn't belong.

THE DAY PASSES. IT'S TOO HOT, AND I DON'T HAVE LUNCH, BUT cold pressed juices. Then I have a quick call with the old man. The conversation is businesslike and formal, with him asking about some deal I inked last month. He doesn't even ask how things are, how Daniela is. I don't know why I thought he might.

I stop working late in the afternoon, and by the time I've showered and gotten changed and headed back outside, Daniela is stretched out on a four-poster cabana on the sand, near the sea. Waves lap gently along the shore. I can't take my eyes off my wife.

She's lying on her stomach, face down, resting on her hands. Her back bare and her skin glowing as a masseur works along her body. Wearing only her bikini bottoms, she looks too comfortable. Too at ease in this temporary paradise.

Too damn tempting.

I should walk away, but I can't. The sand shifts under my feet as I stare down at her. "Hey, sweetheart." My shadow looms over her and she lifts her head slightly, shielding her eyes with her hand.

I suppress a groan.

"Hey, *darling*." Her eyes twinkle with amusement and I wonder if she's having a laugh at my expense. "Hard day at work?"

I clench my jaw. Again. She seems unbothered, like this isn't affecting her, but me? I had to jerk off before I came out just now, because after the call with my father, and the subsequent emails and pesky matters I had to deal with after, I couldn't focus.

Couldn't get the image of Daniela in her bikini out of my head. And now, my bottled-up frustration ratchets even higher as the man's hands knead my wife's bare back.

I don't like another man's hands on my wife. In my head, it's *my* hands that bracket her back and skim the length of her spine. My hands that knead, and slide over her bikini bottoms and move between the apex of her thighs ...

"Is that too hard, ma'am?" the masseur asks.

"No, no," Daniela murmurs. "You could go harder still." She lifts her face and her gaze drops to my crotch.

Jesus. My dick stiffens as she blinks.

"Would you like a massage, darling? Something to ease out the knots of tension."

I shift, turn to the side, trying to hide the boner that's tenting my pants. It infuriates me how easy this is for her. How she doesn't feel anything. How she has no clue of the effect she's having on me. I should tell her to cover up. I should tell her she's taking this too far. Instead, I say, "No."

Then my mind blanks because I can't think of anything else to say. My brain is processing images, not words, and the image I have is of Daniela sitting up, topless. Daring me to make a move.

She laughs. "Are you okay, darling? You're not suffering from sunstroke, are you?"

"Overwork, if anything," I manage to say, wondering how I've gone from being in control of my thoughts and feelings, to *this*. A weak man who can't take his eyes off this woman, my gaze inching over her body. "Just wanted to check in and make sure you weren't feeling lonely."

Daniela hums in response, then lifts her shoulders as if she's stretching them out. Then, to my utter delight and shock, she starts to push up on her elbows. If she lifts any higher, I'll see everything.

"Don't," I caution, my erection fighting to escape my ever-tightening pants.

She halts, blinking up at me. Then, slowly, she moves up a fraction. Barely an inch. Not enough to reveal anything. But enough to remind me of the threat of what could be.

"I'll leave you in peace," I manage to say, before turning around to find mine.

CHAPTER TWENTY-FIVE

DANI

Dexter has spent the second day of our honeymoon working away, cooped up inside, while I made the most of the weather, the time to rest and think, and the cocktails.

The massage was sheer bliss and now I'm so relaxed, I feel loose all over. Being at this beautiful resort has me more upbeat than I expected and I'm determined to make the most of this time because I don't know what to expect once I'm in New York, living in Dexter's apartment, encroaching on his territory.

Him being sullen, and pretending to work all day long, makes it easy for me. I understand that he's a businessman, and the Knights have a global empire, but still ... I would have expected him to make more time than he currently does.

Which leads me to believe he's avoiding me.

I like that.

Because it tells me something.

He's finding it difficult being around me, and yet he can't seem to stay away for too long.

"I'm going to the gym," he announces, much to my dismay, as soon as I step inside after a wonderful day. I was hoping we could talk more, have dinner and try to have the type of deep conversation we had once before.

But he sounds a little wound up. I noticed it as soon as he came over to see me getting my massage. I try not to stare at him, because he's the sexiest I've ever seen him, in his workout gear. Black performance shorts, a fitted sleeveless top clinging to his body like a second skin, showing his muscle definition. He looks like a professional athlete, not a businessman. I'm aware of how hard my heart is pounding.

I'm still damp from the pool, and my coverall clings to me. Smoothing my hand through my hair, I try to appear unaffected, but I'm failing miserably. My gaze lingers over his shorts that cling to him. I try to look away but not before I catch him looking at me. No, looking *through* me. Like he can't bear to meet my gaze.

"Enjoy," I say, keeping my tone light.

His fingers flex, and he appears to hesitate. "Are we having dinner together?"

"Do you want to?"

His jaw ticks. "We don't have to."

I hate that he's so hot and cold. Like an on-off switch. I hate dancing around him, not knowing where I stand. "Just go, Dexter. Go to the gym and vent your frustration."

His expression hardens, and every muscle in that steel hard body seems to flex. If he keeps this up he might snap. "Who says I'm frustrated?"

"Tell me you're not."

"It's work pressure, sweetheart. Don't kid yourself its anything else." He strides to the door and leaves.

It's clear that we're starting to grate on each other. Things started off smooth at the wedding reception, leading to tired flirtation at the honeymoon suite, and then, when I caught a glimpse of him naked, it all started to get harder.

Now it feels like he can barely tolerate me. If he wants to be cold and dismissive towards me, fine. If he needs to keep his distance. He can. This is still my honeymoon and I intend to enjoy what's left of it.

I walk over to the refrigerator, grab a bottle of champagne, and pour myself a glass. I watch the bubbles fizz and pop as I lift the flute to my lips and take a sip. It's delicious. Ridiculously expensive, too, I imagine.

Perfect for an indulgent evening, just for me. I should enjoy these last few days here, before I fall under Paul Knight's radar. I shiver when I think of him being around my parents.

Pushing the thought away, I walk into the master bedroom, champagne glass and bottle in hand, and open the balcony doors. I decide to have an indulgent evening in the hot tub. It would be a shame to let this go unused. No one can see us because it's shielded from view by lush tropical greenery. A hidden jewel offering tranquility and privacy.

I turn on the jets, and the bubbling water steams in the warm evening air. Soft lighting built into the stone lends this a cozy, intimate ambiance.

Waiting for it to fill, I call my mom. She picks up after the second ring. "Daniela, meu amor! How are you?"

Her soft and familiar voice is like warm honey flowing through my veins. I run my hand in the warm water. "I miss you Mãe"

She sighs softly. "Papai went into work today, with your father-in-law."

I don't like the sound of her strained voice. "Why?"

"He said he would," she replies, but there's something off in her tone.

"And?"

She pauses a beat too long. "To see how the business runs. With the Knight alliance, we can make things better." She's trying to sound happy, but I sense the truth. Her pretend reassurance doesn't calm the unease swirling in my gut.

Paul Knight is a snake. A manipulator. A spy. But I force myself to breathe, to focus. This is an alliance. Maybe he's in São Paulo to assess, oversee and strategize. To see how he can get oversight on the business while he's in New York.

My father should be able to hold his own. He's a smart man, if a little older and frailer. He built a multi-billion-dollar company from the ground up, piece by piece. The world has changed, technology, communications, marketing, but he's still the man who made it all happen.

We'll be okay. We have to be.

"I'm sure he's just trying to get to know what he invested in, Mãe," I tell her, hoping to reassure her in the way I can't reassure myself.

"How are the newlyweds? Enjoying yourselves?" My mother teases.

I press my lips together. "Mãe, you know this is an arranged marriage. Dexter has been working most of the time."

"Working?" she shrieks.

"It's an alliance, Mãe."

"I saw the two of you, Daniela." I freeze, the flute stills in my hand. "I saw the way he looked at you, and the way you looked at him."

The memory comes flooding back, of Dexter's mouth on mine, and his hands on me. But nothing has changed. This is still a deal and we are still strangers in an arranged marriage. Even if I've seen him naked, and we've had one night snuggled up in bed.

Last night, I wanted him. Maybe the recent events

overwhelmed me and I let down my guard. But Dexter decided to sleep in a separate room.

"Oh, Mãe," I give a nervous laugh. "We're just playing a part," I whisper, as if the walls have ears.

"I know what I see, filha."

"You see what you want to see, Mãe."

"I see that you both are good together."

I won't win with my mother. She chooses to see what she wants to happen. "I have to go, your father needs me."

"I love you, Mãe. Tell Papai I love him."

I hang up and think of my mom's words. Her deeper dreams and wishes. What she saw when we kissed was for show. It doesn't exist for real. Dexter has put his walls back up again, and he's picked work over me.

Now, he's disappeared to the gym.

It's like the guy can't put enough distance between us. I hope he stays there for hours, because I intend to enjoy my evening alone. I try Raquel's number but she still doesn't answer.

It's not surprising. She told me she could only come for the wedding day and we barely caught up. She's always busy with work and her life is hectic, but hopefully I can see more of her when I move to New York. I'll go and visit as soon as I've settled in.

Settled in.

The thought of living with Dexter, of coexisting under the same roof, makes my pulse race. I try to be present, to enjoy this beautiful view, and this warm bubbling water. Setting the ice bucket on the ledge, with my glass of champagne, I slip into the hot tub, eager not to dwell on my worries.

As soon as my body sinks into the warm water, I feel instantly calmer, as if all my tension soothes away. I rest my back against one of the powerful jets which pulse beneath the surface, and moan with gratitude as they massage me. But then, naturally, instinctively, my thoughts trail back to Dexter. I thought we could be friends, if nothing else, but he doesn't even want that.

What am I supposed to do?

The tension bleeds out of me and my limbs loosen under the hot, pulsing jets. It's better than any massage, better than any forced attempt at pretending everything's fine.

Tomorrow is our last night here. Maybe I'll spend all day in the hot tub instead of out at the infinity pool or in the sea. Being out there alone feels too exposed. People might wonder why Dexter's inside while his new wife lounges outside all alone.

The last thing we need are rumors.

I set my champagne flute down and settle back into the heat. My arms are splayed out on either side, with my head tilted back, I close my eyes, and relax. It's sublime. Peaceful. Everything I need until … the door swings wide open, as do my eyelids, and Dexter strides in. He looks hot and sweaty, his breathing labored, and his T-shirt clinging to him in a way that makes me feel hotter.

Hard, defined muscles ripple beneath the fabric. Strands of dark, damp hair curl over his forehead. I can't help but soak him all in, savoring him like I've savored my champagne. His is a body worked hard, with endorphins no doubt whizzing through him. The towel around his neck catches the beads of sweat trailing down his face and all I can do is gawk at him like a rockstar groupie.

I can't even make myself look away.

I've only seen him in sharp designer suits or casual T-shirts and jeans. Or naked, and sprawled out like the king of the jungle. But even though he's clothed this time, he might as well be bare, raw and unfiltered for the effect he's having on me.

"Having fun?" His voice is surprisingly relaxed, his gaze dipping from my face to my chest, undressing me slowly.

I shouldn't encourage him. I should keep this line between us clear, and sharp, but I'm feeling flirty and in the mood for fun.

"I'm having the time of my life. You should join me." I try to feign nonchalance as I reach for my champagne flute again and bring it to my lips.

He steps closer, into my personal space, his fingers grazing the towel draped around his neck. "Don't mind if I do."

My mouth fills with sand as he approaches. Now he's so close I can see the slight tent in his shorts. I sip more champagne to moisten my mouth enough to quip. To show him that I'm unaffected. "You are allowed to have some fun. We're on our honeymoon, darling." But my insides are in turmoil.

His lips curl. "That, we are."

To my utter shock, he grips the hem of his shirt and peels it off. My breath catches as he stands there. Just as I thought. This man likes the gym. He's all carved muscle, with dustings of dark hair on his chest, and his stomach a landscape of ridges and valleys. This man was sculpted like he was born to make women's jaws drop. When the corners of his lips curve into a lazy smile, fireworks go off in the base of my belly and I press my thighs together, trying to rein in my arousal.

"I'll take a shower first. Wouldn't want to get in there with a layer of dirt all over me." He scrapes his hand across his jaw, the movement causing his bicep to flex in a way that makes my heart miss a few beats. I'm in dangerous territory, my defenses splintering like glass.

"How thoughtful of you." I try to take a casual sip as my heart hammers in my chest.

Dark eyes, *dangerous* eyes, feast on me. My breasts turn heavy and I'm pretty sure he can see that I'm aroused.

His gaze dips to my bikini. "Someone's happy to see me." His voice is pure silk as I sink lower in the water, so that only my face is above water. "Don't do that, sweetheart. I'm your doting husband, remember?"

"How could I forget, darling." I stay submerged, with only my neck upwards visible.

"Wait for me." He heads for the bathroom and I shiver. Not from cold. But because my skin is flushed, my breath is shallow, my body heated.

Everything inside me is burning. Because I want him. And if he comes back … I don't know if I'll have clarity of thought to stop him. I lift the glass to my lips again but set it back down without taking a sip.

I need a clear head.

I need to think carefully.

To him, this is a game.

To me, it's about surviving the year.

Dexter will have the upper hand in New York. I'll be in his territory. His kingdom. His world. Away from my friends, my family, everything I hold dear. I have to stay strong. Why did I stupidly ask him to join me in the hot tub?

I didn't think he'd call my bluff.

I thought he'd still be the distant husband and turn me down, but instead, no. The man's coming in.

It's not long before he strides back into view, and my stomach bottoms out. Charcoal-gray lounge shorts hang low on his hips. They're loose, but not loose enough. The fabric clings to him, outlining every sharp line of muscle, every inch of hardness.

He's a tease.

And I am … *gone.*

I swallow.

He steps in, thick thighs slicing through the water, the

powerful curves of his calf flexing as he sits down with slow, deliberate ease. My eyes betray me, moving to where his shorts cling tight, the fabric tented, and leaving nothing to the imagination. At the same time, the faint scent of lemon wafts over me, crisp and clean, mingling with the humid air.

Dexter doesn't sit next to me. Instead, he settles at the opposite end of the tub, his muscles flexing as he leans back like he owns this moment. His gaze is dark and unreadable and when he splays his arms out on the ledge, my attention settles on his flexed biceps.

This isn't going to be easy. "You didn't get a glass." I try to keep my voice neutral. "Don't you want some champagne?"

"If I did, I'd drink from your glass." His lips curve, and his voice dips lower. Heat coils deep in my belly. I decide to wait ten minutes. No, five. Five minutes before I tell him my skin is wrinkling, that I need to get out.

And escape.

Because I already know. I *do* need to get out. I need to get away. I'm in dangerous waters as Dexter's lingering gaze rakes over me. I sink lower, the water dancing just under my chin, using the bubbles to shield me.

"Good gym session?" I ask, needing to fill the silence.

"Great." His voice is rough. "Managed to vent my frustration."

I nod in agreement.

He snorts, shaking his head. "My father. Work. The usual shit. That kind of frustration."

I hesitate, then push. "Your father's being shown around the business."

A muscle tics in his jaw. "Yeah," he mutters. "Wish he'd just go home."

I don't blame him. Paul Knight is a storm in a suit, and storms don't leave without destroying something first.

"Must be tough for your parents," he adds, watching me closely. "I'm sorry they have to suffer him."

"They haven't said anything." I force a small smile, trying to ignore the knot tightening in my chest. But Dexter doesn't elaborate and so far hasn't hinted at any problems, so I feel reassured.

"Have you heard from Raquel?"

I shake my head. "No. Why?"

"Rio's gone silent." |

"I can't get a hold of Raquel either." I wonder if they're up to something.

"They looked to be getting on that night we had drinks at the hotel," Dexter adds.

The night *we* got on well.

That sneaky little espertinha. *The clever little one.* "I'll have a million questions for her when I next see her."

"I'm sure you will."

The tension around us softens. It becomes less about us, more about the people we can't reach. I remember the two of them in the bar that night. "You think …?" The question hangs in the air.

"I don't know what to think," Dexter mutters.

It's strange, the way all our lives have suddenly merged, how mine and Dexter's lives are tangled together, and how Rio and Raquel's might be, too.

"So," Dexter draws my attention back to him. "Tell me, what kind of men does Daniela Oliviera usually go for?"

I tense, not liking this probing into my personal life.

But he's my husband.

I swirl my fingers through the water. "Wouldn't you like to know?" I say, seductively.

His smile is subtle, yet dangerous. "I would, actually."

I roll my eyes, but my heart is hammering. "Nothing

scandalous. No friends-with-benefits situations." I give him a pointed look.

His grin fades, just slightly. "Not all of my arrangements are meaningless," he says. "Some people want an understanding. No strings. No expectations. We are allowed pillow talk."

I shudder, not wanting to have a visual of him in bed with another woman. "That's not me," I murmur.

"I gathered, given your utter revulsion at the idea." His voice is quiet, but heavy. The steam rises around us, curling in the air, thick with something that's not just heat. His eyes search mine. "And what about Oscar Ramos?"

I still. I knew he'd ask about him again, sooner or later. This time, I don't hesitate. "He wanted to marry me."

Dexter's jaw tightens. "What the fuck?"

"When the deal with Jett fell through," I explain, carefully, "Oscar Ramos stepped up."

His expression darkens. "How did he know about the deal with Jett?"

I hesitate.

Because I know something he doesn't. That my father's business isn't as wildly successful as the Knights think. I don't know the extent of it, but Oscar Ramos obviously had intel.

"How, Daniela?" Dexter pushes.

I shrug. "Oscar's practices are questionable. The way he works isn't always above board. He has people, eyes and ears everywhere."

"And he wanted an alliance to help your family?"

"Like the Knights did. We all want something from this alliance, don't we?"

Dexter's disgust is palpable. "That slimy bastard," he growls. "He's old enough to be your father."

"I would never marry him." I ground down on my teeth as bile snakes up my throat, bitter as venom. Oscar Ramos makes me shiver, but not for the reasons Dexter does. I could never entertain the idea of being married to him. While Dexter would respect our boundaries, Oscar wouldn't.

He shifts closer to me. "So when Jett backed out, you must have been worried?"

I take a shaky breath. "It made me realize I had to do something. That's why I flew to New York. To meet your father and to try to negotiate something better."

His eyes search my face. "God help you if I'm supposed to be your 'something better'."

"You saved me, Dexter." My voice breaks slightly. His eyes drop to my lips, his body inching even closer. I'm shivering, but I'm not cold.

"I'm glad I saved you from that fucker, and I'm glad you picked me." His voice drops an octave lower.

Our knees are almost touching. I'm still seated, but he's squatting in the water. "I'm glad we got married," I whisper.

"If it keeps that fucker at bay, then so am I."

Our eyes lock, and then my gaze falls to his lips, and I remember how he branded me with them. I lick my lower lip, memories of his hot searing kisses come rushing back. He shifts closer to me, water trickling down his hard body as he leans towards me. His face merely inches from me. He dips forward, so close now, that my heart beats loud and fast and ferociously. Before I know what's happening, his tongue swipes over my lower lip. I exhale a breath, and then his tongue slides between my lips. It's heady. Pure, raw desire. It was always going to happen again. It was inevitable. I just wasn't sure that it would happen *here*.

On our honeymoon.

I mewl as our lips press together, his hands frame my face. His mouth on mine makes every coherent thought turn to steam.

The kiss is lightning and gasoline; a hot, desperate spark that ignites everything we've tried to suppress.

This wasn't supposed to happen, but it's impossible to resist. Dexter's hands drop to my waist and he pulls me against his hard body. A low growl rumbles in his chest as our kiss turns frenzied, more urgent, the water sloshing around us. I'm vaguely aware of warm bubbles caressing my skin, but it's nothing compared to the feel of his hands bracketing my hips, the feel of his hardness poking my belly.

A shudder of need spikes through me, and a distant voice tells me, I should stop this.

I should. But the way he devours me sends every promise we made straight to hell.

"Dexter …" I manage to gasp when he momentarily frees my lips, but he doesn't let me finish. He cups the back of my neck and claims my mouth again, even harder. My protest evaporates into a whimper as I run my hands over his broad, muscular shoulders. His skin is slick from the water, hot to touch, and I can't help but dig my nails in slightly. He hisses at the slight pain or pleasure. I'm not sure which, and then I'm lifted clear off my feet. The motion sends a wave of water over the edge of the tub.

I yelp softly as he lifts me up, water streaming off my skin as my legs wrap around his waist instinctively. He's hard and firm all over. Strong and built. I relish every new sensation as our bodies meld together.

The night air is cool on my exposed skin until he lowers us both back into the bubbling heat. But he's sitting down, and I'm straddling his hips. My arms lock around his neck, and the space between my legs presses against his hardness. My core ignites, and my head falls back as his lips blaze a trail down my throat. Nipping at the tender hollow where my neck meets my shoulder, he gives a sharp little bite, and I cry out.

It's all so overwhelming, his hands, his hardness, his body.

"Daniela …" He growls my name like a prayer and a curse. It only makes me need him even more. And then his hand finally slips down to my bikini bottoms.

We pull away, eyes latched on one another. He's asking for my permission. In answer, I widen my knees, half kneeling as his fingers slip inside me. I shudder out a sigh, and when his thumb finds and circles my core, I choke out a strangled sigh.

Pleasure lances through my body, sparking at my breasts and shooting downward. I grind myself against fingers, needing friction, utterly lost in the fire consuming us both.

He wasn't supposed to want me like this.

We weren't supposed to have feelings, or show any emotions.

We weren't supposed to get close.

But every fevered kiss and possessive touch of his hands tells a different story. He's drowning in me, and I'm drowning in him, and there's no saving either of us now. My eyes find his through the hazy steam.

"This is wrong," I pant, the words barely audible over our ragged breathing. "But it feels so right." My body yearns for him, but my mind gives one last feeble protest. Dexter's eyes flash with something that looks like guilt, and longing.

"This belongs to me, wife." He tweaks my clit and sinks in another finger. He doesn't give me a chance to respond as his mouth crashes onto mine again, and the argument is lost in a tangle of tongues and teeth and need.

One of his hands pulls down my bikini triangle, exposing my breast which he hungrily kneads, tweaking my nipple mercilessly. Between that and his fingers sliding over my slick folds under the water, it's too much.

"You're so wet," he mutters against my lips, his tone a mix of heat and desire. A wild laugh bubbles up in my throat at the unintended irony. Of course I'm wet, we're in a hot tub, but it dies the instant he strokes me again. We devour one another with our mouths, desperate with need. I break the kiss with a strangled moan. His thumb presses against my clit, rubbing slow, torturous circles that make my thighs quake around his hips. My head falls back, and Dexter takes advantage, latching onto my breast and sucking hard, extracting every ounce of pleasure he can from my body as his mouth and fingers work their magic.

I cry out again as he sucks hard, his tongue flicking over the sensitive peak while his fingers curl deep inside me. Pleasure radiates through me, every nerve ending on fire. I'm so close already; heat coiling tight in my belly with each pump of his fingers. His teeth graze my nipple at the exact moment his thumb presses down firmly on my clit, and I shatter. Euphoria pulses through me, wave after wave, and all I can do is cry out Dexter's name. He groans and keeps working me with his hand, prolonging my climax until I shudder and fall apart in his arms.

An animalistic sound comes from deep in his throat. "Come for me, Gatinha," he whispers, his voice low and husky. He watches me as I unravel, his fingers still inside me as the orgasm crashes over me, sudden and violent, clenching every muscle in my body.

We pant, and I sit on him, falling into his chest, burying my face in the crook of his neck. Bubbles cascade over me as withdraws his fingers from my trembling body. His arms come around me, caging me against him, and I hear his heart beating wildly. As wildly as mine as we cling to each other.

Dipping his head, he drops a kiss on my shoulder. I shiver, then savor his tenderness, the way he's holding me. How he feels against me. Protective, strong, hard. I love it when his hand soothes back my hair and I can't help but drop a kiss on his damp chest. I inhale, sniffing him like I have no manners.

The truth is, I could stay like this all night. I don't want to move. I don't want this bubble to burst. The secret, sultry place where Dexter and I finally got to share a few moments of intimacy.

Now I want more, because I've had a taste, and it's not enough.

"I'm in danger of falling in love with you, Dexter."

His body tenses. A tremor runs through me that has nothing to do with the cooling night air. I loosen my hold around his neck, suddenly aware of how closely we're joined. He seems to realize it at the same time.

He lifts me easily and sets me down beside him. Hot water swirls between us and I rearrange my clothing so that I'm decent again. I made a mistake saying what I just did, because the way he's looking at me? He doesn't like it.

I start to shake, then panic sets in as I hold his gaze. There's a rawness in his expression I've never seen, and when he drags a hand through his soaked hair, I see it trembling.

"This … shouldn't have happened," he says hoarsely. A spear through my heart. I wrap my arms around myself, suddenly cold despite the steaming water. "It was just supposed to be a marriage on paper." His jaw tightens. Water drips from his hair into his eyes, and he swipes it away, refusing to look at me.

The only sound is the churn of the tub's jets. I rub my arms, trying to hold myself together.

"Do … do you regret it?" I ask softly, bracing myself for his answer. It's like a slap, when he doesn't reply. His silence sends a fissure of hurt through my chest. "Don't," I choke out, anger rising to battle the hurt. "Don't do that."

His eyes snap to mine. "Don't do what?"

"This." I hate the way my voice trembles. "Don't shut me

out and act like nothing happened. Don't you dare pretend that meant nothing."

His face twists, pain etched in every angle. "Daniela ..."

"No!" A bitter laugh bubbles up in my throat. "You swore you didn't want me, remember? That this would never happen." I gesture between us, my hand shaking. "Well, guess what? It did happen. You want me. You need me. You just proved it."

He flinches as if punched, his eyes going glossy. "Of course I—" He cuts himself off, biting down on whatever he was about to admit. A harsh breath shudders out of him. "Wanting you was never the problem."

"Then what is?" My voice cracks. "Because I'm sitting here, and I care about you and I ... and I want this, Dexter. I'm not in love with you, okay? If that makes you feel better. This isn't some grand forever promise. But I care about you, and it scares me. And I'm here. We're in this together, whether we're meant to be or not. And after what just happened between us, you still choose to run away."

He winces, as if my words have wounded him. "I'm trying to protect you," he grinds out.

"Protect me?" I stare at him, incredulous. "From what? From you? You think you're some kind of curse?"

He says nothing, but the flicker in his eyes is answer enough. A hot tear slips down my cheek.

"You don't get to decide how I feel, or what I risk," I whisper. "I knew being with you could hurt. I knew you were wounded, and you think you're to blame for what happened to your mom. That you can't love—" His eyes pierce through me and he frowns.

"Don't talk about love. I got you off in the water. That's all that happened here."

His words hit so hard, they feel like a slap. But I don't back down. "I had an idea you'd be complicated. That you'd fight this at every turn. And I still ..." My voice catches. "I still jumped in, eyes wide open."

"You shouldn't have," he whispers, agony in every syllable. "You should walk away. Right now. Before I hurt you any more."

My heart cracks at the sadness in his voice. "I can't do that. We're in this for a reason. For a financial reason. This is part of a deal." But I need to know more about the source of his pain, his belief, how he sees himself. "Why do you think you'll hurt me? Why can't you just let someone care about you? Why can't you care about them back?"

His head jerks up, eyes blazing with torment. "You want the truth?" he rasps. "You really want to know why I can't do this?"

"Yes," I say, overcome with a desperate need to help him. "I deserve that much." His throat works, and for a long moment I think he'll refuse. But then something in him crumples.

"Because I sent my mother to her death," he bites out. His words hang in the night air like a hangman's noose.

"Dexter ... that's not true," I say, my words tumbling out in a harsh whisper.

"Don't tell me what's true and what isn't. You never knew her."

CHAPTER TWENTY-SIX

DEX

THIS SEEMS LIKE A MARKER IN OUR JOURNEY, AND I WANT TO cherish this moment because it feels like everything has changed.

But it's precisely for that reason that I need to back away. Daniela is sweet and warm, and she trusts me. She fits against me like she was made to be mine.

Like she belongs to me.

Like she's part of me.

Like I've known her for years.

But I will hurt her. I'm a mess, and she's not. I'll ruin her, and I can't do that to her. But now we're sitting apart like angry lovers. Getting her off was fucking sublime, but then she had to go and ruin it by telling me she was falling for me.

Those words set off every alarm in my head. Five-alarm fire.

Get out. Get out now.

I'm getting attached, and I can't afford for that to happen.

This could turn dangerous, become complicated. It could be all the things I don't need or want.

I walk away in seven months, and then this marriage will be nothing but a broken contract. I was never supposed to feel anything real for her, only my fucking dick got in the way. *Again.*

My head is all over the place, a riot of all the wrong emotions; regret and frustration. I need space. I need to shut this down before it's too late. But when she looks at me with her moist lips—lips that demand to be kissed and so help me God, I so badly want to—I hold back. It's not easy, having this restraint.

"I need to take a shower," I tell her, scrambling to find a way to break the moment, to put my barriers back in place.

"Don't run away, Dexter."

"I'm not."

"You are."

"I'm taking a shower."

"You just had one," she murmurs.

"I did, but you just came all over my fingers."

Her expression shifts in an instant. She flinches, like I just slapped her. The truth is, I wouldn't need to have a shower for that. What I want to do is lick my fingers and taste her, but this can't go any further.

The hurt flickers across her face before she hides it, but I see it. And I hate myself for it.

I step quietly out of the hot tub, putting distance between us, trying to ignore the battle waging inside me. I don't want to leave. I want to pull her into me and go further. But it's better that I walk away. I can't.

I force myself not to look back as I try to erase the image of her sitting in that hot tub, looking so very deliciously fuckable. And then I spend most of my shower fucking my fist, remembering her moans of pleasure. How wet and swollen she was for me. How her eyes glazed over as my fingers pistoned in and out of her.

I'm in danger of falling in love with you, Dexter.

Her words bounce around in my head. Their depth and heaviness conjuring up scenarios I can't let myself be part of.

I avoid her later by dealing with non-important emails and pretending to be busy at my desk. When I walk past the bedroom, Daniela is already in bed, curled up under the sheets, facing away.

I want to crawl in beside her, but I force myself to go to the spare bedroom instead. Shutting the door behind me, my shoulders slump as I lean against the door and wonder what the hell I just did.

A silly, needy part of me expected her to ask me what was wrong. To come to me and coax it out of me, but Daniela isn't the sort of woman to chase after a man. I see that now. She is more than I first thought. She gives me the space I need and, unlike other women, she leaves me alone, even when I really don't want to be alone.

She's the type of woman a man would be lucky to have, and stupid to let go. I'm at risk of giving into my feelings, of giving into my emotions, because I'm starting to feel so much for her, but when she crossed a line with those words, my guardrails slammed into place.

She says she could fall in love with me, but I know I'll hurt her. Sleeping in the spare room is the right thing to do, yet I can't help but wonder where the fuck do we go from here?

CHAPTER TWENTY-SEVEN

DANI

I wake up alone, my thoughts filled with Dexter. He's more wounded, more broken, more complicated than I ever imagined.

He does things I don't understand. Kissing me, being so close and intimate with me, touching me and making me come apart in his hands.

I believed it would lead to more. I believed he felt something for me, because I felt something for him. But I made the mistake of telling him I was falling for him. I slap a hand over my face and groan. *Dios*, what was I thinking?

I don't like him being like this, all cold again. Away from me. As if he can't stand being around me.

Now we're back to playing that charade again.

Only, I can't.

It's exhausting.

I want to reach for my phone and call Raquel, but I can't

disturb her again. She's always so busy. I feel so utterly alone and wretched, but it's the last day of the honeymoon and tonight we fly back to São Paulo for dinner with my parents. Tomorrow morning, we leave for New York.

I'm going to stay away from Dexter. I won't confront him, or ask him what the hell he's playing at. Instead, we'll spend the day dancing around each other, pretending like last night never happened.

BY THE TIME I GET UP, SHOWER AND GET DRESSED INTO another bikini and coverall, Dexter is already at work, seated in the office chair, laptop open, his focus locked on the screen.

"Good morning," I say. Clearly he doesn't want to have breakfast out on the terrace with me. He's focussing so hard, his brow creases.

"Morning," he murmurs, barely glancing up.

Seeing that he's not going to move, I bring him a cup of coffee, setting the cup beside him. He doesn't acknowledge it.

"You're working again." I can't be silent. I can't pretend last night didn't happen. I can't be cold and distant.

"Busy day." His tone is dismissive and detached. Like last night meant nothing. Like *I* mean nothing. So much for spending the last day here together. So much for that stupid, fleeting hope that maybe, just maybe, he might be different this morning.

Silly woman. What was I thinking?

He looks up then, and blinks when I don't disappear. Then he blinks again, his eyes dark as they slowly inch over my body.

He's noticed my outfit. *Good.*

If he's going to bury himself in work, then fine. I won't waste my last day here sulking over a man who clearly doesn't care. I decide to make the most of the infinity pool, the sun and the recliner. I'll finish my book and relish the sound of the waves crashing against the shore.

A sound I'll miss this time tomorrow.

BACK IN SÃO PAULO, MY PARENTS GREET US WARMLY. MY mother's eyes brim with unspoken questions. I sense that my father is stressed and when I catch him alone in a rare quiet moment, I ask him. "Papai, o que foi? What's wrong?"

"Nothing, meu amor." His voice is warm but I detect the hesitation. "Are you happy?"

I swallow past the lump in my throat. I smile and lie. "Yes, Papai."

"Has he been good to you?"

I force a brighter smile. "We get along, Papai. You don't have to worry. He's a *really* nice person. Don't worry. I know what I'm doing."

But, do I?

I reassure my parents, play my part, but inside, my heart is bruised and battered. Dexter keeps his distance, slipping effortlessly into his role as the aloof businessman, the dutiful son-in-law, but I know this is just a role, and it's only temporary.

I hate that he's pretending to my parents, even though we all know the deal. Tomorrow I start my new life in New York, and I wonder what awaits me.

By the time we land in New York, reality starts sinking in. A few special moments in our honeymoon gave me a false sense of security, a fleeting feeling that this marriage might not be so bad.

Dexter is softer than he lets on under his hardened exterior. He's not Oscar Ramos. I need to keep reminding myself that I'm with the better man. I also need to keep reminding myself that I'm helping my father.

Awkward tension fills the air as we step into Dexter's apartment. It feels like a different world. A different time zone. A different *something*.

Like Dorothy from Kansas, I have the strangest sensation of being transported from São Paulo and dropped into my new life in New York. He casually mentions that he's on the second floor of the apartment block he shares with his brothers. That Jett has the penthouse at the top and he's sandwiched between Jett and Zach who has the first floor.

"There are amenities on the ground floor," he mentions, and advises me to go and check them out whenever I want. "This is my humble abode," he says, tossing his keys onto a sleek marble console by the door.

I look around in quiet awe. "This is a *gorgeous* apartment."

"Thanks. Let me give you the quick tour."

I follow him down the hallway, my eyes sweeping around the vast property. His place is modern, and slick. Clean and clinical. It looks like it belongs in a magazine. Dark woods, black leather, silver accents. Everything screams Dexter.

"Bricks?" I trace my fingers around the rough wall.

"Exposed brickwork. It's raw, not dressed up. What you see is what you get."

"Like you," I murmur, walking over to the windows and looking out. "Cobbled streets. How charming."

"You're not mesmerized by the views of the Hudson River, or the rooftops and water towers of the Tribeca skyline. But you're in awe of the cobblestone streets below?"

"Simple, and not ostentatious. Like me."

"You're not simple." He gives me a peculiar look, like he doesn't understand.

I wonder what he's thinking. "How would you describe me?"

I see the flex of his jaw, can tell he's choosing his words carefully. Might be that he won't even tell me the truth.

"You're charming, and refreshing, and intelligent. You're also extremely smart and—"

"Okay. Stop." I cut him off. Clearly, he's laughing at me, and I don't like it. "We're alone here, you don't need to humor me. Continue with the tour." I move past him, eyeing the rest of the apartment. He moves fast, barely pausing as he gestures.

"This is the master bedroom." He pushes the door open. I survey it in silence because he doesn't give me any details. It's sleek and masculine and looks impeccably clean. The color palette is charcoal grays, blacks and whites. A king-sized bed dominates the room. Crisp white pillows with a textured slate-gray duvet. There's a fireplace, built-in shelving holding high-end watches, and a half-empty tumbler of scotch on the nightstand.

"Your room is here." He steps away, across the hallway and pushes the door open to the room directly opposite his.

I step inside and stop, my eyes sweeping over the king-sized bed and the dressers and what looks like the entrance to a walk-in closet. This room is such a contrast against the gray, black and white of the rest of the apartment. It has a dash of color. My eyes fix on the soft green walls and that's when I realize. They're the same shade of eucalyptus green from home.

"Don't you like it?" He sounds oddly anxious.

I detect a subtle hint of fresh paint. Like someone tried to disguise it and failed. "Did you do this *for me?*"

"Yes, for you," he says reluctantly. Like it's a chore and now he wishes he hadn't. "You told me it was your favorite color."

"You remembered." My heart pitter-patters fast and my insides suddenly feel light. I try to compose myself. "I like it very much. You're … you're so thoughtful and kind, and you didn't have to do this, but you did," I say softly. I look away before he sees my eyes turning misty. I've been strong throughout this entire process, but now, this tiny act of kindness has me on the verge of blubbering. I can't break down, not in front of him.

"It's just paint, Daniela." Dexter leans against the doorframe, watching me. "Figured I'd make it a little more homey for you."

I walk around slowly, taking in the plush bedding, the small details, things that aren't just generic luxury but personal, and thoughtful. Things that make my throat constrict. Framed prints of São Paulo, a candle that smells of jasmine, a quote framed on the wall in elegant lettering: *Onde o coração está, é onde está o lar*.

Where the heart is, is where home is.

He probably used Google translate, or his assistant did, but my heart is overwhelmed and I blink furiously, trying to fight back the tears that threaten to fall.

Such kindness and consideration … it chokes me.

Dexter thinks he's being subtle, hiding how he feels behind rolled-up sleeves and gruff one-liners, but it's all bleeding through anyway. Like the scent of fresh paint, his intentions linger in the air, impossible to miss. He remembers things he shouldn't. He cares more than he's willing to admit, and it blows me away.

I want to throw my arms around him and fall into his chest.

I wish I could.

I swallow, trying soften the knot that forms in my throat. I felt so alone coming here, but these gestures from him soothe my hurt and loneliness in a way that I never expected. "Thank you."

"Like I said, it's just paint and a few pictures."

"It makes me feel less homesick."

A sliver of concern flashes through his eyes. "I guess this feels strange. Living here, away from your family, your friends …" He hesitates. "At least Raquel's not too far. I guess you'll visit her often."

I sigh. "I hope to, but she's busy. Corporate lawyer, even though she found the time to crash our drinks evening. Remember that?" Because I revisit that scene many times. How easily Dexter and I got on, once we'd warmed up. How naturally our stories flowed when we were trying to convince Raquel that we were in love. We have rapport and chemistry. We have get on. We have a foundation on which we can build.

But I went and messed it up.

His lips curve slightly, and I wonder if he's remembering that night as fondly as I do. I wonder if he remembers when we were a little tipsy, when we got a little too close, when we kissed for the first time. But he doesn't and we just stand there, the space between us small and filled with unspoken reminders of what could be.

He retreats into the hallway, into his safe space away from me. "I don't cook much. I usually eat out, so I'm not sure what you want to do this evening."

"I'm not hungry. Don't let me ruin your evening. You just

do what you normally do." I don't want to get in his way. Ruin his normal routine.

He cocks an eyebrow. "Do what I normally do? What does that mean?"

I don't understand why he's so grumpy. I'm aware that this is his place, and I'm in the way. I don't want to make him feel uneasy. "It means ... just that."

"What?"

I stare at the floor because I can't bear to look at him. I can't bear for him to see this would hurt me so much. We're supposed to be following the rules.

No emotions.

No getting involved.

No hint of a scandal. But we've already done things we weren't meant to do. He's a man with needs. Maybe he's planning on getting those needs met. Just not from me.

"If you want to meet a woman, please be discreet so that we can keep our happily married charade going." My heart breaks just thinking about him with someone else.

He takes a few strides and then he's in my face, tipping up my chin with his finger, his dark eyes boring into mine, a little dark and dangerous. My heart pounds.

"I don't need to see anyone." His gaze falls to my lips, and his brow creases. I hold my breath, wondering if he's thinking of the hot tub. "I'm not doing anything like that, Daniela. I have no plans whatsoever. This might be a marriage of convenience but while we're married I'll take my vows seriously. I'm not my father. Loyalty means everything to me." His words, low and meaningful, wrap around and hug my heart.

My mouth falls open.

"I'll be at work tomorrow," he tells me, nonchalantly. "What about you?"

"I'll be working from home. I need the Wi-Fi password."

"Of course. Let me show you the study."

He shows me the study and then quickly shows me the rest of the apartment. "Obviously, I'll get you a credit card for expenses."

I scoff. "I don't need your credit card. I'm not a child. I'm a woman who works and I have access to my own money."

He looks surprised, for a nano-second. "Of course you have." He lets out an exhale, and seems a bit nervous. "I don't know how this will work out."

Such a fast turn of conversation. It makes me think maybe his doubts and reservations are bubbling just under the surface, that maybe he's not as composed and as okay with this as he's making out to be.

"It has to work out," I tell him. "Just one year. We can do that."

"You seem so sure. So confident."

"Aren't you?" I peer at him, trying to work out what he's battling inside.

"There's a gala." He rakes his hand through his thick hair. A few curls rebound back, falling over his brow. "It's a charity event. We have to go. My brothers and my father will be there. The old man probably arranged it for New York society to see that we're married."

A charity gala? I can handle that. "We'll have to play the happy couple again, no problem."

"Just for a few hours."

I hate that he's so nonchalant about it. Has he forgotten the hot tub and how he made me feel? Did it mean nothing to him?

"There are already pictures of us from the resort circulating online," he adds. "Papers, blogs. People are curious. None of the Knights have ever gotten married before."

"Then we'll need to dazzle everyone."

"Something like that." He's already moving away from me.

He painted the room for me, got me a few things to remind me of home, I know he feels something. "Think you can do it?" I ask. "Play at being happily married?"

He rubs the back of his neck. "I've played at being happy my whole life. What's one more year?"

My heart sinks. *Played at being happy*, must be some of the saddest words I've ever heard. I don't want that for anyone, but I especially don't want that for Dexter.

CHAPTER TWENTY-EIGHT

DEX

"You survived. How was it?" Jett asks, leaning back against the soft leather of the booth and staring at me expectantly.

Zach grins, looking every bit like he already knows the answer. "Yeah, Dex. How was playing house with your new wife?"

I take a slow sip of my drink, measuring my response. "Fine. Just fine." I'm with my brothers in a bar. It's my first day back at work, and we've come out for some lunch.

Daniela was up and in the study as I had my protein shake. I asked her if she wanted one, but she told me she'd get her own breakfast. I hate the tension between us even more now that I know how things could be if I let down my guard. If I gave her a chance.

"*Fine?* That's it?" Jett sounds like he doesn't believe me.

"What else do you want me to say?" I growl. "We went to

the resort. Did the obligatory couple's things. Daniela played her part. I played mine. We're back now. End of story."

Zach peers at me. "No honeymoon bliss? No cozy nights by the fire? No candlelit baths?"

I exhale sharply, wondering why I accepted this invite. "You two sound like gossip columnists. Nothing happened."

Nothing that I'm going to tell them. What am I supposed to say? That I kissed her? That I touched her? That for a few stolen moments, I let myself want her? The way I feel about her scares me. I want her and need her, but it's dangerous for her to be in this family. Daniela is too kind, pure and big hearted to live among the Knights.

I'll always protect her, but if the old man discovers she's my Achilles heel, he'll use it against me. Somehow he'll find a way. He always does.

That's why it's better for me to shut her out. It's torture for me, but it's the right thing to do. "Nothing to report," I say flatly, tossing back the rest of my drink.

My brothers exchange glances but don't push. They shouldn't. Because if they knew the truth, if they knew how dangerously close I was to wanting Daniela beyond this deal, they'd never let me live it down.

This is tough. Harder than I thought, not just because I want to kiss her again, but because I remembered how she felt under my hands. The way my fingers played her like a violin, every movement pulling a reaction, her body responding to my touch like a melody meant for me alone.

I don't know what the hell I was thinking when I let my guard down. When I let us go further than I ever intended. Thank God we didn't go all the way. We *can't* cross that line.

I shoot a somber look at them both, desperate to change the topic. "Tell me what's been going on here? Did the old man have anything to report when he got back? Anything about AO Eletronica?"

Jett sighs. "He's said nothing."

No surprise there. I didn't expect him to divulge much. "The old man is tight lipped anyway. He only tells us on a need-to-know basis."

Jett nods, looking pensive. "I'm sure it's all fine."

"Is he in?" I haven't seen him around the office, not that I'd go out looking for him. I haven't seen the man since we left for our honeymoon, but I thought he might come by and ask me how it was.

"Dad's around. I'm sure he'll come and see you." Zach, the old man's pet, pipes up.

"Lucky me," I grumble.

———

MY FATHER STRIDES INTO MY OFFICE. I DON'T STAND TO GREET him. Just lean back in my chair and wait for him to get to whatever the hell he wants.

He wastes no time. "The honeymoon?"

I keep my expression unreadable. "It was fine."

He nods, studying me like he's dissecting my every move. "We should have dinner, now that you're both back. A family affair."

My gut churns at the thought of subjecting Daniela to a Knight family dinner. "Not necessary."

His gaze sharpens. "It wasn't a suggestion." He adjusts his cufflinks and paces slowly around the room, which I find unnerving. I wish he'd just sit the hell down in one place.

"There's a charity gala coming up—"

"You already told me. Orchestrated by you, no doubt."

"This isn't just a powerful alliance; it's the first Knight wedding. People are interested in you as a couple, but more intrigued about your new wife."

"Great. That's all I need."

"You just need to survive a year."

My nostrils flare at his nonchalance. I wonder if he thought of marriage to my mom as something to *survive*?

"I'll get Patty to send you all the details. You and Daniela will attend and present a united front. Look deliriously happy and in love."

"We can do that." I lean back in my chair, steepling my hands across my chest. "How was the spying? Find anything?"

His expression gives nothing away. "Excuse me?"

"When you went to work with Daniela's father," I say. "You know, playing the benevolent businessman while digging for weaknesses?"

His jaw tightens ever so slightly.

Bingo. I was right.

"There are things you don't understand," he says smoothly. "Things I'll reveal when the time is right."

A chill runs down my spine, but I don't let it show. The old man never mentions things unless he's already set them in motion.

Some shit is brewing, and when it hits, it won't be pretty.

LATER, ON MY WAY HOME, I VISIT RIO IN HIS APARTMENT. HE slouches against the bar, lazy grin in place, his dark eyes flashing with amusement as he watches me. "Welcome back, stranger. How's married life treating you?"

I grunt. "Don't start."

He chuckles. "How close did you get?"

I say nothing.

Rio's grin widens. "Oh, shit. Did stuff happen?"

"Fuck no." I try not to frown. Try not to look irritated. After this my next stop is my apartment where Daniela is. I'd be lying if I said I hadn't been thinking of her all day. I can't get her out of my mind, and now I'm hesitant to go home. It's not even been a day, and I'm anxious. Worried that I won't be able to hide what I'm starting to feel for her.

Maybe I don't walk out in seven months. I can't see how I'll last that long, anyway. Maybe I do it sooner, like in two or three months.

"You actually like her," Rio says, quietly.

I level him with a glare. "I didn't say that."

"You didn't have to." His jaw drops. "You got close. You kissed. And let me guess … you went all cold afterward?"

I hate that this guy is so fucking perceptive. "I had to."

He lets out a low whistle. "You slept with her?"

"No!"

His brows push together and he peers at me. "Then … *what?*"

I squeeze my eyes shut. See me and Daniela in the hot tub. Hear her sighs. Fuck. My eyelids fly open. I'm doomed. She's always in my mind. "We kissing and … *stuff.*"

"Man, you're in trouble."

I'm relieved he didn't push for details. "I've got this."

Rio shakes his head, laughing to himself. "Dexter Knight, the one who swore he'd never fall for anyone, out here catching feelings for his fake wife. This is fucking good."

I scowl. "It's not good."

"You care about her, don't you?"

I twist my neck, trying to ease out the knot. "I feel sorry for her being here away from everything she knows."

"Sounds to me like she was getting to know you." Rio winks.

"You're insufferable. She's … *different,*" I say, thinking about our days at the honeymoon resort.

"Define different."

"She's not clingy, or needy. Or desperate for me." I think about how she was so vulnerable in front of me, of how she trusted me enough to have me stroke her clit and make her come, but she doesn't act like she's tied to me. It unnerves me slightly, that I'm becoming obsessed by her. Maybe it's because most women fall at my feet. Or get on their knees for me. They do it so easily, but Daniela doesn't.

"I can't work her out," Rio confesses.

I bristle at his words. "Don't even try, brother." I don't want him looking at my wife.

"Dude! It's not like that, I promise you. I like the chase, remember?" Rio rushes to reassure me.

I do remember. "I forgot. You're chasing her friend."

"Who?" He tries to put on a confused look, but I can see right through this guy.

"Nice try. You don't fool me. You weren't on the flight home with the others. What did you get up to?"

"My lips are sealed. Don't even waste your time asking."

I stare at him incredulous. "You're *not* chasing her?"

"Conquered and ditched."

This man impresses me. He can so easily put his emotions to the side. I thought I could, too, except that I've now met a woman who seeps into my cells and has left her imprint. A woman I can't easily forget or discard. The coming months are going to be a test, which is why I need to get out of this sooner than I planned. "I can't get emotionally involved."

"Are you?" Rio leans forward, dark eyes wide open, the

perfect picture of shock. When I don't reply, "Damn. You really do have feelings for her. Dude, you're an idiot."

I scowl. "You got anything helpful to say?"

"You feel for her. You care. You weren't supposed to make this complicated."

"You think I don't know that? I'm walking away in seven months. Maybe sooner, I haven't made my mind up yet."

"*What?*" Rio's face twists in disbelief. "What the fuck? *Why?*" He stands up, his muscles tensing like I've dissed him.

"I was always going to. I just didn't tell anyone."

"Why are you telling me now?"

"I don't know." Maybe a part of me wants him to talk some sense into me.

"Dex?"

"I have to." But even as I say it, something inside me twists. I'm falling for her, and I don't know what the hell to do about it.

Rio takes a sip. "You sure about this, walking away?"

The fucker doesn't even try to talk me out of it. "Yes." But it doesn't sound convincing.

"Then I guess you should, because it looks to me like you're suffering, and you've not even been married for long."

"I'll get over it." I have to. One thing I've discovered is that this can't go on for a year. Our living situation is dangerously intimate.

Impossible to handle.

I don't know how I'll survive, sleeping across the hall from her. I won't get much sleep, that's for sure. Tossing and turning in my bed. All alone and thinking of her, all alone in her bed.

My right hand is going to be working overtime and I'll probably need a wrist guard. I've been lying in bed wondering what she wears to bed. Wondering what she's doing. Wondering if she's thinking of me like I'm thinking of her.

Soon there will come a time when I'll have to watch her sitting and drinking her morning coffee in my kitchen. Or freshly showered, with her damp long, luscious locks hanging over her shoulders and trailing down her breasts.

I can't touch her or kiss her.

I'm not sure I can handle that.

I want my wife, but I can't have her.

CHAPTER TWENTY-NINE

DANI

MY FIRST DAY ALONE, AND THOUGH ITS NICE OUTSIDE, THE SUN is shining, there's a chill in the air.

I like this apartment block, and that it belongs just to the Knights and no one else. Dexter mentioned that it was only for him, Jett and Zach. I wonder where the others live. I've seen the swimming pool, gym and jacuzzi on the ground floor, and hope to go there one of the mornings.

Dexter and I barely speak. He ordered take out last night and I had a shower, unpacked, and went to bed. I was exhausted from the trip, the traveling, the changing time zones, and emotionally drained from this charade we're acting out.

We move around each other in the apartment like strangers, polite but distant. His walls are up, hard as steel, impenetrable, and the only way I can deal with this, with him, is to leave him be.

I worked all day, because there was so much to catch up on. As soon as I logged on, I was inundated with hundreds of congratulatory emails from coworkers and friends. Many of my colleagues commented on how handsome Dexter is and what a beautiful couple we make. The photos have already been splashed around online, and have also appeared in some celebrity magazines.

Curious, I go online and search our names. A plethora of images come up. I gaze at them for longer than is good for me and I must admit, Dexter and I look good together. A photo from our wedding day catches my eye. Dexter is looking at me, and my heart stops, because his gaze is serious, but weighted by something heavier, something deeper. He's really looking at me. Almost like he's in love with me.

Staring at this lie makes me despondent and I soon click away. I force myself to get to work, and later go out for a walk nearby, past cobblestone streets, shiny sleek glass storefronts, and the kind of stylish locals who look like they belong in magazines. The city buzzes around me, but I feel strangely out of place. Feeling a little homesick, and missing my mother's cooking, I decide to make something simple but familiar for dinner. Dexter can get takeout or eat out, but I like to cook and I yearn for home cooked food.

But as I leave the supermarket, I notice people beginning to stare at me, and it leaves me feeling self-conscious and awkward. When I look over my shoulder, a man with a camera is following me, and now I feel hounded. A wave of apprehension washes over me. I rush ahead, almost speed walking the whole way back to our apartment. I kept looking over my shoulder to make sure he wasn't following me, and I only felt relieved when I saw our friendly concierge.

MAKING DINNER LATER THAT EVENING TAKES MY MIND OFF THE stalker, and my uneasy feelings.

The kitchen fills with the aroma of rice, beans and steak. I bought a steak for Dexter, in case he wanted some, but I'm not betting on it. Nor am I waiting for him, like the dutiful wife, who has nothing better to do than to serve her husband.

We aren't that couple, and I'm not that kind of wife.

I'm at the stove, stirring the beans when Dexter walks in. My heart jumps that he came home. A part of me thought he'd be out, meeting friends, enjoying being back in the city, but he's come home, to me. He sniffs loudly. "You ordered takeout. Smells good."

The audacity. I pretend to be outraged, because his mood seems lighter, and I like this version of him compared to grumpy Dexter.

"I cooked this with my own two hands, thank you very much." He leans in, inspecting my plate like it's a business contract. "Rice. Steak. What are those?" He jabs a thick finger at my beans.

"Black beans, cooked with garlic and onion in olive oil with a bay leaf. It's a simple dish."

He eyes the food. "Huh." Our faces are so close, I catch a whiff of his cologne before he walks away, loosening his tie.

"Want some, *darling*?" I ask, still stirring the pot, and pretending to be the dutiful wife.

"It smells pretty damned good." I hear his raspy voice behind me, and startle. I feel something on my neck. Not a touch, but *something*.

Did he just sniff me *there?*

Or is he talking about *me?*

Maybe I'm going insane, being cooped up here alone all day, reliving our sizzling moments and wishing they were real.

"Thank you." I pretend to not be affected and start to plate up my food. He doesn't move, and instead looks at me, like he's waiting for something. "Are you going out or ordering takeout?"

"Wasn't planning to. I was going to eat in tonight, seeing that it's our first day back."

My heart lights up like a lamp. Why does this simple little thing make me so happy? "I made some for you, in case you wanted it."

"You made some for me?" He looks shocked, like this is a big thing. Someone making him dinner. Piecing together these little insights into Dexter's life make my heart ache.

"It's easier to cook for two. I just had to buy an extra steak. Why don't you sit down, and I'll plate your food, too?"

"You don't have to do that." He cocks his head, looks at me as if I've slaved over the stove for six hours making a five-course meal.

"I made extra, Dexter, and I'm glad you're hungry, and brave enough to try it."

"It looks and smells out of this world. Thank you."

"It's my world. I hope you like it."

We sit across the table, steam rolling off the plates. This is nice and familiar. Homey. Something I could get used to. He picks up his fork and takes a bite, then chews, and pauses. His brows lift a little as he savors the food. I wait with bated breath, like a good little girl at school wanting her teacher's approval.

"Well?"

He swallows, nods, sets his fork down and fixes me with a serious look. "This is a typical Brazilian dish?"

I sink back in dismay. He doesn't like it. "A simple one, but yes."

He leans back in his chair, nodding slowly, before taking up his fork again. "I have no idea why you ever left."

"You like it?" I ask, sounding like he did when he wanted my reaction on the green room.

He takes another bite, chewing with a thoughtful expression. "I'm not saying I'd fire my private chef over it, but … yeah. It's good. Comforting."

I mock gasp. "Good? Comforting?" I hold a hand to my chest. "Such high praise. I'm honored."

He grins. "Don't get used to it, *amor*. At least it's edible."

"Edible?" I cry, secretly joyous that ge called me amor. He's also playing the part, I remind myself. He seems to really like it, because he's wolfing it down, and that makes me happy.

"Don't be so dramatic," he says, before stealing a bite from my plate.

BY THE END OF THE WEEK, DEXTER AND I HAVE FALLEN INTO some sort of routine. He's been out the last few evenings, and that disheartened me. I didn't question where he went but I didn't like being left alone.

Being with this man is like a roller-coaster ride, and I've resigned myself to the fate of just going along with it. Taking the highs and the lows, while somehow trying to be emotionally detached.

When Cari texts me asking me to come to The Living Room, the café where she's opened her little flower shop, I jump at the chance.

She greets me warmly as soon as she sees me. Too warmly, given that most of our interactions have been formal so far.

"I'm so glad you came," she says, ushering me over to a table. "I'm mostly at Jett's apartment now, and I know we're both in the same apartment block, but I thought it would be nice to catch up somewhere else, where it's just the two of us."

"I prefer this," I tell her, looking around. "This is a lovely place."

"Thank you."

I immediately fall in love with this place. It's filled with bookshelves and has a quiet and cozy ambiance. People around me are sitting and reading, and the scent of freshly brewed coffee fills the air. We sit at a table, drinking coffee and eating pastries and every so often Cari gets up and serves a customer.

"How long have you had it?" I ask her.

"Only a few months." She tells me how it came to be, and in the telling of her story, I find out about the tragic news about her mom, and how this flower shop came to be.

"I'm so sorry about your mom." I want to throw my arms around her and comfort her like I would Raquel, but I don't feel that we have that type of relationship. Not yet. Though I can already see that Cari is lovely and warm, and loyal. I'm glad she's here. Not just because it's good to have another woman in the Knight world, but because I could do with a friend.

"You okay?" she asks, when I fall silent.

I smile, keeping my voice light. "I'm fine. Actually, Cari, there's ... there's something I need to talk to you about."

"Oh?"

It's been weighing on my mind for a while now. Now that I'm a part of this family, whatever that means, I feel I owe her an explanation. "It's about ... the alliance" I say, tentatively. "This marriage of convenience."

She looks immediately concerned. "Are things okay, between you and Dex?"

I flap my hand dismissively. "Yes, that's all good." I feel like I'm starting to blush.

"Because that kiss, after that dance, at your wedding reception ..." Cari fans her face with her hand, signaling heat. "It was scorching hot! It looked *so real*. You're both such good actors." She lowers her voice and looks. "Because everyone in that room bought it. The romance, the sizzle, the passion. Even I did, and I know the truth."

I blink a few times, remembering that night. The memories come flooding back, but I push them away. It's not good to dwell on things that can never be. "I wanted to talk about Jett," I say. Cari looks puzzled. "Nothing ever happened. We never even got talking. We were never in touch. You've been so kind to me, so graceful, and many women in similar positions wouldn't have been, and I just wanted to explain things."

Cari's expression turns soft, her eyes fill with understanding. "You don't have to explain, Dani. May I call you Dani, or do you prefer Daniela?"

I smile. "Dani." I lean in. "I want to explain. I just need to say it. It was *never* romantic. It never even got off the ground. I never knew, neither did my father, that Jett and you were together—"

"It's not your fault," she rushes to console me. "Paul Knight pushed for that deal. Not Jett."

"Even so, with his father pushing, I just want you to know that Jett and I have never communicated. You both make such a lovely couple, and such a lovely family. I don't want any bad feelings between us."

She tucks her hair behind her ear, blushing. "Thank you. He makes me so happy. And Brooke. It all feels so natural, like it was meant to be. Please don't stress about the alliance. I know you had nothing to do with it." She smiles at me. "There are no bad feelings between us. I've been looking forward to being here," she says quietly. "How are things working out with you and Dex?"

How do I answer such a question? I don't even try. I flash a smile. "He's been working a lot, so ... I don't see him much."

I catch a flicker of surprise on her face, before she hides it.

"They're Knights. They like their legacy. They work a lot. I want to know about you. How are you finding it? It must be daunting being away from everything you're used to."

"It's not easy leaving my family and friends and my way of life as I knew it."

"It's a brave thing you're doing." She looks at me, but doesn't push.

"I'm doing it for my family …" I hesitate.

She reaches for my hand. "You don't have to tell me anything."

I nod. We talk about the wedding, about my life in Brazil, and, because it's so obvious, and hanging in the air, I tell her a little about the honeymoon. I mention how Dexter was busy working, and I was busy reading and relaxing. I don't talk about the kiss, or the hot tub, or how he's put distance between us now that we're back.

"Dex doesn't bite, even if he acts like he might," she says. "He can come across as rough around the edges, almost as if he doesn't care. I thought he was like that, but he's got such a good heart now that I'm getting to know him better."

I don't know why she's telling me this, why she thinks I need to hear it. But I appreciate it.

"I should go," I tell her. "I have something to finish before we wrap up for the weekend."

"You're working?"

"Yes. I deal with brand and strategy. Communications and all that, and luckily, I can work remotely. We can have meetings online. It hasn't proved to be a great disruption, so far."

"We'll have to get together again," she says, when I get up to leave.

"We will. I could do with a friend in this corner of the world."

She takes both my hands in hers and presses them lightly.

"You're not alone. If you need anything, or want to talk about anything, you just call me."

I hug her this time, because it feels right to do so. By the time I leave, I feel a little happier, and not so lonely anymore. I can always come down here if I need some female company. I step outside, pulling my coat tighter around me, as I wave down a cab.

Then, it happens.

A hand yanks at my bag, but I don't let go.

My adrenaline spikes sky high. I turn sharply, yanking back. A tall, built guy tries to pull me toward him, but I react fast, the way I was trained. My instincts kick in and I shove a sharp elbow to his ribs, I barely register my funny bone stinging with the impact, before I land him a powerful, well-placed at the perfect spot between his legs.

He grunts, staggering, but doesn't go down. Instead, he reacts violently, shoving me hard with one arm as he clutches himself with the other. I stumble backward, off balance, my face smacking the edge of a parked car's side mirror. Pain shoots across my mouth as metal grazes skin and I taste blood, sharp and metallic. A line of heat cuts across my upper lip, and I feel the sting, the warmth, and the wetness.

"Filho da puta," I mutter, wiping at the blood. But he's limping away. Defeated. Passersby gawk at me, and I stumble a few steps, my breath shaky, my heart pounding. At least my bag is still in my hands. He didn't get to take it.

I take a steadying breath, hailing a cab again, and when it comes, a few seconds later, I get in.

What I don't do is call Dexter.

DEX

· · ·

WHAT THE EVER-LOVING FUCK?

My wife has been attacked, and the only reason I find out is because Jett told me. And the only reason *he* found out is because Cari's customers were talking about a woman getting attacked outside the café. The description of the woman matched Daniela's, and Cari got worried. She called Daniela, but when she couldn't get ahold of her, she got extremely worried, and called Jett.

I rush home immediately when my calls to Daniela go unanswered. I pray it's not her, but it terrifies me all the same.

I slam the door open, pulse hammering, wondering what I'll find. Insidious thoughts have run rampant in my mind which fills with images of a battered Daniela.

When I charge into the living room, she looks up, startled. She's sitting on the couch, holding an ice pack to her swollen lip. My gaze locks on her face and my gut turns to steel when I see the blood.

It was her.

"Who the fuck hurt you?" My voice is sharp, too sharp, but I don't care. I rush to her side, my hands reaching for her face.

"How did you find out?" Surprise lights up her face, then disappears quickly.

"Cari's customers. She's been trying to get hold of you. I have, too."

"Sorry. I was in a meeting. I had my phone on mute and—"

She was in a *meeting*? After getting attacked? "Doesn't matter." My hands are already on her jaw, tilting her chin up and assessing the damage. "You should've called me." Her upper lip is cut badly. There's blood on the tissues scattered around her on the sofa.

"You didn't have to rush home for me, Dexter." Her tone is

light and casual. Like what happened to her is the most normal thing.

"Yeah, I did." She's in shock. My fingers brush her chin, and my thumb hovers to the side of her lip. Fuck. She has a cut, just on the upper lip. "He cut you."

"It's nothing," she whispers.

"It's not nothing."

"It looks worse than it is."

"That sonofabitch." My adrenaline spikes. She's my wife, and I wasn't even around to protect her. This happened on my watch, and it should never have. *Ever*. Whoever did this to my wife is going to pay. I'm ready to hunt the fucker down, but first I need to make sure Daniela's okay. I grimace at the sight of her beautiful lip, tracing my thumb gingerly over her cut, wanting to kiss it better. She winces and something deep in my chest tightens.

"I'm fine, Dexter. I handled it, I told you."

"Are you hurt anywhere else?"

She shakes her hand but my hand stays steady on her.

"Don't ever scare me like that again."

"I'll try not to." She giggles.

"It's not a laughing matter. You're the victim of a mugging."

"He didn't take anything."

"The fucker tried. Tell me what happened."

She does, reciting it like it's the most boring piece of news she has for me.

"Unfuckingbelievable." My blood boils. Daniela is my responsibility. She's my wife. I'm supposed to protect her and I let her down. "I'm sorry this happened to you."

"It's not your fault, Dexter. I'm not hurt."

"Your lip is cut. It's bleeding. You'll have a scar. I'll get my assistant to set up a meeting with a plastic surgeon tomorrow."

She roars with laughter. That same rich, vibrant laugh I've heard before. "You will do no such thing, Dexter. If this leaves a scar, I really don't care. I'll wear it like a badge of pride."

I shake my head, staring at her in disbelief, trying to understand her reaction. How this is no big deal to her.

It's a big fucking deal. My wife was attacked, and I was nowhere in sight. Rage courses through my veins and I feel the urge to punch the wall.

Daniela points to her lip. "This wasn't him. I hit the side of a car wing mirror. But you should see the guy." Her face lights up, like she's telling me a funny story. "I elbowed him in the ribs and kicked him between the legs." She looks gleeful, but it does nothing to assuage my guilt or worry. This could have been so much worse. Someone could have kidnapped her, stabbed her. Shot her.

"I failed you."

She dismisses my comment with a wave of her hand, and a giggle. "I'm a black belt in jiu-jitsu. I can take care of myself. You don't have to worry about me."

"You're my wife."

She sits up, blinking at me. As if my words don't make sense. We're husband and wife on paper, but right now, she's my wife for real. She's someone I care about.

"I'll be right back." I rush to get my first aid kit, then come back, with a sterile wipe with which I clean her wound gently. She watches me the entire time, saying nothing.

"You need a security detail," I mutter more to myself than to her. "I should have thought about this before." I've overlooked the most basic and most important thing of all. We all have bodyguards. They're discreet and invisible. We don't need all need our individual ones when we're together, like we were for the wedding in Brazil. But Daniela clearly needs her own detail for when she goes out.

I'm sure Jett must have provided something for Cari because people can get to us through those we love. I make a note to deal with this straightaway.

Of course, the news spreads. The police weren't involved, but the media picked it up because people recorded it and when they found out who Daniela was, my wife, the media outlets got interested.

My father calls, and he's livid. He has to answer to Daniela's parents. I do, too. Later that evening Jett, Cari, Brooke and Zach all come over, bearing flowers and chocolates and magazines for Daniela, who beams and looks so happy. She recites her ordeal all over again. Then Rio calls, and has a word with her and then he puts Matteo and Enzo on the line, too.

I'm a little overwhelmed by all this attention, and a part of me wonders if the Italian Knights are going along with the act, pretending we're all family and showing concern for Daniela who has married into it. She's an innocent bystander in this dysfunctional group related only by blood.

But maybe, despite everything, we are a family?

CHAPTER THIRTY

DANI

DEXTER IS MAKING SUCH A BIG DEAL ABOUT THE CUT ON MY
lip. I've looked in the mirror and while it's noticeable, it's no
big deal.

He thinks I need to go to the hospital, see a doctor,
maybe get a stitch or two. I assure him I'll be fine. He's
being too much. Too concerned. Too worried. Too
overprotective.

"You're beautiful. I just don't want you to have a scar."

He's trying so hard not to look like he cares, but I see it in
his eyes. I push back "You don't need to fuss over me so
much."

He gets up slowly, looking resigned. "It's up to you. Do
what you want." He sounds a little weary, like maybe I've
overdone the "I can take care of myself and don't need
anyone."

"I'm fine. The kick I gave—"

"Yes, you keep telling me how you dealt with the guy. I

want to find the fucker. I want to find him and kick the shit out of him."

I reach out, touching his arm. He's rigid, tension twisting under his skin, anger coursing through his veins. "Don't do that. Please don't do that."

His jaw tightens, but I see something in his eyes. Something that softens my heart and makes me think he really cares for me. Or is he like this with everyone, because he's rough and rugged, and a protector by nature?

Is this just who he is? Or is this because I'm his wife?

"I hate that you got hurt," he mutters. "You're my responsibility."

"I can take care of myself."

"Yeah, you keep saying that. I understand that you can take care of yourself, but you're my wife."

This constant referral to me being his wife makes me sit up. "In name only," I say, keeping my tone light and teasing.

"You said it, Daniela. In name only." His jaw hardens.

"We're not husband and wife, Dexter. We don't do the things husbands and wives do." I don't like goading him unnecessarily, but I sense he feels things, even if he won't admit it. He'll be running scared for the next eleven months. I can see it, lingering just beneath the surface, that he cares for me. I need to know how deep that goes.

His eyes snap to mine. I want to break down his barriers. I want to talk to him. I want to delve into all the things he buries and the things that hurt him. I want to reach into that shell where he keeps them all locked away. If only he'd let me.

Later that night, he comes into my room. Checking on me. Watching over me.

"What are you doing, Dexter?" I ask, still half-asleep. I wake up for maybe the third time that night to find him bent over by my bed, stroking my forehead.

"Checking to see that you're not concussed or anything."

"I'm not. Now please, leave me alone so I can sleep."

He slowly straightens and walks towards the door. "We can sleep in the same bed if you want."

My eyelids fly wide open. "Will you come into my room, or shall I go to yours?"

"Any way you want." He stands there, hovering in my doorway like a skulking beast. A man who'd kill anyone who dared to hurt me again.

I turn on the bedside lamp and wipe my hands over my face. His eyes falls to my skimpy satin tank top. Without even looking down I know my nipples have peaked. He sees it, too, because he shoves his hands in his pockets and looks away quickly.

"You want me to sleep with you?" I ask, having fun with the innuendo. This man is so guarded and emotionally shutdown, but a little light flirting might just coax him into opening up.

"I want to protect you."

My fickle little heart lights up. *So you do care? You do have feelings for me.* But I don't say what I'm thinking, because I've learned my lesson. I won't assume anything. I won't lay my emotions bare. I try a different tactic. "You think you can protect me by sleeping with me?"

"Sharing the same bed, Daniela. There's a difference."

I sit up taller, rest my back against the soft headboard, watch his eyes drop to my breasts. "The mugger, or kidnapper, or beast, or mythical scary monster, isn't going to break into this apartment and do anything to me, so, please go to sleep, in your bed, and leave me to sleep peacefully in mine."

He drags his gaze away, mutters a "Good night," and leaves.

But the next day, and for the few days after that, he doesn't go to work. Instead, he stays at home with me, pacing around like some caged predator, prowling, checking on me constantly.

On the third day of him being at home. I can't focus with him skulking around, watching me like I might fall apart at any second. "Dexter, if you don't go to work, I will. And I'll do it from the coffee shop where Cari has her flower stand. Near where I got mugged," I add, for emphasis.

"Not happening." Then he casually announces that he's assigned a security detail to me for whenever I leave the apartment.

I sigh. "Then, I'm safe, and you can go to work again. We need to go about our lives as normal, remember? We're married on paper only."

It kills me to say it because I'm beginning to get used to this, living with him. Leaving at the end of the year will break my heart.

"I just wanted to be around in case you needed anything. Like, for me to heat you your lunch, or get you a coffee."

"I appreciate that. You really are a sweet and thoughtful man, even though you try to show the world that you're a heartless beast, but I don't need to be fussed over."

"Fine. Have it your way."

He backs away from the door, and I finally get an inkling of the thickness of his steel walls, the ones that guard his heart and emotions. Maybe he's scared that I'm going to start talking about his past, somehow weave it into our conversation, if he stays here.

He's like a changed man. Soft and caring, and he wants so much to be here for me. To take care of me. Snippets from our earlier conversations keep coming back. I like him being like this. He's got a good heart. But he's also the man who doesn't commit. Who likes sex. Who has hookups instead of relationships.

What if he's so caring and devoted to me just because his

last girlfriend is out of the country? What if he has plans to get back with her once our year is up?

Forget what if. He probably will. And where will that leave me?

This man has many dimensions, many faces. The last thing I want is to get used to the good Dexter.

Thankfully, he goes to work the next day.

I haven't told my parents about what happened. Dexter said his father was going to call them and explain, and he would have as well, but the news hasn't broken in the press over there.

But here? It's a different story.

Photos were taken at the scene. People recorded the assault on their phones, then leaked them to the press.. Someone snapped a shot of me mid-kick, taking down the guy and from that they were able to get the guy and arrest him. I feel better that he's been found.

BEFORE WE KNOW IT, THE DAY OF THE CHARITY GALA SNEAKS up on us.

"We don't have to go, if you're not up for it," Dexter says. He's standing in the doorway, watching me hanging up the dress I plan to wear tonight.

"Your father expects us to."

"I don't care about that. You were attacked and—"

"That was a week ago, and I took care of it! I hope you're not planning on doing anything stupid now that they've found him."

He exhales sharply. "The old man told me to stay away. He said it'd be bad for our reputation if I kicked the shit out of him."

"He talks sense."

"Sometimes. We don't have to go to this," he says again.

I trace a finger over my lip. The cut has scabbed over, and with enough concealer, I can attempt to cover it a little. "I can go."

"Fine. If you're up to it. We should get dressed then." It sounds to me like he doesn't want to go. "That's a nice dress." He eyes my outfit that I've laid out on the bed for longer than seems normal. "Huge slit on the side."

"You disapprove?"

"Not at all. You wear what you want. I just meant that you'll look gorgeous, and sexy."

My chest flutters. I shouldn't let it mean anything. We're not supposed to flirt or say anything that might hint at how we really feel, not after everything that's happened, but the way he says it, like the words escaped his pride to reach me, makes it impossible not to smile. I file his compliment away in a quiet corner of my mind to dissect and replay later, when I lie in bed wishing things were different.

He's become possessive since this incident happened, but looking at him, I think I detect a hint of jealousy. I don't understand it. He's got no one to be jealous of.

"I thought this slit might distract from my war wound."

He grins, his gaze so soft and reminding me how much I love basking in his full attention. "You wear that dress, sweetheart. The old man said we needed to make a splash, and you in that … you're making a splash."

"Okay." I try not to look as despondent as I suddenly feel. His 'sweetheart' takes away from his compliment and reminds me that this is just an act. Instead, I smooth my hand over my deep emerald-green color, cut from slinky silk which clings to my body. It has a plunging neckline which hints more than it reveals, and I especially like the spaghetti straps that cross over my back. It's revealing in a way that the black sequined dress I wore that when we met wasn't. The night Paul Knight summoned me to a soiree at his penthouse. The night I met the Knight family. The night my fate with Dexter was sealed.

"I've got just the thing for it." He disappears. I frown. He's been acting strangely ever since I got mugged. Overly tender and concerned, to the point that it leaves me feeling flustered sometimes.

"Here." He reappears, holding a bright blue Tiffany box.

"What's that?" I peer at it, then at him.

"Open it." I step closer, heart in my throat, because while fussing over me is one thing, buying me jewellery, Tiffany & Co jewellery, says something else. I tentatively open the box and gasp in complete shock. Inside are a pair of the most beautiful emerald-cut drop earrings and a fine platinum chain with a single emerald pendant. It's simple and elegant, just how I like it.

I gape up at him. "Dexter ... you didn't have to."

"Do you like them?"

I nod, overcome with emotion. "How did you know that I was going to wear this?" But then I remember. He asked me last week what I was going to wear to the gala, when he told me we had to make an impression and make people believe we were madly in love. "I love them. Thank you." I'm beyond touched by his thoughtfulness.

"It's nothing."

I hate how quickly and casually he says it. "It's not nothing. This is *everything*." Our gazes lock and we stay like that for a beat. Words rise up on the tip of my tongue. A burst of bittersweet emotions wrap around my heart.

"Let's get ready and make a splash," he says, pushing away from the door and leaving.

It feels like he can't get away fast enough.

I TAKE MY TIME GETTING DRESSED.

With my makeup done, and my hair up, I slip on the necklace and earrings. When I step out of my bedroom. Dexter is already waiting, standing outside my door like some kind of sentinel.

Except he's not.

He's my husband. And he looks breathtakingly handsome in a tuxedo. His gaze drags over me, dropping to my ears, my neck, then all the way down and back up again.

"You look devastatingly beautiful. Almost regal," he murmurs.

"Thank you. You look devastatingly, unforgettably, handsome. Like you're about to break a million hearts."

"The only heart I ever think about, is yours."

His words hit me hard, like a secret he didn't mean to say out loud. I don't dare to breathe, but time slows down and in this precious moment all I'm aware of is his voice, his eyes, and the way those words imprint themselves on me like a promise I need him to make. Listening to him almost like he's rambling to himself, I see admiration in his eyes.

"You're made for this life, Daniela."

Don't fall for it.

I remind myself that he's playing a part, and this is the rehearsal before we step into New York's high society and dupe them.

"A pretend wife?" I say, with some difficulty. Because nothing feels fake anymore. He fixes me with a heated stare and something in my belly does somersaults. I think he's about to say something, but he doesn't. It hasn't been easy being around him lately. We keep our conversations neutral, not venturing into those areas which might lead us to talk about our feelings. We sometimes eat together. Once or twice he's come home late after meetings. The weekdays are easier to navigate. The weekends not so much.

We try to stay out of each other's way, but the simmering tension between us amplifies a hundredfold sometimes. I go to bed feeling aroused, and I lie there wondering if he's aroused and thinking of me at all.

This is how the past few weeks have been like and there are days when I don't think I can survive a year like this.

Now this. Stepping out into the limelight, both dressed up and looking our best. Tonight we'll have to put on a show for everyone.

It's going to be impossibly difficult.

WE GET OUT OF THE SLEEK CHAUFFEURED LIMO.

There are crowds here, held back by barricades. A strong police presence. Cameras everywhere, and people yelling out for Dexter, and for me. I'm surprised they know my name. Dexter leans in, slipping his arm around my waist. "You're famous on account of your mugging." His lips brush close to my ear, his breath warm against my skin.

To anyone watching, it looks intimate. Natural. Real.

To me, I wish it were real.

I smile and try not to shiver as the scent of his cologne intoxicates my senses.

"You look more breathtaking with every passing minute," he says, making my breath catch. That's when I feel it again. That spark. That heat. What he did to me in the hot tub.

"You're a really good actor, darling," I whisper close in his ear. So close, my lip grazes his earlobe. All around us, the lights dazzles magnificently. A sea of lightbulbs explodes. Dark eyes stare down at me. Steady, and sure. "Who says I'm acting?"

A firework explodes in my chest. I don't have time to fully process his words because he grabs my hand and leads me into a plush hotel. Shimmering crystal chandeliers hang majestically above us, and marble floors echo with the sound of my heels. Thankfully, we've left the chaotic madness of the press and paparazzi behind us.

As I look around me, I'm aware that this world, Dexter's world, is all about power, about perception. And tonight, we are the performance.

We play our roles perfectly. Smiling at people. Mingling. He strokes my arm, keeps a constant touch on me, reminding everyone, reminding me, that we belong together.

That I belong to him.

That I am Mrs. Knight.

We work the room well, and I forget the blur of faces and the names in so many introductions. Cari finds me and we hug and talk. She fusses over me, asking how I'm doing and we make plans to meet up again. Dexter is pulled away but Rio approaches and Cari excuses herself, saying she needs the restroom.

Rio grins, leaning in. "You're a badass, you know that?"

I laugh. "So I'm told."

"You really are. You have a reputation and now you've given the Knights some street cred."

"Is that a compliment?"

"I'd take it as one." He coughs lightly. "I hear Dexter's been fussing over you."

"Too much. I had to tell him to go to work, he was fussing so much it was starting to grate on my nerves."

Rio throws his head back, a rich laugh spilling from him. "I had a feeling something like that might happen." The way he says it, his voice laced with something cryptic, makes me wonder if these two have been talking about me.

Something cold and heavy lands in my stomach. All I really want is for my husband to talk to *me*.

DEX

WE'RE SURROUNDED BY NEW YORK'S ELITE. BILLIONAIRES, politicians, models draped over aging tycoons like expensive accessories. The usual.

The gala is a performance orchestrated by the old man. He's here and so are my brothers, Jett and Zach, and the Italian Knights. Everything about tonight, the cameras, the whispers, the knowing looks and tender touches, is a perfect PR stunt, courtesy of Paul Knight.

It's his way of controlling the narrative. In his world the Knights don't marry for love. They marry for power.

And I married Daniela.

But lately, every time I look at her, there's a constant battle between my mind and my heart. I want her, but I can't have her. I need her, but I will be the end of her. I pull her to my side, keeping my hand on the small of her back, a proprietary touch as we work the room. She's good at this, like she was born for it, all soft smiles and polite nods, accepting congratulations on our marriage as if it were real.

And maybe it is.

Maybe it was when she shuddered beneath me, when her body arched, when my name fell from her lips in breathless, broken gasps.

I don't know what's real and what isn't anymore.

What I do know is that I hate this. The performance. The pretending. The way she's here but not really with me.

Now that we're living together, there have been many moments when she looks at me and everything blurs and slides to the background. Sometimes I almost forget we're pretending. Especially when she got hurt. I was ready to do some serious damage to the fucker who hurt her, but I've been warned by the old man, and Daniela, to refrain.

She still thinks it's funny and she laughs about it because she fought him off. I'd be lying if I said I wasn't impressed that she held her own, but some men can be dangerous.

If he'd had a knife, or a gun, it could have been a different story; one I don't want to think about. I didn't sleep the first night it happened, worrying about what might have been. Daniela thinks I fussed too much, but it would kill me if anything happened to her.

Cari comes up to us, just as someone beckons me over. I leave, telling Daniela I'll be back shortly. But even as I converse with a business acquaintance, my eyes are on my wife. She's not just beautiful. This woman is temptation wrapped in silk and I look away, because I want her.

I want her with me. I want her to be mine, the hypocrite that I am. I'm the one who told her we can't get close. I look away, to catch my breath. To calm myself down. To tamp down the feelings I have for her. When I next look over, when I can't help myself, I see her and Rio standing in a corner, away from everyone else. They seem comfortable in a way that makes my skin itch. She's leaning into him, her body turned toward him, her smile relaxed and soft. He's beside her, drink in hand, his usual lazy grin firmly in place. Whatever the hell he just said made her laugh.

He's looking at her the way I do.

Like he wants her.

Like he could have her.

My grip tightens around my glass and my jaw locks. I tell myself it's nothing. That I don't care, and I force myself to walk away before I do something reckless. When we leave, I can't bring myself to look at her, or talk to her. She senses it, because from the periphery of my vision I can see her looking at me every now and then as the car glides back to our apartment.

The second we step inside, the tension snaps.

I throw my keys onto the console table, and loosen my tie. My pulse is still hammering, my blood still running hot, and it has nothing to do with the whiskey. I can't control my rage anymore and storm into her bedroom. "What the hell was that?"

She turns, her large green eyes blinking. "What?"

I stalk toward her. "You and Rio."

She lets out a short laugh, crossing her arms. "Are you serious?"

"You were all over him."

Her mouth falls open. "Excuse me?"

I take another step, closing the space between us. "You laughed with him. You leaned into him. You—"

"Careful, Dexter, before you say something stupid."

Her words are like a red flag to a bull. "What the fuck was that?"

"I'm sorry." Her voice drips with sarcasm. "I didn't know I had to ask your permission to have a conversation, especially with your brother of all people."

My hands fist by my sides. "Daniela—"

"No." She waggles a sleek finger at me. "You don't get to do this." Her voice rises, sharp with anger. "You don't get to treat me like a possession when you've spent weeks pushing me away."

I clench my jaw, my chest rising and falling too fast. "I haven't—"

"Yes, you have," she hisses. "You hold me close when people are watching, but the second we're alone, you shut me out. You act like I'm nothing, and then you act like I'm yours. Which is it, Dexter?"

My pulse pounds. My vision tunnels. A charged silence fills the air between us. "You think I don't want you?" My voice is hoarse, uneven.

She stills, her breath catching. "I think you don't know what you want."

My last thread of restraint snaps. It's been hell, trying to not think of her. Days and nights of tensions, unspoken words, pushing and pulling until neither of us knows what's right and what's wrong. What we can do and what we mustn't.

I can't take it anymore. I grab her face, my fingers tangling in her hair, backing her up against the nearest wall. She meets me with fire, her hands shoving at my chest before fisting my shirt, dragging me closer instead of pushing me away. Her nails dig into my arm, as my body presses flush against hers.

She pants, mouth open, tilting her chin up, I can't help but crush my mouth to hers. She gasps, but I don't give her a chance to argue, to resist, to do anything but feel this the way I do.

This is everything. Heat colliding with frustration, possession taking over. I'm on her, kissing and ravaging, taking what's already mine. She matches my fervor, her hands working my jacket off my shoulders. She can't quite pull it down, so I do it for her. Then she works the buttons of my shirt, and I try to figure out how to get her out of her dress. I need her naked, I need to feel her, because this is all I've dreamed about. Touching her, tasting her, fucking her.

My hunger unleashes in a torrent of heat and I drop fevered kisses along her jaw and neck, along her shoulders. I kiss and nip, and drag my mouth across her skin. She moans, low and gentle, and when my hand palms her breast, a guttural groan falls from her lips.

I can't be gentle. Not tonight. I'm a desperate man who's been starving for her, and now I need urgent release.

"You want to know what I want?" I murmur lifting my face, dragging my hands down the curves of her body. "I want you ... all of you." I frantically search for the zipper, grow frustrated when I can't find it.

"It's at the back," she murmurs. I turn her around, and see the hidden culprit at base of her neck. I try to drag it down, but the fucker is stuck, and my patience has gone.

"Jeez," I mutter, then I just bunch up her dress. It's easy to bunch up because of the huge slit on one side. I lift it as high as I can, just above her lower back.

"Better," I rasp, pulling her back against me, needing to feel her naked against me. My hands run over her body. She's wearing the tiniest thong, and the sight of her beautifully rounded bottom, naked save for a wisp of string, elicits a grunt from me.

I need to fuck her, and I need to fuck her *now*.

My hands run all over her, sliding across her front like a horny dimpled teenager who's never seen a half-naked woman before. I touch and explore whatever I can of her. Her nipples are peaked and perfect, but still covered by the dress.

My hands dip down and I claim her pussy, find her soaking, swollen lips. My fingers sink in and she arches against me, sighing with contentment. I dip in a finger, then another, my cock hardening even more. She's drenched, and ready. My tongue moistens in preparation, and I almost drop to my knees, wanting to taste her, to push her legs wide apart and feast on her. But she arches against me again, her back to my chest, pushing her soft, silky buttocks against my cock.

I lose it.

"Face down on the bed, Daniela. I need to fuck you."

There's no hesitation. She climbs on the bed eagerly gets on all fours, face down, bottom up. A beautiful sight that makes me salivate. Makes my cock strain against my pants. Her silk dress falls over one side, and I stare temptation in the face, barely able to hold back.

CHAPTER THIRTY-ONE

DANI

I need Dexter inside me.

So when he orders me to get on the bed, face down, I obey, then wait with bated breath, a hot, aching pull between my thighs.

"Ready for me, Gatinha?" His gravelly voice reaches deep inside me. I brace myself, face down on the bed, goosebumps prickling all over my skin as he massages the small of my back. I lean down on my elbows, quiver with shock when he runs his hand over my behind, his fingers slowly lingering over my flesh.

Then I feel it. The hot, wet tip of his cock against my silkiness.

"Meu Deus," I gasp.

His face is close to my ear. "May I?" His lips brush my ear, his hot breath kissing my cheek.

"May you, what?" I pant, trying to hold it together. As

desperate as I am for him, I'm not sure if this is one of his little tricks. To test me. To see if I'll give in first.

"May I fuck you."

"Yes." I grind out a moan as he rubs his tip over me, tempting me, teasing me. When he won't push in, like I'm desperate for him to, I writhe against him, pressing back, trying to capture an inch of his cock, something, anything. He slides his steel hardness up and down, like he's marking his territory. "Tell me you want me."

Quivering with want, my brain fogs over. I'm soaking and wanton with need. The logical part of my brain has vanished, and it's not conversation I need right now, but this man insists on making me wait. "I want you, Dexter." His fingers reach between my folds, slipping, and sliding, making me whimper and mewl, as he starts to fill me. First one, then another, and another. I feel full, stretched, and grind out a sigh, bucking backwards, savoring the sensation.

"You're soaking wet for me, amor."

I sigh again as his fingers work their magic. His fingers glide in and out, and I chew my lip, trying not to hold on, trying not to come. Filthy sighs, wild and feral, fall from my lips.

"Ready for me, amor?"

"Y-yes." I buck against him, feeling myself on the edge, but his fingers still.

"Not yet, amor. Hold …"

"I need your cock."

He leans over, his skin hot where it brushes my back. He nips my earlobe gently. "I'm big, amor."

"Then I want you now."

"I don't want to hurt you." His thumb glides over my nub, and I shudder as he plays with me, rubbing my clit. Pleasure lances through me. My knees turn boneless.

"Nice and wet ..." he rasps. "You're ready for me now, amor."

I grunt out a reply, unable to speak because my insides are pure heat and liquid. My nipples are taut under the dress. I shift my hips, lifting my bottom higher, presenting myself for the taking. I need him inside me. I need him like I need air.

He gives me another nip on my earlobe.

"Please," I beg."

He moves away, and for the life of me I can't work out why he's waiting. But then I hear the rip of a foil, and I know what he's doing.

Then, his hands bracket my hips, and I smile in anticipation as he nudges my opening. It's delicious. Heavenly. The thought of what is to come. I cry out when he pushes inside me. One hard, fast thrust.

"Sorry," he whispers. "I should have gone slow." He stills inside me, and all I can do is pant. I feel the sting, a frisson of pain as my pussy fits around his cock like a glove. When he tweaks my clit, I mewl like a contented little kitten. Waves of pleasure start to build, and I savor the feel of him, stretching me, filling me up.

I try to buck against him, willing him to move, to thrust in and out, but he stays still while my arousal heightens, and I wait with slow growing irritation. He fists his hand into my hair, then kisses the back of my neck, along my shoulder blade, raining gently little kisses over my heated skin.

My eyes haze over. I feel full with him inside me, but I need friction of movement. I want him to fuck me, hard. And I need it now. The release of months of frustration. He pulls out slowly, and I sigh, heat coiling inside me. Just as I enjoy this pleasure, he drives in, hard and brutal. It feels sublime, and I cry out, my face falling onto the bed as I whimper. He parts my butt cheeks, then pulls my hips higher as he pistons in and out.

Each thrust jolts my body, and I sink into a state of ecstasy as he sets up a rhythm that will have me coming in no time. My senses are heightened, my heart thundering inside me, blood racing through my veins, my skin hot and sticky. The slopping wet sound as his cock slams into me.

"Dexter." I can barely talk. Can barely breathe. His name is all that falls from my lips.

"You feel fucking divine," he groans, slapping into me, then holding for a few seconds before pulling out. With each thrust I move closer to the precipice. To the edge from where I will fall. He reaches for my breast, curses when he can't feel the nakedness, only the silk fabric of the dress. "Need you naked."

"You ... should ... have ...unzipped me ..." He's driving so fast and hard, I feel my orgasm rising.

"Your pussy is so wet and soft." He pounds away, his balls slapping against me. I feel it building to a peak, and then, a wave rips through me, consuming me, taking me under. I lose myself in it, crying out, unraveling completely, my body loose and boneless. Dexter still thrusts in and out of me, until he comes, too, panting and huffing behind me, his hands still on my hips as he grunts his satisfaction. I rest my cheek against the sheets, wait for my body to come back down to earth.

"That was fucking ... intense." His breath is ragged, as if he's run ten miles. Pulling out of me, he falls onto his back, and I turn onto my back, too, my breathing uneven. The room fills with the sound of our breaths trying to calm down. After a few moments, he sits up and takes care of his condom, before lying beside me again.

I try to shimmy my dress down, try to cover my nakedness, but he takes my hand. "Leave it. I want to see you naked."

So I leave it. His hand entwines into mine, and I feel complete.

"I've been wanting to do that ever since we left for the gala," he confesses.

"Just the gala?" I turn to him, saddened that it only happened for him now.

"Ever since I saw you in that dress, all I wanted to do was take it off." His eyes assess my reaction, like he's waiting to see if I'll recoil, or not. He turns to his side, so that we're facing one another, and his finger strokes my cheek. Dark, hooded eyes, staring at me. "I've been wanting to fuck you ever since the first night on our honeymoon. Hell, ever since the night of our wedding day."

I smile. He felt it too, the sparks between us. As if reading my mind, he says, "Even though I wanted to, I knew we couldn't, so I did my best to block you out."

I give his hand a squeeze. "It took Rio to push you over the edge," I tease, playing with fire. Knowing that this is what riles him up, I should back down, but I don't. I want him inside me again. I want him to be jealous and crazy for me. I need the intimacy we just had. I need all of him.

"Rio's got someone else in mind, I think." He runs his finger over my breasts. My nipples poke through the silk fabric, and he rubs his thumb over them, making them peak more. As if he's entertained by the cause and effect of his actions, he keeps doing it, and I like it, so I lie back and enjoy the sweet thrum of pleasure that sweeps over me again when I've barely recovered.

He sighs. "I'm tired." Then lays down again on his back again. The room is dark, save for my bedside lamp which comes on as automatically when the light is dim.

I wonder how long he'll stay here, in my room, how long we'll lie like this. I decide not to ask any questions, and try to savor this moment with him. I turn on my side, then rest my head against his chest, move my hand along it. I feel his strong and steady heartbeat beneath my palm.

It's quiet, and only our breathing can be heard.

"I don't know how to love someone," he suddenly says. This room, this moment feels ripe for secrets, for a confession. My ears immediately go on high alert, because this is rare, Dexter offering something about himself. "It's because I'm unlovable," he says, his voice low, barely more than a whisper.

My eyes widen at him talking about love. He didn't have to tell me that. He chose to open up, to share a part of himself he's probably never given anyone. That means something.

"You're not unlovable, Dexter," I say softly, looking down at his sad, thoughtful face. "You're not some monster who needs to be alone. You deserve love. You deserve everything."

He closes his eyes, then turns his face into my hand, and sighs like it's giving him comfort. "You barely know me," he whispers. "If you did, if you knew the darkness in me, you wouldn't want to be with me. And I … I wouldn't blame you."

I let out a heavy exhale, but keep my hand on his cheek so he can't look away. "You think I don't see you? I see you, Dexter, as much as you let anyone see you. I know you put up a tough exterior, because you want people to think you don't care, but I see you. I know you're kind, and thoughtful and caring when you drop your guard. I know you blame yourself for things no one could control. I know you spend every day convinced that if you care about someone, they're doomed." My voice softens. "I know you're scared, Dexter. But I'm not going to break if you care about me. And I won't break you."

My eyes fill with tears, and in the blur, I see him studying me, anguish battling with hope in his expression.

"I don't know how," he confesses. "I don't know how to be with someone, not just to enjoy their body, but to really be there for them. Unless it's just sex, it feels like I'm putting their life at risk. It sounds insane—"

"It's not insane," I cut in. "It's trauma. It's understandable, but you can't let it rule you forever."

I feel him pulling back emotionally, retreating behind that wall of guilt. Panic rears its ugly head in my chest at the thought that I'm losing him again, when I've only just gotten him back. "You're not alone." My voice is hoarse but resolute. "Don't walk away from me again. Don't leave me waiting and wanting you, like the last time."

He takes my hand in his, but says nothing.

"I can help you. We can work through this together," I tell him.

His eyes soften and he nods. And my insides turn all warm and fuzzy. There is a way to keep this man, to show him that his fears are what keep him away from people. I want him to see that he doesn't have to live that way.

I'm starting to understand now why most of his relationships have been arrangements. Friends with benefits. No strings. No mess. No entanglements.

I flinch at the idea of him with someone else. But I get it. I understand this man whose walls are high, whose heart is hidden. He doesn't allow emotions or feelings to get in the way. Running my fingers slowly across his chest, I trace invisible lines over his warm skin.

And now I feel torn, and wonder if I should tell him the truth, about my father's business not being as great as Paul Knight thinks it is. It's also not *that* bad. Besides, Paul will have had ample time and opportunity going around the offices with my father. He would have snooped around and found out the extent of it all. I decide not to say anything to spoil the moment. Dexter and I are just opening up to one another, and I can't risk doing anything which will push my husband away.

My husband.

The words feel so right on my tongue, in my heart. I love how we are now, like this, lying entwined in one another in bed, tangled in his sheets, bare and close. I feel warm and safe in his arms, like I belong here. He's also not rushing to leave. He's not pulling away. Instead, he lingers.

"Is this a friends-with-benefits type of relationship?" I ask, needing confirmation, but also preparing myself that if it is, I'll take it, if that's all he can offer.

He sits up. Brows pushed together more than I've ever seen them. "What the fuck, Daniela?"

I sit up, fearing I've ruined the night. "You're my wife. *My wife*. You're so much more, can't you see that?" His fingers stroke my cheek, and my heart fills like a balloon. "I'm lucky to have you. I don't care about the contract. I just care about this, you, me, now." He takes my hand and kisses it. This was supposed to be just an alliance, but it has grown into something much more.

"What do you say, wife?" he asks, when I stare at him still speechless, but happy. This man has changed since I first met him. This Dexter was always there, hiding under the mask of the grumpy and distant Dexter I first met.

I feel blissfully happy. "I think you're overusing that word."

He moves closer then chuckles near my mouth, his lips brushing mine. "I haven't had a chance to say it like I meant it before, and now I do."

My heart does little cartwheels inside my chest as he kisses me, softly, cupping my face, his thumb brushing the side of my cheek. His tongue sweeps in and makes my brain fog over, rendering me incapable of thought. A fire burns low in my belly and my body gets ready for more. More sex. More intimacy. More secrets and sweat. "I don't think I can ever spend a night alone in my bed after tonight."

"You won't," he promises. "Come sleep in my bed."

"Your bed?" I tease, raising a brow. "What's wrong with my bed?"

He leans in, brushing my cheek with his fingertips. "Our bed, Daniela." His voice is husky and low. His hand skates along my waist, fingers splayed, possessive yet gentle. "I want you in my bed, *wife*."

A surge of excitement explodes inside me, warmth flooding through my chest like a thousand tiny ripples. I blink up at him, breath catching. We move off the bed, and make our way, kissing and hugging, and this time I tug at the zipper of my dress, hard to reach behind my back and so cleverly hidden. Hard to undo. Between us, between kissing and touching, we manage to unzip it. It pools like jade at my ankles, only now, we're in his room.

The master bedroom.

The energy here is different. Slightly colder. The air is fresher. He turns on his bedside lamp, his heated gaze moving slowly over my body like he's seeing it for the first time. Like he's appreciating it. I don't need to be told. I already know what I want. I hop onto the bed, and wait, lying on my back, my arms crossed lazily behind my head.

He joins me, his mouth immediately latching to my breast which he suckles hungrily, feral noises falling from his lips, as he tends to each one carefully. This man takes pleasure from me and gives me so much back. I arch my back, ready again.

"This time I don't want to fuck. I want to make love to you," he says, in between sucking.

And just like that, mouth still latched to my breast, he positions himself between my legs, taking turns to squeeze my nipples as he kisses me slowly, languorously. I feel so loved. So taken care of. So wanted.

We're skin to skin with nothing between us. I wrap my legs around his waist, caging him against me. He presses his forehead to mine, dark eyes fixed on me as our breaths mingle and he positions his cock at my opening.

A sigh falls from my throat as he slowly inches inside me, stretching my pussy so perfectly as I accommodate his hardness. I should be used to him, but my body is still adjusting to his size. He stills, buried to the hilt, and for a heartbeat neither of us moves. My walls clench around his thickness, slowly getting used to the intrusion, a mix of pain and overwhelming pleasure stealing my breath.

"Daniela," Dexter groans, voice strained. "You feel so perfect. This pussy … this pussy was made for me." He chokes out the words like they scare him, then pulls back and slams into me again. He finds a punishing rhythm, my entire body shaking with each powerful thrust. I moan and mewl, arching my back, letting him suckle, in between thrusts.

"Don't stop," I beg, gasping into his mouth, only to meet his tongue, delving in and out of my mouth just as his cock slides in and out of my pussy. A delicious combination that ignites something raw and desperate inside me. I feel so connected to him. It's hard to tell where my body ends and his begins. It's rhythmic, perfect and divine. My arms slide around his neck and I cling to him.

"I never want to leave your pussy." He looks down at me, eyes glistening, watching my reaction as he pumps me. My mouth falls open, because he moves slowly, and I relish the sweet friction that inches me to the edge again.

"You're never leaving this bed," he rasps. When I don't reply, he presses, "Are you?"

"I'm not." I being to pant, feeling my orgasm start to climb again.

"You're not what?" He studies me carefully, awaiting an answer. This man has so much stamina. I can barely think, but he's moving, shifting above me, fucking me slowly and it is the most fulfilling feeling. I never want it to end.

"I'm never … leaving … this … bed."

He thrusts into me like he can't get deep enough, like he wants to fuse us into one. And I want it. I want him to consume me, to claim me and ruin me.

My pulse begins to skyrocket again, pleasure coiling tight and urgent. I shouldn't be able to come again so soon, but the way he's pounding away, hitting a sweet spot deep inside, has lights flashing behind my eyes.

I'm already there. "Dexter…" I moan his name like a plea and a warning. I'm falling apart as he slams into me, driving me over that edge again.

His hand snakes between us, his fingers find my throbbing clit. He rubs hard, sending me hurtling into oblivion. I come with a cry, nails digging into his shoulders, my entire body clenching wildly around his cock.

"Fuck! Daniela—" He bites out my name, thrusting once, twice, before he loses himself with a raw groan. He comes, his release hot and pulsing deep in my core, spilling into me in the most primal way. Ripples of shock flood through me, but then, suddenly and without warning, he pulls out, streaks of cum shoot over my breasts and stomach. "I forgot to wear a condom. Shit." He looks at me, worry filling his eyes. "I tried not to come inside you, but I might have, a little."

I blink, trying to think through the haze.

"I'm sorry." He grabs the edge of the duvet and starts to wipe away the cum from my body. I do some mental math. Then I grab his hand and sit up, to console him. "It's okay. It's going to be okay. I just finished my period two days ago. We're in the safe zone."

It still doesn't stop him from looking worried.

"And ... I haven't had sex in over a year," I continue, "I'm not on the pill but he used protection." In case he was worried about that.

He pulls back in disgust. "I don't want to picture you having sex with anyone else."

"I was just telling you about my last boyfriend—"

He shakes his head, his face stony. "I'm the only one who gets to be with you."

The intensity and anger in his voice secretly thrills me. "I only told you because I don't want you to worry about me giving you anything." He stares at me, like he's about to say something. "But you," I press, "With your hookups. Are *you* clean?"

"This is a very clinical conversation to be having after the hot sex we just had. But to put your mind at rest, I got checked before we got married," he confesses, sitting back, leaning against the headboard.

"Why?" I'm puzzled. "On account of what? You said we weren't to get involved. Or where you hoping to?"

"I'm sorry." He looks sheepish, sitting up, sinking back against the headboard. "I wasn't sure if after our that night at the hotel, when we got talking, when we had to convince your friend Raquel, I wasn't sure if we might just want to ..."

"Have a hookup?"

He looks pained. "Not a hookup, Daniela." He cups my face. "I thought we had incredible chemistry, and I wanted to be prepared in case something happened between us."

"It almost did, that night in the hot tub. You're the one who walked away," I remind him.

"I couldn't stay."

"Why?"

"Because you're different. Feelings got involved. You

started to mean something to me. More than I wanted. Hookups are just about fucking. No emotions. Sometimes not even conversation."

I frown, but a sadness settles over me, and the thought of this man, so cold and closed off, craving human interaction, having bodily needs, but pushing away from real human connection.

There's a quiet pause, just the sound of our breathing, our skin cooling.

"This isn't pure, carnal, base fucking?" I ask, my hand reaching for his cock. My fingers close around it and I start to stroke. We're naked, no sheets covering us, sitting up in bed, feeling comfortable.

"I'm in love with you, Daniela. It's something I never expected or planned for."

My hand stills. His words explode in my chest like a firework, bright, beautiful and unstoppable. It feels like the air suddenly turned thicker, like my lungs need to work harder just to catch some air.

"What did you say?" I whisper, unsure if I imagined it, or if I just want it too badly to trust it.

"I'm falling in love with you." His voice is softer this time, as if he's handing me something fragile, and I suppose he is.

Dexter Knight is giving me his heart.

"It scares me," he whispers.

I let go of his dick and sit astride him, my hands going around his neck. "That's just perfect, then."

"Oh?"

"Because I love you, too."

I dip my head and kiss him again. His breath is sweet, his mouth warm and soft. I love his man with every fiber in my body. I think he feels that way about me.

His eyes turn so glassy, that I wonder if I've said something that will trigger him and the beliefs he holds. But he smiles and pulls me into his chest. I feel something wet just under my breast and look down to see a few streaks of his cum that he missed wiping off. I rub it into my breast, then suck my finger.

"Jeez," he murmurs, his pupils turning darker than ever.

And just like that, Dexter's glistening hardness pokes at me again.

WE WAKE UP THE NEXT MORNING, AND THE MORNING AFTER that, entangled in one another.

We sleep in the master bedroom now. The nights are hot and steamy, and the mornings, hazy and warm. We discover things about each other, find out our pet hates and our likes. We discover one another slowly peeling back the layers that once cocooned us.

I discover New York through Dexter. He takes me to museums and art galleries—the places his mother used to take him and his brothers, he casually mentions one day. Places that matter to him, that hold memories he cherishes, and I love that he's sharing these all with me.

We stroll around the city, holding hands, laughing rich and deep, talking soft and secretly. Sharing our innermost desires and fears, recall poignant moments from our childhood and teenage years.

We skirt around the deeper things. About his mother, and the weight of the guilt he carries. About this marriage, and what it is and isn't. There will come a time when we'll talk about those things, but not yet.

We make love all over his apartment. The couch, the

shower, up against the refrigerator. On the floor. We can't get enough of one another. He makes me feel complete. Happy in ways I never thought were possible.

I never thought this would happen, that I'd fall in love with my husband, and he'd fall in love with me.

But it has, and now this city suddenly feels like home.

CHAPTER THIRTY-TWO

DEX

WEEKS PASS. I LOSE COUNT OF HOW MANY.

I love this woman in a way I have never loved anyone. She makes me whole. She takes away my pain, my guilt, my wound. She makes me happy. More than I have been in decades.

I wasn't supposed to want her.

I wasn't supposed to need her.

We weren't supposed to get involved.

But now, I don't know how I'll ever live without her.

The only thing that matters is that Daniela wakes up in my arms every morning, and I go to sleep with her every night. With her working from home, I'm not rushing to the office the way I used to. Unless there's a meeting or a scheduled call, I take my sweet time in the morning. Mornings spent making love with my beautiful wife.

She's glowing. Laughing more. She told me that her mother

said she sounds different. Happier and lighter, like something's shifted.

She's right. Everything's shifted.

We talk more. We laugh. We lie in bed, sharing secrets, tangled together like we've done this forever.

One night, we lie in bed, panting and sated, holding hands and discussing an email the old man has sent me, asking if perhaps we, the Knight family, should have a celebration, something not like the Knight family dinner, something in an expensive restaurant, with a private chef, to welcome Daniela into the family.

"We've been married almost a month and a half, and *now* he wants to have a family celebration?" Daniela laughs.

"I've already welcomed you, in my own special way." I squeeze her hand, before turning to my side and lifting up the sheet. Seeing her naked body, my cock starts to stiffen as I'm reminded me of the things we do when naked.

"And what a way to be welcomed." She waggles her eyebrows, prompting me to lean over and kiss her, long, and deeply. Then we settle back down again. Me on my back with her snuggled against my chest, her arm thrown across it as if we're melded together. I never want another woman in my arms again.

"He wants to welcome you to the family," I scoff, imagining another uptight family dinner. "The location doesn't matter, whether it's the old man's penthouse or a fancy restaurant. He will preside over us like a king, and our family dynamics will be strained, because he's there."

She kisses my chest, her fingers tracing around the dark dusting of my hairs.

"It would be different if mom were here."

Her fingers still. I can tell she's all ears. Waiting for me. Being patient and kind. It feels easier opening up to Daniela.

"I miss her. I miss her very much." I stare up at the ceiling, my body tightening as sadness engulfs me. I picture mom.

Mom would be happy for me, if she saw me and Daniela together. Another light kiss lands on my chest. A kiss that says, *tell me, in your own time.*

"It was the shocking news of his affair, of him having a secret family that tipped her over the edge."

The room is silent, and all I hear is our breathing.

"Something like that would break a person," Daniela says softly. "Your mother must have been in so much anguish."

"It upended her world. She started to retreat then. We could tell, looking back now, that something about her changed. How could it not have? The man she'd been married to and had a family with, was a liar and a cheat, with a mistress and a secret family. Mom was so loving, but she became distant in the weeks that followed. I wanted my mom back, the happy, smiling, carefree mom who was always there for us. I didn't like who she'd become."

"You were all so young, Dexter." Daniela lifts up on her elbow, her large eyes filled with concern. "This situation was awful for you all. I can't imagine what must have gone through your mom's mind. She probably didn't realize she was shutting you all out. She must have struggled to deal with the shock of the news in her own way."

"I should have backed off, but I was angry. I would snap at her, and argue with her. Jett, who was a few years older, kept telling me to cool it. To shut the hell up. He'd been hurt by the news, too, but he was sullen and moody, and he was always out with his friends. Zach was nine, not old enough to fully understand the ramifications of the affair and its effect on our mother, and too young to take sides. I still remember the day it happened. My Dad had missed my baseball game again. I called him Dad back then. Mom was sitting at the kitchen table, her head buried in her hands. Jett was away, on a school trip or something. I don't know where Zach was.

Dad missed the game again, I whined to her. He'd promised me he'd come. Mom had already made excuses for why she couldn't. It should have been a trigger, a warning shot, but I was too young to know that then. That she was starting to lose interest in life, because she would always come to our matches and school plays. She looked up at me. *He's busy, Dex. He's trying his best.*

He's not doing anything! I yelled at her. *He's never here, that's 'cause he's with her. Even when he is here, you act like everything's fine, but it isn't.*

Excuses. She was making excuses. Like that monster needed anyone defending him. It was odd how we tried to continue our lives, despite the news about the mistress and the half-brothers we suddenly had.

Mom got up slowly, walked over to me and placed her hands on my shoulders. She crouched down, and I still remember her bloodshot eyes. *I'm trying to hold this family together,* she said, her voice odd, flat, with no emotion.

I should have noticed the crack. The change in her. The coldness and distance that was edging us further apart. I should have hugged her and said I was sorry, but I didn't. I kept on turning and twisting my words deeper.

Maybe he cheats on you 'cause you're always like this. You're always so sad and weird now, and you're always crying. I hate it. I yelled at her, when I shouldn't have. I was such a despicable child. So angry and evil. I saw the way her hands fell to her side, but she didn't yell. She didn't say another word. She just stared at me like I was a ghost and she could see right through me. And it made me even more mad."

I struggle to hold it together, take a breath as the pain of that moment lacerates me. "I was evil." I say, my voice wavering.

The gentle press of Daniela's body against me, takes me out of the past, gives me a cushioned reminder of the present. I wish I could turn back time. Wish I could take back those words. Wish Mom were here with us now.

"I went further," I tell her. "I yelled at my mom and said, *I don't want to be here. I don't want you as my mom, and I don't love you. I wish you were dead.* And then I stormed upstairs before she could say another word. I felt like I'd been punched hard, and I needed her to feel the pain like I did."

It takes me a few moments before I can speak again. Daniela is up on her elbow, looking down at me. Stroking my face.

"I never saw my mom again," I croak. "She was gone before we woke up. Drove off a bridge. For the rest of my life I've wondered if only I'd shut the fuck up. If I'd told her I'd loved her, and that it didn't matter, and that she was the best mom in the world. Maybe then she'd still be alive."

"You didn't send your mom to her death, Dexter," Daniela says softly. "You didn't. You must believe that. You were eleven. Your mom loved you, and she knew you loved her. She would never have taken your words, the words of an angry boy struggling to make sense of his world, as the truth. She knew you didn't mean it. She knew it. You must believe that, Dexter."

Tears run down Daniela's face. She feels my pain as deeply as if it's her own. I wipe them away, but she shakes her head.

"Your mom was hurt by what your father did. Not by what you said. But I understand how it must feel for you, and I get that. I get how you linked the two things together. The last words you ever said to her, and then you never saw her again. But moms know their children love them unconditionally. Don't let that misbelief take up space in your head, Dexter. Or your heart. Don't be so hard on yourself."

She rests her chin on my chest, waiting, giving me the time

and space to work through my emotions. She doesn't prod, or push, or demand. She's everything I could ever want and need.

I WAKE UP ONE MORNING WITH DANIELA CURLED UP BESIDE ME. It's a weekday, and I have nothing scheduled. It's going to be one of those lazy, sexy, feel-good mornings.

I'm about to slide under the sheets, wanting to wake her up by licking her out. But a notification on my phone freezes me just as I slide under the covers to position my head between her legs.

Unfortunately I make the mistake of reaching for my phone, quickly reading the message. It's from my father. He wants to see us both in his office. Today. I toss the phone away, hating how this fucking piece of metal has derailed my day. I sit up and move the sheet off me. Daniela stirs, then turns on her side, her hand brushing my thigh.

"Daniela," I say quietly.

"Hmmmm."

"We need to go into the office. My father wants us both in for a meeting."

Her eyelids flutter open and she blinks a few times. "Today?" Her voice is still husky with sleep.

"This morning."

She blinks up at me, her brows pinching. She's become very wary at any mention of my father. "Why both of us?"

"I don't know. But I've got a bad feeling about it."

That low throb in my gut won't go away.

We get up and get dressed. I tell her that we'll go and see him, deal with whatever it is, and then do something nice this evening. Maybe a nice dinner, followed by hours of debauchery in bed. I tell her it's always better to have something nice to look forward to. She cheers up. I try to keep my tone light. Try to ignore the pit of unease that's filling my stomach.

We walk into the office together. People look up and nod as we pass. They smile at Daniela, whom they barely see. But all of New York knows she's my wife on account of the mugging and the many photos of us in the press after the charity gala.

I knock on the door of the old man's office. He calls us in. He's sitting calmly at his desk. Daniela glances at me, eyes searching. I look at her and give a slight shake of my head. No idea what this is about.

"We've signed a new contract," the old man says abruptly, looking right at Daniela. "Your father and I." His voice is calm and measured and I feel like a storm is coming.

Daniela's face tightens. "Why?"

I turn to her. She sounds more nervous than she should. Which makes me wonder if she knows something that I don't.

My father doesn't answer her question. He just keeps going, calm and infuriatingly vague. "Things have changed."

"What things?" I ask sharply. "What are you talking about?"

"Daniela's father agreed to the new terms," he says coolly. "The goalposts have shifted."

I frown. "What goalposts? Why are you being so cryptic?"

His gray eyes fix on me, making me shiver. "I don't like being bamboozled."

"What the hell is that supposed to mean?" I snap.

He turns to Daniela. "Your father's company is not in the shape it was presented to us. But you already knew that, didn't you?"

A dead weight settles in the middle of my gut. One look at my wife, and I can tell that she knew. My jaw tightens. "Daniela? Did you know?"

Her eyes go wide. "I'm sorry," she whispers. "The numbers

were sliding, yes, but ... we needed a cash injection. Some investors pulled out, but we were holding steady."

An ice-cold fissure explodes in my chest. "You didn't tell me."

"If only that were the case." The old man examines his fingernails, before adjusting his cufflinks. "If only a few investors pulled out, but the real situation is worse. Your father's business is doing very badly. To make matters worse, he fabricated the accounts. Or his accountants did."

Daniela's face goes white. "No," she gasps, eyes large. "He would never do that."

My father sits forward, like he's about to drop a punchline to a joke no one's in the mood for. "He did exactly that."

"He fabricated the accounts?" Daniela gasps, like this is news to her.

"He did. I have proof, in case you don't believe me."

She crumples back in her seat, at the weight of her father's betrayal, then turns to me. "I didn't know it was that serious." Her voice cracks. "I swear, Dexter, I didn't."

But I can't unsee the look on her face when my father dropped the bomb.

She knew *something*.

And now ... so do I.

CHAPTER THIRTY-THREE

DANI

"How long have you known about this?" Dexter asks when we leave his father's office.

My breath catches in my throat. "I knew things weren't as good as they used to be …" I trail off, unable to shake the way he looks at me because he thinks I've betrayed him.

We head toward the elevator bank. "So you already knew?" He wipes his hand across his face. "Why didn't you say something? Why weren't you honest with me from the start, Daniela?" He looks like he's seen a ghost and I'm scared he's going to use this to push me away again.

"I didn't know! I don't believe it even now. My father would never do this!" I cry. "I work there, Dexter. I didn't see any signs that things were *that* bad."

He exhales loudly. Wearily. Like a man defeated. "You were in the brand strategy department. Maybe you wouldn't have known." It sounds like he's trying to convince himself and that he really does want to believe me.

"I didn't know the extent of it, I swear." I so desperately need him to believe me. There's also another explanation. "Is there a chance your father might be exaggerating?" I'm hanging onto this as if it's my only lifeline. Because it's possible. Paul Knight isn't transparent, and I don't trust the man.

Dexter's eyes cut to mine. "Not a chance in hell. Though it explains why he stayed behind in São Paulo, when everyone returned, when we went on our honeymoon." He inhales, his brow creasing as he mulls over his words. "The old man was going into the office with your father, most likely looking over things. Snooping. I had a feeling he would, and I'd go so far as to say he probably hired people to work there."

"People living in São Paulo? How?" I'm shocked that he would do this.

"Yes, local people. He has contacts everywhere. I'm guessing he got an independent group to audit your father's books. That's why it's taken him a while to tell us." His eyes hold me captive. "You don't understand this man, Daniela. You don't know what we're dealing with here. I do. This man doesn't make a move unless he has the facts."

I swallow, feeling a bitter taste in my mouth at Dexter's ominous words. "That's why he attacks like a snake. Because he can."

Dexter sounds so sure and now, suddenly, I start to doubt my own father. The thought turns me cold. Papai sent me into a marriage of convenience, without telling me the truth. I feel betrayed by the man I thought I knew and the ground beneath me seems to sway. It feels like a sinkhole, ready to gobble me up and swallow me whole.

"The old man doesn't like being tricked, Daniela. You don't know how bad this is. You don't know what the consequences are."

We get into the elevator and descend in silence, my mind a

whirlwind of questions and denials. This is bad. This is *really* bad.

We walk straight across the marble floored lobby, heading for the front entrance. I glance up just in time to see Rio sauntering past, not stopping to talk to either one of us. There's just a quick nod between him and Dexter.

"The old man wouldn't have called us into that meeting unless he had proof. You need to speak to your father," Dexter urges, his face haggard and lined with worry. "I need to go back into the office and work, but I have a car and driver arranged to meet you out front. The driver will take you home."

Just like that, we're strangers all over again.

DEX

RIO SENDS ME A TEXT.

> Wassup dude? You guys looked miserable
>
> What you gone and done now?

I shove the phone back into my pocket. I can't deal with him right now.

Jesus.

I made the mistake of telling him, Jett and Zach how good things were between me and Daniela. They all joked about not seeing me, that I hadn't met them for drinks or anything lately. I wish I'd never told them that I liked spending time with my wife.

My wife.

What a fucking joke.

The warmth between us? That electric, easy intimacy we've lived in these last few weeks? Gone. Evaporated in an instant. I should've known a meeting with my father would end badly, but I didn't expect *this*.

Now it feels like my whole world has been hit by a meteor. It's a miracle we're still standing, still breathing.

I try to work all day, closing the door to my office, telling my assistant that I can't be disturbed. But I'm hiding from everyone and everything, trying to process this news. Daniela might not have outright lied to me, but she didn't come clean.

And her father?

A joke.

Not only is he a bad businessman, but he also sold Daniela out to help him. He doesn't deserve a daughter like her.

The day passes, and I realize I'm avoiding going home. Used to be that lately I didn't like going into work. All I wanted was to be at home with Daniela, and now? I can't bear to walk into my own apartment and confront the truth: This marriage is nothing but a sham, and she used me.

That's not true, my heart whispers. *Believe Daniela*. She doesn't lie. She's too decent, and honorable for that. It's possible that she didn't know the full extent of what was happening with her father's business. If that's the case, it means she's the innocent party here, and if anyone is at fault it's her father, because he sold his daughter to the wolves, knowing that his company was in dire straits.

Something rises inside me, frustration, helplessness and rage, all tangled up in a knot I can't loosen. I don't know what to do with it. So I do the only thing I can do.

I call Rio.

He's in the middle of a game of squash when I reach him, but I don't care. I tell him I need to talk to him urgently. He tells me to meet him at his place in thirty minutes.

When I get to his place, he opens the door, his eyes scanning my face for answers.

"What happened?"

I tell him everything. About the meeting. What the old man discovered. The fabricated accounts. Daniela's face when he dropped the news.

Rio goes still. "You knew this was a game of chess, dude. Where Paul Knight is concerned, it always is."

I nod, jaw clenched. "But this time, he didn't fuck up. My father-in-law did."

"But this was a deal," Rio says. "You marry her. Two families merge. Two powerful families. At least we know it's not just the Knights who are fucked up. Problem is, you've gone and fallen in love—"

"I haven't." I try to deny it, even though Rio's speaking the truth.

"I know you, dude. Look at you. Spending time with your wife? Dexter Knight? That can only be possible if one thing is true. You love her." He laughs, a rich, effortless laugh of someone who knows me better than I know myself.

"I was lonely," I insist. "My hookups stopped, and we're living together. How can I not indulge? We fuck. That's all it is," I snarl.

"You can fool Jett and Zach, dude, but you can't fool me."

I don't even try to push back. I'm angry. Fucking angry. More at the old man than with Daniela. I don't want him to have leverage over me, and this gives him leverage. Rio knows, and anyone who knows me would know. It's clear to see. I'm in love with Daniela, but it spells trouble ahead for both of us.

"The old man has me in a chokehold."

Rio stares at me. "So what's your next move?"

I laugh, but there's no humor in it. "That's the problem. I

don't have a move. He's played us. He says he's changed the contract."

"What did he change?"

"I don't know. That's the worst part. He called us in to tell us the contract's been changed, but he didn't say how. I don't trust him. Not with this."

Rio cups his chin, turns pensive. "It's never just about the deal. It's always about control."

I agree. "It's not me I'm worried about. It's Daniela."

"There you go. This is more than just fucking, dude. You care about her."

"Yeah, yeah," I say, dismissively, and get up to leave.

I don't trust the old man but what scares me is that I don't know what he'll do to punish Daniela, or her family. I can't let that happen.

What I do know is that there will be retribution. But first, I need to come up with a plan, and fast.

CHAPTER THIRTY-FOUR

DANI

I call my father and ask him what happened. "You signed another contract, Papai?"

I hear a deep sigh at the other end. "You know." The fact that this comes as no surprise to him tells me everything.

"When were you going to tell me, Papai?"

"I was hoping it would never have come to this, filha."

"He made you sign another contract. What changes are in the new one?"

"I don't know. I didn't read it."

My mouth falls open. I'm glad my father can't see the shock on my face. "You didn't read it?" I gasp. This man isn't the businessman I knew. My father is a shrewd man, and ordinarily he would check and triple check everything. That he didn't on this instance tells me just how far he's fallen and how desperate he must have been.

"Paul Knight was so angry when he discovered that the accounts had been touched, he was furious that we'd gone to such great lengths to mislead him. He warned me that it's a punishable offense, but I was so desperate so ..." His voice peters away.

Desperate men do desperate things.

"We'll find a way out of this, Papai." I do my best to try to reassure him but I feel empty inside. Hollow, like there's nothing holding me together and I'm about to crumble into a heap of nothingness.

"He threatened to expose me. He said bad publicity would make things worse, and if I wanted to avoid that, it was better to sign the new contract. That's what I did, filha."

What worries me is that he did so without reading it. I need to see what has changed. "Please, just send me a copy of the contract."

"Do you really need to see it, filha?" My father sounds tired. He doesn't sound like himself, and I feel him slipping away from me again, lost in his own world.

"Yes, I do. You've spent time with Dexter's father, and you should know the type of man he is. This isn't good."

"Are you in danger?" My father sounds even more worried, so I try to lighten my tone.

"No," I laugh, but I know I don't sound convincing. "You should have told me the company was in a worse position than I believed. Why didn't you?"

There's silence on the other end and I can only guess how guilty my father feels. "Why did you mislead Paul Knight?" I ask, my voice softer.

"I didn't know what to do, filha."

"When did he find out? Was it when he stayed behind, when Dexter and I went on our honeymoon?"

"It might have started then, perhaps. He must have suspected something, because he had his own people in and going through the accounts. I'm sorry, filha. I've put you in a terrible position."

My father's betrayal and the consequences of it, finally sink in. "I would never have married Dexter Knight if I had known this. We would have found another way. Why didn't you tell me before?"

I hear labored breathing at the other end of the line. "I failed you as a father. I failed the company... but mostly, I failed you, my daughter. As a father, what I've done is unforgivable, expecting you to marry a man you barely know."

I soften when I hear the pain in his voice. I can't let this destroy him. "It was only ever on paper, Papai. Nothing happened. You don't need to worry." Now it's my time to lie. I suck in a breath to stop myself from saying anything that might hurt him, but I'm furious and disappointed that I walked into the lion's den without knowing what I was getting myself into.

What makes it worse is that I've given my heart to Dexter, and now he's going to hate me. I feel so torn. I sacrificed everything to save my father's company, but now it's worse than before. Papai blames himself and I can't let him do that. I can't let this be the end. I can't let Paul Knight win.

"Please email me the contract, Papai. Does Mãe know?" I hold my breath and pray she doesn't.

"She knows only what you knew. That things weren't great. She doesn't know the truth."

"Don't tell her anything." I can't have both of my parents worried sick.

"The truth will come out soon, filha."

"Maybe not. He made you sign another contract. I just need to know what's in it. Please send it as soon as you can, Papai, *please*." I hang up and feel lost as I pace around the apartment, not knowing what to do.

Do I stay? Do I go?

I won't know what to do until I see what my father has signed. I need the facts. It was not having the facts in the first place that landed me in this situation. Paul Knight thinks he's the grand chess master, and that I'm just a pawn.

Not so. I'm determined to exact my revenge, but I don't yet know how.

I spend the evening alone. Dexter still hasn't come home, and I doubt he will. He was furious when he discovered I'd been keeping something from him. I shouldn't have kept this from him. He wouldn't keep anything from me.

If my father had told me how bad things were, would I have done this?

Yes.

The answer comes back in a heartbeat. Because if the company was in as bad a state as I've now discovered, we would have needed *something*. It would have come down to Oscar Ramos or the Knights.

I couldn't imagine a life with Ramos, but meeting Dexter Knight was the best thing that happened to me. I've met the love of my life. Only, I don't know if he wants to be with me anymore.

Tonight I'll sleep in my own bedroom, because Dexter probably doesn't want me anywhere near him. I have a feeling that he'll withdraw again and this time it will be worse than before.

When he walks in, much later, looking at me like I'm a stranger, everything we had between disappears.

"I'm going to bed," he announces.

I want to ask him if he wants to eat. Or if he wants to talk. But no, he's *that* Dexter again. Guarded. Closed off. He doesn't want anything to do with me.

He tosses the car keys into the marble console, like he does every day. But he looks weary and aged. As if he's been carrying a heavy weight ever since the news broke. "I wish you'd told me," he says again, the blame heavy in his tone.

"I told you, I didn't know."

"You knew *something.*"

"I didn't know it was this bad, Dexter. You must believe me."

"But you knew it wasn't exactly how your father presented it. Fabricating the accounts." He swipes a weary hand through his hair, looking defeated.

"I'm sorry," I whisper. "Don't put your walls up, Dexter. Let me in."

He walks toward me, eyes sad, like this is insolvable. "If you'd told me, we wouldn't be in this mess."

It's over. That's what he's really saying.

He takes my hands in his, his dark eyes meeting mine. "I just need some time and space. I'm not pushing you away, Daniela. I'm not, but I need to work through this myself. Just let me be, for a while, please."

He's trying to make me feel better, but I'm already scared. I nod, then retreat to my bedroom and close the door, feeling desolate and broken. My attention shifts when I hear the ping of a notification on my phone. I check it to see that my father has sent me an email with the new contract attached. My eyes scan across the document quickly, and then my heart stops.

Papai has signed away control of his company to Paul Knight and the snake now has the majority share. My insides twist so hard I feel sick. Rage bubbles up, thick enough to choke me. I want to scream, to break something, to tear Paul Knight's empire down brick by brick and watch him burn in the ashes of what he did to us.

He tricked my father. Manipulated him when he was vulnerable. Pressured him into signing a contract he didn't read, didn't pass to legal, didn't even question because he trusted the devil in a suit who smiled while sharpening the knife.

This is my worst nightmare come to life. I went into this marriage of convenience thinking I was helping my father, but now Paul Knight owns fifty-one percent of everything my father built.

I read and reread those paragraphs again, disbelief warring with anger. Nostrils flaring, my resentment for this man boundless.

"Papai!" I call my father back quickly, barely able to control my rage. "Did you mean to sign away control of your company?"

He cries out, like he's in agony, and it tells me he didn't. I blame myself. I shouldn't have told him over the phone. I should have flown back home and sat my parents down and explained the seriousness of the situation.

Because I now understand it myself, and what this means for us, for our business. It wouldn't surprise me if this was what Paul Knight wanted all along. If he made my father relinquish control of his company, what was in the *original* contract? I remember that he never gave us a copy of it, even though Dexter and I both asked for it. Something doesn't smell quite right.

Paul Knight claimed that he wanted this alliance to get his foot in the South American market, but he's a wily man, where my father is not.

What if that snake had ulterior motives from the start?

What if this was his goal? And the serious offence of my father misleading him by fabricating the accounts might just have given Paul what he wanted, but much sooner. No wonder he threatened to expose my father, who probably signed under duress. There was a reason we didn't get a copy of the original contract. I won't be surprised to discover that Paul Knight planned this from the start.

I tell my father not to worry, that we will fix this. We'll find out a way. I urge him to get some sleep and promise to call him again tomorrow.

Defeat and resignation are quickly replaced by rage as I rush out of my room and knock on Dexter's door. He needs to know. He opens the door quickly, an ugly frown on his face. "What?" He's just come out of the shower, towel around his waist, body dripping wet.

I force myself to look at his face, trying to suppress the memories that light up in my head. "Your father … your father tricked mine." I'm so filled with rage that I can't get the words out. I wave my cellphone at him. "He tricked my father into signing over the majority share in the company."

Dexter shakes his head slowly. "That sonofabitch," he says, slowly, wiping a hand over his face. "I knew the old man would try to pull a fast one. I just wish it wasn't this."

"But it *is* this. He's done it."

Dexter walks around in his room, water droplets trickling down his muscled torso. He looks tortured. Defeated, too. "If I had known I would have been better prepared to prevent something like this."

"I keep telling you, I didn't know the whole truth. I wish you'd believe me. But this, your father tricking my father into signing over the majority share in his company, what are we going to do about that?"

Dexter isn't listening to me. He seems to be caught up in his own world. "Dexter!" I shriek. "What are we going to do?" I'm trying hard not to become hysterical, but I worry that he'll repeat his old patterns again and retreat into his safety zone. He'll choose to be alone.

I found a way to reach him. Made him see that old wounds

can be healed, that the past as he believed it was wrong. I thought I was getting through to him, but these recent developments haven't helped. Yet, I still believe we can overcome this. We love each other. We're perfect for each other. We want one another. We can fix this.

I reach out and place my hand on his chest. It's warm and slightly damp, and brings back a flood of memories. "We can fight this, Dexter. We can fix it."

To my quiet surprise, he doesn't flinch or recoil from my touch, but his face twists as if he can't bear it. "I need to tell you something," he says, in a voice that sounds unfamiliar. Vulnerable. Soft. My stomach hollows out, because his voice, the way he looks at me, the vibes rolling off him, they all scream trouble. I brace myself for the worst. "I was never supposed to stay."

It takes a few seconds for his words to sink in. I stumble back a few steps. "What do you mean you were never supposed to stay?"

He closes his eyes and buries his face in his hands.

"What are you saying, Dexter?"

He looks at me like I'm the problem; like this is my fault. "This was never supposed to happen. I was supposed to walk away."

I stare at him in shock. "Walk away? From me? From us?"

"From this arrangement. I thought I'd do it after seven months, but then I started thinking, maybe I could do it in three months ..."

I gasp in shock, unable to utter a word. *Three months?*

"I'd decided early on, before we got to know one another."

My mind goes into overdrive as Dexter continues, my heart shattering while I try desperately to compose myself in the face of such news. He was going to walk away before the year was up.

"But now I'm implicated in this mess," he says, more to himself. "It means my father will find a way to get one over me. The only reason I agreed to marry you was to get one over him. To spite him."

My head starts to spin. This can't be real. After everything we shared, everything we did, the intimacy we had. Those hot, passionate nights in bed. Were they lies? Was he using me? "You don't mean that," I whisper.

"I just want to be honest with you. In the beginning, I married you out of spite, not love, but then it turned into love."

A heavy rock sinks in my belly. He married me out of spite. Whatever he said after that doesn't register. I barely have time to compose myself. To force myself to stand straighter. To remember who I am. That I am built strong. That I can handle men who treat me badly. "It was never supposed to be about love," I remind him. "It was just an alliance."

"Yes," he says, agreeing easily, while my heart sinks further down my stomach. "It was an alliance, but now ..." His gaze settles on me. I like to think it's because he cares about me, but I can't trust my stupid heart and my silly feelings. "But now, not only am I involved with you, it so much more complicated. As you've now discovered, unfortunately, the old man's found a way to punish your family. He'll punish us, too. I know this, Daniela. Because that's the kind of man he is."

He's angry. He's angry at himself for giving into his feelings for me. That's what my heart tries to tell me. *He thinks we'll both have to suffer for it.* But the logical part of me wants the truth. "Did none of it mean anything? Our nights together? The things we said to one another?"

"They meant everything but I just need to figure things out."

It's the "but" I hear, loud and clear.

"I told you we'd have to pay for it. This is what my father

does. I've never trusted him, and I told you to be careful. Why do you think I initially stayed away from you, Daniela?"

"There are so many reasons and you keep giving me new ones," I snap. "Every time I come to you, you push me away. Every single time."

"I need to come up with something. Please trust me, Daniela." His eyes search mine, like he needs confirmation.

But I know who he is. I've seen it with my own eyes. I know that he was raised by a monster after his mom passed away. I've met the Knights, and Dexter is a product of a fucked-up family with more money than morals.

He's a man who doesn't commit. Nothing confirms this more strongly than his admission that he was going to walk out on this deal. Not after seven months, like he originally decided, but *three*.

Three.

It hurts more than I can bear. He's just told me he'd planned to never keep his end of the deal. To make things worse, his father is the one who ruined my father's business, and possibly his health.

I can't be a part of this anymore. Dexter didn't care about me. He didn't care about the alliance. He only agreed to this deal to seek some sort of twisted revenge on his father. I was just collateral, and now he wants me to wait for him to come up with a plan?

No way.

He clearly wasn't falling for me, despite his hollow words, because if he was, he wouldn't have an exit strategy in place. This man is used to hookups and friends-with-benefits arrangements; fickle entanglements.

I'm not. I'm done with him, and I'm done with his family.

I go back into my room and read the contract again. Dexter and I will be sleeping in separate rooms again and our passionate nights will be nothing more than a memory. I'll just have to find a way to live through unbearable, slow-burning, maddening tension.

The only thing that matters right now is how I'm going to fix this. I'll find a way, or make one because Paul Knight will control my father's company over my dead body.

I call Raquel and tell her everything, the state of my father's company's, and what he did. The facts he withheld from me, and Paul Knight's ultimate revenge. Then I drop the biggest shock of all—that Dexter and I had a marriage of convenience. It was fake, and we tricked everyone. I tell her I'm sorry, and that I hated lying to her.

Her reaction is everything I expected. She's shocked, and dramatic, and then calming and strategic. She understands why I did it, and then, dispensing with emotions, she cuts to the chase. Asks me to send her the new contract, as well as the original one that my father signed before the wedding. The one Dexter and I asked to have a copy of, but which Paul Knight never gave us.

I promise her I'll get a copy from my father and send it to her tomorrow. I tell her that I love her, that I'm sorry I deceived her, but she cuts me short and tells me the past doesn't matter, that we need to fix things now. She tells me not to worry, that she'll always be there for me, no matter what.

I realize then how it's the men in my life who have fallen short, but the women? They've always been there for me.

After speaking to Raquel, my future path is suddenly clear. Dexter is too complicated and too wounded. I don't trust Paul Knight and I refuse to be trapped just because he tricked Papai. I've come to see that the Knights are just as bad as Oscar Ramos. It's common knowledge that Ramos's empire is built on questionable business practices, just like the Knights, but with Ramos, I know what I'm getting into.

Underneath their veneer of respectability, the Knights are no better.

I don't need them.

But I do need a billionaire to save my father.

My father was wrong to mislead the Knights, but I will never accept Paul Knight's trickery, and I can't let this be the end of my father's legacy. If it means marrying Oscar Ramos, I'll do it.

I try to push down the revulsion I feel at the idea of being with him. I'm not in the slightest bit attracted to him, but I have no choice. I'll do it, because for me, family is everything. Something Dexter doesn't understand, and maybe never will.

CHAPTER THIRTY-FIVE

DEX

I'M SITTING AT A TABLE AT THE OASIS, WAITING FOR RIO. I'VE already ordered his bottle of beer. Me? I'm drinking water.

Jett and Zach have texted, asking me if I want to have drinks, but I've told them I'm busy. Naturally, they assume I'm busy with my wife. I figure the old man hasn't told them about the dirty sneaky thing he's done with Arminio, my father-in-law, because if they knew, they'd be at my door. Jett would storm into the old man's office, throwing chairs and demanding blood.

As for Zach? He'd find some way to excuse it. Say it was just business. Say that "Dad" had his reasons. I don't need to involve them. I'll tell them when the time is right. When the wrong has been righted.

Rio struts towards me, dark glasses, designer suit, running his hand through his long hair, which falls forward falls into his eyes. He's wearing that signature lazy grin again. "You look like hell." He slaps me across the back.

"I feel like shit."

He walks to the edge and looks out over the skyline. "You bring me all the way up here to mope? Thought we were going to get to work?"

"We are. I couldn't sleep, but I have a plan. Been thinking about it all night. Need to run it by you."

Rio rubs his hands together. "Bring it on."

"The old man thinks he's outplayed everyone. He's taken fifty-one per cent of Daniela's father's company, and he thinks it gives him leverage over me. He thinks I'll fall in line."

"True. But you married her, I don't get how he's going to keep you in line when you already stepped up and did the thing he wanted."

Now comes the part I've been keeping from him. "He thinks I'm desperate for the money. I get one million dollars for every month I'm married."

Rio whistles. "What … the … *fuck*?"

"I know. It's not why I married her."

Rio sits back, his arm lazily draped over the chair next to him. "Dude, I know. You're not about the money. Revenge and spite are more your game."

"Only, it's backfired now. I'm not walking out after seven months, or three."

"The hell you aren't." Rio chuckles.

"But we're getting control of Arminio's company back."

Rio sits up. I lay it out for him, everything I know. My father-in-law's health is failing. Daniela's desperate. My father's holding all the cards, and we need to flip things around. "I want you to make him an offer. One he can't ignore. Something that comes from your side. I need you, Matteo, and Enzo in on it."

Rio gives a low whistle. "You want me and my brothers involved?"

"The old man will never see it coming."

Rio smiles. Broad, wide, confident. "I like it. I fucking love it, dude. You want me to pretend I'm swooping in for control?"

"Exactly. The old man naturally assumes we're all divided. He doesn't know we're close. He has no idea that we talk. Hell, he still thinks you'd stab me before you'd ever help me."

Rio laughs. "He's not entirely wrong."

"Are you in?"

"You really love her?"

"Yeah," I say quietly. "I do. More than I've ever loved anyone, brother."

"This isn't just a friends-with-benefits type of deal?"

"It was never that," I say feeling wistful. Daniela was always so much more.

"Then I'm in, and I'll get Matteo and Enzo on board."

"Do it now, because we don't have much time. I told Daniela I need to figure things out, but I know this has hurt her too much, not just what the old man did to her father, but what her own father did, when he didn't come clean with her. I know this woman, and family means everything to her. I want to make things right for her."

"I'm on it." He slides out his cellphone and calls Matteo. Tells him to bring Enzo with him, since they're both still in the office. We sit, drinking quietly while we wait. I see the bar's owner walking by. "Luke!" I raise my arm when I see my friend.

"Congrats, man, I hear you got married." Luke greets me warmly, before shaking hands with me and Rio. "You didn't waste any time."

"I remembered your wise words. Once you meet the right woman, never let her go."

"Glad you listened."

I thank him for recommending The Bluebell Manhattan, the place where Daniela and I had our first date.

"Cool. I'm glad you liked it."

"Awesome hotel. You did it up real nice."

"It's won quite a few awards already," he announces proudly.

"Rightly so, brother." I'm already imagining candle-lit dinners there with Daniela.

"I don't know if you noticed, but we have a rooftop sky garden, right at the top. Anytime you have a special occasion, let me know. I can get the whole thing set up just for you."

"Thanks. I appreciate it. You going to buy every hotel in sight?" I ask. This man started off with bars and nightclubs. The Oasis is still going strong, but The Vault, the club in the basement is no longer there. Luke's been slowly acquiring real estate and has now moved onto buying hotels and doing them up.

"I'm working on it. It keeps me busy." He grins. "Let me know if I can help, if you need another special date with your wife."

"Thanks, brother."

"Cool dude," Rio comments when Luke walks away. I agree, because Luke looks extremely content, like he owns the world.

"He's a good guy. A family man."

"Wife?" Rio asks.

I nod. "Still happily married. I think he has three, maybe four boys now."

"Nice if you can find that kind of happiness."

"What's the deal with you and Raquel?" I ask.

"I have no fucking idea," Rio replies. Just as I'm about to question him further, Matteo and Enzo stroll towards us. Matteo with that casual, laid back swagger that seems to be his trademark, and Enzo, cool and sophisticated. Like he's on a runway, modelling for Tom Ford or Lora Piana.

Matteo whistles. "If this is some ambush, I swear to God—"

"It's not," Rio cuts in. "It's important."

"Important? Why are we meeting here?" he regards me with suspicion.

"Because they don't want our father to know about it", Enzo replies, ever the observer.

"We're forming an alliance," Rio says.

Matteo glances in my direction. "An alliance? With *him?*"

Rio doesn't flinch. "Dex needs our help."

"Since when do you two even talk?" Enzo asks.

Rio glances at me, then back at his brothers. "We talk. We just don't advertise it. Because if the old man ever knew we were working together, he'd do everything in his power to destroy it."

They go quiet and the silence slices through the tension.

"We're family," Rio continues, calm and clear. "We shouldn't let the likes of our old man divide us."

That seems to settle things. They sit down. Matteo rubs the back of his neck. Enzo just sits and waits. A server comes and takes their order.

"Is this about Daniela?" Enzo asks, finally. This guy? He's a dark horse. Perceptive and sharp, he's observant, too. Moving like he's always three steps ahead but never has to raise his voice or impress, to prove it.

"Let me explain," I say, once the server has set their drinks on the table. I tell them what's happened, about the contract, and Daniela's father, and the old man taking the majority share in his company. A part of me feels bad that I'm not telling my own brothers first, but I can't afford for Jett to go in guns blazing trying to sort this out.

I explain our strategy. "We're not going to outright fight the old man. We're going to do what he's good at. We're going to trick him into signing back the fifty-one percent without realizing it."

"You want us to go to him and offer to buy the company?" Matteo asks.

"Not buy," Rio replies. "We contact outside investors who have a vested interest in AO Eletronica."

"Are these people legit?" Enzo asks.

"Yes, they will be," I reply. "That's the beauty. We're not going to fabricate anything. We're just guiding the narrative."

Enzo peers at e. "How are you going to find them?"

"My father-in-law, will help," I answer smoothly. "I've already spoken to him and apologized about the way the old man handled things, about how he tricked him into signing over the shares."

"That must have been a heavy call," Rio says.

"It was, but he apologized. Said he felt bad for what he'd done, cooking the books and all that. Said he felt the worst for Daniela, for not being honest with her. I told him we're not going to dwell on the past. We're going to fix this. The guy's not in a good place himself, and I can see why. He didn't tell his daughter the whole truth, and she walked into a marriage of convenience blind. That kind of guilt eats you up. I know it does." I take a moment to inhale. To think about how Daniela saved me, how she made me see. And now I want to fix things for her. "If something happens to him she'll never forgive herself. I'll never forgive myself." I reflect on how much Daniela loves her parents. How much they love her. "I want him to recover from this. He had to be in a desperate place to do this." A quiet murmur goes around the table. "I told him it has to be our secret. That he can't tell Daniela, or anyone, not even his wife."

"How's that going to help?" Matteo asks.

"We just drop the right whispers in the right ears and let their interest do the rest," I reply.

"How?" Enzo peers at me.

"We quietly stoke real investor interest in AO Eletronica by talking to people who already have an interest in the company. Arminio has a list of old players, some of whom have history with the company. Some just see it as undervalued tech ready for revival."

"I still don't see how that will help," Rio pushes back.

"These whispers build buzz and speculation that will reach Paul through his own channels; his legal team, PR advisors, industry journalists and so on. Then we manufacture a crisis. Maybe a foreign investor consortium is preparing a hostile takeover of AO Eletronica or some regulatory risks if Knight Enterprises holds a majority in a foreign-run tech company, something like that. Something that would hurt Knight's quarterly numbers, and maybe even trigger shareholder panic. The purpose of this crisis is to scare the old man into thinking that AO Eletronica is now a liability. It's classic corporate manipulation."

Rio sighs as if he's been enlightened. "The old man ends up hearing exactly what we want him to hear, but it feels like it's coming from independent sources. He never suspects that we're behind it."

"Exactly."

"Smart," Rio says. "You've been working hard, dude."

"I haven't slept."

"You look like shit," Matteo comments.

"Thanks, *brother*."

Enzo looks thoughtful. "You should take care of yourself. This isn't going to be easy, going up against our father."

"It's easier compared to the thought of losing Daniela."

Matteo and Enzo look at me. *You care about her?* Is what I read on their faces.

"Let's stick to the task at hand." Rio points a finger at me." So, the old man takes the bait. He'll panic, thinking AO Eletronica is a liability now, and he'll look to quietly dump the fifty one percent holding before it implodes."

"That's exactly it. Then, a shell company, it's probably better that you three form that," I say to the Italian Knights. I trust Rio implicitly, and I trust Matteo and Enzo because I know they'd do Rio's bidding. Keeping my name out of it entirely is probably a better bet. "You're behind the shell company and you offer to buy the fifty-one percent. The old man thinks he's outsmarted the market, but the shell company is secretly owned by you three. The moment the deal is done, you own the majority stake."

"And then what?" Enzo asks. "You give it back?"

Rio nods. "We return control back to Daniela's father. It's all done through the shell company. The old man will never see it coming."

"Why would he give up the shares in the first place?" Matteo asks.

Rio clicks his fingers. "Focus dude. The hostile takeover or regulatory issue."

I nod. "Exactly that. We leak the news that holding onto the company could bleed Knight Enterprises. Something like that. I'm still working on the finer points. The old man doesn't like losing money and he'll offload the shares."

They exchange glances. No one speaks for a long beat.

Finally, Matteo grins. "Damn. I kind of love it."

Enzo lets out an exhale. "He'll be pissed when he figures it out."

"That's the point," I say. "He doesn't figure it out until it's too late."

"How does this help you?" Enzo asks.

I look at Rio. "It helps me get my wife back."

Matteo cocks his head. Enzo's dark eyes glitter, and I can sense he has questions, but doesn't push.

"Are you guys in?" Rio asks them.

They nod.

"Then let's drink to it." Rio calls a server over and places the drinks order. But to me this doesn't feel like a celebration just yet.

It won't do until the shares are signed over to Daniela's father.

The tension is sky high.

Where I used to lie in bed with Daniela in my arms, now I'm alone in my bed. We're sleeping in separate rooms again. I leave for work early in the morning. I hit the gym at five a.m. to take out my frustration. By 6:30, I'm at the office, buried in deals. After work, in the evenings, we convene at Rio's place. Me and the Italian Knights. During the day it's business as usual in the offices, but after work, we all work hard putting this deal together.

I'm grateful to Matteo and Enzo, that they're helping, and our bond becomes stronger over drinks and takeout as we work around the clock. It's been a week and the silence is unbearable.

Daniela's been working from home and we barely see each other. Sometimes she goes out in the evenings. I check with her security detail and discover that it's usually to meet Cari at a bar or restaurant.

I've tried to talk to her, to get back some of the friendly banter we used to have, because I care deeply for her, but she's frozen me out. Maybe I shouldn't have told her about me wanting to walk away after seven months, but I didn't want any more lies between us. It's the lies that destroy people.

She's still distant, and I don't want to push too hard. She needs her time and space, and I need to give it to her. I just can't tell her anything about what I'm working on because I can't risk news of this plan getting out.

I feel confident that it will work. And once my father-in-law gets his company back, Daniela will see that we're going to be okay.

CHAPTER THIRTY-SIX

DANI

THIS WEEK HAS BEEN HARD. I'VE BEEN FIGURING OUT THE course of my life, and now I've landed back in my beloved São Paulo.

It's late in the evening and I'm going to surprise my parents. I've deliberately kept them in the dark until now, and showing up on their doorstep seems like the right way to break the news to them.

I feel happy to be back, though I've carried a dull ache with me on my journey, like extra baggage I didn't need. It's been with me ever since I left Dexter's apartment. I've kept my head down, figuring out my plan, with Raquel's help. He's been working long days. He's out of the apartment before I'm up and he's been coming home later than usual every day.

I don't even bother asking him where he's been or who he's been with. I want to forget everything we shared, all our precious memories which will soon be replaced. While I still miss him with all my heart, Paul Knight's betrayal cuts deep; as deep as the shock of Dexter's exit strategy.

I knew it was never about helping me. He despised me as soon as he saw me. It wasn't about him helping his father, a man he clearly hates. I should have dug deeper to find out why Dexter decided to marry me in the first place, but I didn't. What I shouldn't have done was gone and fallen in love with him.

It all makes so much sense now that I know what truly motivated Dexter. Hate. Revenge. Spite.

And getting close to me? He wanted what most men who meet me want. He wanted my body. This was all about desire, about him getting his pleasure from me. I'm trying to keep my distance and I didn't see the point of telling him about the latest bombshell, the one I discovered when Papai sent me the original contract. There, in the fine print, was a clause buried in a ton of legalese, that I only managed to decipher with Raquel's help.

It revealed the biggest shock of all.

Paul Knight had baked this into the contract from the start. He'd intended to take my father's share of the company at the end of the year. The yearlong ruse gave him just enough time for his people to learn everything they could about the business, so that by the end of the one year, they were already in position to take over.

I would have returned to São Paulo, thinking I'd helped my father, only to discover that Paul Knight had wrestled control of the company from my father.

Obviously that happened sooner rather than later, when Paul Knight discovered the real state of AO Eletronica. The new change to the contract was to sign the shares over with immediate effect, instead of waiting the year.

My decision was cemented once I learned that, and now I'm home again, where I belong.

Mãe opens the door, her eyes wide and red-rimmed when she sees me. She doesn't speak but wraps her arms around me, clinging to me like I'm her long-lost child. I cling to her, needing her strength, her guidance, her love.

"I had a feeling you might come back," she whispers. "Papai told me about the contract." She doesn't know about the original contract. No one does, except for me, Raquel and Paul Knight. I'm not sure I want to tell my parents just yet. I can see that my mother's already looking fearful and confused that I'm here.

Worry fills me when my father doesn't come to the door, when I don't hear or see him. "Papai?" I ask.

"He's in the study," Mãe whispers, brushing my hair back with trembling fingers. "He's not well."

Of course he's not.

As soon as I step into the study, I see my father hunched over his desk, slumped in his old leather chair, the one he used to sit in when I was a little girl, lecturing me on business ethics while I pretended to listen and secretly doodled flowers on a notepad.

His posture is so bad, I'm tempted to go over and straighten him. He looks smaller, and fragile, and nothing like the giant of industry I used to look up to. Though he was starting to look better at our wedding.

Our wedding.

I brush the thought away, and focus on my father. It won't do to think of Dexter. Not now. Not ever. If I'm to survive this, I need to erase that man from my mind and my heart.

My father looks up slowly, his eyes dull. He's back to looking like a shell of his former self. "Daniela …"

I cross the room and kneel in front of him before I can stop myself. "I'm here." He touches my cheek, and I see all too clearly how weak he's become. It's heartbreaking. "Why are you here, filha?" He looks surprised.

"I had to, Papai." I take his hand and hold it between mine. "I'm back where I belong."

"You belong with your husband."

A silence stretches between us, heavy and sharp. I haven't said a word to them about what I've done. That I took Raquel's advice and flew to the Dominican Republic before I came here.

"I wish I'd never gone to New York," I say quietly. "If I hadn't, I never would've met Paul Knight. I never would've married Dexter."

My father flinches. "Daniela ..."

"I loved him, Papai. I still love him." I hate that my voice cracks. "But it doesn't matter now. What matters is fixing this."

He leans back, weary. "Fixing what? What's done is done. Paul Knight has the majority, but ... maybe we should just wait."

"Wait?" I stare at my father in disbelief. "Wait for what, Papai?"

He doesn't answer me.

"I'm not letting that man take this company from you. You spent your life building it up from nothing. How can you give up so easily?"

I'm disappointed in him.

"Leave it be, filha," he says, wearily, like the problems of the world sit on his shoulders.

I blink at him, stunned. "I can't leave it be. I can't believe you want me to give up. I can't believe you're giving up."

My father looks away, defeated and resigned. It breaks my heart to see him like this. "Papai, what happened to you?" I whisper. "Where's the man who used to tell me that integrity matters more than profit? That we build legacies, not just balance sheets? Where's the fight in you?"

His lip trembles. "Don't you see? I wasn't upfront with you. I was desperate, that's why I did the cowardly, weak thing and ordered my accounts department to mislead Paul Knight. God forgive me."

"Why would you do such a thing? That's not who you are."

"I was trying to protect you."

"By lying to Paul Knight?" I ask gently, trying to keep the bitterness from my voice.

He lowers his head. "I didn't want you to marry Oscar Ramos. If Paul Knight saw the state of the business, he would never have agreed to an alliance."

"You made the business look better than it was so he'd agree to the alliance?"

"I didn't want you to marry Ramos. Not that man. He had an idea that we were struggling and he made me an offer, before Paul Knight came along. He told me he'd invest in us, help us to regain our power, but he wanted something in return. You."

I remember Oscar Ramos. How he glanced at me, put his hand on my bare shoulder and gave me a wolfish smile that made my insides fall. This man would devour me the moment we closed the door to the bedroom on our wedding night. I shiver, just thinking about it.

It's what made me go to New York to speak with Paul Knight. I swallow. The thought of the slimy Ramos being anywhere near me, makes me want to retch but that's something I'll now have to overcome.

"I couldn't do it, Daniela. I couldn't sell you off like that, and I was trying to figure out our next move, but you flew to meet Paul Knight and when you told us you'd met Dexter, and that everything would be fine, I thought my prayers had been answered. I thought Paul Knight would protect the company, and I stupidly thought he'd do it from afar. Not only did he come into work with me, poring over the books and examining all our processes, but he also hired a top audit firm to go through everything. That's how he discovered the truth."

It explains why Dexter was so worried when his father stayed behind. He knew his father was up to something. And now my heart is a mess of contradictions. Of rage and sorrow, love and betrayal. All of it tangled up in the hollow space that Dexter once occupied.

"I walked into the deal blind," I whisper. "I was walking into a fire pit, Papai. I wish you'd forewarned me, at least."

"How could I? I was ashamed of myself, of using you. But the Knights were young, good-looking, and everything about them looked perfect."

I look away.

"Is it not perfect?" my father asks, his dark, baggy, saggy eyes on me.

"You should be careful of Paul Knight."

"You shouldn't do anything hasty, filha."

I place a hand on my father's arm. "I'm going to fix it."

"How?" My mother stands in the doorway. Her face is pale. "What are you planning, filha?"

I stand slowly, meeting both of their eyes before I make the announcement. "I'm going to marry Oscar Ramos."

They both go still, like I've caused their hearts to stop beating.

"No," Mãe breathes. "You cannot do this."

"I'm already divorced," I say softly. "It's done."

My father looks like I slapped him. "You … you divorced Dexter?"

I nod once. "In the Dominican Republic, before I came here. Divorces can be finalized quickly there than in the U.S or Brazil. I had to do it."

I was able to file unilaterally, and without Dexter, Paul or media attention. I needed it to be quick, because I wrestled with the decision all the way there. Raquel kept telling me not to rush, and thought I needed to calm down before I made a rash decision. Even after I told her that Dexter and I had tricked her and everyone around us, she somehow seemed to think I should talk things over with him first. Her advice shocked me. She's supposed to be my wing woman. I can't deny my love for Dexter, but everything I've learned about the Knights makes me sick to my stomach. I will get over him, but Raquel doesn't seem as convinced. I've sworn her to secrecy, and made her promise not to say anything to Dexter, or Rio. I haven't told her about my other plan. She would never let me go ahead with that.

My mother looks stricken. "What did Dexter say?"

"He doesn't know."

My mother claps a hand to her mouth, in horror. "He doesn't know?"

"You've divorced Dexter, and he doesn't know, and now you're going to marry Oscar Ramos? Daniela, what's gotten into you?" my father cries, worried more about my future problem than the one I've left behind.

"He's not Paul Knight," I say. "And if I marry him, I can convince him to help us get the majority stake back to you. He's so rich, he can help us. He can fix it."

"You will not sacrifice yourself," my father says, his voice tight.

"It's my life, Papai. It's my decision."

"He's not right for you, filha." My father raises his voice, startling me.

"You think the Knights were?"

"Dexter is a good man," he insists.

"Dexter ..." I want to tell them that he's complicated, but they seem to think he's the best son-in-law ever, and I don't want to talk about him.

"You're playing a dangerous game."

"I don't care," I snap, my voice breaking. "I loved Dexter. I gave him my whole heart. And now he's just like the rest of them; silent, cold and gone. But you?" I turn to my father. "I still believe in you. I still remember the man who taught me how to fight. So let me fight for you now."

"Don't do this, filha. Wait. Have patience."

"Wait for what?" I try to keep my voice steady.

The air turns silent again, but this time, it feels different. My mother reaches for me. "What about your heart, meu amor? Will it survive this?"

I look away, because I don't know the answer. I'm not sure it will. But I nod anyway. "It has to."

CHAPTER THIRTY-SEVEN

DEX

I wake up and find that Daniela isn't around.

At first I don't think anything of it. Maybe she went to the gym. Maybe she just left early. For what, though? To meet Cari at the flower shop? Maybe. But when I come back home later that evening, she's still not there.

Her phone rings four times before going to voicemail.

Again.

I stare at my cellphone, willing Daniela's name to light up. I miss my wife more than ever, and I only have myself to blame. I asked her for some distance, but when she's not around in the apartment, when I can't get a hold of her, her absence hits me like a punch to the chest.

This silence might not just be space. This emptiness might not just be time.

She might really be gone.

Not to see Cari. Not to a spa.

Gone gone.

My vision mists and the walls of the room close in. I feel like I'm suffocating. Like I can't breathe. It all comes back to me, how I told her I needed space, but what I really needed was *her*. I told her I needed time, but all that matters is every moment spent with her.

I fear I might have made it too easy for her to leave me. I call her security detail in a panic. Only to be told that Daniela hasn't left the apartment, as far as he knows.

"She's not here, you idiot!" I yell down the phone.

"She hasn't left the apartment, sir. I've been stationed in the lobby all day," the guy says.

My blood runs cold.

"She fucking has! She's not in this apartment." I nearly put my fist through the wall. Has he let her slip past him?

Asshole. Daniela gave him the slip. She got away, I don't know when and I don't know how, but I intend to find out. It's clear she didn't want me to know.

I call Rio and show up at his place moments later, falling to pieces like a frantic, hot mess. I pace around his apartment. "She's gone. She's disappeared. Something's happened to her." I stop and gape at Rio. But he's calm, arms folded. Not feeling my panic.

"I'll tell you what's happened," Rio says. "But I don't know if you can handle it."

My head whips to him. "You know where she is?"

"I just found out, an hour ago. I was going to tell you."

"Tell me what?"

"She's back in Brazil."

The words hit like bricks. I stumble back, bumping into the edge of Rio's kitchen island, gripping it like it's the only thing holding me up.

"She *w-what?*" My voice splinters, I feel it sharp across my throat. "She's back in São Paulo?" My knees threaten to give way. "She left the country?" I choke out. "Without telling me? Without her security?"

It's almost like she was escaping.

From *me*.

Rio doesn't answer. He looks at me, eyes wide with worry. "Take a breath, dude. We can fix this. There's also something else you should know. Something Raquel told me."

My lungs struggle to work. I'm not sure I can take any more. "What?" I croak.

"The old man was going to do it anyway, get control of AO Eletronica. It was in the original contract, pages of fine print and bullshit, but this was his intention all along."

I shove both hands through my hair, fingers digging hard into my scalp. The room starts to spin and I feel uncertain and unsteady, like my life is not worth living. "That sonofabitch. He just can't help himself can he?" I hiss. "I would never have married her had I known."

"That's just it, dude, you didn't know." Rio's voice is steady and calm. Everything I'm not.

"How do you know all this?" I recall asking the old man for the contract, but he never gave it to us. I hazard a guess. "Raquel?"

"Don't even ask," Rio mutters. "She says she's not supposed to say anything, but she thinks you need to know. She figured you'd be worried." He clears his throat. "Daniela went to the Dominican Republic, likely for a quickie divorce."

"What?"

What fresh hell is this? I hold my stomach, feeling like a wrecking ball's hit me. The only reason she'd be getting a quickie divorce is because she's not just divorcing me.

She's planning to marry.

And if she's back in São Paulo, I know exactly who she's planning to marry.

Oscar Ramos.

I press my palms to my face. I want to scream, but I can't find the air.

Daniela hasn't just left me to get some space.

She's gone forever.

And now she's planning to marry another man. A corrupt man. A man who doesn't love her.

"Dude." Rio's voice is soft. He's by my side. "Calm the hell down. You fall apart like this, you won't stand a chance. It's all well and good getting the company back from the old man, but I can take care of that. You need to take care of *you*."

I suck in a deep breath, stand taller, nod as I see Daniela's face in my mind's eye. I told her I needed time, but she took it to mean I'm letting go.

The fuck I am.

The fuck I'll let her marry that sonofabitch. I need Daniela like I need air to breathe. I can't function without her. I can't imagine a day of my life without her by my side.

What have I done?

Instead of giving keeping a distance between us, instead of working around the clock with Rio and his brothers, I should have told Daniela what we were doing. I should have involved her. Let her know I was working on a plan to fix everything.

"What will you do?" Rio asks.

I realize it in an instant. My father never expected me to fight for Daniela. He expected me to walk away, like I always do. He thought that's what I'd do again, but Daniela has changed me. There's nothing I wouldn't do for her, but damn it, I messed up. I was so desperate to fix everything that I forgot the most important thing of all—keeping my wife. I was desperate in the way her father must have been when he asked her to make that deal.

This woman has suffered enough, and I let her slip away from me. There's only one thing left to do now.

Win her back.

I look Rio dead in the eye. "It's time I brought my wife back home."

CHAPTER THIRTY-EIGHT

DANI

I wonder what I am walking into this time. I wonder if marrying Oscar Ramos will be the answer to my problems.

The receptionist greets me with the same too-perfect smile. I walk in, a sick feeling in the pit of my stomach. I can't work out which was worse, walking into the office to meet Paul Knight that first time, naively and ignorantly unaware of what my father had done, or now—going to meet Oscar Ramos.

Asking him for a favor.

I tell myself it's just nerves. Just the weight of what I'm about to do, but the truth is this man scares and repulses me. The only reason I'm here is because I am out of options and I hate myself for coming here to beg Oscar Ramos for help.

He keeps me waiting. Typical. By the time I'm ushered into his office, I've rehearsed every line, every counterpoint, every calm, emotionless argument I'm going to make. But the moment I see him, leaning back in his chair like a man who's already won, I know I'm in trouble.

"Daniela." He rises, slowly. "You look tired."

I hold my head high. "I didn't come for compliments."

"No?" He gestures for me to sit. "But you obviously came for something. What do you need from me?"

He knows.

That's the only reason I'd be here.

"Sit." He motions for me to take the chair but I refuse to sit down in. "I'm not your enemy, Daniela. Talk to me."

"I'm divorced," I say, tone clipped.

His mouth twitches. "Dexter Knight let you go. Just like that?"

"It didn't work out." I finally sit, my legs shaking. Back ramrod straight. Nerves tingling in the base of my spine.

"What happened?" Oscar gets up and walks toward me, his steps slow and deliberate. "Why the rush, querida?"

I tense. "Please don't call me that." He's being familiar, and patronizing. Manipulative, too. I shiver inwardly because I'm suddenly not sure about this.

"You were only married a few months," he presses.

"That's none of your business."

"But it is," he murmurs. "You've come to me. That makes it very much my business."

"I'm here to make a deal."

He sits back down, and steeples his fingers. "Let me guess. Paul Knight now controls the majority share in your father's company."

I don't flinch. "You already knew."

"I'm a man who pays attention." His smile is thin and cruel. "And you? You're a woman who needs help."

He's smart. Or psychic. Or, as my father said, he probably has a few people on the inside, working in my father's company. People who will happily sell important information for a price, just like Paul Knight probably does. There's no difference between them. It's suddenly very clear to me that Oscar Ramos is the type of man who will pay any price for anything.

And that includes me.

I tilt my chin up in defiance. "I want my father's company back. I want Paul Knight out. You've always wanted in, and now I'm offering you that chance."

He raises an eyebrow. "Explain."

"I'll marry you," I say, the words bitter on my tongue. "In public. On paper. If that's what it takes. I'll make the alliance look legitimate."

Oscar leans back, studying me. "You'll marry me?"

"You said once you'd help my father if I agreed."

"You refused me then."

"I'm agreeing now."

He tilts his head. "You were willing to marry Dexter Knight for a business arrangement. Why not me?"

I don't know what to say. How to tell the truth without offending him.

His eyes darken. "I saw the photos, Daniela. That charity gala in New York. The way he looked at you. The way you looked at him. You could have fooled the world." His voice turns low. "But you didn't fool me."

My pulse spikes.

"I'll fix things," Oscar says smoothly. "I'll use my lawyers, my leverage, my contacts. I'll make sure Paul Knight relinquishes control of the company without destroying your father, of course. I'll even keep your father's name clean so that fabricating financials won't get him in trouble. We'll bury it and say it was an accounting error. It's easy enough to blame it on an external audit firm." He shrugs. "Knight Enterprises won't want that scandal made public either."

A long pause.

I say nothing.

And then he drops the final blow on my neck like a guillotine. "But in return, you'll be my wife. Not just on paper. Not just for the press." He leans forward, eyes glittering and I feel so very thankful his large desk is border between us. My eyes settle on his thick, stubby fingers, and I bite back the bile which claws up my throat. "You'll share my home. My name. My bed. You'll bear my children."

Something cracks in my chest. "No," I whisper, shaking my head as my insides hollow out.

"You already said yes," he replies, cool and quiet. "You just didn't realize what the yes meant."

I stand too fast, the chair scraping behind me. "This is blackmail."

"This is business." He rises too, calm and smug. "And you know the terms. I suggest you take the night to think it over. But we both know you'll come around."

I turn and walk out before I scream, before I cry. But the second the elevator doors close, the tears come, hot, angry and silent, trailing down my cheeks and burning.

This is the second time I've made a deal with a devil and I've walked into hell all by myself.

Again.

CHAPTER THIRTY-NINE

DEX

I've been texting Daniela all night long.

> Can we talk? Please. Just let me know you're
> okay.

No response.

I wait an hour. Then another.

I send an email. I call twice, once from my cell, once from the office line. Straight to voicemail both times.

I leave another text.

> Just get in touch. Please. I need to know
> you're okay.

Still nothing. I check my phone again. Still no message. Still no ticks turning blue. Is she ignoring me? Or has she shut me out of her life completely? I hold onto the hope that it's because she's in love with me and she knows that if she reads a single word I sent, she'll crumble.

In trying to fix the problem the old man has created,

because I know what matters to Daniela, and what is right, I took my eyes off us, got distracted, and now she's gone.

I love her, and this isn't the end of it. I'm getting her back. I haven't slept a wink and now I'm getting ready to board a flight to Brazil. I tell the old man, and my brothers that I'm away on business. I don't take the private jet, because everything must be done stealthily.

But every time I close my eyes, I see her with him—Oscar Fucking Ramos. I let my wife slip through my fingers, the only woman who's ever had my heart. What if she thinks I don't deserve the chance to make it right?

The thought rips me to shreds. But my one and only goal in life now is to get her back. My brothers are working the plan. Rio has personally contacted the trusted legacy investors, rival firms and quiet allies of Daniela's family. The buzz is building and has created just enough market noise that the old man's intel network starts to pick it up.

In a few days' time, Rio will engineer the "crisis" that will help a quiet rumor to spread. The old man will start to take notice and by the end of the week, he'll panic. Sometime in the next week or two, the shell company will step in anonymously offering a generous, but not suspicious, buyout of fifty-one percent.

I call Rio for an update because I need to know he's got this.

"Don't you worry, I'm on top of it," he reassures me. "The old man will take the bait, and I guarantee that by the time you get back with your wife, he'll be discussing a transfer."

"You're sure?"

"I told you. I've got this."

I press a hand to my chest, trying to calm the thudding panic beneath my ribs. "Anything I should know about?"

"It's all working as planned. He'll get the company back,"

Rio confirms. "Through the shell company as agreed and he won't be able to trace a damn thing."

I exhale, feeling a sharp relief. "Thanks, brother."

I have a battle looming ahead of me, but I'm prepared for it. I can handle Ramos. It's Daniela I fear. It's her answer I'm afraid of. That she might not want me back.

"What are you waiting for, dude? Go get her."

I hope I can. "You think she'll listen?"

"I think," Rio says carefully, "you've got a small window before Oscar Ramos convinces her she doesn't have a choice."

My blood turns cold, because that's also what worries me. I've moved as fast as I can and now I'm about to fly out. I know how fast my wife, my *ex-wife*, moves when she puts her mind to something. "You think she'd really go through with it?"

"She flew all the way here to talk to Paul Knight. Who the hell does that? She fought off a mugger. Dude, your wife has bigger balls than you."

I smile. "She does, and I love that about her."

"But you telling her about your exit strategy? Probably one of your dumber moves."

I frown. "I didn't want to have any more lies between us." And then I think about it. He's right. Daniela suffered too much betrayal that night. Me telling her about wanting to walk out was probably too much.

"Dude, *love?* You used the 'L' word. You really are turning all soft."

"I've come to my senses. I just didn't realize it till I lost her." I thought love was something I couldn't have, but Daniela showed me I can. She's given me the strength to go after what I need and what I want. She's given me the strength to love.

"Get on a plane," Rio urges. "Go to Brazil. Go get the love of your life."

I stare out at the skyline. New York feels gray today. Empty. Like something's missing.

Daniela's missing.

"If it's not too late," I whisper. Daniela didn't just love me, she *saw* me.

All of me.

And she stayed.

Until I gave her no reason to.

———

BY THE TIME I ARRIVE AT DANIELA'S PARENTS' HOUSE IN SÃO Paulo, I'm soaked in sweat and regret. Her father answers the door, and his expression says it all.

"I'm too late, aren't I?"

He shakes his head. "Not yet." He steps aside to let me in. The familiar scent of the house, spices and fresh flowers fills the air. This is a cozy home, a home you'd want to come back to. Nothing fancy or sterile or cold about it. It's the type of place where I can see Daniela and her parents sitting down and having a good home-cooked meal. The type of home I want to come back to.

Just like that, I remember the first meal Daniela cooked in my apartment and suddenly, I long for that time again, being with her, living with her. The simplicity and security of domestic bliss, and I'm not sure how much of that was pretending. She changed me. For the better.

What kind of man lets a woman like her slip away from him?

An idiot like me.

Daniela's mom comes rushing. "Dexter?" She keeps her distance as though she's not sure how to welcome me, but I sense she wants to hug me.

I make the move first, stepping towards her. "Forgive me." My voice falters.

She throws her arms around me. "You came for her." We pull away and I see her eyes are filled with tears. "Save my child, please," she begs.

My head snaps to her father. Daniela isn't here, so where is she?

But I already know.

"She told me not to say a word, but she's out with him." Her father's voice is heavy. "Oscar Ramos. A private dinner. Somewhere quiet and exclusive for just the two of them. It scares me."

My blood pressure spikes. "Where?" I grind out.

"Brisa." He sighs. "The restaurant at the top, with a rooftop view of the city."

Perfect.

Just public enough for a scene. Just private enough for a declaration. I turn to leave, but he catches my arm.

"She told us she was doing this to fix everything." His eyes are glassy. "I know you're working on something, Dexter, but you have to run. She can't marry that monster. I don't care what happens to my company. It can burn. It can rot. But I can't watch my daughter marry a man like that."

I stare at him, stunned. "You won't lose the company, sir. Everything's going to plan."

"Please save my daughter from him."

"I will."

"Go quickly," his wife pleads. "If you love Daniela, go. Stop her from throwing her life away."

I nod once.

Then I run.

IT'S A FANCY RESTAURANT. I'LL GIVE HIM THAT.

It's the sort of place I'd like to take Daniela myself. Perched on the edge of the skyline, candlelit and sleek, where two people in love can just be. Where they can stare into each other's eyes and plan their evening, their future, their life.

Soft jazz plays alongside the clink of silverware and the muted conversations of São Paulo's elite. Amid this quiet tranquility, I storm past the hostess before she can stop me.

And then I see her.

Daniela.

My wife.

Ex-wife.

There's a pang in my chest, and the realization that she divorced me, sits heavy atop the pile of regret. She's sitting across from Ramos, wearing a black silk dress that makes her look like something untouchable. Her posture is tense, her smile, forced, her makeup minimal. She's not in the least bit made up, like she was on the night of the charity gala. She doesn't look happy, and that makes me happy, as twisted as that is.

Soon, I'll rescue her from this. *From him.* I stride across. She's looking down at the table, while Ramos lifts a champagne flute and smiles at her. "To our future—"

"No fucking way," I growl.

He flinches and Daniela's eyes snap to mine, wide, stunned. Her long eyelashes flutter as she blinks a few times, as if she can't believe what she's seeing.

"Dexter," she murmurs, my name falling from her lips like a release. I can't live without her. I can't breathe without her. Daniela is the only woman who gives my life meaning.

Ramos stands up defiantly, his face darkening. "You have five seconds to get out."

I ignore him. "Don't do this, Daniela. Please."

"I have to." Her voice croaks. "You don't understand—"

"I do. More than you know."

I step towards her, my heart in my throat. My life in her hands. "You think this is your only option, but it's not. You don't need to do something you'll regret forever."

Ramos steps between us, eyes hard. "If she regrets anything, it's marrying you."

"The fuck she does," I snarl.

"She can't trust you." Ramos signals for something or someone. "Your father stole her father's company."

"I'm fixing that," I snap. "All of it. What my old man did, what he took. He's going to lose it all."

"Empty promises," Ramos jeers. Just then I hear a skirmish behind me. Plates smashing, glasses shattering. I turn around to find two burly men in a fisticuff. My security detail, and I'm guessing someone from Ramos's team.

"Call yours off," I hiss. "The last thing we need is a goddamn fucking spectacle." "I'm sorry." I hold my hands up helplessly to someone who looks like the manager. Next to him, a team of servers quickly and quietly work at clearing up the mess.

"Don't listen to this buffoon," Ramos urges Daniela. "These people cannot be trusted. You know that now. You've learned the hard way."

"Don't listen to him. I'm putting things right," I plead with her. "We're working on a deal to give your father his majority share back."

Daniela's eyes widen. "What? How?"

Ramos pokes me in the chest. "You little—"

"Get your fucking paws off me." I turn to the woman I love. "I was a fool. I never planned to stay, but you changed that. You changed me."

Ramos pokes me again. "You crazy American—"

"Let him talk." Daniela's voice, cold and cutting, stops Ramos in his tracks.

I'm desperate for her to believe me. "I know about the original contract," I say, my voice low so that Ramos won't hear. She stands up, her body slightly turned towards me, like we're blocking Ramos out. Like it's just the two of us here. "I know he intended to do the dirty from the start. He was just waiting for the year to be up."

Her brows push together. "Your father ..."

"Is evil. Yes. He is. I warned you from the start."

"I didn't understand just how evil."

"You wouldn't have, because your heart is pure. There's not an ounce of nastiness in you. I love you, Daniela. I love you so damn much, and if there's even a sliver of a chance you still love me too, please don't make this mistake."

Ramos slams his hand on the table, reminding us that he's still here. We flinch. "If she walks away now, Knight, you'll never get the company back. She won't either. I'll make sure of it."

"I won't either? Is that a threat, Oscar?" Daniela's voice has a deathly quiet edge to it. Ramos narrows his eyes, like the demure woman he thought he was dealing with is suddenly ready to slay. "I see what this is," she continues, chin tilted up, eyes defiant. "It was never about helping my father. It was about owning me."

The old man's jaw ticks. "You made a deal, and you must keep it." He starts to reach across the table for her hand.

I see red. "Touch her and I swear—"

The man stops. Daniela presses into the table, rising slowly. "I agreed to the deal, but I take it back."

Ramos waggles his finger at her. "You'll regret this. My men will destroy you, your family, and your father's so-called legacy."

I face Ramos, my voice calm but lethal. "And my family will eat you alive."

Daniela steps forward, anger blazing in her eyes. "You don't get to decide what happens to me, Oscar. Not you, not Dexter, not anyone. I choose my future, and who I spend it with. And I choose Dexter."

She gives me her hand, and I grab it firmly, like my life depends on it, and it does. I see that now. Her palm, warm, soft and familiar, makes my skin break out in goosebumps. From the moment she walked out of my life, I've been on tenterhooks. Now, with her hand in mine, I find my footing on solid ground again and I can finally breathe again.

Ramos pounds the table with his fist. "You're doing this? You're going back to the American? The one who broke you? The one who let you walk away? He's not your future. He's your worst mistake."

"I don't love you, I never will. But this man, he loves me, and I love him, and nothing can break that. He is my future. He always was." Every word Daniela speaks is certain and solid. She scoffs. "You want to know my mistake? Coming to you thinking I'd run out of options." Her eyes turn to mine, shiny, bright. "I should have trusted you, Dexter, like you asked me to."

I nod.

"But you left him," Ramos hisses, breaking our tender moment. "What makes you think he won't go back to his old ways?"

"I know this man. I know the deepest parts of him, and still I choose him. He might not be perfect, but he's mine, and this time, I'm not walking away."

Ramos's face is flushed, his chest heaving. "You think this is over?"

I step in front of Daniela, shielding her with my body. "This is me being polite, old man. Disappear. Now." He blinks. I lean in just enough for only him to hear. "You come near her again and I won't sue, I won't negotiate. I'll bury you so deep your own men won't find your body."

Ramos stiffens, but I don't give him the satisfaction of waiting for a reply. I take Daniela's hand and we walk out of the restaurant without looking back.

"Asshole," I mutter, as we stand outside in the balmy night air.

"You came for me, Dexter." Daniela's voice is soft, with a hint of surprise, like she can't believe I'm here for her, claiming her back. My thumb brushes her cheek. Behind her, Ramos leaves a few minutes later, with his bodyguard in tow. I bring my gaze back to Daniela. "I can't live without you," I confess. "It took me losing you to realize that."

Tears glimmer in her eyes, but she smiles through them, soft and fierce. And in that moment, I know. We've survived betrayal and trickery. Power dynamics and the old man's scheming. We've come out the other end. I know now that we can survive anything.

But there's something I need to know.

"Why did you do this, Daniela? Why did you run to him, when I told you I needed some time and space?"

"How could I trust you?" she whispers, looking at me like she's torn in two. Like she so badly wants to believe I'm going to do the decent thing, but she's been so broken by all the lies, too distrustful of anything touched by the Knights.

"But I asked you for some—"

"I know, Dexter, but I thought you were pushing me away again."

I shake my head, catch her hands in mine, pressing them firmly, like I never want to let go.

"Never. I was trying to figure out what to do. As soon as I

heard what the old man did, I knew we needed to fight back. All I could think about was how to get your father his company back. I'm sorry I didn't put you first. I thought you knew how I felt about you. I know how much your family means to you. I know what you did was out of love, you sacrificed your happiness to fly to the US, to meet a nasty American billionaire from a dysfunctional family. I knew your main worry would be your parents. That's all I was thinking of, and how to put things right. I thought you and I were tight."

I lift one trembling hand to her face, brushing my thumb along her jawline, feeling the way she shudders at my touch. I love her so much. I don't just need her, I can't *live* without her. She's my oxygen, my redemption, my soul mate. She saved me from myself.

"But you were already thinking of an exit strategy. You weren't even going to last the year."

My face falls. "I wasn't thinking of you at first. I'll admit that. I wasn't thinking of anything but revenge back then. You have to believe me. It was before I went into this."

"But you wanted to leave after three months."

Her eyes widen, and she flinches. I put my hand to her face, needing her to listen and understand. I don't want any lies between us. "Hear me out, amor. That was after we came back from our honeymoon, when I was battling with my heart, warring with my emotions, denying that you meant anything to me. Denying that I was falling in love with you. Love is scary, Daniela," I whisper. "I thought I wasn't capable of love," I continue, my voice wavering. "But you proved me wrong. I can't let you marry someone else, because you're the only woman who's ever seen me. *Truly* seen me, and loved me anyway."

Her eyes shine. A solitary tear slides down each cheek. "I

ran because I thought you were retreating again," she says, her voice small. "You were pushing me away."

"Never."

"It felt like it."

"I understand, and I'm sorry." I wipe away her tear.

"I wanted to believe you," she whispers. "But I've been burned so many times, Dexter. Lied to. Used. And you're a Knight. I didn't know if you were any different. I thought you were back to your old tricks, coming home so late."

I sigh with exasperation, seeing it through her eyes now. "I was working on a plan the second you told me about the majority share."

"How do I know this isn't just another Knight maneuver?" she asks quietly. "Another play to protect the brand?"

Smart woman. I see her brain working, trying to triple-check this is real. Not taking my word at face value. "Because there's no angle here, Daniela. No strategy. I'm not saving a company, I'm saving *us*."

She presses against me, her head resting against my chest. I've missed this. Her touch, her words, her wisdom. I hate being alone and I plan to never be without her. I wrap my arms around her protectively. "I didn't sleep much that night, or the nights after," I explain, needing her to know why I worked such late nights. "I hatched a rough plan. The next day, I called Rio. Together with Matteo and Enzo, we worked on it."

She moves her head up, her brow lifting in quiet surprise. "You worked with them all?"

I nod. "Amazing, isn't it, what family will do." The weight of it settles in my chest like a punch. I've always called them the Italian Knights, like we were somehow different species, not born of the same blood. But somewhere in the simmering resentment, something changed. Despite everything the old man did to divide us, we stood together. We fought together. And in that moment, I realized he can never win.

Because blood is thicker than all the lies, and there is strength in unity. In family.

"We would work late into the night, at Rio's place. We couldn't do it at work because we needed the old man to think we were still enemies." A smile crosses my lips remembering those days. "We worked at Rio's, over pizza and beer. That's where I was. I couldn't tell you, because I didn't want to endanger anything. I didn't want to give you hope until I knew things were working. It was a delicate plan, requiring lots of little parts, and it will take time. I'll explain it later, but I need you to believe me that I was there. You can ask Rio, Matteo and Enzo."

"I believe you," she whispers, her eyes searching mine.

"I couldn't let you go because I didn't realize just how much I needed you, until I lost you. I believed I hurt the people I love, and I destroyed them, and you taught me better. You showed me there was another way, and now …" I press another kiss against her lips. "We win together, your family wins. Paul Knight loses."

"Does he know?" she asks.

"Not yet. This deal will take a while to shake out, but it's happening. Don't you worry." I nuzzle my nose against her, eliciting a giggle. Her expression relaxes. The tightness around her eyes disappears. I realize how close I came to losing her. Dinner with Ramos. A wedding would have followed soon. I can't bear to think about it.

"You broke me, when you left, Daniela."

"I'm sorry." She lets out a shaky breath, her eyes boring into me. Then her fingers curl around my wrist, and she leans into me. "I hated myself for leaving," she breathes. "Every second was hard. But I thought you'd already made your choice."

"I did." I step closer, our foreheads nearly touching now. "I chose you. I've always chosen you. I just didn't say it fast enough."

Her lips tremble and her arms wrap around my neck. My arms slide around her waist and I take a deep inhale of her heady scent. She intoxicates me, soothes me.

"I missed you, amor." I press another kiss to her lips.

She snuggles closer to me. "I've missed you, Dexter, and I don't ever want to be apart again."

"Then don't ever run from me again, amor." My voice is a whisper, to her upturned mouth. "You're the only one for me, Daniela. Always."

CHAPTER FORTY

DANI

I worry that Ramos might do something vengeful to Dexter, but then I remember the Knights are a formidable force. Oscar Ramos would never touch them.

That night, Dexter and I sit around the table with my parents. We're talking, laughing, sharing. Just like families do.

Later, before we go up to sleep, Dexter gives me a moment. I sit on the veranda with Papai. He's tired. Still recovering from everything, but there's a light in his eyes I haven't seen in weeks.

"Your husband is a good man," he says, voice low.

I chuckle. "He's not my husband, Papai. We're divorced."

I hear a low gasp.

"But this time, I feel that when we marry, it will be for real." I say it without hesitation, as if getting married again to Dexter is the most natural thing in the world. As easy, as natural and as necessary as breathing.

"He's not Paul Knight," Papai adds. "He's earned our respect. Yours most of all."

I smile softly. "Dexter did more than that. He gave us a second chance." I don't voice my next words, but Dexter rescued me. I never thought I needed rescuing, because I've always prided myself on being a strong woman, but I was about to sign a pact with the devil; a pact that meant I'd have to share Ramos's bed.

Just thinking about it sends a shiver down my spine, but I exhale a sigh of relief because Dexter rescued me from that. He knew I'd do anything for my family. Even *that.*

Papai squeezes my hand. "You were always strong, filha. But the two of you are stronger together. Did you know he would come for you?"

"I think I did."

I'd blocked him out, not wanting to trust again, but I wasn't completely surprised when I saw him. I wondered if he remembered how good we were together, just like I did in my many despondent moments. I wondered if he remembered how perfect we were for one another.

Turns out, he did.

We sit quietly, the breeze carrying the scent of gardenias and the sound of the city beyond the gates. It's a scent I'll cherish and take back with me when we return to New York in a few days' time.

EVERYTHING FEELS DIFFERENT.

Lighter.

Brighter.

The heaviness of recent weeks has lifted. It's like when rain has fallen and scrubbed everything clean again.

Dexter holds my hand in the car. He doesn't let go. Not once.

When we get back to his penthouse, our home, I pause in the doorway of the bedroom. For so long, this space represented distance. Lines we never crossed. Feelings we never said aloud.

He shuts the door gently behind us. I turn to him, heart racing.

"I can't stop thinking about it," he says, voice low.

"About what?"

"That you didn't just change my life. You changed me." He steps closer. "You made me believe I could love someone. That I could be loved back. You didn't see my name, or my money, or the mess I tried to hide." He presses a hand over his heart. "You saw this. The part I buried. And somehow … you loved it anyway."

Tears sting the corners of my eyes. "You made me believe in things again too, Dexter. I'm so used to people writing me off as just a pretty face, but you took the time to get to know who I am. You *see* me. No one else ever dug deep enough."

He pulls me into his arms. "I love you so much, sometimes it scares me."

I lift my head up. "Scares you?"

"If something had happened to you. It was bad enough when you were mugged, but seeing you with Oscar Ramos, sitting across the table from him, looking sad. It was heartbreaking."

"I was sad. Oh, Dexter. I was *so* sad." I press my face into his chest, breathing him in. He's everything I need. Safety, steadfastness, and home. For the first time since this entire nightmare began, I believe we'll be okay. "I'm just so thankful to be back home, with you," I whisper.

He brushes my cheek. "I'm just to thankful to have you back in my life again, where you belong, meu amor."

Our eyes lock as we hold hands. I'm still trying to process the storm that just tore through my life, and this man before me is a promise I never let myself believe in.

Dexter Knight.

My husband. Or ex-husband.

My heart. My life. My everything. I swallow the lump in my throat, overwhelmed. He cares. He really cares. More than that, this man loves me, and he's not only told me, he's shown me.

"You didn't shave." I run my hand across his stubble. It feels alien on my fingers. He's usually cleanshaven, his skin smooth as a baby's.

"I haven't slept much," he confesses, wiping a hand over his face, like he's wiping away the stress and exhaustion of the past few days. He looks rough, and exactly like he's been sleep-deprived for days.

"Dexter," I murmur, putting my arms around his waist again and leaning into his hard chest. The beat of his heart against my ear is reassuring.

"I couldn't bear the thought that I'd lost you. That I might have been too late."

A few more days, and he would have been too late. I shiver, not wanting to dwell on that ugly thought. I look up at him. "You came, you found me. I'm yours, Dexter," I say softly. "I choose you."

Later, as we lie tangled in sheets and quiet laughter, Dexter turns toward me.

"There's one more thing."

"Oh no," I groan. "Do I need to sign something?"

"Worse."

I raise an eyebrow and sit up. "Worse?"

"You need to attend a Knight family dinner. The old man has no idea what's been going on these past few weeks. What

Rio and the guys have been doing. He thinks we just accepted what he did to your father and he has no idea that you left me and returned to São Paulo, that you divorced me, and that I went after you."

"Some father," I murmur, stroking his face.

"I could be dead, and he wouldn't know, or care."

My face scrunches up in disbelief. "He would care. You're his son, Dexter."

He presses a kiss on my lips, "Amor, do you really still not know what this man is like?"

I refuse to let this man poison what Dexter and I have. I refuse to give air to anything about him. "I love you, Dexter. I think I started to fall in love with you when we were trying to convince Raquel." He smiles at the memory. I clear my throat. "But I love you more with every passing moment, and I promise to take care of your precious heart."

He doesn't speak, and it feels like something old, dark and rotten, something that's been buried deep inside him, is starting to loosen its grip. I'm determined to erase all traces of the guilt and sick belief he has that he didn't deserve to be loved after the way he treated his mother. I want this man to know he is capable of love, and of being loved.

He rests his forehead against mine. "I love you."

"We found each other. We deserve each other. We were meant for each other."

He breathes out a sigh. "Yes," he murmurs. "Yes, we did, we do, we are." We fall into another kiss, and I already know that we're not going to sleep much tonight.

"You said I had to attend a Knight family dinner," I remind him. "Cari told me about them."

"She's only been to one."

I chuckle. "She said that one was enough."

"You'll come?"

I groan dramatically. "Fine. But if your father says something smug, I'm throwing wine in his face."

Dexter grins. "I'd pay to see that, and don't worry, I'll back you up."

"You better."

He kisses me again, slow and deep. "Welcome home, Mrs. Knight."

"Dexter, we're divorced."

"Need to fix that."

CHAPTER FORTY-ONE

DEX

Knight family dinners are always tense, but tonight seems especially bad. It feels like a battlefield. And I walk in last. With Daniela on my arm.

Everyone's seated at the long dining table in my father's penthouse. No drinks in the Great Room, just straight to the dining table. Jett and Zach are on one side. Rio, Matteo, and Enzo are on the other.

A hush falls for the longest time, and my father looks up, eyebrows lifting. "Well. The prodigal son returns, with his wife."

Daniela doesn't flinch. She looks flawless in navy silk, her spine straight, chin high. My father may be powerful, but my woman is unbreakable.

"Let's just try to get through tonight," Zach mutters. "We don't need more drama tonight."

"I disagree," I say, stepping forward, "we do."

My father exhales loudly, clearly irritated. "You obviously have something to say, Dexter. Say it."

"It's about the fifty-one percent share of AO Eletronica that you took from Daniela's father."

Jett tenses and Zach goes quiet. My father sips his wine, smug as ever. "I didn't steal anything. I protected our interests."

"That's your opinion. The way I see it, you manipulated a desperate man and took advantage of a family in crisis. That's not business. That's cowardice."

My father narrows his eyes. "Careful there, boy."

I nod toward Rio, who leans back in his seat, grinning.

"Rio?" My father's tone is wary now. "What is going on?"

Rio shrugs. "You were so busy underestimating us, you didn't see what was right in front of you."

We all watch our father do something he rarely ever does. He looks unsure.

"You've been duped," I tell him. "We faked a hostile takeover rumor. Played on your fear that AO Eletronica would drag down Knight Enterprises' quarterly report. Leaked whispers about regulatory risks tied to the acquisition."

Matteo jumps in, voice smooth. "Our outside investors? All carefully selected. People with long-standing confidence in AO Eletronica. Industry players who want it to succeed because they've benefited from its innovations or partnerships in the past. And none of them trace back to Dex."

My father's nostrils flare; something else we rarely see.

"You thought you were outmaneuvering us," I continue. "So you offloaded your majority share in AO Eletronica to a shell company."

My father leans "Whose shell company?"

Rio tosses a folder on the table. "Ours. Mine, Matteo's and Enzo's."

The old man tears it open and his face drains of color. For a second, he's immobile. Then he clenches the papers tightly in his fist until they crumple. A muscle jumps in his jaw. We're witnessing something we've never seen before—the unraveling of this usually cool and calculated man, whose chest now rises and falls in shallow, angry breaths, like he's trying not to accept the cold hard fact that he's been outplayed by his sons. We're all witness to real gut-wrenching fear flashing across the old man's face.

I don't feel the smug satisfaction I expected.

I feel pity. And sadness.

"You can't reverse it," I say calmly. "Not without looking like a fool to the board. You signed off on it yourself. Won't look too good, what with you not realizing the fabricated reports initially. People might think you're losing it, Father. Getting old, not able to cope anymore."

Zach looks dismayed, and shifts uncomfortably in his seat. The old man glances around the table at all of us seated around the dining table. His voice is quiet. Lethal. "You've been working together."

"*Getting on,* is a better description," Rio says. "Because we're family, whether you like it or not."

The old man turns to Enzo and Matteo. "You two were in on this?"

Matteo grins and lifts a shoulder. "We're family."

Enzo blinks.

"This is for you, Daniela." Rio passes a folder around the table. "I've signed over all controlling interest. Your father owned forty-nine percent. We, the shell company that Matteo, Enzo and I formed, hold fifty-one percent on paper, but the documents transferring control are right here and now your father has it all."

Daniela blinks, stunned.

"You got your company back," I say softly, looking at her beautiful face. "All of it." She clutches my hand beneath the table, and nods, speechless.

The old man rises slowly, livid. "You'll regret this." He glares at me. "You think love makes you strong? It makes you weak."

"Love made me smart enough to know that it's never wise to bet on fear. Oh, one more thing. We know," I wave a hand between me and Daniela, "and I told these guys," I gesture at Rio, Matteo and Enzo. "And I was going to tell you—" I nod at Jett and Zach who are staring at me in total shock. I eye the old man. "That you'd planned this all along. To steal the majority share from the start, before you even found out about Arminio's people fabricating the accounts. You were fine with screwing her father over from the get-go. You were just going to wait out the year."

"You did what?" A vein pulses along Jett's temple, and his body tenses, like he's holding himself back from launching across the room.

"It's called business," the old man replies, sipping his wine.

"But ... *Dad* ..." Zach's open mouth can't find the words to end that sentence.

"Is this what we are now—dirty, sneaky players?" Jett looks like he wants to throw something. Beside him, Zach rests his hand on his shoulder, trying to placate him.

"Like I said. It's called business." The old man has no moral compass and now he looks at me, eyes blazing with cold fury. "You played me."

I meet his glare head-on. "You raised me to be ruthless. I finally turned it against the right target."

Rio lifts his wine glass. "To family dinners."

"There's something else." I remember something. "The million dollars a month I'm supposed to have received for each month we were married. We made it to about six weeks. Which means you owe me one and a half million dollars."

"Six weeks?" The old man frowns, as if the math doesn't add up. It doesn't, and I don't want to give him an answer. I don't want him to have any more personal information about us. He knows none of this: my brothers working behind his back, Daniela leaving and divorcing me, and planning to marry Ramos before I raced to get her back. He never even asked about her, or me.

"You need to pay him what you promised." Jett's voice is as hard as his gaze.

Rio nods in agreement. "You sure do. One point five mill. You owe him that much."

The others murmur the same. The old man looks shocked for a few seconds before schooling his hard, defiant, shameless mask back on and storming out of the room. As soon as the door slams, Rio bursts out laughing. Matteo pours himself a drink. "That went better than expected."

Enzo smooths his hand through his hair. "I was expecting a chair to fly through the air."

"I can't fucking believe this," Jett mutters.

Zach's quiet; the old man's actions sinking in.

I turn to Daniela. "You okay?"

She nods slowly. "I am now."

The servers come in setting large bowls of food on the table.

"I'm starving," Matteo announces, lifting the lids off to see what's on the menu today.

A delicious aroma fills the air. I take a long inhale, and decide I'm starving too. "Me, too."

I watch Jett. He gets up and paces around like he's going to erupt with all the bottled-up anger. "Come and eat, brother. Don't let good food go to waste."

"Might as well fucking eat, if he's gone," he mutters. Then

he sits back down again. And just like that, we start talking. Wine glasses are refilled and we pass around the bowls of food.

The tension that hung thick in the air, seems to have left with the old man. It's just us, the Knight boys, my brothers, and we're eating, for the first time, like a real family.

EPILOGUE

DANI

Dexter told me to meet him here, in The Midnight Lounge, the place where we had our first date. Where we started so see each other for who we were.

It was here that we were trying to work out our backstories. What we'd tell people who asked questions about how we met and how he proposed.

We were like fire and ice. Opposites who somehow complemented one another perfectly.

We just didn't know it at the time.

As the air between us crackled between us, we thought we were getting on while pretending not to care.

Tonight feels different yet familiar. I'm curious as to why he asked me to meet him here. It's not quite Valentine's Day yet, and it's not even the weekend. He's always so busy working hard at the office, and I'm still working from home.

Home.

My heart floods with warmth when I think of home. It's not Dexter's apartment that's home. Home is wherever he is.

The elevator dings and opens onto the familiar view. But as I step into the lounge bar, and look around, it's empty. Except for the tall and vaguely familiar man standing before me.

"Daniela, it's me, Luke. We met before." Dressed all in black, with his copper-colored hair and the bluest eyes, he looks intense and commanding. I remember now. He was the guy who sent us the bottle of Cristal champagne.

"Hi. What's going on?" I asked, feeling confused.

"Everything's fine. Dexter's outside, waiting for you."

"Outside?"

"He has something arranged for you." A hint of a smile. "Please, come this way." He gestures for me to follow him back into the elevator.

"Where are we going?"

"You'll see."

The doors close and my heart races. I have no idea what to expect. But we're hardly in there are a few seconds when elevator doors glide open and I let out a gasp as my eyes sweep across the twinkling lights.

"I didn't know you had a rooftop garden."

Luke chuckles softly. "Hope you like it."

Twinkling fairy lights are strung above a glass canopy. Warm shadows fall over frost-kissed ivy and delicate white roses tucked into sculptural planters along the perimeter. I feel the warmth coming from heaters, but I don't see them anywhere. I see only marble benches.

In any case, the crisp February air feels warm enough that my long camel coat suddenly seems a tad too thick.

"This ... this is like being in a fairytale."

When I turn to Luke again, he's gone. I walk around, taking in the skyline and then I see him.

My ex-husband.

My darling Dexter.

He's standing tall, tailored, and visibly tense, his hands bracketing the iron railings. He sees me, and turns, shoving his hands into the pockets of his long black cashmere coat as he walks towards me.

That's when I see it, behind him.

A small round table draped in deep navy velvet, with a silver champagne bucket resting on top. A bottle of champagne inside, flanked by two tall flutes and a single pale blush rose in a crystal bud vase.

"Dexter …" I whisper, my breath leaving a trail of white curls in the cold air.

"Are you cold?" he asks, concern lining his brow.

"Not anymore." We meet in the middle, standing face to face, the view before us a glittering galaxy. Snow flurries swirl lazily in the air like confetti.

The world below fades away and all that remains is the quiet hum of city lights and the way he looks at me, like this is a dream. His dream, and it's come true.

It's my dream, too, and I fight the urge to pinch myself. Dexter's hand reaches for my face, the same time as I place my hand on his chest.

He inhales a steadying breath. "I didn't know how to do this the right way," he says. "There's no manual for falling in love with the one person who sees through all your bullshit."

Oh my.

I choke up at his words. "Dexter …" I stare up at him. Thankful for everything I have in my life now. "We had our first date in the bar below," I whisper.

He chuckles under his breath. "We had stories and details to iron out."

"I came here knowing that you hated me for choosing you,

but by the time I left, I thought we had more in common than not."

His brow furrows. "I spent so long carrying the burden of my guilt, that all I could ever think about was hating and exacting revenge." His voice softens. "But then you walked in, and you made me see things. You made me believe things. You gave me peace. That's what I really wanted. Peace, not power, not revenge. I wanted you."

I let out a shaky laugh, looking up at him through a hazy blur. Batting my eyelashes to try to stop the tears.

"I don't like the idea of you being my ex-wife."

I giggle.

"So, I need to fix that. Quickly."

He looks at me for a long moment before reaching into his coat pocket and slowly dropping to one knee.

Oh my.

I gasp, my hand flying to my mouth.

He's not, *is he?*

Everything fades into the background. All I see are Dexter's eyes on mine and when I look down, he pulls out a black velvet box and opens it. Inside is a breathtaking ring.

"An emerald?" I gasp. I love the color green, and Dexter remembered.

"It's a rare Colombian emerald," he says quietly. "Flawless, untreated, and worth more than most diamonds, because nothing about you was ever ordinary."

The vivid green stone glows in a platinum setting, flanked by two tapered diamonds on each side.

I love it.

"I don't want a life without you in it. I want your coffee breath in the morning and your smart-ass comments when I'm being an idiot. I want your trust, your laughter, your fire. I want it all, Daniela." He looks up at me. "No contracts," he says. "No timelines. No expectations. No loopholes."

I can't breathe.

This is *a proposal.*

A real one.

My eyes turn glassy, and his face loses focus for a few seconds until I blink back the tears.

"Will you marry me, Daniela? Again. For real this time."

I nod, laughing through the tears. "Yes, again, for real, forever. Of course, yes."

He slips the ring onto my finger, and it's not flashy or ostentatious. It's elegant. Simple. Perfect. I remember the last time we did this, hurried, like an afterthought, him handing the ring to me under the table.

"Emerald," he says, rises to standing. I throw my arms around his neck. "A symbol of love reborn, truth and loyalty. Like the love I have for you. Something that started under false pretenses and grew into something real."

I didn't think it was possible for my heart to overflow with even more emotion, but it does. "Dexter, I love you, so, so, *so much.*" There's a wobble in my words, and a tear falls down my cheek. It's emotion, pure and raw.

He wipes the tear away with his thumb. "You'll marry me?" he asks, again, his scent intoxicating.

I press a kiss onto his lips.

"Yes."

It feels like we've come full circle, having gone on a hell of a journey; we've been strangers who disliked one another and then got married, and then we were a couple in love who divorced.

This time, it's real. We're madly in love, and now we're engaged to be married.

"I love you, Daniela." This time, when he kisses me again, it isn't for show.

It's love in its purest form.

Thank you for reading Dani and Dex's story! I had so much fun writing it and it was so difficult to let go of these characters that I ended up writing TWO BONUS EPILOGUES for their story. **You can get these bonus epilogues by signing up here:** http://www.lilyzante.com/bonusdex

Please note: If you're already subscribed to my newsletter, there's no need to sign up again. You will automatically get these bonuses.

I was expecting to write Zach's story next … but *this guy* walked onto the pages and refused to leave. Can you guess who?

RIO!

The next book is based on Rio and one of the bonus scenes mentioned above shows what happened when Rio and Raquel met at Dex and Dani's fake wedding.

He's the billionaire who swore he'd never be like his father. She's the fearless lawyer who swore she'd never fall for a Knight.
When Rio Knight is sent to Belize to smooth over problems with an eco resort, the last person he expects to find standing in his way is Raquel Monteiro—the sharp-tongued, red-lipped attorney who already haunts his thoughts.
She hates his name.

He can't stay away from her fire.
And when their attraction ignites, neither of them is ready for the fallout.

You can read an excerpt of RIO at the end of this book

Also, if you're intrigued by Luke Hunter, the owner of The Bluebell Manhattan where Dex and Dani have their dates, you can read his story in THE HOOKUP.

EXCERPT FROM RIO

RAQUEL

*C*ARACA. M*Y* STOMACH FEELS ALL FLUTTERY.

I have a Knight in my hotel room. It feels so dangerously wrong on so many levels, and yet I'm the one who invited him in.

A Knight of all people.

He was kind enough to see me back safely, and that scorching hot chemistry between us is as strong as ever. That surprises me. Shocks me, that someone like me could ever feel anything for something like *him.*

I don't know why this man has such an effect on me, but he does, and I haven't stopped thinking about him since that night at the Manhattan bar when I was spying on Dex and Dani. Tonight, at their wedding reception, it was impossible to ignore how much in love they are, but it still strikes me as odd that everything has happened so fast.

The Dani I know wouldn't do this. She's not just a friend, she's like a sister to me, even though we were from such different worlds when we met. Against the odds, we became best friends at the private school I was lucky to attend. Our paths would never have crossed were it not for the government-funded scholarship I got to one of São Paulo's most elite schools. The type of school I never knew even existed. The type of school that had what I imagined only the grandest homes would have: marble staircases, tennis courts, swimming pools and perfectly landscaped grounds.

When I stepped into that school, I entered a world that was alien to me. A world I didn't belong in. In my early days, armed with nothing more than a sharp tongue and death stares, it made me more determined than ever to rise. To show these people that I was more than my tattered shoes and clothes. That's when I met Dani. She was nothing like the others, even though she looked perfectly at home here.

I taught her how to swear and she taught me how to control my anger and use it to fuel something I could control. I vowed then to be someone who could make things better.

We grew close and kept in touch through the years, and then we lived together in the U.S. while I was doing my LL.M. at Georgetown. We've always known what was going on in each other's lives, but I never thought she'd keep something like this from me. Her marriage to one of the Knight billionaires. She kept Dexter a secret for so long, I wonder if she fell in love and lost her head.

Some women do.

But the way Dex kissed her this evening, in front of everyone, it was plain to see that they're in love. I'm so happy for her. I am. But I'll be watching Dexter. He's a Knight, so he doesn't get a free pass from me.

"Nice room, princesa."

"Why do you keep calling me that?" I ask, turning to the Knight in my room.

"Because you are."

I kick off my heels to find Rio stands, taking up the space like he owns it. Hands in his pockets. Calm. Relaxed. He laughs. His voice is too low, too smooth, too flirtatious. He's the kind of man who's hard to forget, and I know he's bad for me. I know he spells trouble, which is why I keep my distance. But now, he's only a few strides away, filling the room with his aura. His magnetism.

He's Dani's new brother-in-law. I mustn't forget that. I was tempted to kiss him in that Manhattan bar when I thought he was just another sharp-dressed, cocky businessman. Then I discovered who he was.

As a corporate environmental lawyer, I know all about the dirty tactics Knight Enterprises uses. I've seen too many cases where they've wreaked havoc across the globe.

The Knights mean trouble, and I've only let this man in to be polite. I'm going to send him back to the wedding reception soon. Dani might not realize I left the celebrations early, but I had to.

Work commitments, unfortunately.

The law firm where I work, Tovey & Roth, is one of the best firms in Miami. It was founded by two partners, but only my boss Pierce Tovey remains at the helm. William Roth retired years ago and faded quietly from the legal scene.

Pierce has been on my back all week. Pressure from the job, I can take. But a shiver of revulsion slithers through me every time I think of him. He's a corrupt, misogynistic blot on my day. The subtle innuendos he makes when others aren't around, the way he looks at me, how he brushes past me "accidentally" are all things that can't be used as evidence against him. He's careful, and knows exactly what he's doing, but he knows how to stay clean.

I love what I do. It's my passion. It's what fuels me. I'm a corporate environmental lawyer who occasionally takes on pro bono cases, though Pierce prefers I stick to billable hours that keep the firm's profits flowing.

Having Rio around is a little distraction. A little harmless fun. Nothing will happen, but I'm curious, and I have been, about him, for months. This one is rare, I feel it in my gut, but I've just got to find a way to stop thinking about him.

Though sometimes I can't help but wonder what he'd be like in bed. I don't usually think like that. But with him? I haven't been able to stop. He should've been easy to dislike. Easy to walk away from. I knew we'd meet at the wedding and I managed to keep away from him for most of the day, but then he found me in the gardens. And now he's here.

"What'll you have to drink?" I head toward the wet bar.

"You're offering me hospitality?"

"Just one drink. Knight, before I send you on your way. What will it be?"

"I'm not going to drink. I just wanted to make sure you got back to your hotel room safely."

He's chivalrous, if a little forward. I turn around to see if he's joking or being real and his eyes dip down to my bare feet. I'm suddenly feeling hot and bothered. I reach up and undo the big bow at the side of my high neck; not that it's going to help much. This dress which tapers in at the waist and fans out into a wide skirt, is elegant and perfect for a wedding, but now, with its full sleeves and that neck, it feels suffocating. The silky fabric clings to my skin, too hot and sticky, even though the air conditioning is on.

"You don't need to strip for me, princesa," he murmurs. The corners of his lips turn up into a lazy smile.

"In your dreams. I'd never strip for you."

"You have no idea of my dreams." His voice, thick and raspy, makes my brain fog over because his words sound like a confession. I'm suddenly too afraid to fire back. My mouth usually doesn't let me down. I can match wit and humor, easily. But tonight? I'm at a loss.

Despite my earlier resolve, I need a drink, so I reach for a small bottle of white wine, but then I remember I can't have it. I need a clear head, for work but also because I also can't let my guard down, not with this man in my room, looking like he wants to eat me.

How I want him to.

I shake my head, hating myself for feeling so hot, and tingly all over and grab a bottle of sparkling water instead. He hasn't even touched me yet, and already my breasts feel heavy. Heat begins to coil low in my belly.

Needing to show that I'm in control, even if I don't feel it, I turn around, place a hand on my hip and stare at him. He's made himself at home, dropping onto the edge of the armchair like he owns this room, but now his gaze trails over me slowly, and I fold my arms in disapproval. We stare at each other, tension crackling in the air. Suddenly everything feels too intense. The hot, sultry night fills with heated anticipation.

"I've changed my mind. I'll have uh ..." He pauses. "I don't suppose they have much in there?"

"Stale peanuts or overpriced chocolate?" I ask him. Then, "There's no aged tequila."

That earns me a grin. "You remembered, princesa."

Me and my mouth. "Jack Daniel's?"

"That'll do."

I grab a mini bottle of the Jack Daniel's, walk over and hand it to him. The rough calluses of his fingertips scrape lightly across my skin. It's heat and fire. Electricity and shock. Just from one touch. A delicious shiver tingles along my spine. I assumed that as a pampered Knight, with his smooth suits and inherited money, his cocky self-assuredness and not a worry in the world, he'd have baby smooth skin. But now my imagination runs wild as I wonder what it might be like to have those big, rough hands all over me.

I immediately step away.

"You been thinking of me, huh?" He twists of the cap and downs half of it without blinking."

I don't bother replying, but move away, needing to keep some distance between us, even as my heart hammers in my chest and I try to phase out sinful thoughts running rampant in my head. My breasts feel heavy, and as I stare at Rio looking so comfortable, so casual, I wonder if he can tell I want him. He looks so at home with his legs wide apart, one hand resting lazily on the armrest, the other holding his Jack Daniel's.

"I see you've made yourself at home."

"You haven't kicked me out." His gaze slides over my body again. If looks could undress, I'd be naked now. I shift from one foot to the other, feeling the need to squeeze my thighs together, to relieve the buildup of pressure making my insides combust. "I think you like me being here but you're too stubborn to admit it."

The audacity of the man. "My mother raised me to have manners and I'm too polite to kick you out just yet."

He's nothing but a pompous, confident ass, sitting on my armchair, looking like he's never going to leave. I almost, *almost,* look him over again.

"You're not nervous are you, princesa?" He grins before taking another gulp.

I laugh. "I don't scare easily—"

"I didn't say you were scared. I asked if you were nervous."

"Same thing, Knight." I sip my water, the bubbles fizz as they go down my throat. He watches me so intensely, I feel goosebumps skittering across my skin.

"We're two adults in a hotel room, alone. Very innocent, princesa."

"I said no flirting."

He holds up a hand. "No flirting. Just sitting. Watching you pace around barefoot like some kind of goddess who hates me."

I snort. "Goddess?"

He nods. My eyes avoid his, but it's the heat I feel, from everything being so overpowering—his gaze, his presence, his cockiness.

"You hot?" he asks.

I stifle the sigh threatening to cut loose from my throat. This man can read me like a book, and this is something I'm not used to. This is why he intrigues me. Why he's constantly in my head. I feel sweaty all over, with a dampness under my arms, between my legs, down my back.

He sits forward. "You left your best friend's reception early. Why?"

I shrug. "Too many people. Too much noise. And I hate small talk."

"Hmm." He studies me, like he doesn't believe me. "That wasn't all of it."

Damn him. I have work to do. Pierce is going to call soon and demand an update. But Pierce and work are the last thing I want to think about right now. "Dani's happy. She has someone who sees her. Fights for her. It made me realize … how lucky she is."

He frowns, and I feel like I've said too much. "You could be lucky." He winks. "All you have to do is not push me away."

"I know what kind of man you are."

"You know what kind of man my father is. Please don't ever make the mistake of thinking that I'm another version of him. I'm not."

He stands up and places his now empty mini bottle of Jack

Daniel's on the table next to him. My heart thunders inside my chest, but I manage to hold my ground until he closes the distance between us.

"You think I'm dangerous, arrogant, and spoiled," he challenges, his husky voice reverberating through me.

"I don't *think* you're spoiled. I know it, Knight. You brothers with your billion-dollar trust funds."

"We're not trust fund brats, but you have been thinking about me." He reaches out and brushes a strand of hair behind my ear. Gone is the cocky grin, replaced by a more serious, intense look. He's looking at me like I'm the only woman in the world. Like we're already intimate and he knows everything about me. I look up into his eyes—so dark they look black, just like his hair, slicked back today. He looks sharp and dangerous, like he could sling me over his shoulder, and walk out of here, and no one would dare stop him. That charm of his sometimes borders on predatory, and my insides heat up in a way they shouldn't.

My eyes go to the soft dimple in his chin, and I'm tempted to touch it; to run my fingers over the dip. But I don't. I scarcely breathe. His tone is softer now, almost a whisper.

"You still let me into your hotel room, and I have a feeling you're not about to tell me to leave anytime soon."

My breath hitches, but I don't move away.

He's right.

"What are you doing?" I manage to say, feeling a trail of heat where he touches me.

His hand lingers around my jaw. "You can keep hating me tomorrow, but right now, tell me you don't want this."

I swallow, and my voice is barely a whisper. "I don't."

"What's changed, princesa?" He walks back a few steps like the shock of my words physically punched him. "When we first met in Manhattan, you were all smiles and flirtation."

"I didn't know who you were back then."

"But you shut me down fast enough."

I don't flinch. I don't smile either. "Because once I found out, everything changed." It's not that I hate the rich. I don't. There are many rich people who do good, but the Knights are not those people. I was raised by a single mother in a favela on the outskirts of São Paulo. I've seen poverty up close. I've experienced the struggle and the injustice.

"Because of my last name?"

"Because your last name destroys rainforests and bribes politicians," I snap. "Because Knight Enterprises is the kind of monster I've built my whole career fighting."

The words seem to land harder than I expect.

"Then tell me, what am I doing in your hotel room?"

I narrow my eyes. "I know how to keep my distance."

"By letting me in?"

"By being nice to you because you saw me back to my room safely."

"You think you're safe from my charm here?" he murmurs. "I think you still want me."

He's infuriating, and not wrong. But I'd rather die than admit that. I tilt my chin up in defiance. "You think very highly of yourself. All of you Knights do."

"I think very highly of what I see, and what I want." He does it again, his gaze taking its sweet time trailing over me, slow and deliberate, every cell in my body vibrates. Heat flares at the base of my belly. I want to lift my dress up and have him be on his knees, pleasuring me.

Damn this man.

Damn my thoughts.

I force a light laugh, but it's laced with challenge. "You're wasting your time here. I don't do men like you."

"*Do?* That's an interesting choice of word, princesa." His

eyes glisten with mischief. "What exactly do you mean by men like me?"

"The type of men who think the world revolves around their name, their money, and their ability to get whatever they want."

His smile is lazy, full of undisguised interest.

"What type of men do you *do*, then, Raquel?"

My name on his mouth sounds like temptation and sin. I love the way he says it. Slightly dirty, and in his voice thick, and raspy. Stupidly, I step forward and place a finger on his chest. "I do men who can keep up."

I start to walk away, but he grabs my wrist, gently, but firm.

"I can keep up, princesa. What are you offering?"

RIO IS AVAILABLE FROM ALL RETAILERS.

BOOKLIST

Buy direct from Lily and save!

NEW SERIES

Knight Empire: A series of steamy billionaire romances based around a family of six brothers and their tyrannical and controlling father.

The Darkest Knight (prequel)
Jett
Dex
Rio
Zach

The Seven Sins: A series of seven standalone romances based on the seven sins. Emotional, and angsty romances which are loosely connected.

Underdog (prequel)
The Wrath of Eli

The Problem with Lust
The Lies of Pride
The Price of Inertia
The Other Side of Greed
The Seven Sins, Books 1-3

The Billionaire's Love Story: This is a Cinderella story with a touch of Jerry Maguire. What happens when the billionaire with too much money meets the single mom with too much heart?

The Promise (prequel)
The Gift, Boxed Set (Books 1, 2 & 3)
The Offer, Boxed Set (Books 1, 2 & 3)
The Vow, Boxed Set (Books 1, 2 & 3)

Indecent Intentions: This is a spin-off from The Billionaire's Love story. This two-book set consists of two standalone stories about the billionaire's playboy brother. The second story is about a wealthy nightclub owner who shuns relationships.

The Bet
The Hookup

Honeymoon Series: Take a roller-coaster journey of emotional highs and lows in this story of love and loss, family and relationships. When Ava is dumped six weeks before her Valentine's Day wedding, she has no idea of the life that awaits her in Italy.

Honeymoon for One
Honeymoon for Three
Honeymoon Blues

Honeymoon Bliss
Baby Steps

Italian Summer Series: This is a spin-off from the Honeymoon Series. These books tell the stories of the secondary characters who first appeared in the Honeymoon Series. Nico and Ava also appear in these books.

It Takes Two
All That Glitters
Fool's Gold
Roman Encounter
November Sun
New Beginnings

A Perfect Match Series: This is a seven book series in which the first four books feature the same couple. High-flying corporate executive Nadine has no time for romance but her life takes a turn for the better when she meets Ethan, a sexy and struggling metal sculptor five years younger. He works as an escort in order to make the rent. Books 4-6 are standalone romances based on characters from the earlier books. The main couple, Ethan and Nadine, appear in all books:

<u>Lost in Solo (prequel)</u>
The Proposal
Heart Sync
A Leap of Faith
Misplaced Love
Reclaiming Love
Embracing Love

Standalone books:

Tomorrow Belongs to Us
Love Among the Ruins
Love, Inc
An Unexpected Gift

ACKNOWLEDGMENTS

I would like to thank Maria at SteamyDesigns for creating this awesome cover. A huge thanks to Nicole McCurdy at Emerald Edits.

As always, a huge 'Thank You' to my wonderful team of proofreaders:

Charlotte Rebelein
Dena Pugh
Marcia Chamberlain

ABOUT THE AUTHOR

Lily Zante lives with her husband and three children somewhere near London, UK.

Connect with Me

I love hearing from you – so please don't be shy! You can email me, message me on Facebook or connect with me here:

Buy Direct from Lily and SAVE
https://shop.lilyzante.com

TikTok |Instagram | Website | Facebook Email

Newsletter sign-up:
http://www.lilyzante.com/news
Follow me on Bookbub
Follow me on Goodreads

facebook.com/LilyZanteRomanceAuthor
instagram.com/authorlilyzante
bookbub.com/authors/lily-zante
goodreads.com/authorlilyzante

www.ingramcontent.com/pod-product-compliance
Lightning Source LLC
Chambersburg PA
CBHW050605170726

48283CB00001B/117